Whispering
Shadows

Whispering Shadows

A Novel

JAN-PHILIPP SENDKER

Translated from the German by Christine Lo

37 INK

—

ATRIA

NEW YORK   LONDON   TORONTO   SYDNEY   NEW DELHI

ATRIA BOOKS   37INK

An Imprint of Simon & Schuster, Inc.
1230 Avenue of the Americas
New York, NY 10020

First 37 INK/Atria Books hardcover edition April 2015

37 INK / ATRIA BOOKS and colophon are trademarks of Simon & Schuster, Inc.

For information about special discounts for bulk purchases, please contact Simon & Schuster Special Sales at 1-866-506-1949 or business@simonandschuster.com.

The Simon & Schuster Speakers Bureau can bring authors to your live event. For more information or to book an event, contact the Simon & Schuster Speakers Bureau at 1-866-248-3049 or visit our website at www.simonspeakers.com.

Interior design by Kyoko Watanabe

Manufactured in the United States of America

10 9 8 7 6 5 4 3 2 1

The Library of Congress Cataloging-in-Publication Data has been applied for.

ISBN 978-1-4767-9364-1
ISBN 978-1-4767-9366-5 (ebook)

For Anna, Florentine, and Jonathan

Whispering Shadows

PROLOGUE

He was a small child. Even at birth. Six and a half pounds; barely more than a preterm baby though he had stayed in his mother's body a week past term. No cause for alarm, the doctors had assured them. He would catch up.

His skin was pale, almost transparent, and ever more delicate than that of other newborns. Tiny blue veins shimmered on his temples, his chin, and his hands even after the first few weeks, when suckling infants normally turned into well-padded babies.

His cries were less shrill, less piercing and shorter than those of the others. He grew tired easily, even later on, as a three- and four-year-old. While the other children at the playground on Bowen Road or, later, on the beach at Repulse Bay, barely knew what to do with their energy, while they climbed, charged about, or ran into the water shrieking wildly, he sat on the sand and watched them. Or he climbed onto his father's lap, lay his head on his shoulder, and fell asleep. He was economical with his movements, as if he felt that he had to conserve his strength, that his time was limited. No cause for alarm, the doctors thought. Every child is different.

He remained a delicate child. Thin legs and arms with no muscle tone, like sticks, so that at six years of age, he was still so light that his father could pick him up with one arm and throw him in the air. At school, he was one of the quiet ones in class. When the energetic Mrs. Fu asked him a question, he almost always knew the correct answer, but he never said anything without being prompted. During the break, he preferred to play with the girls or he sat alone in the schoolyard and read. In the afternoon, when the other boys either played basketball or football, he had ballet lessons. His parents had objected. Was he not enough of an outsider as it was? An oddball with no close friends. He had not needed to beg them for long. The quiet disappointment in his face had been a fervent plea that his father had not been able to refuse.

A few weeks later, he had complained for the first time about pain. His limbs hurt, his legs especially. That was perfectly normal, the ballet teacher said comfortingly. Many children felt the same when they first started dancing, especially when they threw themselves into it with the dedication that made him stand out from the others. Muscle cramps as a result of movements he wasn't used to, suspected his father. An orthopedist whom his parents were friendly with offered reassurance. The boy was probably growing, so a strong tugging sensation in the bones was not unusual. It would pass. Nothing to worry about. Then the unexplained exhaustion began. He fell asleep during lessons, had difficulty concentrating, and spent most afternoons on the couch in the living room.

Would they have consulted a doctor sooner if they had not been able to lay the blame for the pains on ballet? If he had been a boy bursting with good health, a boy whose every prolonged spell of fatigue or weight loss would have immediately seemed strange? Should they have taken his complaints more seriously? Had they been inattentive or careless? It would have made no difference, ultimately. The oncologists took every opportunity to emphasize this. Paul wasn't sure if they only said that to calm him down—so that on top of the panicky fear he had about his son's life, he would not be tortured by his own conscience—or if they were telling the truth. Unlike other types of cancer, with leukemia, early diagnosis made no difference the doctors told him over and over again. As though they assumed that he had feelings of guilt. As though those feelings were justified. But even if they were right, even if an earlier visit to the doctor would have changed nothing about the illness, the treatment, the prognosis, or the chances of survival, what was the point? Was that supposed to comfort him? Paul and Meredith Leibovitz had failed as parents; he had no doubt about that. Their son had been given to them to care for; they were responsible for his well-being, for his health, and they, Paul and Meredith Leibovitz, had not been able to shield him from this illness. What were a father and mother for if they could not protect their child against this?

"Don't blame yourselves. Blame God, if you like. Blame fate. Blame life, but not yourselves. You can't do anything about it," Dr. Li, the oncologist in charge, had said to them in a conversation shortly after the diagnosis. Meredith had taken that advice seriously and, over the next few months, been able to free herself of the guilt she had felt at the beginning. Paul had not. He did not believe in God, he did not believe in Karma; there was nothing and no one he could make responsible for the illness, who he could blame for it. Nothing and no one apart from his own complete inadequacy.

Paul stood by the window and looked out. It was early in the morning. There were several tennis courts and soccer fields right in front of the hospital. A couple of joggers were taking advantage of the still-tolerable temperatures at this time of day and running their laps. The dark gray clouds that had hung low over the last few days had disappeared and given way to a cloudless blue sky. The monsoon rain had washed the smog out of the air and the view was clear, which was rare in Hong Kong. He could make out the Peak clearly, the narrow IFC tower and the Bank of China in front of it. Between the skyscrapers of East Kowloon and Hung Hom the silver-gray water of the harbor gleamed, already crisscrossed by dozens of ferries, tugboats, and barges. Traffic had already come to a standstill on the Gascoigne Road and Chatham Road South flyovers. He thought about the beach in Repulse Bay and about the sea and how often he had gone out with Justin to build sandcastles at about this time of day on the weekends, while Meredith was still sleeping. Just the two of them, father and son, with the warm and humid summer air of the tropics blowing around them, bound by a mutual understanding that neither of them needed to speak. How he had allowed Justin to spread mud on him and how they had returned home laughing, and how Meredith, heavy with sleep, had always been a little put out by their good mood and needed some time and two coffees to be able to share it with them.

He turned around. The room was tiny, hardly bigger than a storeroom. He could cross it in two or three big steps. Justin's bed was against the pink wall. Next to it was the stand for the drip, a chair, a nightstand, and a foldout armchair, on which Paul spent the night. On the nightstand were two books that Paul often read aloud and a pile of cassettes, which Justin had still liked listening to a couple of days ago. Now he didn't even have the strength to do that. Paul watched his sleeping son. His skin was as white as the bedclothes; his face had lost all color. His eyes lay deep in their hollows and a soft, light blond down covered his head. His breathing was shallow but quiet.

Paul sat down and closed his eyes. *I'm sorry to have to tell you . . .* It had been nine months since the pediatrician had, in a low voice and with a sorrowful expression, told them the results of the first blood test. Since then these words had rung in his ears. They had taken hold of him, and they echoed in his head even nine months later. Would he ever be free of them? Would he ever hear anything else? *I'm sorry to have to tell you . . .*

Why my son? he had wanted to scream, but he had kept silent and listened to the doctor talk about myeloid leukemia, hemoglobin counts, bone marrow tests, and procedures. Why Justin? Why did Meredith no longer ask herself this question?

Relief came only in the brief moments when Paul started awake at night and thought he had dreamt it all. He sat in bed for a few seconds and had the feeling he had woken from a nightmare. It wasn't true. The blood count was normal. Justin still had his head of strawberry-blond curls; his hair had not fallen out. He was lying next door in his room, in bed asleep. Paul felt such relief then, such indescribable joy, almost foolishly happy, as never before in his life. It made the crash to reality seconds later all the worse.

Where was Meredith? Why was she not with them? She was on a plane. Probably forty thousand feet above Pakistan and India right now. Or over Kazakhstan and Uzbekistan, depending on whether the plane had taken the northerly flight path or the southerly one out of London. A very important conference, she had said. About the bank's new strategy in China. About investments and share-holdings worth billions. As the head of the Hong Kong office, it was impossible for her not to be there. She would be in Europe for two or three days at the most. They would be able to keep Justin in a stable condition until next week. The doctors had assured her of this. And the morphine had knocked Justin out; he slept practically all day, so he wouldn't notice his mother wasn't there anyway, she thought. She had looked at Paul, and they had looked into each other's eyes for a moment, for the first time in a long time. Should he disagree? Should he tell her that he was almost certain that Justin knew perfectly well whether his father or mother was in the room, if they were sitting by him, holding his hand, stroking his head, or talking to him, even if his body did not display any outward reaction any longer? That was why he had practically not left the tiny room for almost a week now. That was why he sat here, camping on the small cot, which was at least ten centimeters too short for him, and on which sleep was out of the question. That was why he read aloud from books, sang lullabies, hiking songs, and Christmas songs, anything that came to mind, until his voice gave out. He knew that Meredith had felt comfortable with her decision and that she would not have let herself be dissuaded, that she did not even expect him to understand her any longer.

Meredith's workload had increased in proportion to Justin's condition worsening. He had read somewhere that this was not un-common for parents whose children were dying of cancer. What was unusual in their case was that it was the woman who sought refuge in work. Two days after the diagnosis she had unexpectedly flown to

Tokyo. From then on she had shuttled more often between Beijing, Shanghai, and Hong Kong and her long days at work were followed by dinners with clients that went on late into the night.

Paul had noticed that there were two kinds of couples at the pediatric oncology unit. The first kind still looked each other in the eyes; their child's illness welded them together. They shared their fears, their doubts, and their feelings of guilt. They supported each other, gave each other strength or clung together. The other kind crept through the corridors with their heads down, staring at the floor. They were afraid to look into their spouse's eyes because they would see in them what they did not want to see: a reflection of their own fear, their rage, and their immeasurable grief. They were made mute by the prospect of death; they turned away from each other; they retreated into themselves, more and more despairing, as they searched for a place that they hoped would be free of pain. Paul and Meredith Leibovitz were one of these couples.

Just three days ago, making the most difficult of decisions, they had no longer been able to look each other in the eye. They had sat side by side, like two strangers, neither able to find strength or support in the other. The doctors told them there was no hope. The relapse of six weeks ago was as unexpected as it was serious. The cancer cells were multiplying at an explosive rate. They had not responded to the two courses of chemotherapy. All medical recourse had been exhausted. Now it was just a matter of keeping Justin as free of pain as possible. And it was a question of whether his life was to be extended at any price. There were options. They talked about the intensive care unit and ventilators. They could certainly win some time that way, perhaps a week, perhaps two. It was not a problem, medically speaking.

We assume that you wish to do this, Mr. and Mrs. Leibovitz?

Meredith said nothing. She had closed her eyes and she was silent.

The doctors looked at him. They waited. They waited for a decision. Do you have any other questions? Should we talk you through it again? Meredith kept quiet. Paul shook his head.

Should we move Justin to the intensive care unit?

Paul shook his head again.

"No?" the doctors asked.

"No!" he heard himself say. "No." He had decided. Meredith did not disagree.

––––––––

It must have been just after 2:00 PM when the heart stopped beating. Dr. Li could only guess at the exact time of death later on.

A nurse had last been in the room at 1:00 PM. She had wanted to collect the tray with the soup and the tea that she had brought an hour ago, that lay cold and untouched on a small table. She had felt the boy's pulse, which was weak but regular. She had checked the drip, the catheter, and whether Justin was getting enough morphine. Paul Leibovitz had been sitting silently next to the bed, holding his son's hand. He had asked for the ECG machine to be switched off, so the room was unusually silent, unlike the rest of the unit.

Dr. Li entered the room at five minutes to three PM and thought at first that father and son had fallen asleep together. Paul Leibovitz had tipped forward, his upper body lay on the bed with his right arm stretched out, and his left hand clasped his son's delicate fingers. Justin's head had sunk deep into the pillow and was turned to one side. Only when he looked again did Dr. Li realize that the boy was no longer breathing, that his eyes were wide open and staring, and that the father was not sleeping but weeping. Not loudly, not plaintively. It was not pain that was being cried out, as was often the case here. These sobs were terribly quiet, hardly audible; they reached deep inside, and sounded all the more despairing for it.

In the last thirty years, despite all the advances in medical science, Dr. Li had seen many children die. The death of a child was a traumatic experience for all parents, but in most cases there were brothers or sisters who required attention, grandparents who had to be cared for, work that had to be done, and mortgages that banks chased the monthly payments for. Life went on, even though the families could not imagine it in the first weeks and months. Some people, a few people, were broken by the loss. They allowed themselves to be consumed by feelings of guilt or sank into self-pity. They could not bear the emptiness or simply refused to let their children die. They never found their way back into life. Dr. Li thought about those parents as he listened to Paul Leibovitz sobbing.

1

Paul lay still on his bed, held his breath, and listened. All he could hear was the low, monotonous hum of the fans. He lifted his head from his pillow a little. Listened. Wasn't that the first bird calling? The sound came from the other side of the small valley; a faint, lone chirrup, so tentative that Paul was amazed that it hadn't been silenced on its way to him. It was a good sign. It meant that dawn would soon be breaking, that in the village the first cock was crowing, and would be followed by others in intervals of seconds. It meant that in a few minutes the birds in his garden would also start singing, that he would hear the clatter of his neighbors' crockery and pans. That the night was over. That he no longer had to endure the voices of the darkness.

Life goes on, Paul!

Meredith's harsh voice. Over and over again. Paul waited until the first rays of light fell through the wooden shutters and her voice had fallen completely silent. He pushed aside the mosquito net and stood up.

He made his bed, rolled up the tent that protected him from the mosquitoes, switched off the fans, went down to the kitchen, put some water on to boil with the immersion heater, went up again to the bathroom, and turned on the shower. The water was too warm to be really refreshing. It had been a typical summer night in the tropics, hot and humid; he had perspired a lot despite the two fans standing at the foot of his bed. His neighbors thought he was crazy because he refused to install an air conditioner even in the bedroom. Apart from old Teng, he was the only one on the hill who abstained from this luxury of his own free will.

Life goes on.

He hated those words. They embodied the unspeakable injustice and the utterly appalling, monstrous banality of death. Everything in Paul strained against it. There were days when he felt that every breath he took was a betrayal of his son. Days when the survivor's feeling of guilt threatened to overwhelm him, when he was not able to do anything other than lie in his hammock on the terrace.

The fear of forgetting anything. Justin's sleepy face in the morning. His big blue eyes that could shine so brightly. His smile. His voice.

He wanted to do everything he could to prevent the clamor of the world from covering up his memories. They were all that he had left of his son. He had to hold on to them until the end of his life; they were not just immeasurably precious to him, but also extremely fragile. They could not be relied on. Memories were deceptive. Memories faded. Memories evaporated. New impressions, new faces, smells, and sounds layered over the old ones, which gradually lost their strength and their intensity until they were forgotten. Even while Justin had still been alive, Paul had felt this loss: a pain that he had felt almost daily. When had his son spoken his first words? Where had he taken his first steps? Was it at Easter on the lawn at the country club or two days later on the trip to Macau, in the square in front of the cathedral? When it happened, he had thought he would never forget, but two years later, he was already unsure of the details. This loss was only bearable because new memories with Justin formed every day as the old ones disappeared. But now? He had to rely on the memories he had. Sometimes he caught himself searching for a few moments for Justin's voice, closing his eyes and having to concentrate until Justin appeared before him.

To stop the memories from being extinguished, he wanted to

protect himself from everything new, as far as that was possible. For-getting would be betrayal. That was why he had moved to Lamma shortly after his divorce and that was why he rarely left the island, and then only very unwillingly. Lamma was quiet. There were no cars, fewer people than anywhere else in Hong Kong, and hardly anyone that he knew. His house was in Tai Peng, a settlement on a hill above Yung Shue Wan, ten minutes from the ferry terminal. It was hidden behind a formidable wall of green bushes and a thick bamboo grove at the end of a narrow path.

He had set himself a daily routine. He woke at dawn, drank ex-actly one pot of jasmine tea under the parasol on the terrace—never more, never less—practiced tai chi on the roof for an hour, went into the village to make his purchases, and ate at the same harborside restaurant—always the same mixture of vegetable and shrimp dim sum with two steamed Chinese buns stuffed with pork. Then he car-ried his shopping home, after which he went on a walk lasting three to four hours. Every day, this took him past the small plots of land in which old men and women were weeding, breaking up clumps of earth, or spraying their greens and tomato plants with insecticide. They greeted him with a nod and he answered with a nod. He was safe with them. They would never think of speaking to him, let alone of engaging him in conversation. He carried on walking to Pak Kok by the sea, took a wide arc back to Yung Shue Wan, and then went halfway across the island to Lo So Shing Beach, which was almost always empty, apart from on a few weekends in summer. Paul went swimming for exactly twenty minutes. Then he sat in the shade for half an hour, sometimes longer in good weather, and looked at the sea, always relieved by the familiarity of the scene. Or he closed his eyes and meditated. There was nothing unexpected to fear here.

The walk back took him over the long ridge of a hill from which he could see the narrow East Lamma Channel that separated the island from Hong Kong. Only seldom did he linger on this path, gaze at the huge container ships with their full loads, and ask him-self what their cargo might be and where they might be going. His only companions were stray dogs or the odd homeless cat. He spent the rest of the day in the garden or on the roof terrace looking after his plants and cooking or cleaning the house.

He did not read a newspaper and had no television; he only listened to the BBC World Service on the radio from seven to seven-thirty in the morning. A day on which he did not exchange a single word with anyone was a good day. A week like any other in which nothing happened to leave traces on his memory was a good week.

He knew today would be more difficult. It was the third anniversary of Justin's death and Paul planned to travel to Hong Kong Island as he did every year and to climb the Peak.

It was not a good day for a hike. The second of September in Hong Kong was never a good day for a walk. The thermometer by the door showed a temperature of ninety-seven degrees Fahrenheit and humidity of 98 percent. The city was sweating. It was groaning in the heat. Everyone who could do so was hiding in air-conditioned rooms during this time.

Paul fetched a third bottle of water from the fridge for good measure and packed it in his backpack. He was wearing gray shorts and a light short-sleeved shirt. To prevent sweat from running down his face and stinging his eyes, he had tied a bandanna around his forehead. His long, muscular legs were evidence of his daily walks, and he had the flat, toned stomach of a young man. Even so, the climb would require all his strength in weather like this. He picked up his trekking pole and walked down the hill to the village at a leisurely pace. He was sweating even before he got to the ferry.

It was the memory of a lie he had told of necessity that drove him to visit the city and climb the Peak twice a year: on the birthday and on the death anniversary of his son. It was a ritual that he could not even explain to himself; adherence to it had become a kind of compulsion. As if he had to make up for something.

Not long before his death, Justin had asked him if he thought that they would climb the Peak together again one day. The highest mountain on Hong Kong Island had been one of their favorite outings; the walk around the summit, which commanded views over the city, the harbor, and the South China Sea, had made a great impression on Justin even when he was only two. To Paul, it seemed that the Peak was a place in which his son felt safe. It was a kind of lookout over the world that Justin insisted they visit in every season: in summer, when, thanks to its height, it offered a little relief from the oppressive heat and humidity of the city; in winter, when the wind blew so cold that Justin wore a woolen hat and gloves and they were almost the only people walking around up there; yes, even in spring, when on many days the clouds covered the summit and you saw nothing but mist before you. They had often sat on a bench up there eating and Paul had explained to his son how airplanes flew and ships floated, why the big double-decker buses suddenly looked as small as toy cars, and why stars were called stars and not suns, even though they also emitted light.

Would they make it there together again?

"Yes, of course," Paul had replied and his son had lifted his head a little, smiled at him, looked into his eyes, and asked, "Really?" Paul had looked into his son's tired eyes and not known what to say. Did Justin want to know the truth? Did he want to hear no, Justin, no, I don't think so, you're too weak for it and I can't carry you two thousand six hundred feet uphill. There is no hope anymore. We will never stand together on the Peak again and count airplanes, and ships, and dream about gliding through the air like birds and leaving droppings on people's heads. Of course he didn't want to hear that. Of course no one in his right mind could have brought himself to tell an eight-year-old that. Why should he? But then what could he do?

"No cheating, Daddy. Tell the truth," Justin had said in a warning tone shortly after the diagnosis, as Paul, in his helplessness, had tried to play down his son's condition and babbled away about a bad case of the flu. No telling lies. The truth. He, Meredith, and the doctor had stuck to it, in as far as a child could understand the kind of destructive force raging in his small body. But this? Will we climb the Peak again? This was not about leukocytes and plastocytes, not about hemoglobin counts and the next blood transfusion. It was a simple question that expected a simple answer: yes or no? Justin looked at his father, his eyes demanding the truth.

"Yes, of course," Paul said reassuringly, for the second time, nodding. Justin gave a quick smile and sank back into his pillow. It was a little white lie, the right reply—who would worry about it? But Paul could not forgive himself for it. Even today, exactly three years after Justin's death, he felt the sting of it. He had betrayed his son. He had left him to cradle an illusion, a stupid, ludicrous, completely ridiculous hope, rather than tell him the truth, to share it and make it more bearable that way. A feeling of shame had crept over him, and it had not diminished, no matter how often he had turned his lie over in his mind and justified it to himself. The feeling of despair remained, and with it, the feeling that he had been a coward at a critical moment.

11

Paul was the last passenger to get off the ferry, and a hellish scene greeted him: two jackhammers pounded at a stretch of asphalt, and, next to them, growling buses expelled black clouds of exhaust. From behind a construction site barrier came clanking and crashing so loud and shrill that he winced at the shock of it, his ears hurting. All around him were crowds of people rushing here and there in a great hurry, constantly passing right in front of him and jostling him as soon as he stood still. He fled into a taxi and took it to the terminus of the Peak Tram; a pedestrian path up to the summit started there. The altitude difference was about sixteen hundred feet; it was a distance that he had covered without any problems before; on some days he had even done it with Justin on his back.

He took a big gulp from his water bottle, picked up his backpack, and started walking. The narrow road passed May Tower 1, May Tower 2, and Mayfair, incredibly expensive residential developments that looked like faceless satellite towns but in which an apartment cost many millions of Hong Kong dollars. He and Meredith had owned two large apartments in Mayfair, which they had sold at more than three times the original prices at the peak of the property boom in 1997. He had used part of the profit to buy the house on Lamma and he lived off the interest on the rest of it.

Paul turned into Chatham Path, which led away from the road into thick tropical vegetation. It was a steep ascent and Paul felt the strain in his calves and feet, his thighs and knees, how they hefted his one hundred and fifty pounds or so upward. A thick blanket of cloud, gray like ash, had hung over the city for weeks. It had cleared somewhat in the morning and now the sun even broke through occasionally, turning the climb into a hike through a hot steam room. The trees were so thick here that Paul found himself looking through a solid green wall; all that remained of the traffic was a dull roar in the distance; instead of cars he heard birds and grasshoppers. He stopped to rest, finished the first one-liter bottle of water, and tried to empty his mind.

He made it in just under two hours. The final thousand feet along Findlay Road were easy for him, and he reached his goal with slow but rhythmic, almost feather-light, steps. Before he circled the summit on Lugard Road he wanted to have a coffee on the Peak and have a piece of lemon cake, a ritual that Justin had introduced. It was terribly cold in the café. He hated the effects of the icy air conditioner; it was as if someone had shoved him into a cold storage room. It always took a few minutes for the body to get used to the new temperature.

The café was unusually empty. A couple huddled in one corner: a young man with headphones and a girl on the telephone. An older man was reading the *South China Morning Post*, and a woman was poring over a map of the city, sitting just behind the table by the window that he and Justin had sat at almost every time. Paul got himself a cup of coffee and a slice of cake and sat down at the place that had so many memories for him. From up here, the view of the city had something surreal about it. Sometimes he had a passing thought that the voracious city below was only a figment of his imagination. These honeycomb apartment blocks built so boldly on the steep slopes, the skyscrapers in the Central and Causeway Bay districts, the harbor with its hundreds of vessels, scuttling back and forth assiduously like ants. To be sure of their existence, he had to trust in his eyes completely. The thick glass in the window turned the view into a spectacle free of noise and smell; the cars, the ships, the helicopters, and the planes moved as if in a silent movie. Paul remembered his arrival here thirty years ago. At the time, he had been certain that the Crown colony was only a stopping point on his way to the People's Republic of China. He had wanted to stay one or two years at most. Beijing was his actual destination; as soon as the political situation calmed down after the Cultural Revolution, he would move there. Paul had stayed on in Hong Kong, at first because the political struggles in China had lasted much longer than he had expected, then because he had been won over. Without him really realizing it, Hong Kong had become his home, the only one that he had ever known. He liked this city, built by refugees for refugees. The busyness of people who had been driven from their homelands set the tone of the days and nights here; the anxiety of the homeless, the fear of the persecuted. Before he had withdrawn to Lamma, the nonstop hustle and bustle and the lack of peace and quiet had not put him off; on the contrary, they had reflected his own restlessness in part and gave him, on good days, the feeling that he belonged, was part of a whole; a feeling that he had never known before in his life.

———

"Do you live here?"

Paul didn't know where the voice was coming from at first. He was so startled he nearly dropped the lemon cake from his fork.

"Or are you here on business?"

It was the woman at the table next to his. She must be American, Paul thought. No one else would start a conversation with a stranger in a public place just like that. How often he had had to defend himself against the hello-where-do-you-come-from? chattiness of an American passenger sitting next to him on an airplane.

"No, I live here," Paul replied.

"Oh, how interesting. May I ask if you've lived here long?"

"Thirty years," he answered briefly. He did not want anything he said to give the impression that he was interested in having a conversation.

"Thirty years! My God, how can you stand this number of people?" Paul looked over at the woman. Judging by her slight but unmistakable accent, she was probably from the Midwest. She was slim, a sporty type, wearing a light-brown trouser suit, white shirt, and a string of pearls. Her hands trembled as she lifted her cup of coffee. They were delicate, refined hands, with long fingers wearing gold rings, one of which was set with small diamonds, but even the precious stones glittering in the light could not detract from the fact that the hands were shaking. Paul was unable to guess her age. Her face looked much younger than her hands; it was smooth and disconcertingly free of wrinkles, but small pockets of skin hung from her neck as they did in an older woman. She could just as easily be in her midforties as in her early sixties. She had one of those very smooth faces that strove to give away as little as possible, that was practiced in concealing hurts and worries, the tracks that life left behind. She was wearing sneakers, but her trousers, blouse, and, most of all, her jacket, were much too warm for the season. She was clearly used to air-conditioning. She had probably taken a taxi straight from her hotel to the Peak, and not even noticed how hot and humid it was yet. He said nothing, in the hope that his silence would end their conversation.

"Don't the crowds bother you? Or do you get used to it with time?"

He took a deep breath and replied, in order not to seem impolite. "I live on Lamma, a small island. It's quieter there."

She nodded, as though that explained everything.

"You must travel a great deal in China, mustn't you?"

"I used to, yes. But not so much now. And you?" He regretted the question immediately. What on earth was he doing? How could he have been so stupid as to ask her such an open question? That was the opening she had probably been waiting for. Now she would tell him all about her trips to China or about her friend's or her husband's travels, about the unusual table manners, about the burping and the farting and the noisy eating at mealtimes. About the toddlers who did not wear diapers but simply shit on the street through the slit in their trousers. Or about the skyscrapers in Shanghai and the expensive Mercedes-Benzes and BMWs on the streets, which she had not expected from a Communist country. And at the end, thought Paul, she would ask if the Chinese really smashed open the skulls of monkeys while they were still alive and sucked the brains out with relish. But instead of holding forth with the torrent of speech that Paul feared, the woman stayed silent and looked him straight in the face for the first time. He shrank. Did they know each other? He felt as if he had seen her before somewhere. In fact, he was quite sure of it. Her big blue eyes. That penetrating gaze. The restlessness in that look. The nerviness. The trembling. The fear. She was so familiar to him that it seemed like he had last seen her yesterday. They had met before. But where?

"Do we know each other?"

"I don't think so."

"You look familiar to me. Do you work in a bank? Maybe you know my ex-wife, Meredith Leibovitz?"

"No."

Paul thought for a moment. Perhaps she had lived in the city before, and they had met at Justin's school?

"Do you have children?"

"Yes, a son." She looked away and stood up. Her strength seemed to desert her midmovement; she held her breath for a moment and dropped back onto her chair. She tried again, holding on to the table, swayed, and sank back into her seat.

"Are you unwell?"

"Just a bit dizzy," she said in weak voice. "My circulation. I can't cope too well with this climate."

"Can I help? Would you like some water?"

"Water would be good. Thank you."

Paul stood up and walked over to the serving counter. Suddenly, he heard the sound of chairs scraping and a dull thud from behind. When he turned around, the woman had disappeared. It was only when he looked again that he saw her lying on the ground between the two tables.

Although the ambulance from Matilda Hospital took only a few minutes to arrive, Elizabeth Owen was conscious by the time the ambulance staff arrived. Deathly pale, she was sitting up against a wall and drinking some water. Paul was kneeling next to her. She did not want to go to the hospital. Under no circumstances. She wanted to go back to her hotel. Her husband was waiting there. She had low blood pressure, had had it for years, and had simply forgotten to take her pills this morning. The heat and the high humidity had taken their toll on her. She would feel better as soon as she took her pills. No reason to put her under the care of a hospital. The ambulance crew packed up their equipment and Paul hailed one of the taxis that were waiting in long lines on the Peak for customers.

———

Elizabeth Owen was staying with her husband at the InterContinental Hotel in Tsim Sha Tsui on the Kowloon side of the harbor. The taxi ride seemed to take forever. They were stuck in a jam on Peak Road because of roadwork; traffic crawled through the narrow road at a walking pace down to Central. The approach to Cross-Harbour Tunnel was congested, as it was almost every day. They barely exchanged a word. Elizabeth Owen kept her eyes closed most of the time. The odd tear ran down her cheeks, but Paul did not hear her sobbing or crying. He wondered if he should ask her what she was sad about, and if he could be of any help, but discarded the thought immediately as a reflex from another life. Why should he get involved? What did this woman matter to him? He would take her back to her hotel and make sure that someone there took care of her and that they called her husband. And he would leave her his telephone number in case she needed it. That would have to be enough. He didn't have the strength to do more, even if he had wanted to. Paul felt that the last hour had taken a lot out of him. He had spoken more than he normally did in an entire week. He wanted to go back to Lamma. Back to his house. Back to his memories.

Elizabeth Owen. The name meant nothing to him. Was he mixing her up with someone else? Or had they really met before? But where? And if so, why was she behaving as if she did not know him?

He hated the sound of a ringing telephone. It didn't matter which ring tone he chose; it always disturbed his peace most unpleasantly. Paul sat on the terrace in the garden, finished the rest of his morning tea, and let it ring. He was not the kind of person who jumped up as soon as someone called him. His mobile phone was in the kitchen. Only very few people had his number; it was probably Christine, but he did not feel the slightest desire to speak to her or to anyone else, and he hoped that she would give up soon. There was silence for a few moments then the phone started ringing again, without pause. He stood up and fetched it.

Paul did not recognize her voice or her name.

"Owen," she repeated slowly. "Elizabeth Owen. You helped me yesterday on the Peak. Don't you remember?"

"I'm sorry. I didn't catch your name the first time. Of course I remember. Are you feeling better?"

Silence. He heard noises from the street and her breathing, but not her voice. "Hello?" he said to her. "Is everything all right?"

"I need your help," she said. "Can we meet?"

"Meet?" he repeated, not sure whether he had understood her correctly.

"Yes."

"When?"

"Now."

"Oh God, that's not at all convenient, I ..."

"It's extremely urgent," she interrupted. "Please, Mr. Leibovitz."

He heard her voice cracking and suddenly its trembling sound seemed as familiar to him as her face had been yesterday.

"Where are you now?"

"In front of the police station in ..."

Paul heard the roar of traffic in the background and a man's voice saying, "In Admiralty, honey."

"I'll be at your hotel in two hours."

———

Elizabeth was waiting for him in the lobby. She was even paler than Paul had remembered from yesterday. Her skin seemed almost transparent: Blue veins were prominent on her temples and her chin. Her eyes were red rimmed and her hair straggled over her face. She took him by both hands and pressed them firmly. "Thank you so much for coming so quickly." She gestured toward the man by her side. "This is my husband, Richard."

Richard Owen stretched his hand out in greeting. He was a bear of a man, and his age was as difficult to guess as his wife's. His hair was flecked with gray but thick, and his face was tanned and taut, as though the passing of the years were nothing to him. He was at least six feet two inches tall, with broad shoulders and a solid torso, though not portly, and had bushy eyebrows and very long arms. His handshake and his deep, insistent voice made Paul wince.

The Owens led him to a ready-laid table in the lobby. On the other side of the window, which climbed over three floors from floor to ceiling, was a picture-postcard view of the Hong Kong skyline. They ordered coffee for all three of them and a whiskey as well for Mr. Owen.

"Mr. Leibovitz," Elizabeth Owen said in a quiet voice. "We'd like to ask you to help us." Paul could see that she was making an effort not to lose her composure. She swallowed a few times and her eyes filled with tears.

"How can I help you?"

"We . . . We're looking for our son. He's disappeared."

Paul felt the blood drain away from his face and he felt dizzy for a moment.

"Your son?" he heard himself say.

"Michael. Michael Owen," she said in a way that implied that he must know him.

"What do you mean when you say he disappeared?"

"He traveled to Shenzhen two days ago and was meant to be back that evening. We've heard nothing more from him since."

"What did he want to go to China for?"

"We have a factory just on the other side of the border, in Guangdong Province," her husband explained quietly, when he realized that his wife's voice was gradually giving out on her. "He had a lunch appointment with our business partner Mr. Tang, Victor Tang. But he never turned up to that appointment."

Paul had no idea what he ought to say. He could feel his heart racing and his breathing growing shallow. He wanted to comfort the woman. He wanted to say to her that she mustn't worry, that surely nothing had happened, that everything would be cleared up in a few hours. That everything would be fine. He was unable to speak. *I'm sorry to have to tell you . . .*

"We talked to the Hong Kong police this morning, but they weren't very helpful. You're the only Western person I know in this city and you said yesterday that you've lived here a long time, so I thought . . ." She did not finish her sentence.

Paul nodded mutely.

She turned to him and gave him a pleading look of desperation that moved him in a way that he found almost unbearable.

"I'm afraid. I'm so afraid. Can you understand that?" she whispered, and started crying.

Richard Owen sat by her side on the couch and shifted from side to side, uneasily. He was clearly uncomfortable with his wife's tears. He went to put an arm around her shoulders, but she shook herself briefly and he withdrew his arm. He cast Paul a look as if to draw him into a male complicity. Paul looked away.

"I think you're worrying too much, honey."

Paul had not heard so much helplessness in someone's voice in a long time.

"Michael is thirty years old. He's a grown man. I'm sure he'll call us in the next few hours and explain everything."

That didn't sound very convincing, Paul thought, and he wondered how he could help. He had no contacts in the Hong Kong police force any longer. The two British police inspectors he used to know had more or less voluntarily taken early retirement and gone back to England when the colony was returned to China. That left only Detective Superintendent Zhang Lin at the homicide division in Shenzhen. If something had happened to a foreigner there he would know about it.

"I have a friend who's in the police force in Shenzhen. I'll give him a call and get in touch with you this afternoon or tomorrow morning," Paul said. "I can't do much more for you right now."

Elizabeth nodded thankfully, and her husband drained his whiskey glass in one gulp. They sat silently for a moment before they took their leave. The Owens walked slowly to the elevators with their heads bowed. Paul had the impression that Richard Owen's left leg dragged a little and for an instant this big man seemed very small to him.

———

"Paul?" Christine must have recognized his number on her phone. The surprise and pleasure in her voice were unmistakable.

"Yes, it's me. Is it a bad time? Should I call back later?" What stupid questions, he immediately thought. He knew from what she told him that her travel agency, World Wide Travel, consisted of a tiny office that she shared with two employees, and that their phones rang from morning to night. He heard a few female voices in the background, punctuated by phones ringing almost nonstop.

"It's no problem. Can you wait a minute, please?" She asked the customer on the other line for his number and promised to call him back in a few minutes.

"Where are you? On Lamma? It's noisy where you are."

"No. I'm standing in front of the InterContinental."

"What are you doing there? I thought you wanted to be on your own."

Christine had asked him out to dinner that night. She thought distraction was good for him. Paul disagreed, and thought her invitation was a sign of her lack of sensitivity. He did not want to be distracted; that was the whole point. He did not want to be occupied so that time would pass more quickly. The more quickly time passed, the more destructive it was to memory. Time faded memories.

"Shall we meet?" Christine offered, instead. "I have time for a coffee."

"Where?"

"Here in Wan Chai. I'll meet you at the MTR so you don't get lost in the crowds."

"I don't know." The more they talked, the worse he felt. It was always the same. She couldn't help him. Why had he called her in the first place?

"Or we could meet later and . . ."

"No," he interrupted her. "I think I'd better go back to Lamma."

She didn't say anything for a moment. The sound of phones ringing, women's voices, someone calling her name. "I could come to Lamma this evening, and we could have dinner at Sampan on the harbor."

"No," he repeated, "absolutely not," as if there was a risk that she might come secretly, against his wishes.

"Paul, you don't make it easy for me sometimes."

"I know, Christine. I'm sorry. I'll be in touch later."

He did not want a girlfriend. He was no longer capable of loving. He did not want to disappoint and be disappointed any longer. He wanted to be alone.

IV

They had met in winter on a cold, rainy Sunday morning on Lamma while he was on his daily walk and she was looking for Sok Kwu Wan village and the ferry back to Hong Kong. It had started raining heavily. He had been taking shelter in a viewing pavilion, looking over the lead-gray sea with its curling crests of white foam. He startled when she spoke from behind him.

"Excuse me."

Like her, he was wearing waterproof hiking shoes and a dark-green rain hood that hung low over his forehead. His face was wet and a drop of water dangled from the tip of his nose; a couple of gray strands of hair were pasted to his brow.

The rain pattered on their backs, and she took a step closer to this strange man, who insisted on standing right in the middle of the shelter on the only totally dry spot, and was staring at her with such surprise that it seemed he thought he was alone in the world.

"Excuse me," she repeated. "I didn't mean to startle you."

He still said nothing. She had the feeling that he might shatter any moment, like a car windshield cracking into thousands of little pieces. She had never seen such a vulnerable expression on anyone's face before. She would have liked to take him by the hand, lead him to a bench, sit down next to him, and look out at the sea until he was able to speak again. But there was no bench, it was cold, and the ferry was leaving in forty minutes.

"Could you tell me how to get to Sok Kwu Wan, perhaps?"

He said nothing but looked at her and, finally, nodded, as if he had thought something over long and hard.

She tried again. "I'm looking for Sok Kwu Wan. Am I going the right way?"

"Why are you going there?"

Did he not understand her English or was he just not listening properly? Why was this man not able to give a simple answer to a simple question?

"To take the ferry to Hong Kong," she replied.

He nodded again. "Continue along this path. You'll see it behind the second hilltop you pass."

"How long will it take to get there?"

He looked out into the rain, which was drumming down onto the roof more and more heavily, and wrinkled his brow. "In this weather? A long time, I'm afraid," he suddenly said in Cantonese.

She smiled briefly, without knowing exactly why. Was it his soft, quiet voice with its strange singsong manner, which was completely unsuited to the harsh, brusque sound of her language, or the round-about way in which they were conversing?

They waited until the rain let up. He wanted to know why she had come to Lamma in such dreadful weather, and she had replied that she was asking herself exactly the same thing. A friend had rec-ommended a walk on this island, but she must have come in the fall. She talked about her Sunday walks on Lantau and in the New Terri-tories and how beautiful the Sai Kung Peninsula and the beaches on it were, and how hardly anyone knew how much green space Hong Kong had, really, or how many nature reserves there were. He lis-tened to her so attentively and patiently, which no one had done for a long time, and gazed at her so earnestly with his deep-blue eyes, as if she really had something important to say, that she just kept on talking and talking. She talked about how much these outings meant to her, how she sat for six days a week from 9:00 AM to 7:00 PM in an open-plan office with two employees and one intern. She told him about her twelve-year-old son, Josh, who had absolutely refused to continue coming on these walks with her a year ago and spent the time with friends instead, wasting his time on Game Boys and video games. She had given up trying to persuade him to come with her or to change his mind with treats or threats. As a single mother she had to choose her battles. She talked so much that she only realized too late how cold she was and how the ever-growing wind had blown the rain under her jacket and through her pants. She shivered. He invited her to warm herself up at his house.

Even though it was still raining, they set off with him leading the way and her in close step after him, trying to shelter herself behind his back. She followed him as he turned right in Yung Shue Wan some distance from the ferry terminal, crossed a small valley, and climbed yet another hill. She followed him, still without uttering a word, onto a path that grew narrower and darker until they stepped through a garden gate and stood before a house that could hardly be seen from the path, as it was hidden behind a wall of trees and bushes.

She followed him into the house, up to the first floor, took off her wet clothes, had a hot shower as he had advised her to, and, as the water gradually warmed her body and the steam filled the bathroom, she felt desire rise in her in a way she had not experienced for a long time. She knew that she would not get dressed after this, that she would follow him to his bedroom and slide into his bed, that he would not need to practice any great arts of seduction for her to give herself to him. He would only have to say a word, make a gesture, give a hint, however subtle, and it would be enough.

Instead, she heard him clattering away in the kitchen.

He had laid out a white bathrobe for her along with a long-sleeved man's silk undershirt, a sweater, a pair of old sweatpants, and thick woolen socks, all much too big for her but dry and warm. She walked quietly down the stairs to the ground floor, which clearly only consisted of the hall, the stairs to the first floor, and two big rectangular rooms. In one of the rooms was a rectangular Chinese table of reddish-brown rosewood and eight matching chairs; at the far end of the room were two couches and a low antique table. The floor was tiled with deep-red square tiles and the walls were painted white; Chinese calligraphy scrolls hung between the windows. In each corner was a palm tree in a giant blue and yellow Chinese urn. The house seemed remarkably tidy to her. There was no clutter, no newspapers lying around, no paperwork, no DVDs. The floor seemed to be freshly mopped and the table just dusted. He must have a hardworking Filipino cleaner.

She entered the room where the clatter of crockery was coming from. Apart from an antique wooden lounger in front of the window to the garden and an old red Southern Chinese wedding chest with a big circular brass fitting, the room was empty. It adjoined the small eat-in kitchen with a wooden counter that was set with two placemats. Steam rose from the teacups; they smelled of lemongrass and ginger. She had never been in a home that presented so many puzzles. This man clearly had money and liked Chinese antiques, but why did he live on Lamma and not in the Mid-Levels or Repulse Bay, like most of the well-off foreigners? Or was the house just a weekend home? His Cantonese was excellent, but she could see no sign of a Chinese wife or girlfriend. Who had he learned it from? Did he live alone? She had noticed a child's coat and rain boots in the closet and markings and dates on a door frame recording the growth of a child.

His voice roused her from her thoughts. "I've made tea and some hot soup. Would you like some?"

"Yes, please. Very much."

When he noticed how the sweater, with its sleeves rolled up several times, and sweatpants hung loosely from her, a brief smile passed over his face.

She felt her heart pound. A gesture, a hint would suffice.

The soup was delicious. A vegetable and pork belly broth that her grandmother had made for her when she was a child.

"This tastes wonderful."

"Thank you."

"Did you make it yourself?"

"Yes," he said. "Yesterday. I just warmed it up."

"Do you cook often?"

"Every day."

She wondered if any of her women friends still cooked for themselves. Everyone she could think of had a Filipina maid who cooked for them, and on Sundays they all ate in restaurants. Her husband, like all Hong Kong men she knew, really, had never even been able to prepare a decent congee.

"I suspect a Filipina maid cooks for you. And on Sundays, when she's off, you go out to eat."

She suppressed a grin.

"And your husband . . ."

She interrupted him. "I've divorced."

"And your ex-husband couldn't even prepare a decent congee for you?"

When had a man last made her laugh?

"You know Hong Kong well, and you speak very good Cantonese."

"You mean, very good for a *gweilo*."

"No. I mean very good."

"Thank you."

"Where did you learn it?"

"In Hong Kong."

She looked at him, how he bent over his bowl spooning his soup into his mouth and slurping as though he were Chinese.

"You were born here, right?"

"What makes you think that?"

"Because . . . Because . . ."

"Because I slurp my soup, can cook Chinese food, and speak Cantonese?" he retorted. "That should actually prove the opposite. Or have you ever met a foreigner who was born here or grew up here because his father was in Her Majesty's Service or worked for a company here who spoke Cantonese or Mandarin or had even the slightest interest in the culture and history of Hong Kong?" He poured more tea for her and for himself before continuing. "No. I was born in Germany. My mother is German and my father is American. I first came to Hong Kong in 1975 via Vietnam and Bangkok. I've lived here ever since."

"On Lamma?" she asked, astounded.

"No, in the city. I moved to Lamma only two years ago. Shortly after my divorce."

"Don't you feel it gets too lonely here?"

He shook his head gently.

"Do you live here on your own?"

He looked her straight in the eye. There was that expression again, that she had felt so intensely before: vulnerable, open, and raw, a kind of nakedness that was unfamiliar to her.

"Some days, yes. Some days, no."

She remembered the child's shoes in the hall. She wanted to ask a question, but his look told her that it would be better to stay silent.

"And you?" he asked her, after a long pause.

It was an invitation that she could not refuse. He was the first person in a long time who was paying attention to her without wanting anything in return. Without demanding a cheaper flight, an upgrade, a pay raise, a day off, or money for a new computer game. The first person for whom she did not have to slip into a particular role: not be the mother, the ex-wife, the boss, or the daughter. He simply sat across from her listening, leaning his head to one side then the other, sipping his tea and asking her questions. She told him about the Catholic school she had attended in Hong Kong and about getting her degree in tourism in Vancouver. About how difficult it was to earn money from a small travel agency in the age of the Internet and to bring up a child at the same time. About the evenings she fell asleep, exhausted, in front of the television, and Josh or Tita woke her at night in front of the flickering screen. About the Sunday dinners with her mother, a burdensome duty that she, like most Hong Kongers, could not escape. She talked about the failure of her marriage. About her husband, who had had a Chinese mistress and child on the other side of the border for years and not told her a thing. Who had supported this woman and their child throughout his marriage to her. That was the real reason why they had never had enough money, why they had to sell the small rental apartment in Kowloon Tong and, later on, even their car, though the business at World Wide Travel had still been going well. She had never really thought about it, or, looking back on it, perhaps she had not wanted to. She had trusted her husband and there had always been good reasons for his many business trips to China. So he claimed, at least, and she had not wanted to doubt him, not even when the first rumors of his infidelity had reached her. She had defended him: to her friends, to her mother. She had believed him, she had wanted to believe him, but he had deceived her, cheated on her, and betrayed her. He had gone behind her back and lied to her. She said all this without self-pity. That was the risk that human beings took when they trusted other people; that was the price they paid. Later, her relations had whispered among themselves that she had brought this on herself; she had been so naïve, so trusting. She had had no contact with her family for months because of their opinions. She would not have done any differently today. Believing and hoping. Over and over again.

As if trusting was only for fools. As if we had a choice.

Darkness had started to fall by the time Christine's torrent of words slowed to a trickle. In the twilight she could make out Paul's shadowy outline; he sat opposite her, motionless. The flickering of the candle, which he had lighted, fell on his face. He looked exhausted, as if he was the one who had been talking the whole time. They sat in silence for a long time; it was not an ominous silence, though, but one that lifted their spirits.

A gesture, a mere hint, and . . .

———

He walked her down to the ferry terminal. It had stopped raining and the light from the streetlamps was reflected in the puddles.

The restaurants in Yung Shue Wan were brightly lit and full of big families who didn't mind the cold wind; their laughter and chatter sounded through the village and over the hills around it. A couple of fishing boats were bobbing up and down in the harbor.

The ferry arrived on time.

They stood facing each other, silent, unsure of how to part. But even though they did not arrange to meet again, parting with a noncommittal "Maybe we'll see each other again," her feeling of intimacy, of being comforted and safe, remained undiminished.

Sleep was out of the question. He lay on the futon, stared up at the ceiling, and listened to the whirring fan and the furious whine of the mosquitoes trying in vain to find a hole in the mosquito net. The rain drummed heavily against the windowpanes once again. He had spoken more today and listened to more than he had in all the previous months in total. Of course he had had to offer the freezing and shivering woman a hot shower and some hot soup; he had not given it a second thought. But why hadn't she left after that? As far as he could remember, he had not prompted her to do so. Neither directly nor indirectly. Why not? Why had he let this intruder in his world not only do as she pleased but even told her where he was born, how long he had lived in Hong Kong, and that he was divorced? He could not explain his sudden talkativeness. Nor his attentiveness when she had talked. Listening and asking questions. Over and over again. What for? Had he really wanted to know all that? In retrospect, this sudden intimacy with a stranger was beyond unpleasant, as if he had stepped over an invisible boundary and given away something precious about himself, betrayed someone or something, though he could not say who or what.

As if trusting was only for fools. As if we had a choice. These words stuck in his mind. We always have a choice, he had wanted to reply to her, but he had kept silent instead. She was a beautiful woman;

he had to give her that. He pictured her sitting in front of him in the twilight, her pageboy haircut, her skin unusually tanned for a Hong Kong woman, her slim but toned arms and hands, her long, tapering fingers. He heard her voice: a soft, agreeable voice that removed much of the aggressiveness and crudeness from the sound of Cantonese, and which made her English unusually gentle and melodic. It still sounded clearly in his ears. Paul remembered far too many details about the day and it disturbed him.

He felt revulsion rise in him. A disgust for himself. His chattiness. His questions. His interest in her.

———

The following Sunday, he went into the village later in the morning, when the ferries with the day-trippers from Hong Kong were arriving, and did something he never usually did: he sat down on the Sampan terrace, which gave him a good view of the passengers arriving. He told himself he wasn't waiting for anybody. He told himself he had followed an impulse. When he saw her from afar among the throng of visitors, he knew that he had been lying.

They spent the day together. It was an unusually mild, pleasant day for the season; the sun shone from a cloudless sky, and the beginnings of the brief tropical spring were in the air. They walked without exchanging many words. They drank tea on his terrace. And from the silence, Paul started telling her about himself, hesitating a little to begin with. Why had he lived in Germany and America as a child? Christine wanted to know.

Where should he begin? With his father, Aaron? The crazy Jew from New York—or Brooklyn, New York, to be exact, he'd always insisted on that distinction—that remarkable man who had gone to Europe as an American soldier and, in Germany, of all places, in Munich, had fallen in love with the daughter of an official in the Social Democratic Party. Or with Heidelinde, his mother, for whom the relationship must have been a kind of delayed act of resistance to Nazi racial policy, for his parents were so ill suited that he had never been able to see any other reason for their union. How his father had paid for his love for a German. His family in New York had given him the choice between separating from his wife or being disowned by them. After he had decided to stay with the German, all contact with the family was broken off and never, as far as he knew, resumed. Paul had been the only relation at his father's funeral.

He told her about that day in the spring of 1962, shortly after his tenth birthday, when his family had moved practically over-night from Munich to New York, without anyone explaining the reason for the move to him. Aaron Leibovitz had come home one night—Paul remembered it very clearly now as he was talking about it—with his pale skin even whiter than usual, his long nose even more pointed, his fleshy lips stretched into a thin line. He had sat down at the kitchen table and said they would be moving, to New York, to Manhattan, to the Lower East Side. In two weeks at the most. His wife had dried her hands on her apron and walked out of the room without saying a word, as she so often did. Aaron Leibovitz said nothing for a while then he stood up, put his hand on his son's shoulder, mumbled something about being sorry and about packing his things, and left the house. Paul would have liked to say to him that he needn't be sorry, not at all, quite the oppo-site, in fact. He had no objections to moving house, wherever they moved to. With a Jewish father and with the daughter of a Social Democrat as a mother, living in postwar Munich was not exactly easy. Paul could not say which of the insults flung at him in school was worse, "Jewish pig" or "Socialist pig," and to be honest, when he thought about moving to America, he could think of no one he would miss in Germany, apart from his grandparents, though he was not even sure about that. He would have missed Heinrich, his only friend, whom he had shared a bench with in class, but he had died the year before from a lung infection that had been diagnosed too late.

Christine listened without asking many questions; perhaps that was why he kept on talking. He didn't know why or how, perhaps it was her way of listening to him without interrupting, without commenting on what she heard, without taking it as an opportunity to tell her own story or make a witty remark, as Meredith used to do. Her comments had often been astute or funny or both at the same time, and at the beginning he had admired her for it, but later, they had irritated him and driven him to silence. He had felt used, as though what he said was nothing more to her than another opportunity to prove her intelligence and her sense of humor. Christine was different. She took in what he said and it moved her, he saw it in her eyes, and she was fine with his silences. It did him good but it felt strange too.

Paul thought about how much silence there had been in his family and how oppressive, unhappy, and suffocating he had found it. It had never been a communal silence, more a brooding over things unsaid. He talked about the six-day voyage from Hamburg to New York, when this family had been even quieter than it usually was. "We spent most of our time on deck. We stood by the rail, looked at the sea, and imagined a new beginning. My father dreamed, I think, of a flourishing business that would make us forget about the debts and the bankruptcy in Germany that had forced us to move. My mother must have dreamed of a marriage without fighting, and I dreamed of a school I could go to without the pit of my stomach aching with dread, and of having a friend."

He stopped talking and waited to see if she would say something, but she was wise enough to stay silent.

"After a week," he continued, "I knew that I would remain a stranger in this new world. The place I came from was not just Munich, it was also, in the New York of the 1960s, a black mark that I would never be free of, no matter how I tried. Here, I was the German, the Nazi, the little Hitler, and hardly any of the boys on the street or in the school playground cared that my surname was Leibovitz, that my father was a Jew and had fought against the evil Germans. My accent gave me away as soon as I opened my mouth.

That's why I only ever spoke after being asked to do so several times, and even then only very reluctantly and hesitantly."

He looked at Christine as if to make sure that she wasn't laughing at him, to make sure that she understood what he was saying. She nodded, but instead of continuing, Paul stood up and began walking up and down the terrace, saying nothing.

No, she had not done anything wrong. No, it was not that she should have interrupted him or said anything, expressed her understanding or sympathy in some way. Why had he suddenly fallen silent, then? He himself did not know.

At the ferry, when they said good-bye, she asked him for his telephone number, but he ignored her request. When she came to the house again the following weekend, he lay on his futon and did not move.

He knew that he was hurting her, but he did not have the strength for explanations. He had burned himself out the previous Sunday, and had suffered from it the whole week. She called his name a few more times, knocked on the door, and waited a few minutes, which seemed endless, until she finally went. The next morning, he found her business card, which she had posted through the slot in the door. He rang her ten days later.

And so the last six months had passed. Pleasurable Sundays, filled with harmony, were followed by days of silence, difficult weeks in which he could only bear to hear her voice on the telephone, in which he asked her on Saturdays not to come but spent Sundays walking up and down on the pier impatiently, full of longing, full of trepidation that she might have come against his wishes. He could only talk to her about Justin in the sketchiest way, and he could hardly bear any physical contact. Their only attempt to sleep with each other had ended after a few minutes. No part of him had moved; he had lain next to her rigidly like a plank of wood. Over and over again, he told himself that he had to end this relationship; the reason he did not do so was Christine's patience with his moods, the considerateness with which she reacted. She did not accuse him of anything. She did not ask him for anything. Why not?

"Because I can feel that you're giving me what you can right now," she had replied.

"And that's enough for you?"

"I think time is on my side," she had said, with a shy smile.

VI

Paul was still sitting on the harbor promenade more than an hour after his meeting with the Owens.

He pulled his cell phone out. Zhang's number was saved somewhere in the phone; all he had to do was find it among all the extras, programs, services, profiles, and functions. He pressed the wrong button a few times until he finally got the ring tone.

"Hello?"

It was always good to hear Zhang's deep, familiar smoker's voice.

"It's me. Am I disturbing you?"

"You? Never. You know that."

"Where are you?" asked Paul. "Do you have a minute?"

"I'm sitting on the other side of the street from the police station, eating a bad noodle soup. Awful."

"Are you alone?"

"What a question. Have you ever seen a Chinese person eating alone? I'm surrounded by . . ."

"I mean, do you have other officers with you?"

"No."

Paul told him about his meeting with the Owens in a few sentences. When he had finished, he waited for a reaction from Zhang, but in vain. He heard the sound of traffic and a couple of men's voices in the background, but not his friend's. He heard the scrape of chairs and tables and someone swearing. "Zhang? Are you still there?"

"Of course. I was just paying and looking for a quieter spot to talk in. Paul, what do you think about coming to visit me again?"

"What do you mean?"

"Exactly what I said."

"Uh, yes, of course, I'd love to, sometime," Paul replied, confused and unsure about whether his friend had heard what he had said.

"You haven't been for a long time. A lot has changed."

"Yes, but you know how I hate leaving Lamma."

"What about this evening?"

At first, Paul thought he had misheard him. This evening? What on earth was Zhang thinking?

"Are you crazy? Do you know what you're asking me to do?"

"I'm not asking anything. I'm simply asking my dear friend to dinner."

"Zhang, that's very kind of you, but Hong Kong is already too much for me. How am I supposed to make it over to you in Shenzhen?"

"Listen, we'll meet at the station, buy some groceries together, go to my house, and I'll cook for you. After that I'll take you back to the border and put you on a train."

It sounded as if he was inviting his doddery old father, who suffered from dementia, over on a visit. Paul paused to think, and Zhang pounced on the hesitation.

"You can do it," he said immediately. "Just for a couple of hours. You climbed the Peak yesterday, right?"

"Hmm." Zhang would not leave him in peace.

"When was the last time you saw Mei? She'll be so pleased to see you."

Paul liked Zhang's wife very much and, apart from at Justin's funeral, it really was years since he had seen her. It was quiet now in the background. Zhang had clearly found himself a spot where no one could hear him.

"Apart from that, there are a few things that I'm not too keen to discuss on the phone."

"Has something happened?" Paul asked, startled.

"There's quite an uproar at the station. I heard something about it in the corridor just now."

"About Michael Owen?"

"I don't know. They found a body in Datouling Forest Park this morning. I think it's a foreigner."

———

Hung Hom. Tai Wai. Sha Tin. The Kowloon-Canton Railway train sped from station to station. Paul was still not sure if he had taken far too much upon himself. But his friend had sounded quite definite and convincing; in the end, Paul had placed more trust in Zhang's encouraging voice than in his own feelings of weakness. He also felt a strange sense of duty toward Mrs. Owen, a mother who was worrying about her son. If he could be helpful to her, he would try it for one afternoon.

Tai Po Market. Tai Wo. To Paul, the station names sounded like a distant echo from another life. He had often made this journey before, not just to see Zhang in Shenzhen but also on weekends, to escape the hemmed-in feeling and frenzy of Hong Kong and its bustling, noisy heartbeat. He had sought refuge here with Wendy Li, back when he thought their love had a chance. For two years, they had traveled to the New Territories nearly every time they had a day off; they had gone hiking and camping, made love in the night on the warm sand of the Sai Kung beach, and, in the candlelight, dreamed of having children together. They had seen each other for the last time in Sai Kung. She had told him that she loved him, and how grateful she was to him, because no one else in the world could make her laugh the way he did. Three days later, she had married the man that her family had chosen for her, a man whose existence Paul had not known anything of. How long ago was that now? What had happened to the Paul who had been so good at making women laugh? Who had liked to present a woman with a picnic on the beach by candlelight or spoil her with breakfast in bed? Who had been able to love so passionately? When had he ceased to exist? After Wendy got married? During his marriage to Meredith? After Justin's death? "That must have happened in another life," he used to say so often. How many lives did a person have? Two? Three? Or just one, after all?

The train slowed down and before long, in the blink of an eye, paddy fields gave way to barbed wire fences, roads, cars, concrete walls, and buildings that towered in the sky. Skyscrapers clustered together like trees in a thick forest. The train stopped with a jerk and people jostled to get out in a frenzy, as if not everyone was allowed to get off, as if whoever did not manage to get off the car in a few seconds would be forced to make the journey back immediately.

Paul followed the crowds up the stairs as they pushed and shoved him through various dimly lit corridors to the automated immigration control. He slid his Hong Kong identity card into the machine and, seconds later, passed through the turnstile. He walked through the arrival hall out onto the station concourse and rang Zhang.

"Are you there already?" he asked, amazed. "I still have work to do in the office. Do you want to wait or shall we meet at four in Starbucks? It's around the corner from our apartment. Then we can go get the groceries and I'll cook. Okay?"

"Okay. Where's the Starbucks?"

"In CITIC City Plaza. That's the big new shopping mall."

"Is it far from the station?"

"No, not at all. Take the new metro line 1 to Ke Xue Guan Station. Exit D there is the south side of Shennan Zhong Road. Walk up the road to the shopping mall. On the right is Seibu, the Japanese department store, and on the left is the Chillout Lounge. You'll see Kentucky Fried Chicken, Pizza Hut, and . . ."

"Zhang, you've got to be kidding me."

"What do you mean?"

"A chill-out lounge?"

"You haven't been here for a long time."

"Not for years."

Zhang sighed. "Would you prefer to wait at the station for me, then?"

Paul thought for a moment. "That would probably be better, yes."

"Then wait for me in the station concourse. I'll be there in forty-five minutes."

————

Paul sat down on a bench and thought about the first time he had crossed this border. It must have been in the summer of 1980, shortly after Deng Xiaoping had declared this insignificant backwater a special economic zone. Back then he had had to cross the Lo Wu Bridge on foot and rent a bicycle at the station. There were no taxis, not even a bus service then. He had cycled through the puddle-strewn streets made muddy by the monsoon rains, past pig farms and basic single-story buildings. Shenzhen had been nothing more than a small town where people made a living from fishing or cultivating rice. The passersby had worn blue or green Mao suits, he remembered quite clearly, and their looks of surprise, often fear, had followed him wherever he went. Whenever he had stopped, a crowd had gathered around him and he had been marveled over and stared at, touched and patted. Two children had pulled at the black hairs growing on his forearms. He had encountered searching looks and sometimes confused expressions; none of them had let him out of their sight for a second. When he had used a public toilet, the curious people had trailed him to the door and waited outside to see what would happen. In the toilet hut, several Chinese people had been squatting over holes in the ground with their trousers down. Paul remembered well their loud cries of horror when they saw the foreigner come in. Two of the men had almost fallen into the drop latrines in shock. The commotion acted like a marching order for the curious onlookers. They flooded in through the small doorway, and in an instant, Paul was surrounded by dozens of people in a space that stank of piss and shit. At first they still stood at arm's length, but the more people crowded in, the smaller the distance between him and them. Soon they were standing so close to him that he could feel their breath on his skin. He tried smiling at them but there was no response. They whispered and murmured among themselves. At the time, Paul's Cantonese was not good enough to understand everything they said, but he made out the words "foreign devil," "spy," and "class enemy." He would never forget how the looks of amazement and curiosity gradually faded from their faces, to be replaced by a look of brooding distrust. He tried to make his way to the exit, but the men standing in front of him were crammed too close together. Even if they had wanted to make room for him, they could not have done so. He was pouring with sweat. He wanted to get out, just to get out there. Suddenly he heard a deep voice calling loudly, which made the crowd fall silent. A policeman was standing in the doorway. He looked around the room and, after he had spotted Paul, he barked orders for everyone who was not using the toilet to leave at once. Before long he and Paul were alone.

They stood facing each other in silence, sizing each other up. The policeman was wearing an ill-fitting uniform that was much too big for his slight build. They must have been about the same age. Paul noticed the man's features were soft and did not match the stern, brisk voice.

"Now you can continue in peace," he said, and turned his back to Paul. "I hope you don't need toilet paper. There's none here."

That was how Paul Leibovitz and Zhang Lin met for the first time, and a friendship that had lasted over twenty-five years now had grown from that meeting. There had been times when Paul had traveled to Shenzhen nearly every week, and later on, when it had become easier for Chinese citizens to travel to Hong Kong, Zhang had also visited his friend several times a year. After Justin's death, Zhang was the only person whose company Paul could bear. Zhang came to Lamma for a day every six weeks. They did not do much; just sat on the terrace, drank tea, played Go or chess or listened to music. The first year, Zhang had often cooked a big pot of soup in the afternoon that Paul would finish off the following week. Zhang was able to listen and also able to be silent. He was wise enough to know that there was no possible comfort and honest enough not even to try to hide the fact that he knew this. For this, Paul was immeasurably grateful. Otherwise he would have had to ask him not to come again. Some days they had not exchanged more than a few sentences. Nevertheless, Zhang would come again six weeks later without fail.

Zhang's most recent visit was over a month ago, and the thought of seeing him again now filled Paul with a feeling of calm that did him good. He stood up, looking to catch sight of his friend, and soon he saw him coming toward him from a distance. He walked with a slight limp, and his blue jacket and his shoes were more worn out than they should have been for a detective superintendent; a cigarette that had gone out hung from his lower lip. They hugged each other briefly, and Paul could see in Zhang's eyes that he understood exactly what this visit meant for him. He had never experienced this mutual understanding, which needed barely a word or a gesture, with anyone else before.

"Always good to see you. Here today, especially," Zhang said in greeting. He smiled. "Have you eaten? Shall we go and buy the food?"

"Sure."

They walked across the station concourse to the metro station. It had opened just a few weeks ago, and everything was still so empty and clean that Paul felt as if they were on a trial journey. They had the last car almost to themselves. Zhang, who looked exhausted, flopped onto one of the shiny aluminum seats.

"You can't imagine what's going on at work right now," he said, lowering his voice. "Everyone's running around like crazy, as if they've been told to practice self-criticism in public. Or give access to their bank accounts. Even the mayor's office has called."

"Why?"

"Why? The dead foreigner is driving everyone into a frenzy. Let's say he's not just a tourist who sadly happened to die of heart failure while taking a walk. Let's say he's an investor, an entrepreneur from America, who manufactures lights, rain boots, or Santa Clauses in China and has died a violent death. That would be . . ." He searched for words. "That's never happened here but I imagine that would lead to one or two headlines in Hong Kong and in America. What do you think?"

Paul thought for a moment. "Probably. At least in Hong Kong. What do you know about the dead man?"

"A foreigner, and a Western one to boot. About thirty years old. Six feet two inches tall. Blond hair. Identity not known as yet; he had no ID on him. Cause of death unknown. We get the autopsy tomorrow morning. Two gardeners found him this morning in Datouling Forest Park on the bank of a small lake, supposedly with a smashed skull, but that's a rumor. I've not been able to talk to either of the men yet."

"Are you thinking it's murder?"

"It's not decided yet. It wouldn't surprise me if there was an official announcement tomorrow saying that he died a natural death. Otherwise it would be a pretty bad story and we'd have a lot of trouble. Who'd want that?"

"Are you one of the investigators?"

"No idea. You know they don't like assigning me anymore. Apart from that, there's not a lot to investigate yet."

"And if it's really a murder?" Paul asked.

"Then I might be able to get one or two people to help me. Does the description match this Michael person?"

Paul racked his brain. "No idea. I forgot to ask the Owens what their son looked like."

Zhang sighed loudly. "You'll never become a detective."

"But the age is right. His father is tall and blond and . . ." Paul fell silent. He thought about Elizabeth Owen. He thought about her fainting fit, about her tears, about her husband sitting next to her silently, and for the first time, he realized that this dead man could be Michael Owen. The image of the mother's face distorted with fear and pain came before him. He shook his head as if he could rid himself of it that way.

They got off and slogged up a long staircase back into daylight. Clouds of dust hung in the air, and a cement mixer almost ran him over when it turned into a construction site without paying any heed to pedestrians. This place had nothing in common with the town he remembered. When exactly was it that he had last visited Zhang? He had come with Justin then, before he fell ill, so it was four or five years ago. Even then he had noticed the effects of the economic boom in how quickly Shenzhen had changed. Now he barely recognized the place. A metro system, even wider streets, even more cars, even taller buildings, even more people. There had been fifty thousand on his first visit. How many were there now? Seven million? Ten? Twelve?

The CITIC City Plaza was a modern gray block of steel, concrete, and glass, a sight Paul was familiar with from Hong Kong. Even the fountains in front of it had been copied by the architects. Paul and Zhang walked through the shopping mall and crossed the street behind it to the police detective's apartment. Paul gradually began to recognize the place: On the corner was the small Muslim noodle-soup restaurant that he had eaten at so often. Just as before, a young man covered in flour was standing in front kneading a lump of dough and unhurriedly making fresh white noodles out of it. The cobbler on the other side of the road was also still there. Next to him, a new shop had opened. It was brightly lit and decorated with red lanterns. Two young women in long, dark-red evening dresses were standing at the entrance and a well-dressed man was standing at a rostrum in front of the door. At first, Paul thought it was the entrance to a restaurant, whose dining area was to the back, and the man was responsible for valet parking. But there was no area at the back, only a narrow marble staircase that led upstairs. The shop front was entirely made of glass; behind it sat at least two dozen heavily made-up young women in pink clothing, whose eyes all followed Paul. They reminded him of the big teddy bears displayed as fairground prizes that he had seen at Coney Island in his childhood. "Come on in, sir," the man at the rostrum called. "They are yours, sir. You can choose anyone. Come on in, sir."

Zhang walked on without paying the least bit of attention to the man.

"What was that?" Paul asked.

"Do you still want to have a few wontons before?" Zhang asked, instead of giving a reply.

"I'd love to," Paul said, only half listening. He could not believe how much Zhang's neighborhood had changed. Where were the many grocery shops? Where was the genius tailor who could sew a button on quicker than Paul could fetch a yuan note from his trouser pocket in payment? Where was the dentist who, at the entrance to his practice, had a display case of extracted teeth in front?

They turned into one of the narrow side streets where they used to buy fruit and vegetables. Now it was full of hairdressers and beauty salons with scantily clad women squatting outside, smoking, eating, whining to each other, or painting their nails. The younger ones stretched themselves as soon as they saw Paul, or thrust their breasts out at him briefly. The others just looked on, bored. They were experienced enough, he thought, to see straightaway that he was not interested. On one of the buildings hung an advertisement for different breast implants that purported to come from America: Bless You, Glorified Beauty, and Always Number One. Next to it was a Shenzhen police placard with an emergency telephone number for the serious fraud office printed in extralarge type.

Zhang was now deep in conversation with the owner of the last remaining greengrocer about the best recipe for a bitter gourd soup. Paul tugged at his sleeve. He felt like an impatient young boy pulling his father away from a conversation with a neighbor.

"What on earth has happened here?" he asked in a whisper, as the vegetable woman disappeared back into her shop.

"What do you mean, what's happened?"

"What's happened to your neighborhood?"

Zhang stopped for a moment, leaned his head to one side, and looked at Paul as if he still didn't understand what his friend was talking about.

"What are you so surprised about? Would you like to go to the hairdresser? Should I make an appointment for you? I get a regular's discount."

Paul looked at him in astonishment. Only a very slight, barely discernible twitch of a smile around his mouth betrayed the fact that Zhang had understood exactly what he was asking about. Zhang's very subtle sense of humor was one of the qualities that Paul prized most in him. It had taken a while for Paul to discover it, and even now, after so many years, there were still times like these, moments in which he could not immediately be sure if Zhang really meant what he said.

"No thanks."

"Okay. The rumor is they're not that good, not those in my block, anyway." After a short pause, he added, "That's what I hear."

"And where are the tailor and the dentist?"

"Do I really have to explain the laws of capitalism to you?" Zhang asked by way of reply and laughed. "The rents here have tripled, no, quadrupled. The brothel-keepers can pay it, the others can't. We're now the last ordinary family left in our building. The whole of the first three floors is a whorehouse."

"With Detective Zhang in the middle of it all?"

"On top, to be exact."

"What does Mei think about it?"

"We've already offered to move out. But our landlord said, 'Certainly not, Comrade Zhang, certainly not. Please stay.' And to make sure we did, he reduced the rent by thirty percent on the spot. To make up for any possible disruption from the noise. That convinced Mei right away. You know my wife. When he heard that I'm a Buddhist and that I meditate on the roof, he even arranged for an awning to be erected. I think they feel safer with a policeman in the building. At any rate, everyone always greets not only Mei and me but our son very politely and treats us with great respect. If we moved, we'd have to move to the edge of the city. We can't afford an apartment in the city center anymore. We wouldn't want to do that, so we're staying here."

"How much do you get from it?" Paul asked.

His friend gave him a long look and did not reply. Finally, he asked, "Who exactly do you mean when you say 'you'?"

Zhang's tone of voice unsettled Paul. How could he have formulated his question so clumsily?

"I didn't mean you personally when I said 'you.' You know that," Paul said, almost apologetically.

Zhang smiled. It was one of those smiles that started somewhere deep inside, raised the corners of the mouth gently, and quickly reached the cheeks and the eyes, until the whole face beamed. A smile that was so calm and relaxed that Paul envied him for it.

"I don't know how much 'we' get from it. When I look at my fellow policemen's and my bosses' cell phones, wristwatches, apartments, and cars, I guess it's not a small amount. But you know, if you're going to drink wine, don't forget where it comes from."

"An old Chinese saying?"

Zhang nodded. "A modern version. 'Updated,' as my son would say."

They walked on to the butcher and while Zhang was buying mincemeat for the mapo doufu, Paul waited in front of the door and watched a prostitute disappear into the back room of a hairdressing salon with a client. Everything that he had seen in the last few minutes was illegal. But no one made even the slightest effort to pretend to be obeying the law to save face. Why were the police doing nothing about this? Where was the party secretary for this district?

VII

Zhang diced the eggplant with deft movements, put it in a bowl, and sprinkled salt on it liberally. He took a smaller knife and chopped fresh ginger and garlic into tiny pieces, sliced two bunches of spring onions, cored the bitter gourd with a few twists of his hand, cut the tofu into small pieces, and fetched several jars containing pickled chili, chili paste, and fermented black beans from the cupboard. He was dry frying some Sichuan peppercorns in a pan on the side. Once they were done, he ground them to a fine powder in a mortar with slow, rhythmic strokes of the pestle. Paul set out a folding table and three stools in a corner of the tiny kitchen, sat down, and watched Zhang's every movement.

Many, many years ago, on his list of Things That Make Life Worth Living, "Watching Zhang Cook and Having the Meal Afterward" had been in one of the top spots. He had never seen anyone else prepare food with such love and dedication.

Zhang barely spoke in the kitchen. He did not reply to any questions; he didn't even hear them. Guests who arrived didn't get a look from him; he was deep in a world of smells and spices, of herbs, oils, and pastes, of steaming, slicing, and woks. Mei and Paul thought that cooking was another form of meditation for him and he had let them believe this for over twenty years. There were things in his life that he could not talk about, not even more than thirty years later. Neither with his best friend nor with his wife. How could they understand that food was never just a simple meal for him? That he envied everyone for whom it was so simple. That he could never put a piece of tofu, a chicken's foot, no, not even a single, tiny grain of rice into his mouth without thinking of Li, Wu, Hong, and all the others in his work brigade who, like him, had been sent into the mountains as children during the Cultural Revolution to help the farmers with the harvest, where they had been forced to labor for six long godforsaken years. Six years in which they thought they had been forgotten by their parents and by the rest of the world, in which they had almost nothing but rice to eat, and, when that was not enough, because the inexperienced city folk were a burden rather than a help during the harvest, they ate grass, leaves, and bark. Six years in which not one summer or winter passed without one—weakened by starvation though surrounded by a natural world that had more than enough for everyone if only it were properly managed—succumbing. Six years in which he could think about nothing for days at a time but the dumplings his mother used to make. Not about his mother; Zhang thought about the dumplings.

For him, every meal was a celebration. A small, quiet triumph of life over death. Of love over hate. Of beauty over ugliness. Of good over evil. And the more effort he made, the better it tasted, the more the taste buds were stimulated or the nose pleasured, the more the stomach was filled, the sweeter the triumph. Who said a pinch of pepper was just a matter of taste? Who said coriander, chili, aniseed, caraway, ginger, and cloves were only spices? Who said life was so simple? He had seen how the Red Guards had shouted at Old Hu just because he had tried to give his watery broth a little taste with some of the pepper he had secretly stored away. The peppercorns were said to be proof of his decadent bourgeois past and of the impossibility of reforming him. The soup had to taste the same for everyone. Who did he think he was? He had better not dare think of trying that again. And what did the mad old fellow do? What did this fool, who had worked as a chef in a French restaurant in Shanghai before the Revolution, do? He seasoned his food. He seasoned it again, he seasoned it without showing any remorse. As though pepper were a form of resistance against barbarism. The Red Guards had been watching him; they beat him until he no longer moved. The whole village watched: the children, the old people, the men, and the women, and no one helped him. Instead, they screamed, "Punish the counterrevolutionary Hu!" "No mercy for Hu's betrayal!" And the sixteen-year-old Zhang Lin stood there and screamed with them, and if they had ordered him to hit him, he would have done it. Three peppercorns. Who was he supposed to explain that to? Beaten to death because of three lousy black peppercorns. Who on earth would ever understand that?

He could only begin to relax once the food was on the table. The white cubes of tofu lay like morsels of deliciousness in the luscious oily red of the chili sauce. The eggplant had exactly the right soft and creamy consistency, he could see that at a glance, and the bok choy, lightly steamed with garlic, had retained its freshness; he tasted it with his eyes and felt it on his tongue before he had even tasted the vegetable. And the bitter gourd! The many shades of its green! Tender and light in some places, almost transparent, and dark and moist in others, like the color of the paddy fields just before the harvest. He loved its bitterness. He loved the dominant taste of it, which did not suck up to anything else, was not overcome by the next-best flavor, and lingered in his mouth until the might of the Sichuan pepper finally covered it.

Hu would have been proud of him.

He waited until everyone else at the table had tasted the food; he always helped himself last. After a few bites Paul sighed with bliss. "Unbelievable. Wonderful."

Mei nodded in agreement. "Now I remember—

"—why you married me," Zhang said, finishing her sentence. She rolled her eyes in response. Did she know how much these small intimacies meant to him?

Zhang tried a piece of mapo doufu, one of his favorite dishes. The smoky, earthy spices filled his mouth immediately, followed by the typical taste of the Sichuan pepper, which bewitched the tip of the tongue and the lips then numbed them a little; he felt the kick of their unique spiciness in his throat and even in his ears.

"Why don't you open a restaurant, seriously?" Paul asked, with his mouth full.

Zhang responded with a brief smile. It was a rhetorical question, a ritual, and the answer was the same today as always. "Too dangerous."

They laughed.

Mei and Paul took it as a joke. They were thinking about dissatisfied customers, about drunks, rowdy guests, and policemen asking for protection money. Zhang was thinking about Old Hu and about how times could change so quickly in China.

"Danger aside, at least you'd earn a decent amount with it," Mei said, helping herself to another piece of eggplant and shooting him a challenging look.

Just that morning over a quick breakfast, they had had another one of their bad quarrels over Zhang's attitude toward his work and the poor chances of his career taking off.

Zhang had been a member of the Shenzhen police for over twenty-five years, but in all this time, he had been passed over for promotions with notable regularity. He had been moved one rank higher three times, until he had made it to a lowly inspector in the homicide division, but every modest recognition of this sort had been conditional on self-criticism in public. His most recent promotion was now fifteen years ago. The official reasons for this were his Buddhist beliefs, or, more precisely, the fact that he publicly acknowledged these beliefs, and his refusal, in the face of several requests, to rejoin the Communist Party after they had expelled him in the 1980s during a campaign to cleanse the party of "spiritual pollution." Both of these black marks could perhaps still have been overcome, but, in the eyes of his superiors, what totally ruled him out to take on greater responsibility was his honesty. Zhang doggedly refused to extort protection money from restaurants, bars, hotels, businesses, or illegal workers, and he even politely but firmly refused the envelopes of cash, the cigarettes, the whiskey, and all the other presents at Chinese New Year. He even paid for his noodle soup lunches at the street stalls around the police headquarters from his own pocket. This honesty was a regular cause for quarrels in the Zhang family. The basic salary of a detective superintendent and that of a secretary, even one like Mei, who worked for the office of an international company, was not enough to enjoy all the advantages of these new times in which they lived, especially not when some of this income went toward supporting parents in Sichuan and donations toward the building of a Buddhist temple. It was not enough for an apartment. It was not enough for a car. It was not even enough for a regular shopping trip to one of the new shopping malls with their many international brands. The computer in the Zhang household was a Chinese make. The video camera, the digital camera, and the television too. Mei's Prada bag and Chanel belt were imitations of the cheapest sort, just like her son's Adidas shoes, Levi's jeans, and Puma jogging suit. Mei could accept the time-consuming search for bargains and the crude imitation goods in her home, but what she could not forgive her husband for was the fact that she could not send her son to one of the many new private schools. Out of the five secretaries in her department, she was the only one who did not send her child to a private school. The only one! Did he really understand what that meant? What a loss of face. The people who could not afford one of those expensive schools did at least send their child to one of the private language schools in the afternoon or in the evening so that the child learned English well or at least received a certificate claiming that he or she had done so. But they didn't even have enough money for that. Not even for a shitty second-class certificate.

Why did their fifteen-year-old son have to suffer from the moral strictures that his father applied to himself? What kind of job did he think their son would get later on? He was welcome to play the hero, but not at the expense of his family. It was his responsibility as a father to provide the best education possible for his son, that was what Confucius had stipulated, Mei used to remind her husband on a regular basis. Since Zhang did not accept the master as an authority on such things, she had buried herself for weeks in the writings of the Buddha to find something in them that would bring her husband to his senses. Sadly, Siddhārtha proved to be fully unsuited to justifying the acceptance of money and gifts in the name of the higher good. Quite the opposite: Greed and desire were constantly mentioned by him as the causes of human suffering, strengthening Mei's conviction that this religion would never succeed in China and that her husband was a terrible eccentric in his beliefs. She could only appeal to his feelings of responsibility and his common sense: Could he tell her, please, how it could harm anyone if he merely did what everyone else in his position did, that is, let himself be paid commensurately for his work? And if the government did not pay enough, a person had to secure his livelihood by other means. In the past, he had replied to her with a long monologue saying that nothing, absolutely nothing, that a person did in life was free of consequences, and that we, not the government, not a political party, not a boss of any kind, were responsible for them.

In more recent times, he simply responded to her questions by saying that he, Zhang, would be harmed if he took bribes; he didn't want bad Karma, after all, and he had to think about his next life. Who wanted to be reborn as a snake or a Japanese person? The hint of mockery in his voice told her that it would be foolish to object.

They were tough quarrels, long and fruitless, which ended with Mei refusing to speak to her husband for days. She would probably have left him long ago and accepted one of the many advances from her German boss if not for the fact that his stubbornness, his honesty, his courage, and his unbending nature were also the very qualities that she loved most about him. She could not really be angry with him. He saw that in her eyes, even in the moments when they were full of displeasure while looking at him. He could rely on

Mei, and this knowledge gave him the strength to put up with the hostilities and the temptations he faced at work.

He looked at Paul, how he was scraping the bowl of mapo doufu clean and smiling at him gratefully from the side. It was good to see him sitting in this kitchen again. Mei did not understand why Paul had withdrawn himself so much; she thought he should have done the opposite and not turned away from life but thrown himself into it until it swallowed him and his pain up. Zhang, on the other hand, marveled at how resolutely his friend grieved for his son, how he took the time that was necessary for himself to do this, even if he would grow old in the process.

Paul looked at the clock and panicked. It was late, almost ten thirty, and on no account did he want to miss the last ferry. They made their way to the metro station, and were just crossing the plaza in front of the shopping mall when Zhang's cell phone rang. He flipped it open, looked at the small screen, and picked up the call. His face darkened with every sentence he heard. He interrupted the caller with questions every so often, but in a dialect from Sichuan province that Paul did not understand. After he had ended the conversation, he turned to his guest again.

"Sorry, that was Wu, one of our pathologists. He's from Chengdu and he cooks the best mapo doufu that I know. Amazing. He's an old friend of mine and I asked him to ring me as soon as he had news. He hasn't quite finished yet, but it turns out it's true that the skull was smashed. Apart from that, the left arm is broken in several places and the right shoulder is dislocated. Whoever the victim is, he didn't give himself up to his murderers without a fight. He'll tell me the rest tomorrow."

They walked down the west side of Shennan Road to the metro station in silence.

"Shall I take you to the border?"

"Thanks, but I'll manage on my own. Do I look that tired?" asked Paul.

"Yes. Exhausted."

"I am. It was all a bit much for a hermit."

Zhang nodded understandingly. "Can you do me a favor, though? When you speak to the Owens tomorrow, please ask them if their son ever injured his left knee."

"Why?"

"The body has a big scar on the left knee, probably from an operation. Wu thinks it's from an accident or a sports injury."

VIII

The voices of the night were no more than a whisper. The water lay smooth as a mirror in the glow of the red and blue neon advertisements, and a lone barge or tugboat made its way across the pond every now and then. Tiny waves lapped against the walls of the quay in exhaustion, as if the harbor had been transformed into a deserted, windless lake. The white lights in the office blocks had almost all been switched off, bit by bit, like lighting for a celebration that someone had carefully blown out candle by candle. Even the never-ending roar of traffic during the day had fallen silent. The hour after midnight was the time when the city that never otherwise stopped allowed itself a rest.

Paul stood at the pier from which ferries to the outlying islands departed and thought about what he should do. He had missed the last ferry. At this hour it was impossible to find a private vessel that would take him to Lamma, and there was no one he could stay the night with. Undecided, he sat down on the steps that led down to the water. He had slept in the train, and felt wide-awake in some strange way, yes, almost a bit hyper, but not unwell at all. The air was still pleasantly warm and smelled not of gas but of the sea and the humid, sweet, and heavy air of the tropics. He thought about what could be making him feel so keyed up. The many impressions of the past few hours? The pleasure he always felt when he saw Zhang and Mei? Did he care more about the fate of Michael Owen than he admitted to himself? Or was it the smells, the music of the streets, the faces, the sights of Shenzhen, which were different from Hong Kong's, that stimulated him so? That awakened memories in him that he thought were buried so deep that two lifetimes would not be enough to unearth them?

China! The other side of the world. The better side.

He had first read about Li Si and her father, the emperor of Mandala, in a German children's book when he was eight years old. The little princess was the first girl he fell in love with. In her country lived an imaginary giant and there grew wonderful trees and flowers in the strangest shapes and colors, and they were all transparent. Plants made of glass! There were rivers there with porcelain bridges swinging over them! Some of these bridges had strange roofs with thousands of small silver bells hanging from them, which tinkled with every puff of wind and glittered in the morning light. In the capital city of Ping the streets were full of hair counters, ear cleaners, magicians, acrobats, and hundred-year-old ivory carvers, who carved away at a single piece of wood for their whole lives. From that time on, he had dreamed of traveling to Mandala, and when his father explained to him that there was no such country and that China was the country the book meant to describe, a huge empire on the other side of the world with a big wall around it and a secretive Forbidden City in which the emperor used to live, he had set his sights on traveling to China.

The life that he longed for was in China. In China the people were smaller, not so heavily built; there were no children there who were a head taller than him and who bullied him to chew the gum they spat out. In China no one cared if his father was Jewish or his mother German. In China parents did not quarrel and it was easy to make friends. In China the people were just much friendlier and more honest and cleverer; it was not for nothing that they had invented gunpowder, paper, and the compass.

China! The word alone drew the young boy to it like magic. Full of wonder, he discovered Chinese characters, tracing his finger across the paper over and over again, copying the strange lines with slow, respectful movements. What kind of country was it where the people drew small pictures instead of using letters like *A* or *Z*? Where the same sound could have completely different meanings depending on which tone it was spoken in? In New York, while the other boys played baseball on weekends, he went to Chinatown and hung around the vegetable and fish stalls, trying to catch snatches of words and to identify them again, because he was so incredibly fascinated by the sound and the color of the language.

Later, he spent a great deal of time in the public library on Tenth Street at Tompkins Square Park. There, surrounded by old men and women who kept coughing in winter or blew their noses noisily into handkerchiefs the size of pillowcases, he studied Marco Polo's accounts of his travels, Confucius, Laozi, and Mao, understanding little of what he read. But that did not bother him, as long as the books helped him to keep dreaming of China.

On his travels later, he learned how little his fantasies had to do with the Chinese reality, but bidding farewell to the land of his dreams was not too difficult for him. The reality in the 1980s, the period of gradual opening up, was even more exciting and interesting that he had ever imagined, and he no longer needed China as his castle, a place in which he could seek refuge in his dreams. With the birth of Justin, his interest in the country and in traveling there had waned, and after the diagnosis, it had been totally extinguished. He had refused Zhang's repeated invitations over the past few years for him to visit or for them to take a trip to Shanghai or Beijing together. China no longer moved him. Or did it? Just a few hours ago he would still have said that with conviction.

Paul stood up, thought about which hotel was nearest on foot, and walked slowly up the empty streets toward the Mandarin Oriental.

The quiet murmur of the air-conditioning, a low hum from the bridge, and a cell phone that kept on ringing somewhere. Paul opened his eyes and reached for his mosquito net. It was a few long seconds before he realized where he was. The cell phone stopped ringing, only to start again shortly after. Eyes heavy with sleep, he looked at the display. He did not recognize the number; it was neither Christine's nor Zhang's. Probably the Owens. Paul switched his phone to silent. He did not want to speak to anyone, least of all to the Owens. The alarm clock showed it was 7:15 AM. There was a piercing pain in his head and his whole body hurt, as though he had drunk too much alcohol last night. Had he gone to the hotel bar? He could not remember anything. He turned on his side, pulled the light blanket up to this chin, and fell asleep again.

When he woke the second time, he felt even worse. The headache had gone but now he felt as if someone had bound him tightly around the chest. He tried to lie there quietly, but still could not breathe. He felt hot, even though he had felt cold the whole night through because of the air-conditioning and the blanket that was much too thin. He was afraid. Afraid of speaking to Elizabeth Owen. Afraid of too many impressions. Afraid of too many voices, sounds, smells, people. He could feel this fear growing with every moment that he lay alone in this strange bed, in this strange room.

He got up and called Christine. Her voice calmed him a little. Yes, she had time, always had time for him. He could come to pick her up for a lunch in an hour.

Paul went to the metro entrance on Statue Square. He wanted to take the MTR to Wan Chai, but the deeper he descended into the station, the worse he felt. When he saw the crowds of people waiting for the train and got shoved in the back by the first elbow, he turned around and hurried back up onto the street. On the tram, there was a seat free in the first row on the upper deck; he held his head out of the window, and the breeze from the movement of the tram dried the sweat on his brow.

The stairwell at 142 Johnson Road was even narrower and dirtier, and the World Wide Travel office was even smaller than he had imagined from Christine's description. She and her two employees sat in front of three computer screens; all of them were wearing headpieces and in the middle of conversations with clients, talking loudly over each other in order to be heard above the air conditioner rattling in the background. The desks were piled with catalogues, brochures, bills, and tickets. The walls were covered with yellowing pages from a Cathay Pacific calendar, with photographs of pagodas in Japan, Thailand, Sri Lanka, and Vietnam. The room had no window. Paul wondered how she put up with these cramped and noisy conditions every day.

Christine led him to a dim sum restaurant not far from her office. She wove her way through the bustling throng of people on the overcrowded sidewalks so quickly and so skillfully that it was only with some difficulty that he was able to keep up with her.

The restaurant was as big as a soccer field and as noisy as a rock gig. Every table was occupied, and as soon as anyone stood up the people waiting would rush for the empty seat as if there was something to be had for free at that table. After a brief exchange between Christine and the maître d', a waiter led them past a row of fish tanks to the back section of the restaurant, to one of the few tables for two. Christine checked the boxes for their order on a piece of card, and Paul told her in a few sentences about what had happened in Shenzhen and about the phone call he had to make that he had been postponing for a few hours now.

"What is it you want to hear from me? Advice?"

Her voice had lost its lightness of tone. She sounded stern and tense.

"I don't know," Paul said quietly. "Maybe."

"I would call these people and tell them that you're sorry, but you can't help them, and that would be the end of that. The police in Hong Kong or in Shenzhen or the American embassy in Beijing can worry about the rest. You have nothing to do with it. I would stay out of it."

She looked at Paul, her lips pressed firmly together. Her tone had probably been much sharper than she preferred it to be, but she could not help herself. Paul was thankful that she did not even try to cover it up. He knew her face and he knew that she did not trust the mainland Chinese. And how could she, after everything that had been done to her family? Any attempt to do so would be marred by the memory of the sound of the boots of the Red Guards, the creaking stairs, the sound of the wooden door splintering as it was kicked in, her father's face filled with the fear of death. The jump from the window. An accident, they said. An accident! That was still what they said today, nearly forty years later. If it had been possible, she would have emigrated to Canada, America, or Australia before 1997. She did not want reunification. Her family had fled China for Hong Kong in 1967 only to fall under Beijing's control after all, thirty years later. Of course, a lot of time had passed and the government of today apparently had nothing to do with the government of all those years ago. She knew the arguments, she knew them all; she had argued often enough with her friends about this, had tried to explain something that perhaps could not be explained. But the same party was still in government, and this party had never apologized to the people for the crimes that it had committed; as long as it did not do so, as long as it did not ask for forgiveness from the victims of all its campaigns and purges, Christine Wu would not trust it. And she would not attend one of the Mandarin language schools that now dotted every corner of Hong Kong. Nor would she organize any tours to China or travel there herself. She had tried once, and taken the train toward Shenzhen. She had grown more and more tense the nearer the train got to the People's Republic. Finally, she had stood at the border to the land of her birth, her heart racing with fear. She had heard the voices of her parents. The voices of her grandparents. After a long struggle, she turned back. Because the shadows of the past were too long. Because the whispers would not fall silent.

Paul said nothing. He felt annoyed at himself for having asked her in the first place.

"I'm sorry. What I'm saying sounds very selfish and is perhaps not what you want to hear."

As two waiters brought the first few bamboo baskets of dim sum dumplings to the table, Paul's phone rang. It was Zhang.

"Hello, Paul. Did you catch the last ferry?"

"No. I spent the night in a hotel."

"Sorry about that."

"Don't be. It was the Mandarin Oriental. It's right next to the ferry terminal."

"Where are you now? It sounds as though you've been put to work in a restaurant kitchen."

"I'm sitting with Christine in Wan Chai, having dim sum."

"Then I'll make it quick. Have you spoken to the Owens yet?"

"No."

Zhang did not say anything for a moment. "I know that it's not going to be pleasant conversation." He did not sound formal, but it was impossible not to hear the detective superintendent in him speaking. "But I have to know as soon as possible if the body is Michael Owen. Even if it turns out this afternoon that he died of heart failure. With murder, time is mostly on the side of the murderer."

"I know," Paul whispered into the telephone.

"What did you say?"

"I know," he repeated, a little louder.

"Can you tell those people to stop rattling their plates? Why do the Chinese have to shout so while eating? I can't hear a thing."

Did Zhang really not hear him or was that his way of telling him that he should call the Owens as soon as possible?

"I know that I have to talk to them," he said, loudly and clearly.

"That sounds better. Decisive."

"Can I wait till after lunch?"

"The sooner the better. Do you know if Michael Owen has an apartment in Hong Kong?"

"No, but I assume he must have."

"Can you ask his mother? And if he does, go and look at it today, if possible?"

"How am I supposed to do that?"

"His mother must have they key. Think of an excuse."

"What am I supposed to look for?"

"If he really was murdered, there are probably clues in the apartment as to why he traveled to Shenzhen two days ago and who he was meeting there, also whether he had friends or acquaintances in the city. And even if he's not the dead man, he's still missing. Maybe he threw himself off the Tsing Ma Bridge and left a farewell letter."

"If he is the murdered man, shouldn't the Hong Kong police be searching the apartment instead?"

"They'll be doing that, yes. But I want us to be the first to look at it. I'll explain why to you later. Now, have you got Mei's cell phone number?"

"Yes."

"Will you call me on that number from now on about this?"

"But why?" Paul couldn't help asking.

"Later, I'll tell you everything later. Will you call as soon as you have news?"

"Yes."

"Enjoy your meal, then."

Paul switched his phone off and put it in his jacket pocket. He would have liked to sink it in the sweet-sour soup that was in front of him. He did not want to call the Owens. Not now. And not later. He did not want to know whose child the dead young man was. He wanted even less, much less, to have to tell the man's parents that they had lost their son. He did not want to be moved by this sadness, this pain, this distress. He did not want to be moved at all. He wanted to have a meal with Christine and then, since he was in the city, to buy a few things he needed and then take the quickest route back to Lamma. His house, his plants, and Justin's rain boots were waiting there for him.

Paul sipped his tea, pulled his chopsticks out of their paper wrapper, and helped himself to a vegetable dumpling. Better than expected, he thought. What had he to do with the Owens? He dabbed a steamed shrimp dumpling in the red chili sauce. Wonderful. What did a dead body in Shenzhen have to do with him? The stuffed rice-flour rolls were a little overcooked and the dough was too thick. A pity. The jasmine tea was extraordinarily good, though; strong, but not bitter. Christine was right: he should stay out of it. Not get any further involved. Just one more phone call.

Christine had followed his conversation with Zhang. She was now sitting opposite him, bolt upright, not touching the food.

"Are you not hungry?" Even as he was asking the question, he could hear how stupid it sounded, how ridiculous he was making himself. As if he did not know what she was thinking.

"No," she retorted.

"I'll follow your advice. This situation is a matter for the police."

"Do you really mean that?"

Paul nodded.

"Promise?"

"Promise."

Christine helped herself to a pork bun. The finest in all Hong Kong.

———

Paul walked through the narrow alleyways of Wan Chai looking for a place where he could call the Owens. But no matter which street he turned into, which entryway he stood in, or which coffee shop he sought refuge in, the roar of jackhammers, construction machinery, cars and buses, and the clamor of the voices of passersby and street vendors made such a conversation impossible. He thought about the Grand Hyatt Hotel with its big, wide lobby; surely he would be able to find the necessary peace and quiet in a secluded corner there. Paul crossed Lockhart Road and Gloucester Road, passing the immigration authorities and Wanchai Tower before he arrived at the hotel.

———

"Mr. Leibovitz. I've tried so many times to reach you. Where have you been?"

"I'm sorry. I . . . my cell phone . . ."

Elizabeth Owen did not wait for his explanation. "Have you spoken to the man you know in Shenzhen? Do you know anything about my son's whereabouts?"

"No." Paul had no idea how difficult it would be for him to tell this lie. He had thought he could be able to pronounce these two letters and put down the phone shortly after. Instead, they echoed through his head like dark, muffled drumbeats that did not die away but grew louder and louder. *NO.* You coward.

"I mean, of course I spoke to my friend. Several times, in fact, and he talked to his coworkers, but no one had heard of a Michael Owen." *No cheating, Daddy. Tell the truth.* "So that's really a good sign, isn't it?"

Elizabeth Owen said nothing.

Paul heard nothing but a quiet rustling. He could not stand the silence, so he continued talking. "I'm sure that everything will be cleared up soon. Your son will turn up today or tomorrow. My friend in Shenzhen promised to call me as soon as he hears of anything. What does he actually look like?"

"Who?"

"Your son, of course."

"Tall, blond, blue eyes. I don't know how I should describe him."

"Does he have any distinguishing marks?"

"What do you mean by that?"

"Any special marks. A liver spot on the forehead or something like that."

"No."

"A scar on the cheek?"

"No."

"No old scars or injuries?"

"No."

"From a car accident, perhaps? A fall from a bicycle?"

"No."

Paul got up from his armchair. He had to move; he had to express the relief he felt somehow. He walked up and down, rocking on his heels, with the phone pressed to his ear.

"That's great."

"Michael was always a very healthy boy."

"I'm glad to hear that. Very glad to hear that. Then I'm sure that everything will soon be sorted out, Mrs. Owen."

"He always did a lot of sport."

Paul did not want to know any more.

"He was a very, very good sportsman, you see. He was captain of the football team in high school."

Paul wanted to end the conversation. A press of the button would suffice.

"He even got a sports scholarship from Florida State University."

Fantastic. An amazing guy; no doubt about it. And why couldn't the story end right there? He did not want to hear any more.

"Mrs. Owen, I'll get in touch if I hear from my friend in Shenzhen, okay?"

"Florida State. You know what that means. Florida State! They have one of the best football teams in the whole of America. But then he had that stupid accident. After that he was never able to play football properly again."

"What kind of accident?" Paul couldn't help asking.

"He was hit by a fellow player during a training session; it wasn't intentional, but Michael's ligaments got torn. He had to have three operations."

"Where?"

"On his knee."

"His knee? Which knee?"

"The left one. Why are you asking? Hello? Mr. Leibovitz? Are you still there?"

———

Michael Owen's apartment was on the thirty-eighth story of Harbour View Court, one of the condominium complexes typical of the Mid-Levels of Hong Kong, with its identical high-rise blocks containing cookie-cutter apartments piled on top of each other like little shoeboxes. Elizabeth Owen was waiting in the lobby for him. In the taxi he had already felt his heart pounding harder and harder and his hands growing cold and clammy. How should he greet her? He had said nothing to her on the phone, and did not want to tell her anything now either. That was not his job. The police or the American consulate in Hong Kong or whoever it was should take care of it. He had come to Robinson Road because Zhang had asked him to do him a favor; he would take a look at the apartment, tell his friend about it, and then take the next ferry to Lamma.

Mrs. Owen looked him up and down and kept her eyes fixed on him as they walked through the lobby and into the elevator. As though any one of his movements or his gestures would shed light on her son's whereabouts. Did she know that he had been lying? Could she tell by the way he was avoiding her gaze, by the way, as they stood next to each other silently in the elevator, he was staring at his shoes? Or was she simply nervous? Had his request to see the apartment roused her suspicion? Her husband had been in the apartment yesterday and said that he had not found anything suspicious. Might he have overlooked something? A message? A note? A farewell letter?

Elizabeth Owen's hands trembled as she unlocked the door. With a brief movement of her head, she motioned for Paul to go ahead.

"Hello, is anyone home?"

No reply. He could only hear the sonorous hum of the air-conditioning. A jacket and a suit were hanging in the hallway, with two pairs of shoes beneath. It was cold and smelled strongly of disinfectant and cleaning agents.

"What did your friend say we should be looking for?"

"Nothing in particular. He just thought we should have another look just in case. Perhaps we'll find a clue of some kind."

"What kind of clue?"

"I have no idea, Mrs. Owen. A travel itinerary? A hotel reservation?"

Paul pulled aside a curtain that separated the hall from the living room. It was a large room with a dark-wood floor, polished to a high shine, white walls bare of pictures, and floor-to-ceiling windows. The windows faced the harbor, but the view was almost completely blocked by new buildings. There were two black leather couches and a wooden trunk in the middle of the room, opposite an oval dining table with four chairs. Paul saw neither newspapers nor any kinds of papers, letters, or documents lying around. The Filipina housemaid had probably cleaned the place yesterday or this morning, and tidied up. He looked in the kitchen; everything there was also clean: no food remains, dirty breakfast dishes in the sink, or half-empty coffee pot or teapot on the counter. A narrow corridor, with the bathroom and two other rooms leaving off it, led to the back of the apartment. The bedroom was small and dark; there was hardly any space next to the bed—which was made—and a chest of drawers, on which a few ironed and folded shirts lay. The other room, however, was big and light and, unlike the rest of the apartment, untidy. There were several piles of papers, newspaper cuttings, and books on the floor and the shelves were full of document files. There were two flat-screen monitors on the desk, along with two cell phones, a notebook, a calendar, pieces of papers with handwritten notes on them, and a small pile of unopened mail. Under the desk was a large computer hard drive. At first glance, Paul could not tell what seemed suspicious or conspicuous. This was the typical Hong Kong apartment of a young person from Europe or America who lived for a few years in the city, often alone, in order to earn as much money for himself and for his company in as little time as possible, working as a banker or a lawyer. These business people were as interchangeable as their apartments. Paul tried to think if he had noticed anything personal in these rooms, any clue about a particular interest, a preference, a passion. Souvenirs from traveling? Photos of people who meant something to the occupier? Books or music that moved him? Nothing occurred to him.

Elizabeth Owen had followed him through the rooms like his shadow; now, she stood by the door and continued watching his every movement. Ever since they had entered the apartment, they had barely exchanged a word, and the silence had grown intolerable to Paul. She knew that he was lying, and if she did not know then she at least felt it, smelled it, saw it in the way he walked, in his eyes, in the way he shied away from her. He could not bear the fear in her face any longer; he turned away.

"If you knew something, Mr. Leibovitz, you'd tell me?

Paul was silent.

"Why don't you answer me?" Words that should have sounded like a decree, like an order, came out like a pleading entreaty.

"Answer me." Her voice was now so loud and shrill that she stumbled forward. Paul turned around suddenly. Elizabeth Owen was standing directly in front of him, sobbing and trembling. He took her by the arm, a reflex; he could not do anything else except take her gently into his arms. He felt her body shuddering and shivering and heard her crying, a crying that knew no tomorrow, no hope, and no comfort. It was so familiar to him. He led her to the living room, laid her down on one of the couches, fetched a glass of water and a towel, and sat down next to her. She was holding a pill, one that looked like a Valium, in one hand, which she swallowed with the glass of water. Paul waited until she had calmed down and closed her eyes, and her quiet, even breathing announced that she had fallen asleep. Then he stood up, went back into the office, and rang Zhang.

"Michael Owen had a sports accident as a young man. He had three operations on his left knee."

Paul heard Zhang sigh heavily. "I'm sorry. Have you told her anything?"

"No. And I won't be telling her anything."

"Good. Where are you now?"

"In his apartment," Paul said, describing the state every room was in.

"Have you read through the handwritten notes?"

"No. There's a whole book's worth of them. Mrs. Owen could wake up any minute. How should I explain myself to her if I were to be rifling through her son's things?"

"Can you look in the chest of drawers in the bedroom or behind the files in the shelves?"

"Mrs. Owen would wonder what I was up to if I started searching the place."

Zhang thought for a moment. "What about the computer? Can you take it with you without her noticing?"

"Impossible. It's a big machine."

"Do you see a laptop?"

"No." He pulled open the top drawer in the desk. "There's a small hard drive here. Perhaps he used it to back up his data."

"Good. Take it with you. Anything else?"

Paul pulled the other drawer open. "Assorted papers. Cash. A digital camera. A case of telephone SIM cards and memory chips, I think."

"Take it."

"Shouldn't I be leaving this to the police?" Paul asked.

"No, on no account. We can discuss this later. Take as much with you as you can keep hidden from her. The cell phones, the memory chips, the notebooks, the calendar on the desk; everything from which we can find out appointments, places, and the names of his contacts in China."

"And what should I do with the stuff?"

"Bring it to me. As quickly as possible."

Elizabeth Owen was still asleep when Paul returned to the living room. He went into the office again and put the two cell phones and the small digital camera into his trouser pockets, wrapped the hard drive, the case with the memory chips, and the notebooks in his jacket, wrote a short note for Mrs. Owen, which he laid on the table in the living room, and left the apartment as quietly as he could.

During the journey to the border, his head was full of Zhang's words. His voice had sounded unusually sharp, almost a little unfamiliar. What was the meaning of his instructions? Paul could understand his suspicion of most of his coworkers, but why did he distrust the investigations of the Hong Kong homicide squad in this case before they had even started on their work? Were there connections between the Shenzhen police and the Hong Kong police that Zhang knew about, or did he just want to play it safe? His behavior was more than strange.

Paul wondered if he should call Christine, but decided not to do so. It would only worry her; he would be back in a few hours and would call her then.

In Shenzhen, he bought a fake leather briefcase at the train station and put Michael Owen's things in it. Although he could not imagine that any secret information was really hidden in there, he felt unsettled nonetheless, and held the case close to his chest with both hands. He felt like calling Zhang to pick him up from the station, but then felt it would be silly to do so.

———

Mei opened the door and greeted him with a smile. Paul had always thought her an extremely beautiful woman, even though she did not fit the ideal image of a Chinese woman; she was too short for that. She had inherited the short, stocky build of her mother, a farmer from Sichuan, but she had a very sensual mouth and eyes, which expressed an infectious joie de vivre.

"Come in. Zhang is still out getting the groceries. He'll be back any minute. Would you like some tea?"

"Yes, please." Paul sat down at the folding table and put the briefcase down by his feet. "Tell me, why is there so much underwear hanging outside?"

"Today is laundry day for the brothel," she said, turning on the gas stove, taking a large spoonful of dark-green tea leaves from a tin and putting them in an old porcelain teapot. She turned to face him suddenly. "It's nice to see you more often again, Paul," she said.

"Thank you," he said, a little surprised.

"We've missed you."

"I've missed you both too."

"Will you come and visit us more often again now?"

"I don't know. Maybe."

He fell silent, unsure whether there was another, deeper meaning in what she said, if there was something she was hinting at.

"There's something I want to talk to you about," she said, her voice becoming unusually quiet. "I'm worried."

"Worried? About what?"

But before Mei could reply, they heard Zhang panting his way up the steps. Swearing softly, he put his key in the door lock. Mei turned wordlessly and poured the hot water into the pot.

Zhang put his shopping bags down with a loud sigh and sank onto the kitchen stool. "You'll have to carry me up here one day," he said.

"Just stop smoking," Mei replied, in a tone of voice that wavered between irritation and worry. "Then you'll be able to get up the stairs again."

"It's not the breathing. It's the legs. They're much worse." Zhang rubbed his right knee with both hands.

Paul knew about his friend's joint pains. They were a constant reminder of the years that he had spent in the countryside during the Cultural Revolution. He had suffered his first inflammation of the knee after he had planted rice for almost forty-eight hours nonstop with a group of young people. They had stood for two days and nights in the paddy field, often knee-deep in cold water, in order to prove that they were not spoiled brats, not the pampered city kids of soft intellectuals, but that they could serve the Revolution like everyone else. Two in the group had died of lung infections a few days after that; for Zhang, it was only his knee that swelled and was intolerably painful for weeks. The pain had developed into a kind of rheumatism over the years and got worse with increasing age.

Mei passed him two hot towels, which he wrapped around his knee.

"Have you eaten?" he said, turning to Paul and starting to unpack the grocery bags without waiting for a reply. Before long the whole apartment smelled of sesame oil, garlic, coriander, and ginger, of fried spring onions and chili peppers. On the table was a plate of cold chicken, several saucers of black and red sauces, fried pork belly, deep-fried mushrooms, watercress, and rice. Zhang took his place contentedly.

"Are you going to tell me why I should only call you on Mei's cell phone now?" Paul asked, after he had praised his friend for the food.

Zhang helped himself to a good chunk of pork belly before he replied.

"Because I'm not sure who might be listening in to the cell phone I use for work. It doesn't normally bother me, but this case is different."

"Why?"

"Why?" Zhang spat a bit of rind out. "I tried to explain to you yesterday. The murder of a foreigner in China is not simply a murder. It's a loss of face. It damages the country's image. And in some cases it becomes an economic problem. The authorities do everything to make foreigners feel safe. I can't think of anything like this ever happening before here in Shenzhen. I can't imagine that anyone would be so stupid as to attack a foreigner and to rob him and kill him too. There are enough rich Chinese people around."

"Who would have a reason to kill a young American man, then?"

"I haven't got the faintest idea, but I'm afraid that's exactly why it's a problem. Can you tell me anything about the Owens' business in China?" Zhang asked.

"Not much. They mentioned that they have a factory here. Or several, perhaps. I can't remember exactly."

"What do they manufacture?"

"I don't know."

"Didn't they give any idea? Toys? Lights? Shoes?"

Paul shook his head.

"Do you know the name of the company?"

"No. I didn't ask them. They did say, though, that their son had an appointment with a Mr. Tang. It sounded as though that was their manager or a joint venture partner."

"Tang Mingqing?"

Paul would think back to this moment a great deal later on. To Zhang's eyes opened wide. To the grimace on his lips. Why had he not taken these unusual reactions as a warning?

"No," Paul replied uncertainly. "If I remember correctly, they didn't mention a Chinese name."

"Also called Victor Tang?"

"Yes, I think that's what he was called."

Zhang stared at his friend disbelievingly.

"Are you sure?"

"Fairly sure. Who is this man?"

"Victor Tang is . . . is . . ." Zhang searched for words and finished his sentence only a few seconds later, "an incredibly influential person." Paul waited for something that would explain his friend's sudden tenseness, but Zhang did not say more.

Mei stared down at her plate, which was still half full.

"What do you mean by influential?" Paul asked, after a pause.

"You don't even know his name?" Zhang said in response.

Paul thought for a moment. Victor Tang? Tang Mingqing? The man must have very patriotic parents. Who else would name their child after three Chinese dynasties at once? "No. The name means nothing to me. But why should it? I haven't been here for a long time and I haven't read the newspapers for years. How am I supposed to know who he is? What can you tell me about him?"

"Not much either. I don't know him personally, but his name is often in the papers. He is an adviser to the mayor and is a member of a few committees in the city and in the party, and he's the head of the CWI."

"CWI? What does that stand for?"

"China World Investment. It's a conglomerate of companies that produce all kinds of things; I've no idea what."

Zhang shoveled two mouthfuls of rice into his mouth with several deft movements and thought hard. "There's an Internet café a couple of streets away. Now we have a name we can see if we can find anything on the Internet that will help us. Where's the stuff you brought from Michael Owen's apartment?"

Paul passed him the briefcase. Mei cleared the table and Zhang spread the things out in front of them.

"I'll have a look at the cell phone and the hard drive later," he said, leafing through one of the notebooks. Michael Owen's handwriting was so illegible that Paul could only make out a few words. There was a business card in one of the booklets:

CATHAY HEAVY METAL

MICHAEL OWEN

Director

The Internet café was very busy, so they had to wait a few minutes. Paul looked around: There were two or three youngsters sitting in front of some of the computers, playing games or pounding wildly at the keyboards. The air was so full of cigarette smoke that his eyes stung.

"This café was closed for a week last month," Zhang whispered. "Someone reported it for spreading pornography."

"And? Did they not find anything?"

"They did. My coworkers checked all the computers. Porn sites had been clicked on almost all of them in the preceding days."

"Why is it open again, then?"

"It was just porn, not politics. They didn't find a politically sensitive website. I did wonder about that, but it must be because of the area. You can get rid of a porn charge with a few generous gifts."

Before they could expand on this theme, a terminal became free and they sat down. Google.com and Google.cn showed eight hundred and twenty-eight entries for Cathay Heavy Metal. The first one was the company's website, which was not very comprehensive. It stated that Victor Tang and Michael Owen were joint directors of the company. Cathay Heavy Metal supplied components to the rapidly growing motor industry in China and had been founded three years ago. The number of its employees—more than three thousand—had tripled since then. All the figures and charts on the website showed vertiginous growth. Their customers included well-known German, Japanese, American, and South Korean car companies.

The other search results that they clicked on were small articles in newspapers and mentions in trade and professional publications. According to them, the Owens were part of a family dynasty in the American metalworking industry. They owned Aurora Metal Inc. in the American state of Wisconsin. The company had been founded by Michael's great-grandfather, a German immigrant from Böblingen, a hundred years ago. Richard Owen had been the president of the industry association in Wisconsin and had been received in the White House by President Ronald Reagan as part of a delegation. This fact did not leave Zhang unimpressed.

"He won't rest until we find out who murdered his son," he said, as he paid the bill. "The sooner we find him, the better."

"What shall we do with Michael Owen's things?" Paul asked.

"I'll hang on to them for now. Perhaps I'll find something that will help us further."

"Why did you insist that I bring them to you? Don't you trust the Hong Kong police?"

Zhang hesitated before replying. Paul was not sure if he was thinking about the question or if he simply felt uncomfortable talking about this.

Finally, Zhang said, "Would you trust them?"

"I haven't had any reason to think about that before." After a pause, he added, "Probably not."

———

On the journey back to Hong Kong, Paul started feeling so troubled that he could not sit still, but paced up and down in the car instead. He remembered that Zhang had ducked his question, and had replied by asking him a question instead. The whole time, his friend had seemed inexplicably, unusually tense. On top of that, Paul could not get the Owens out of his head, no matter how hard he tried to think about something else. He could clearly see the picture of the American president and Richard Owen. The two men were shaking hands. They were laughing. Looking straight at the camera. One of them with routine friendliness, but the other with the boundless pride that you only saw otherwise in photos of children. Mr. Owen must have donated tens of thousands of dollars to get that photo. Apart from labor costs, profit margins, and over a billion potential customers, what had driven the family to China? Had they known what they were letting themselves in for or had they come with expectations of trees and flowers of glass, bridges of porcelain, and bells that tinkled in the wind?

IX

———

The clock on the train platform showed 9:15 PM when Paul reached Central Station. He had changed trains in Kowloon Tong and Mong Kok and would be able to get the 9:30 PM ferry to Lamma without hurrying. Though he had been longing for nothing more than his home and the peace of the island for more than twenty-four hours, he hesitated now. Too many impressions, thoughts, and ideas were whizzing through his head. Where were they to go? He wished he could pack them in cartons, put them on the shelves, take them out one by one, and think them through, examine them until they dissolved into nothing. Or that he could share them with somebody. Talk about them until they no longer raced around in his head, until they ebbed away, like a wave that lost its momentum on the beach and seeped into the sand forever. He felt that he had completely exhausted himself. As though his mind and his senses had taken on another rhythm in the past three years on Lamma, a rhythm that was no longer equal to the pace of the city: its sounds, its people, its hustle and bustle. Should he take a later ferry and have a drink in the bar at the Mandarin?

He called Christine. Her voice would do him good.

She was still in the office working on last month's accounts. No, she had no objection to having a drink at the Mandarin Oriental.

———

Paul felt the effect of the alcohol immediately. He felt it first in his legs and sensed it creeping through his body in waves, reaching his head, and he was overcome by a feeling of ease that he had forgotten existed.

Christine glanced at him, amused. "Is everything all right?"

"Yes," he replied, and had to laugh.

"When was the last time you had a drink?"

"I can't remember. It must be years ago. But it feels good."

"Why have you asked me here? What have you been doing since we had lunch?"

He had thought about whether it would be better to say that he'd had a long conversation with the Owens, run some errands or gone swimming, and had an appointment in the Foreign Correspondents' Club, but then it seemed ridiculous to him to say nothing about his visit to Michael Owen's apartment and the few hours he had spent on the other side of the border. So he told her about his investigations into the murder. She looked at him as though he had told her that he never wanted to see her again. For a moment he was afraid that she was going to start crying or screaming at him. Or that she would stand up without saying a word and leave.

"You don't take me seriously."

"Why do you say that?" Paul said.

"You promised me that you wouldn't get involved. You said you would stay out of it."

"I only did my friend a favor."

"You smuggled evidence over the border."

Paul did not respond. He wanted to take her hand, but she shook her head in rejection.

"You're treating me like a hysterical woman."

"Not at all. Why are you saying that?"

"You think I'm seeing ghosts, don't you?"

"No."

"You think I hate the Communist Chinese because they killed my father."

"No, Christine. No."

"You think I hate them because my husband had an affair with one of them. Admit it." Her voice was now so loud that the other guests in the bar turned to look at them.

He looked at her. Her lips were trembling a little. The skin above her neckline mottled red with rage or fear or agitation. He got up and knelt down next to her and stroked her on the head, and in that moment he felt something that he had thought had completely and utterly withered away, died, been extinguished forever. He felt a faint longing, a desire for her, for her body, for her breath on his skin, for her hands to hold him as tight as they could. He put one hand on her lap and stroked her tenderly on the cheek with the other.

"Can you stay here with me?" he asked quietly.

"Now? But I *am* here."

"Tonight."

She looked at him in disbelief, searching his eyes, his face, for a sign. Did he even know what he had just said? Was he serious?

"Shall we stay the night here, in the hotel?" he asked, and then stood up. He saw in her eyes that she would not say no.

They were so keyed up that they were completely silent as they stood next to each other in the elevator, holding hands tightly.

The room was much too cold. He turned the air-conditioning off and opened the door to the small balcony. Warm, humid tropical air streamed in immediately. Christine disappeared into the bathroom. He stood around in the room undecidedly, not knowing what to do with himself, with his fear and his lust, not knowing whether to take off his clothes, not knowing what was driving him, whether he was aroused, needy, or full of desire. His whole body was trembling. He closed his eyes. He wanted to feel her, do nothing more than feel, without words, without gestures, without a tomorrow, to forget everything else for this one moment, this one, never-ending, long and terribly short night.

He heard her opening the bathroom door and coming toward

him. She stood in front of him, undid his shirt slowly, button by button, then his belt. She helped him out of his trousers like he was a blind man; her hands stroked his chest and her lips caressed him. He could not open his eyes. One look would have spoiled everything. She took hold of his hands and made them push her bathrobe aside, baring her breasts, and he let her lead, let her do what she wanted, as she pulled him onto the bed, as she undressed him fully, stroked him and kissed him in places that no one had touched for years. He began to stir and at some point he did not need her to lead any longer, trusting himself, awakened, to move his hands of his own accord, caressing her breasts, her thighs, touching the opening of her vulva, so carefully, so tenderly and so gently, as if it were the first time, as if it were the last time, her body were the most precious of all gifts. As though he could barely believe his luck. He felt her breathing growing louder and heavier, her writhing under his hands as she grew more and more aroused.

And when the time came, when the air in the room was as warm and as humid as it was in the street outside, when the bed, the sheets, the walls, the carpet, and every corner of the room smelled of them, when nothing more stood between them, when she asked him to come inside her at last to release her from her desire and her lust, his strength ran out. He collapsed into himself and drooped. Unable to fight it, he fell aside and lay still.

He pulled the thin blanket over his head. He wanted to hide away, to disappear, to dissolve. "I can't," he whispered. "I'm sorry."

———

They had breakfast in the room, sitting on the bed in fluffy toweling robes with their feet tucked under them as they drank freshly pressed orange juice, spread marmalade on each other's still-warm bread rolls, and were careful with their words and gestures. Two people who know how delicate every happiness is.

At some point he got up, put the breakfast things away, and kissed her on her forehead, her neck, and her lips until they fell slowly onto the bed. They lay face-to-face, nose-to-nose. He saw his face reflected in her eyes.

"You mean a great deal to me." It did not sound as tender as he had wanted it to. But it was what he meant, and it was a lot.

"You mean a great deal to me too. I worry about you."

"You mustn't."

"Promise me something?"

"What?"

"Promise me first."

"Promise first? Without knowing what? Who ever heard of that?" They giggled.

"Trust in me," she said, putting on a mysterious voice that reminded him of someone. Trust in me. Kaa, the snake from *The Jungle Book*, spoke like that. He held his breath. What made her say that? Why use exactly those words in that tone? He did not want her to say any more. He did not want to be reminded of *The Jungle Book*. It had been Justin's favorite film; they had watched the DVD together so often, sitting on the couch in the living room or in bed, that Justin knew the dialogue practically by heart. *The Jungle Book* would destroy everything now. Everything in this world, he thought, hung by a thin thread that could break any moment. Any moment. You didn't even have to touch it. He put his index finger on her lips and said very quietly: "I promise."

"You promise me that you'll no longer travel to Shenzhen for this thing?"

Paul nodded.

"You have to keep to what you promise, right?" she asked, making sure.

"You have to keep to what you promise," he repeated.

———

Paul took Christine to her office. With her help, he was even able to cope with the overcrowded metro this morning. They stood with their bodies pressed together. He had never seen her looking so radiant before. The sight of her was enough to help him bear with equanimity the crush in the train, which normally made him anxious.

They arranged to meet for lunch. He found it difficult to say good-bye to her, even for only a few hours.

He wondered if he should get in touch with Elizabeth Owen. He felt a sense of responsibility for her that he could not explain, certainly since he had left her sleeping in her son's flat. What right had he to keep from her the fact that there was a dead body in Shenzhen who was, in all likelihood, her son? Was it not his duty to tell her about this? Whoever she received the news from, the impact would be the same. Whether from a Hong Kong policeman, from an official at the American consulate, or from him, Paul Leibovitz, who knew from personal experience what the death of a child meant to a parent. The longer he thought about it, the stronger grew his conviction that he could not shirk this responsibility, that they shared the same fate, that it should not matter whether he liked the family or not, but that what he had suffered and lost meant that he simply had no choice. He rang her number.

Her voice sounded more agitated than worried or frightened.

"Mr. Leibovitz, I was just about to call you. Did you go to my son's apartment again yesterday or this morning?"

"What do you mean? What should I be doing there? I don't even have a key."

"My husband thought perhaps the concierge had one and had let you in. But I told him straightaway that that was nonsense. What reason would there be for you to go to the apartment without us?"

"Why are you asking?"

"Because we're in the apartment now and it's all in a mess. Someone must have been here searching for something. I'm sure it was Michael but then why didn't he get in touch with us? He has our number and he knows how he can reach us. But the more important thing is: Where is he now?"

"Mrs. Owen, wait there for me. I'll be with you in fifteen minutes."

———

The apartment had not been totally trashed. There were no broken bits lying around and neither the couch cushions nor the mattress had been slit open, but someone had been here, and had looked in every corner, making no effort to conceal the search. In the bedroom, there were piles of underwear, socks, sports gear, and shirts on the bed; the chest of drawers was empty and the wardrobe had been emptied. In the study, the floor was covered with countless files. Many lay open and some had had documents torn out of them. The contents of the desk drawers lay strewn all around: pens, paper clips, flight schedules, dollar and yuan notes, coins, rubber stamps, and photos.

Richard Owen sat down on his son's desk chair and looked out of the window in silence, as though he was far away in his thoughts.

"Do you know if anything's missing?" Paul asked.

"What should be missing?" Elizabeth Owen asked in astonishment. "My son can't steal from himself. Apart from that . . ."

"Be quiet, Betty," her husband interrupted her sharply, without turning around.

"Richard thinks I'm crazy."

"Stop it," he commanded.

"But I'm sure that it was Michael," she continued, not listening to her husband. "Apart from us, he's the only one who has a key. And the door to the apartment hasn't been broken into."

"His cleaner has a key. How many times do I have to tell you that, dammit," Richard Owen barked at his wife.

"He was looking for something. He was definitely in a great hurry; that's why he didn't have time to call us," she said, as though she had not heard him. "He'll be in touch in the next few hours. I'm sure about that."

Later, Paul would often wonder if it was what Elizabeth Owen said then that made him finally tell her the truth. Her son would be in touch in the next few hours. She was sure about that. Knowing how absurd it was that she was convinced of this was intolerable to Paul. It made him an accessory, an accomplice to her degrading illusion. He had always told the doctors that he didn't want them to lie to him, and he had been glad that they had, as far as he could tell, never tried to.

"I have to tell you something," Paul said. He felt his heart racing so hard that it seemed fit to burst. His knees went weak and his voice cracked. He gasped for air as though a mighty hand was pushing him down under water. He was about to shatter these people's happiness or, more precisely, about to tell them that it was shattered, but that distinction made no difference to them. Nothing would be the same as it had been for them after what he was going to say next.

"The police found a dead body in Shenzhen yesterday," Paul said.

Elizabeth Owen's mouth fell open but no sound came out.

Richard Owen jumped out of his seat.

"They still don't know who it is. The man did not have any papers on him. But he's from the West and he is the same age as your son."

"That doesn't mean anything!" Richard Owen shouted at him, raising his hands as though he wanted to protect himself or was about to push Paul away.

"The dead man had three scars on his left knee."

Paul had hoped never to look into eyes like these again.

———

He would need a good forty-five minutes to get from Harbour View Court to Wan Chai on foot. Paul thought about taking a taxi, but he would not be able to stand being cooped up in a car stuck in a traffic jam. Not to be able to move forward or backward. To be locked in. He would be overcome with claustrophobia. He had to be out, under the open sky. He walked down Robinson Road, getting faster with every step; the movement was doing him good. He took deep breaths and exhaled with such loud sighing sounds that the few passersby turned to look at him. He walked through the Botanic Gardens, ran down Kennedy Road, and came to the aviary in Hong Kong Park. There, his strength failed him. Drenched with sweat, he sat down on a bench and gasped for air like a sprinter within sight of the finish line. He felt a pounding pain in his head, and heard his blood rushing through his ears. Perhaps Christine would come to see him in the park for half an hour.

———

She brought along two cheese sandwiches, a packet of stuffed rice dumplings, and two half-liter cups of iced tea.

"I don't know anyone else who would be mad enough to sit in the park at lunchtime and have a picnic," she said, spreading a paper napkin out on the bench and putting the sandwiches down on it.

"It wouldn't be my first choice either," he replied wearily, "but I can't do anything else."

"How are the Owens?"

"They wanted to stay on in their son's apartment for a while. They'll go over this afternoon to identify him. I've called Zhang. He'll pick them up at the border."

"Is there no doubt at all?"

"I'm afraid not."

"Will you go with them?"

He shook his head.

"Did they not ask you to?"

"Yes, but I said no."

"Are they going on their own?"

"No. I advised them to contact the American Consulate. One of the officials there will surely go with them. I won't. A promise is a promise."

"You said that yesterday too. A couple of hours later you were over in Shenzhen again."

"That's true. But it's different now. I can't go on. The whole thing touches on a raw nerve for me." Realizing that what he was saying still did not reassure her, he added, after a pause, "And I don't want you to worry about me."

"I'm sorry. I can't help it."

He stroked her hair.

"You think I worry too much, don't you?" Christine asked.

Paul thought for a moment. "After everything that has happened to your family, I can understand why you don't trust the authorities in China. But that's over thirty years ago. I don't think that you still have to be frightened of them. It's no longer the same country."

"No? Is it no longer the People's Republic of China? Have I missed something?" She had wanted to ask this question calmly, almost as a throwaway remark, sounding only a little surprised. But she sounded snappy and aggressive instead.

"I don't know how I would feel if they had my father on their conscience," he said to appease her.

"And your brother."

"My brother?" Paul asked, surprised.

"Your brother," she repeated.

"But you haven't told me anything about that."

"He was ten years older than me, and when he was still at school, he was sent off to work in the countryside during the Cultural Revolution."

"Did he starve to death?"

"We don't know. We fled to Hong Kong one year after that, and never heard from him again."

"Then he's probably still alive."

"Possibly."

"Have you not tried to find him since China opened up?"

"How? My uncles and aunts all escaped to Hong Kong and Sydney. No one lives in Guangdong any longer."

"You can go to your village and look for him. Maybe he went back there, and if not, perhaps someone would know something about . . ."

"Paul," she interrupted him curtly. "You don't get it. I'm never going to China. Never. We were counterrevolutionaries."

"Forty years ago!" He regretted his words almost as soon as he spoke them.

X

Zhang stood at the Lo Wu border, a few meters behind the counter for diplomats and VIPs, waiting for the Owens. It was hot and sticky in the hall; the air-conditioning was either not working at all or only very slightly. Zhang wiped the sweat off his brow with a tissue. He was so nervous that the bunch of keys he was fingering agitatedly slipped out of his hands twice. The identification of a dead body by a family member, a task disliked by almost all his coworkers, was for him one of the most unpleasant responsibilities of the homicide division, and the worst scenario was when parents saw the corpses of their children. In moments like that, Zhang felt, the heart of the world stopped, and nothing, absolutely nothing, could make it start beating again. The expressions of pain that death carved on the faces of the living often haunted him through the nights. Even after twenty years, he did not know how he ought to behave in such situations. Look away? Offer help? Cover up his own speechlessness with a torrent of words? In these situations, his coworkers always spoke of punishment, of revenge or justice, and gave assurances, over and over again, that the person who had done this would be hunted down and that they would not give up until that person, and anyone else involved, was caught. As much as Zhang meant whatever he said, he could never shake off the feeling that he was lying. So he preferred to say nothing, which meant that there was often an oppressive silence.

How would the Owens react? Would grief or rage dominate? Would they ask questions, ones that he had no answers to?

He was tired and worn out and longed to be with Mei. She would be able to calm him down with a few sentences now. Or he would lay his head down on her soft, warm breast, and very soon his thoughts would stop racing around dead people, murderers, and their motives.

Zhang closed his eyes and focused on his breath, trying not to think about anything. He imagined a sunrise in the mountains of Sichuan. He saw a luminous green paddy field, flooded with water, and the yellow-white orb rising behind it, gradually spreading its light over everything. He took a deep breath in and counted to eight, breathed out and counted to ten. After four or five breaths he slowly felt stillness returning to him and he felt his face relaxing, as if he could, for a few seconds, step out of the role of the restless, anxious police detective.

He had started meditating a few years ago. When he began, he had thought that external quiet was needed to meditate, but he had learned that stillness was already within him, and that meditation was merely the path to it. So wherever he was—in the office, buying groceries or at the Lo Wu border crossing—did not matter one bit. He had found it tremendously liberating to be able to soothe himself and not to be helpless in the face of his fears and his inner demons. Since then, he had practiced meditation several times every day, often only for a few minutes. It almost always helped.

Zhang looked around the hall and immediately saw the Owens among the Western business travelers arriving. Paul had described the couple well. She was wearing a dark-blue trouser suit and he was in khakis and a white short-sleeved shirt. Both of them were hiding their eyes behind sunglasses. Hers were so big that they covered half her face. They were accompanied by a young American man from the consulate who spoke incredibly good Mandarin but still stammered slightly at the beginning of every sentence. He was trying to hide his nervousness, which made it even worse. Two dark sweat patches were showing around his underarms, and he clutched a brown briefcase to his chest with both hands, like a swimmer clinging to a plank of wood in the water. The two men towered over Zhang by much more than a head, giving him the impression even when they were speaking to him that they were looking past him or away from him. Was that what made him feel uncomfortable from the very beginning? Was it the dark glasses that they did not remove, making it impossible for him to see their eyes and giving him the feeling that he was looking at a wall? Or was it the foreign language? His attempts to say a few sentences in English as a gesture of courtesy and respect were met with not a single response or reaction.

Zhang hurriedly switched to Mandarin, introduced himself, and thanked them for coming. The consulate official translated what he said, but the Owens did not even nod in acknowledgment. They walked through the station out onto the plaza, where a black Audi limousine was waiting for them. Elizabeth Owen's movements were sluggish; she had probably taken strong medication for her nerves. Her husband came to a sudden standstill and stretched a hand out as if he was looking for a wall or a tree to hold onto. He swayed slightly and seemed about to fall. Elizabeth did not notice or did not want to notice and walked slowly past him. After a couple of seconds, he gathered himself and followed.

On the way to the police headquarters they were stuck in a traffic jam twice; with every minute that passed in the stationary car, Zhang felt the inside of the vehicle shrink, until he could barely tolerate its confines. In the rearview mirror, he saw Richard Owen reach for his wife's hand several times, but she flinched away every time.

At headquarters, the scene at the train station repeated itself. Luo, the head of the homicide division, and Ye, the powerful party secretary, were standing in front of the side entrance, surrounded by their assistants. They greeted the Owens with a few fragments of English; the Owens said nothing in response. It took the elevator only a few seconds to travel from the ground floor to the basement, but they seemed like an eternity to Zhang. Elizabeth Owen was trembling all over and the two men were silent, both looking away as if they had nothing to do with each other. In the basement, Luo led them down a long corridor into the small, badly lit morgue. Elizabeth stood still at the doorway. As if she could not take one more step toward the corpse which was laid out and covered with a gray blanket. The consulate official hesitated briefly, wondering whether to stay with her, before he followed her husband into the middle of the room.

Wu, the old pathologist, waited for them in silence. They were standing in a semicircle in front of the body, in almost unbearable silence. Even Wu, who had carried out so many autopsies, seemed to be nervous. He fussed around the blanket before he finally raised it slowly. Zhang did not look. He stood next to Richard Owen and observed the two American men. The blood drained out of the consulate official's face; he turned chalk white and started retching. Richard Owen did not hear him; he looked down at his son's face without any reaction. He nodded and murmured a few words that made Zhang start, but whose meaning he was not sure he had understood correctly. He wanted to ring Paul as soon as the Owens had left and ask him what Richard Owen could have meant.

In the first few years of his job, Zhang had tried to interpret the reactions of family members in such moments; he had thought they would tell him something about their relationship to the dead person, about their pain, about the meaning of loss. This Zhang of years past would have been disconcerted now; he would have started to harbor suspicious thoughts. He would have equated a lack of reaction with indifference. He would have registered every movement, every flicker of the eyelids, every twitch of the mouth exactly and judged it; he would have asked himself why this man did not burst into tears, why he did not want to touch his son, why he did not close his eyes or start trembling.

Zhang had stopped asking himself questions like this at some point. When parents, siblings, or friends were told of a death or when they identified the body, whether they wept, cried out with grief, broke down, or stayed as calm as if they had barely known the person said nothing, or only very little, about what was really going on inside them or how deeply affected they were by the death.

Grief has as many faces as there are people, Zhang thought. It had that in common with love.

So he felt all the more annoyed with the thoughts that were now whizzing through his mind. There was something not quite right here. He found the Owens increasingly odd. Why was Richard Owen not hurrying back to his wife's side? Why was he not saying anything else? Zhang thought he would see more than pain and despair in his face. As a detective, he had learned to trust in his intuition and his instincts, but he was uncertain in this case. He was dealing with an American, whose culture he did now know.

And something else confused Zhang. Why had Party Secretary Ye come with them to the basement? It had been a matter of protocol for him to greet them at the entrance, but Zhang had never seen him down here all these years. He was a political chief detective superintendent, leader of all the party members at the police headquarters; he organized their meetings, during which they studied the resolutions of the party conferences, the teachings of Deng Xiaoping and of Hu Jintao, the president of the People's Republic of China and the party chairman, and practiced self-criticism and praising improvements. He had nothing to do with police investigative work and therefore had no place down here. What did his presence mean?

The voice of his superior interrupted his thoughts. Zhang heard him say something about a head injury and that they still had no definite answers as to whether it was the result of a fall or an act of violence, but they hoped to have some certainty in the next few hours. They would not bother the family with questions for too long.

So they had not decided yet whether to try to hush up the murder. Most of his fellow policemen secretly hoped they would; Zhang understood that very clearly from their comments. It would save them a lot of work. But Zhang feared such a solution. Every time external influence was exercised on an investigation, whether for political reasons or because someone had pulled strings, and suspects were released, interrogations were suspended, or innocent people had to be arrested, he reacted with physical symptoms, mostly nausea and vomiting. For a time, he had been called the "retching policeman" by the people at headquarters.

They did not say a word on the way back to the train station. The Owens looked left and right out of the car windows in silence, without seeking support or comfort from each other. The unhappy consulate official sat between them, stiff and unmoving like a mannequin, his eyes fixed straight ahead of him.

Zhang took them to the border. The lines of people in front of the counters snaked through the entire hall and only shortened in length very slowly, for the young border officials took their duties very seriously and performed them with great care. He took the passports from the three Americans and obtained exit stamps for them from the station manager. The consulate official was about to thank him, but the Owens turned away without a word and made their way to the train.

When he was out of the station, he tried to call Paul, but there was no reply.

Oh my God, Michael. I am sorry. I am so sorry. Zhang was almost positive that he had heard these words. What did Richard Owen mean by them? What was he apologizing for?

It was not a good sign.

XI

As they waited for the train to take them back to Hong Kong, Richard Owen's thoughts turned to his father, Richard Owen II. He saw him playing with Michael in the garden of his house in Wisconsin a year before he died. It had been an oppressively hot summer day; Richard remembered it quite clearly. The old man had been wearing shorts, which showed his pale, thin legs. That had been unusual. He had been throwing footballs to his grandson, coughing and gasping for breath after every toss. His cancer-ridden lungs had made him short of breath, but they had not known this yet on that day. Michael had been unstoppable. *Just five minutes more,* he begged every time his grandfather tried to end the game. He dived and lunged across the lawn, sprinting tirelessly for the farthest passes, snatching even the most difficult balls from the air, constantly fired up by the rasping, effortful words of encouragement from his grandfather. *Good boy. Great catch. Great catch.* The weak voice could no longer be heard from the house at the other end of the large garden.

Richard Owen had sat on the terrace watching his father and his son, wondering if he should go over to them. He had dismissed the thought immediately. He would not be welcome. He was not even sure if they would let him join in. The day before, his father had only had strength enough for a few tosses, but when Richard had offered to replace him, his son had claimed that he was tired and gone up to his room.

Michael was very close to his granddad. The two of them got along in a way that Richard did not understand, in a way that was alien to him and that he secretly envied. His father had never played ball with him before. He had not even found the time to attend the high school games in which his son had always been the quarterback and undisputed star. Where had the interest and the relaxed manner come from that enabled him to play with his grandson now, and since the boy had been able to walk, even? When he, Richard, played with Michael, they always started fighting within minutes. The boy was so sensitive. Awful. He reacted to every one of his father's comments with an objection and he took every piece of advice as a criticism. He was only trying to give him a few tips to help him to improve his game. But Michael refused to profit from his father's experience. At some point they had stopped playing football together. Now as he observed his son play with his own father, Richard didn't know if there was a greater distance between him and his father or him and his son.

Why were images from that afternoon over twenty years ago coming to him now, of all times? An afternoon that, as far as Richard could remember, had nothing remarkable about it. Why could he not remember a happier time with Michael? One of their fishing trips, on which they had not argued? Their trip to the Indy 500? He knew that they had had these experiences together, but with the best will in the world, he could not recall any details about them. He hated how unpredictable his memory was. He had nothing more important to think about or to remember right now. He was on his way to identify a dead body and he had no doubt that it was his son who lay in the morgue, regardless of any straw of hope Elizabeth still wanted to cling to.

The train to Hong Kong was so full that the young man from the consulate had to stand. Richard sat between his wife and an old Chinese woman who stank of garlic and who nodded off repeatedly. Her head had already landed on his shoulder twice, and only a determined shake had woken her again. He would have preferred to go by car, which the consulate official had offered them, but Elizabeth had insisted on the train, probably because Michael had always taken the train.

They had barely exchanged a meaningful word in the last few hours. Every time he started saying something, she turned away. When he tried to take her in his arms her whole body stiffened. As if it were all his fault. As if he had irresponsibly sent the boy off on some adventure against his will. They had been fighting over that for two days. It was quite the opposite, he reminded his wife over and over again, failing to convince her. If the goddamn family had only listened to him, their son would still be alive.

As the third co-owner and former sole managing director of Aurora Metal, he had refused to invest in China for a long time. How could Elizabeth have forgotten all the discussions between father and son, the arguments that had resounded through the house, often ending in shouting and slammed doors? And when Elizabeth had gotten involved, Michael's faction had seized the opportunity. He, Richard, had made his position clear to her more than once: The American and the Canadian markets were enough for him; they had already provided a good living for two generations before theirs, so why should they change anything? They had provided General Motors and Ford with reliable supplies of specially manufactured screws and motor parts for close to half a century. He had known the buyers at the firms for many years; he was friends with some of them; they had never complained about the quality or the price. Why should he start manufacturing the parts on the other side of the world all of a sudden? China was a place for General Electric, for McDonald's, Boeing, or Philip Morris, the global players, not for Aurora Metal.

Who were they, after all? A medium-size firm, a family business that was managed by a third-generation Owen, that never wanted its shares to be publicly traded on the stock exchange, that was proud of still manufacturing in the same small town, yes, practically on the same piece of land on which his grandfather, Richard Owen I, had founded the company in February 1910. They had grown with the automobile industry, quite organically, without acquisitions or take-overs. The two-man business had grown into a respected firm with nearly nine hundred employees: the biggest local employer, sponsor of the college basketball team and a high school football team, and generous donor to the community hospital, where two operating theaters were named after them. Of course there had been a few lean years—the oil crisis in the 1970s, the subsequent recession under the ineffective Democrat Jimmy Carter—but for the most part it was about cyclical upturns and downturns, which the company had handled well. In the summer of 1995 they had inaugurated their new factory: bigger than a football field, filled with the latest machinery, the best American equipment. Faster. Cleaner. Safer. More efficient. They had spent a hundred million dollars on it, convinced that they were prepared for the future.

Less than two years later a young buyer from General Motors came to Richard Owen's office for the first time. He was barely older than his son, fresh from college, his head full of figures but with no idea how things actually worked. One of those types that universities seemed to spit out from a conveyor belt. He refused an invitation to lunch. He did not smoke, and instead of coffee he drank one Diet Coke after another while negotiating prices. Telling him, Richard Owen, something about the pressure on costs and shorter supply deadlines, about further rationalization in manufacturing and a competitor from Pusan, whose quality was not far off theirs. Pusan? Richard Owen asked, not sure if he had heard right. Pusan, South Korea, that smart-ass had replied in an intolerably arrogant tone of voice. As though people in Wisconsin had to know every crappy backwater in Korea. Richard Owen had come close to throwing him out.

Michael had been in the meeting. He had made notes and barely said anything. One month later, he suggested China for the first time. He wanted to go to Hong Kong, Shanghai, and Shenzhen to do some research to see if moving at least some of their manufacturing operations might make sense. At first, Richard Owen had thought his son was joking. They had just invested a hundred million dollars in a new plant, in the future of Aurora Metal. Why should they manufacture at the other end of the world? In a country ruled by Communists. The savings could not be so great that he would want to do business with them. He was a very conservative person, yes, old-fashioned and a relic, if his son wanted to look at it that way. The very idea of moving abroad just because they could shave a few cents off the price of manufacturing appalled him. They did not have to justify themselves to shareholders. Patriotism was more than a matter of lip service to him. He had bought American all his life. He would never have entertained the idea of driving a German or a Japanese car. When he had ordered his first motorboat, he had insisted on replacing the Yamaha engine with a Mercury. He only drank American wine and American beer.

But Michael would not leave him in peace. Every week, he came up with fresh figures and statistics, with examples from other industries, with comparable family-owned firms that had closed their factories in Indiana, Illinois, or the Carolinas and moved them to India or China. One day, Michael drove to a Walmart Supercenter with him and led him through the long rows of shelves. They started with the shoes. Michael picked out random pairs, turned them upside down, looked at the soles, and showed them to him, without saying anything. There were the words, Made in China. On every pair. And what about it, Richard Owen said. They're shoes, just shoes. They went on to the pants and jackets, to the lights and garden furniture, to the tools, to the toys, and the digital cameras. They pulled televisions and DVD recorders out of the shelves. The same three words were everywhere: Made in China. Walmart, Walmart of all places, Richard Owen thought to himself. How long ago had it been since their stores had had giant billboards in front of them with the words Made in America? Since every customer had had a button proclaiming Buy American! pressed into his hand? Ten years ago? Definitely not. Five at most. Michael asked his father if he knew what percent of Walmart's products came from China. Richard Owen got the feeling that he didn't know anything anymore. He felt old, terribly old, and he wanted to go home. He shook his head and only vaguely registered the answer: almost 80 percent, his son told him with a triumphant tone in his voice.

Despite this, Richard Owen remained obstinate. What was Walmart to him, he said. Aurora Metal did not supply consumers who watched every cent, who only wanted to get things cheaper and cheaper. Its customers were General Motors and Ford, not for their budget models but their most expensive ones, which meant quality was even more important and quality had its price, as their managers knew; the people who bought a Cadillac or a Lincoln knew that too.

In the end it all happened very quickly. In the automobile industry, so it seemed to Richard Owen, the buyers had taken over power from the engineers in a short space of time. He found himself sitting across the table from young men who no longer enthused about the latest technical innovations or the R&D divisions, but cared only about the numbers. Suppliers meant nothing more to them than costs, which had to be reduced by every means possible. They demanded a "China price" from him, the amount for which they could supposedly get the parts manufactured in China. Aurora Metal could either comply or the business relationship between them would have to come to an end sooner or later, regrettable as it was. Richard Owen looked at his figures and felt that he was being made a fool of. He would have liked nothing more than to shove the young managers' paperwork in their mouths. He could not have supplied the goods at these prices even twenty years ago. He thought about how his father or grandfather would have dealt with these fellows, how they would have chased them and their China prices off the premises. But he was no longer strong enough to defend himself.

Michael Owen flew to Hong Kong, Shenzhen, and Shanghai, and when he returned after almost three weeks, he told his father that there was no country on earth that was more capitalist than China, that there was no need to worry about the Communists there, for they dreamed the American dream, and it was a ridiculous anachronism born of sentimentality or ignorance to produce even a screw or a button in America when you could manufacture it for ten, no, twenty times less at the other end of the world. Michael had already spoken to several possible Chinese joint venture partners. With the Owens' experience and contacts, Aurora Metal was a sought-after partner; their only problem would be choosing who they should partner with. It was not a matter of moving parts of the production process there but the entire manufacturing operation. The plant in America had to be closed, the sooner the better, it didn't matter how modern or efficient the machinery was. The hourly pay of their new workers in Guangdong would be twenty-five cents, thirty-five cents at most. There were no trade unions, no pension provisions, and only one week's paid holiday, and anyone who did not do good work could be let go from one day to another. There were enough young men waiting at the factory gates who were ready to take on any kind of work. What was there left to discuss? Out of the nine hundred or so employees in America they would have to keep twenty at most in the office and in accounts.

When Richard Owen continued to hesitate to take this step, Michael threatened to go it alone. The next day, the first orders for the coming year were canceled. He knew that this was no cyclical downturn but a warning from General Motors' Diet Coke men. He had waited too long. China was no longer an alternative. China was the only way out now.

Michael announced the closure of the Aurora Metal factory in Wisconsin at a workers' meeting. He spoke calmly and matter-of-factly, like a teacher patiently explaining a math formula to his pupils. What surprised Richard Owen the most was that the workers' reaction was just as measured. No furious protests raged through the halls; no cursing, no shouting was heard. It was as if it had always been clear to them that the gates here would one day be locked, to be opened again ten thousand miles away. The China price was a law of nature that only fools fought against.

Richard had stood next to his son fighting back his tears. He had not known how good Michael was at giving speeches. The resonant voice, the erect posture, the gaze directed straight over the heads of the workers at the silent machinery. The men had respected him, Richard. He had known many of them by name; they were the second, some even the third, generation of their families to work in this factory. He had not looked over their heads; he did not want to avoid their gazes but to look them in the eyes. He did not succeed. He had stared at the ceiling and the floor and his eyes had rested on the helmets, the blue overalls, and the fire extinguisher on the wall instead. The workers had expected a few words. He ought to have said something; he wanted to. But what? Michael had explained the China price to them. They had stood there silently, listened, and nodded. There had been nothing more to say. Richard had felt ashamed of his helplessness.

The noise of the train arriving back in Hong Kong drew him back from his memories. They walked out of the station onto the plaza, and he suddenly had the feeling that the ground beneath his feet was shaking. After identifying his son's body what else could he expect. And then there was the heat and the humidity, which pressed down on him in the open air almost like a physical force. If only he had the feeling that he and Elizabeth were in this together, but she had been so distant. No matter what his wife thought, he did not love Michael any less than she did, even though he and his son had fought often and hard, especially in the last few weeks. What did that matter? He had explained the reasons to Elizabeth, but she did not listen; she did not want to know anything about the dangerous games her son was playing in China. He had tried many times, had pleaded with her to speak to Michael, perhaps he would listen to her rather than to his father, but she had only shaken her head. He ought not to doubt his son and nag him constantly; he had always done that before, so it was no wonder that Michael was resisting;

he, Richard, should simply trust him more. After all, it was Michael who had pushed to invest in China, who had found Victor Tang and handled the negotiations with him, saving Aurora Metal.

Richard Owen felt his eyes growing moist and he swallowed a few times. Might Elizabeth have been right? Had he done his son Michael an injustice with his skepticism? No tears now, he thought, he couldn't let himself go, not in front of his wife and certainly not in public.

If only Tang were by his side now. Why had Elizabeth insisted that he not come? She liked him; she had always claimed to, anyway. Yet this morning, for the first time, she said that Tang made her uneasy, without saying why exactly. They had gotten into a fight about it, for if there was one thing—apart from the numbers, of course, which had showed the increased profits—that had persuaded Richard Owen that the decision to move production entirely to China had been the right one, it was the meeting with Victor Tang.

Their joint venture partner had impressed him greatly since their first meeting in the Regent Hotel in Hong Kong. Tang spoke perfect English, almost entirely without an accent. He had studied for a PhD at Harvard and had traveled a good deal through the States in that time. Over and over again, he impressed Richard Owen with his breadth of knowledge about American history. He was clearly fascinated by America, and knew more about its history than Richard Owen himself, and certainly far more than Michael did. The scheduled two-hour business lunch had turned into nearly a whole day, with a Chinese dinner followed by a visit to a karaoke bar, where they drank whiskey from Tennessee and sang Frank Sinatra's "My Way" together. No one in Wisconsin would have believed it. A Chinese national who could rattle off whole paragraphs from the American Declaration of Independence and Abraham Lincoln's Gettysburg Address by heart, who claimed that there was a spiritual connection between Deng Xiaoping and Ronald Reagan, and was even able to prove it with quotes. "Greed is good," the American leader had said, while the Chinese one had declared that "to get rich is glorious." Both of them, Tang said, meant the same thing. He constantly emphasized that China could learn a great deal from America, and that it was finally prepared to do so, which flattered the Owens. "The American dream, Mr. Owen, is very much alive. It is dreamed and lived by millions of Chinese people, and their numbers are growing every day, believe me."

And Richard Owen did exactly that from that day onward. He believed Victor Tang. He had looked him in the eye and seen a strength of will and a steeliness that was familiar to him. He had eaten and drunk with him and known that he could do business with this man, that he could trust him.

He missed him today in that cold, dark cave where all eyes were on him, where a man in blood-spattered overalls lifted a dirty cloth, where his wife stood by the entrance and looked at him as though he were the murderer; he had felt as alone as he ever had in his life.

It was Michael. Of course it was Michael. He had guessed, no, known it the whole time. What was wrong with his head? Why was a piece missing? My God, Michael, what have they done to you? You were right, I should have listened to you, but why weren't you satisfied with what we'd achieved? Why wasn't it enough?

For a moment Richard Owen thought he would explode. He wanted to scream and flail around him; he wanted to press his son to him and take him away, carry him out of this miserable tomb. To touch him, at least, stroke him one more time. But he had resolved beforehand not to lose control. No tears. Not there. Not in front of those strangers.

The China price. The words shot into his mind. The China price.

XII

Victor Tang sat in the back of his Mercedes 500, which was so new that neither his driver nor Victor himself, of course, had had the time to familiarize himself with the functions and details of its many buttons, switches, and fittings. Tang heard his chauffeur swear after he had pressed yet another wrong button. With a few brusque words Tang instructed him to turn the music up and to restrain himself; Chinese curse words did not go well with Beethoven's Kreutzer Sonata. "Louder, I said. And a little louder still." The slow opening chords played from the four speakers crisply and clearly without the slightest jarring or distortion, and filled every last crevice of the vehicle. The engine could neither be heard nor felt; Tang felt as though he were sitting in a concert hall rather than a car. The interplay of the violin and the piano helped him to concentrate.

Richard Owen was worrying him. He had called him from his hotel in Hong Kong yesterday evening after identifying the body. His voice had grown shaky after a few sentences, and he had started crying, weeping bitterly. Tang's careful attempts to comfort him had been in vain, and Richard had simply hung up after a while.

Tang had not reckoned with this reaction, not after the conversation that he had had with Owen Senior the previous week, not after all the fights between father and son that he had witnessed in the past three years, which had grown more serious and embittered in the past few weeks. He was unsure of how to judge Richard's tears.

He was either still suffering from the shock of the sight of his dead son or old wounds had been opened. The latter, Tang knew from personal experience, would be dangerous.

He looked at the clock. In about an hour the chief of police, the party secretary of the police headquarters, the leader of the homicide division, and a few trusted employees from the mayor's office would be meeting him in his office. He wanted to emphasize to them once again that telling Elizabeth and Richard that the death was an accident was most definitely not an option. Elizabeth would insist on a postmortem in Hong Kong or America. It was murder and the case could not stay unsolved for long. Elizabeth would not let matters rest until the murderer was found and convicted. They needed a suspect with a plausible motive, and as quickly as possible. That shouldn't actually be very difficult after everything that had happened at the factory in the previous weeks. The longer the investigation dragged on, the greater the danger that the media in Hong Kong reported on the case and thereby alerted the Chinese newspapers to it, or the American embassy in Beijing got involved. Diplomatic representatives, possibly including an FBI detective asking awkward questions, were the last thing they needed now. The murder had to be solved today, tomorrow, the day after tomorrow at the latest. In Shenzhen and in his home province of Sichuan there were only too many envious people who were just waiting to pin something on him to sully his reputation, who wished for nothing more than for him to make a mistake so that they could pounce on him, tear his little empire apart, and divide it among themselves.

The Mercedes came to a standstill with a gentle jerk. They were stuck in an impossible traffic jam on the Shennan Road. Furious broken chords sounded from the loudspeakers in the car.

Tang looked at the city's skyline, and got the impression, as he did every time whether he wanted to or not, that New York lay before him. Needless to say, he could not group these skyscrapers with those in Manhattan. Of course not. Shenzhen was not Shanghai or Hong Kong, but what they had created here from nothing in the past fifteen years, from a squalid and miserable fishing village, was more than astounding; it filled him with pride. No one could deny that this skyline had a certain beauty. Especially not at twilight, when the somewhat monotonous buildings disappeared and all that could be seen was the endless sea of light, reminding him of the American big cities that had fascinated him on his earlier travels, like every sighting of something new had.

New York City. Manhattan. Fifty-Third Street, corner of Lexington Avenue. There were two days in Tang's life, which even today, decades later, were so present in his mind that he marveled at his memory over and over again, over its incredible capacity and precision. It made him a time traveler. Whenever he wanted, his memory took him back to that warm, cloudless day in the early summer of 1985, when he first set foot on American ground at the John F. Kennedy airport. He was there on a scholarship to Harvard, and had been chosen from several thousand applicants throughout China, sent by the government of the province of Sichuan. He had studied English, Economics, and Business Studies at Chengdu University, and was to further his studies with a PhD, get much-needed experience, and, after his return, help to turn a socialist planned economy into a free-market economy. Or at least into the Chinese version of one.

Victor Tang saw himself standing in front of Terminal 1 of the airport once more. He was alone and feeling so unsure of himself that he had difficulty setting one foot in front of the other. This uncertainty was more than the brief disorientation of a stranger who first had to get used to a place. It went deeper than that; it filled him with shame and it wounded him. He was a grown man who, at thirty-three years of age, did not want to feel as helpless as a child. Mixed with this feeling of shame was an indistinct rage; he did not know where it came from or what it was directed against at first, but it was to accompany him like a shadow over the next few years.

The provincial government had given him a meager allowance. In his jacket pocket was an envelope with five twenty-dollar bills; they had also provided him with a dark-blue suit, but it did not fit

him, unusually tall as he was for a Chinese man from Sichuan. The
sleeves of the jacket did not even reach his wrists, and the trousers
did not touch his ankles. They had not provided him with shoes
in his size at all. His old footwear was so worn out that he would
have preferred to go barefoot. He had barely noticed all this when
departing from Beijing, but now he could not fail to see it. In these
clothes he cut a ridiculous figure.

Tang had to get to Manhattan from the airport and report to the
Chinese consulate there before the journey up to Harvard. He saw
an endless line of yellow taxis and politely asked what the trip to
the city would cost. At first he thought the man in the turban had
not understood him correctly. The driver was asking for more money
that his mother in Chengdu earned in a month. He would never pay
such an amount for a car ride; he would rather walk into the city. The
bus was also too expensive, so Tang did something that the consulate expressly advised its exchange students against: He ignored the
warnings about attacks and took the subway to Manhattan.

He felt more confident on the subway. Among the many people
with brown and black skin who were themselves unremarkably
dressed and did not pay him the slightest bit of notice, his odd cos-
tume no longer stood out. The rumbling of the shabby old cars on
the worn tracks reminded him of the pathetic condition of the trains
in his homeland. At some point they disappeared into a tunnel from
which they did not emerge, and Tang felt himself becoming a little
dizzy. He clung to the silvery metal pole in front of him and hoped
that he would soon feel better again.

The station at Fifty-Third Street was full of people. The confined
space and the warm humid air in the underground station made his
dizziness worse. The train platform was uncomfortably narrow. Tang
made his way up the stairs, walked through a tunnel toward the exit,
and pushed himself through a heavy door there. Outside, he took in
several deep breaths, one hand holding on tight to the stair railing
while the other clutched his suitcase. He walked up the subway
stairs one step at a time. Just before the final step, he stopped and

looked around him. He could not believe his eyes. His gaze passed over the sidewalk, the streets, and lighted on a shopwindow full of bags and suitcases, moving up the building floor by floor toward the sky, higher and higher until he had to lean his head back on his neck to see the top of the skyscraper. He had never stood in front of a building anywhere near as high as this one.

Tang turned around in a circle like a child who could not decide which direction to run in. He walked down Lexington Avenue, turning left and right constantly, not knowing where to look first. Sometimes he simply wanted to stand still, but passersby jostled him immediately and their irritation and curses drove him. Aimlessly, he turned into Fifty-First Street and crossed Madison Avenue, then Park Avenue, in the middle of which flowers were blooming, and stumbled many times over fire hydrants and trash cans before finally retreating into the entrance of a building and gaping in amazement. He could not get enough of looking at the canyonlike but dead-straight streets with their traffic lights flickering red, yellow, and green reflected in the glass claddings of the towering buildings, of the many cars, of the shops filled to bursting with goods but with no lines of people outside them.

He felt his understanding of the world, constructed by so many people over so many years, dissolving before his eyes, hissing like a drop of water falling onto a red-hot surface. This was the moment in which his life took a new turn.

Tang understood that he had been lied to. For more than thirty years. Every day. From dawn till dusk. They had told him fairy tales. As a child, as a young man, he had given them the most precious thing he had, his trust, and they had exploited it. Where were they now, the teachers, the party secretaries, the great chairmen, and their many little helpers? What would they say? How would they explain this to him?

He had grown up believing that he was lucky to live in a country that was better than the rest of the world in every way. They did not have a great deal to eat but the teachers had often told him how much worse it was for the children in Europe and America, who ran through the streets dressed in rags, their stomachs growling with hunger. In school, they had not had lunch for a whole week so that the poor children in America could have enough to eat for once. Sacrifice for America, the campaign was called! Starve for America! And they had done it! Eagerly and enthusiastically. With a secure sense of their own superiority.

He had trusted them when they had arrested his father, a loyal PLA officer, at the beginning of the great proletarian Cultural Revolution. There was surely something justified, thought Tang, about the party's accusations. He had trusted them when they had sent him to the countryside to learn from the farmers, when he had joined the Red Guards and they had to carry out the Revolution against bourgeois elements and outmoded thinking, defend themselves against revisionists and counterrevolutionaries, with violent measures if necessary. He had obeyed every one of their orders, not out of fear, but with the deepest conviction. Because he had believed them. Because he had trusted them. Now he walked through the streets of Manhattan and knew that trusting was for the weak. For people who did not have the courage to seek the truth for themselves. For people who lacked the strength to check things out properly, who were too cowardly to live with the consequences of lies. Those who preferred to believe rather than to strive for certainty. It was no longer for him. Victor Tang had wasted enough trust in his life.

Before he arrived in New York he had, of course, known that China lagged behind the West, the United States in particular, in terms of economic development and the standard of living. The Sichuan provincial government had prepared him for his journey: He knew all the figures and statistics, he had seen photos and read books. Despite that, this first sight of the streets of Manhattan struck him like a blow that he could not defend himself against. He was deeply disturbed by how little numbers were able to tell you about a place. Even words and pictures could not encapsulate the essentials.

The first months at Harvard had been difficult; at times, he had not known how he would get through the day. The tranquility and the amount of space around made him nervous. The beauty of the old buildings and the elegance of the surroundings made him feel shy. Almost all the students and professors were extremely friendly and helpful to him, but he often found it difficult to accept their generosity. They invited him to dinner in their town houses, and he spent a few weekends in luxurious houses in the country. He told them about China and his audience marveled politely without really taking an interest in or understanding what he was describing. And how could they? Tang always felt uncomfortable at these dinners. He was the poor cousin; their generosity would not change that. On the contrary, it spelled it out anew every time. He was with them but he did not belong.

What saved him was his diligence, his intelligence, and his desire not to waste a minute that he spent there. He studied obsessively hard, as though there would be an exam that decided whether his family lived or died at the end of the period. He wanted to soak up everything to the limit like a sponge.

He had been forced to throw away the first thirty years of his life. Thirty years in which his American contemporaries had attended kindergartens, normal schools, and colleges. In which they had had time to play, to read what they wanted, and to study what was important to them. Thirty years head start.

Victor Tang did not have a single day more to waste. He was so busy that he did not even have the time to envy his fellow students. He wanted to understand what made America so successful. There had to be a secret to the superiority of the West, and he wanted to find out what it was.

His day began at five in the morning. During his time at Harvard he only had four hours' sleep a day. When there was barely anything left of his English to improve, before and after the seminars he devoured every book in the university library about the American Civil War, the robber baron era, and the Great Depression. He also took supplementary courses in philosophy, economics, literature, and history.

He was well known among the students for his ability to refresh himself with five minutes' sleep. He could fold his arms and put his head down on them for a short nap anywhere—in the cafeteria, during a seminar break, or in the library—regardless of any hustle and bustle around. The others thought he was an oddity but respected him; his capacity for hard work and boundless thirst for knowledge was a little strange to them. How could he explain it to them? How could a well-fed, well-nourished person ever understand the despairing greed of a starving man? Thirty years. Half a life!

During the semester breaks, he traveled on Greyhound buses to several American states. When he accidentally knocked over his plastic cup of iced tea in a coffee shop in Butte, Montana, and read the words on the bottom of the cup, he knew, from one moment to the next, that he had found what he was looking for. Made in China was written on the plastic cup. It was the first time in America that he registered a product made in his homeland. Why were the plastic cups not produced in Texas, Florida, or California? Because they were produced more cheaply in China, even when you added the costs of transport. What was true of plastic cups would also be true of plastic toys. Or rain boots. Pants. Shirts. Sweaters. Or even, much later on, TVs. Phones. Fridges. Cars. If one of the lessons that he had learned from his economic history seminars was right, then in the end, every product would be manufactured by whoever could do so most cheaply. That was as obvious as the fact that water always flowed downhill. A law of nature in economics.

When he told a few classmates this a few days later in the cafeteria, they laughed in his face. China? TVs from China? There were hardly any TVs there. Phones? From a country in which only one out of every ten thousand people owned one? Cars? They snickered and cackled; they slapped their thighs, roaring with laughter as though he had told a fantastic joke. China did not even produce six thousand cars in a whole year. Tang must be crazy. If anything, these products would one day come from Mexico. Or Brazil. Or maybe from India. But not from China, which was poor and had a Communist government.

There were 1.3 billion hungry people waiting for their opportunity in China. Why did they not see what was so obvious? Was he wrong or did these American students lack imagination? In that moment, Victor Tang understood that the first thirty years of his life had not been as much of a waste as he had previously thought. True, he had not been able to attend school regularly during the Cultural Revolution, and before he had come to America he had no idea of history, economics, law, literature, or classical music, but life had taught him important lessons instead.

They had not the faintest glimmering of where he was coming from. Their laughter made clear to him how privileged he was. Not in comparison with the people in his homeland, he knew that already, but in comparison with the young men and women sitting in front of him, who had spent their lives up to now in town houses and homes in the country. He slowly began to understand their world, but they had not the least idea of his. They did not understand how hungry the people in his country were and they would never completely understand it. That was neither their fault nor a failing; it simply was the way it was. And he, Victor Tang, belonged with the others, not with them, even though he ate in the same cafeteria with them, wore jeans, sweatshirts, and baseball caps, could barbecue pork ribs, and knew what a quarterback and a fastball were. Despite this, he did not belong, and he would never belong, even if he wanted to. He was a guest here; he belonged to the world of the others; he knew the hunger, the despair, and the greed, the willpower and capacity for suffering that were over there. They were the qualities he possessed. They had brought him to Harvard, to this very table, and they would drive him onward. On to a point when no one would laugh about him anymore.

———

He stayed four years at Harvard. On the grounds of his outstanding talent, despite his age, his scholarship was extended twice after the two-year period, one year each time. It came to an end in the early summer of 1989. Students in Beijing were staging demonstrations for freedom and democracy in Tiananmen Square at the same time. When the Chinese government was declaring martial law, Victor Tang was traveling through Arkansas on the bus. When the People's Liberation Army began marching and the tanks rolled through the streets of the capital city, he was sitting on a beach in Los Angeles, looking at the Pacific Ocean, on the other side of which his homeland lay.

He could have stayed. Nothing would have been easier. An application for political asylum, a written declaration to follow the American way of life, and a mention of a made-up family member who had been crushed by a PLA tank in the streets of Beijing in his fight for freedom and democracy would have been enough. That was what thousands of Chinese students in America did in the weeks and months after, and they were given a warm welcome. Tang had the prospect of an assistantship at the University of California in Los Angeles, and they would surely have found something for him at Harvard too.

Tang did hesitate, but only for two days.

The interviews on campus and with the professors in Los Angeles put an end to every one of his doubts. In their pity and their appalled reactions to the events in Beijing was too much self-justification; in their offers for him to stay in America was too much self-importance. He did not want to be passed around as an exile at official events and receptions, marveled at as an exotic creature who had just about managed to wriggle his head free from the Communist noose; thanks to help from the Americans, no one would fail to mention that. Tang did not want to serve once again as a living example of the superiority of a system; he had done that for long enough.

He wanted to go back. His place was in China; anything else would have been a betrayal. His time would come. He was still young enough. With his American education, the future was his in his homeland; he had understood that in the run-down coffee shop in Montana, even though he still had to be patient. The exceptional circumstances, the events in Tiananmen Square, were no more than setbacks, and the falling markets were no reason for panic; they were buying opportunities; his professor at Harvard had explained that convincingly. China's market had crashed in the summer of 1989, to the very bottom; it could go no lower. Economic sanctions. Trade embargoes. No investment. Horror over the "Beijing killers." From the analysts' point of view, it was like an extremely undervalued company; there was no better time to get in.

Only a fool could have believed that it would last. Only an ignoramus could have believed that, in the end, everything would not be manufactured by those who could do it most cheaply.

The world needed China. China needed the world.

After four years in America, he was convinced that the land of unlimited future opportunity no longer lay on the American side of the Pacific.

And he did not doubt it over the three years that followed, when China was politically and economically paralyzed as a result of the student protests and the military intervention. There was a leaden heaviness in the country: All the foreign investment that had been on the cards was canceled or suspended and economic reforms that had been agreed on were put on hold or rescinded. The state security apparatus hunted down the leaders of the protests and their followers; hundreds of them disappeared into forced labor camps and prisons. Everyone who had demonstrated sympathy for the demands of the students too openly was thrown out of the party; the liberal and conservative factions of the Communist Party fought over the future of China in Beijing, and what the outcome of these power games would be was unclear. Was the new party chief Jiang Zemin a reformer or did he want a return to a socialist planned economy? Which side was Deng Xiaoping on? What influence did the old man still have? The country was crippled, right down to the lowest levels of the party and the provincial governments. No one dared to make any decisions because everyone was afraid to be found standing on the wrong side of the political divide when the conflict came to an end.

Tang took only a passing interest in all this. He worked in a sort of division for economic development in Chengdu, but had practically nothing to do, so he spent his time networking and laying plans. For him, the continuation of political reform was only a matter of time. There was, as he had learned in America, a kind of economic logic that no one could resist in the long run, and it made a further opening up of the country inevitable.

In the spring of 1992, Deng Xiaoping traveled through southern China with his family. His speech in Shenzhen, his call for further vigorous economic reforms, was the sign that Tang—and practically the whole country besides—had been waiting for. That summer he persuaded the provincial government of Sichuan to send him to the Special Economic Zone of Shenzhen to seek out investment opportunities and establish contact with foreign investors. He established several firms on their behalf, built a shoe factory, one for plastic cutlery, and one for Christmas decorations, and set up a construction and property business of his own, seeing his vision of China as the factory of the world taking form very slowly.

———

The finale of the Kreutzer Sonata came to an end, and Tang told his driver to put on the Beethoven violin concerto. There would be enough time for the first movement.

They passed the site of an accident. Several policemen were waving traffic past it: In the right-hand lane was a smashed-up minibus with a motorcycle in front of it; next to it, Tang saw the outline of a person under a cloth. The Mercedes gradually glided into motion again, and exactly twenty minutes later they rolled through the gates of the Cathay Heavy Metal works. He remained sitting in the car for the final one-and-a-half minutes of the first movement of the violin concerto, looking out at the factory grounds. Thick white smoke was rising from the three chimneys, and several containers were being loaded at the front of the yard; farther behind, two big trucks were delivering fresh steel. The plant was working at the limits of its capacity; it was barely managing to produce enough. It was high time for them to start building a second factory. Tang had counted on a boom in the Chinese car industry from early on. He had started with a shoestring outfit that had grown quickly, but it had only grown into a goldmine in the last three years with the help of the Owens, their years of experience, and their contacts with the big American firms. And that was only the beginning. The best years lay ahead of them. China was growing into the biggest market for cars in the world. Everyone, whether American or Chinese, seemed to dream of having their own car. Tang was profiting from it and he would not let anyone take that away from him. Not for anything.

The limousines of the chief of police and the head of the homicide division were already parked in front of the office building. Both of them were much more than old acquaintances. In a town like Shenzhen a businessman had to have the most important party functionaries and the police on his side. He had taken care of that. He had given the chief of police an apartment and the most senior homicide detective a BMW. He had often taken these men to brothels and been generous with his gifts; he had enough incriminating information about them to finish their careers the next time there was a political campaign against corrupt officials.

He would not have to remind them about that.

XIII

The Cathay Heavy Metal factory was in an industrial park in the northwest of Shenzhen, a good way from the new airport. Zhang had gotten hold of the last one of the unmarked police cars available, an old VW Passat whose seats and suspension were so worn out that every little bump in the road caused him pain in his back. Like most of the manufacturing plants Zhang had visited, the grounds of this one looked like a small fortress. It was surrounded by high metal fences with security guards crouching by watch posts in front; young men in ill-fitting uniforms who stood at attention and saluted whenever a vehicle that they knew passed but who checked on every stranger with an attitude of suspicion. Zhang drove around the factory compound once, slowly; it covered about a block. He saw an office building and several halls, with the workers' living quarters behind them. Next to the entrance, three big Chinese flags and two big American ones were fluttering in the wind.

Black limousines were waiting in the parking lot outside the office, one of them a big Mercedes. He recognized two of the cars by their number plates: They belonged to the police headquarters' fleet. He wrote the numbers down so that he could find out later who the Mercedes belonged to and who had ordered the official cars. Zhang could not remember any of his colleagues mentioning a visit to Cathay Heavy Metal during their meeting that morning.

Opposite the factory were several streets full of shops, restaurants, and tearooms where the workers of nearby businesses could meet after their shifts or on weekends. Zhang searched for a Sichuan restaurant. The migrant workers from that province no doubt gathered there, and he could strike up a conversation with them in their dialect without anyone asking him where he came from and what he was doing there. Coming from Sichuan would be enough for them to accept him as one of their own.

He was in luck; only two streets away, he spotted the Old Sichuan. The neon sign over the entrance promised the best hot pot in Shenzhen. The restaurant was run down, the red carpet was worn and covered with oil and food stains, and the fish bobbing up and down in the tank by the back wall looked half dead. But the place was full. The food must be good, Zhang thought, and he walked slowly through the restaurant, glancing around as if he were looking for someone he knew. He did not see anyone he wanted to sit next to. There were a dozen tables with plastic stools in front of the door; even they were all occupied despite the heat.

A group of men wearing gray overalls with the Cathay Heavy Metal logo on them was sitting at one table talking loudly among themselves. He drew up a stool alongside them, asked for a cigarette, asked if they would recommend the hot pot, whether it was as good as it was in Chongqing, said how happy he was to hear his dialect being spoken, and before he knew it they had invited him to eat with them, ordering another plate, a glass, and a beer for him without being asked.

The men were just starting on their meal. In the middle of the table was a pot of bubbling broth that smelled delicious. Around it were several plates of ingredients: shitake and oyster mushrooms, watercress, cauliflower, bean sprouts, lotus roots, tofu, chicken, smoked bacon, thin slices of meat, and pig's kidneys. The very sight of it all made him homesick. Although he had lived in Shenzhen for over twenty years, he had not taken the town to heart. How was a person to become familiar with a place that changed so quickly that none of its inhabitants recognized it after a few years? New developments had to make way before long for newer buildings, while someone somewhere was already planning even newer buildings. How was a person supposed to put down roots when he was being uprooted every few years? Zhang also did not like the southern Chinese hustle and bustle, doing business here, there, and everywhere. He often missed the relaxed and easygoing atmosphere that he was familiar with in Chengdu. Mei had to constantly promise that they would move back to his hometown once he had retired.

The men around him clearly felt the same way. They told him how homesick they were and how difficult it was for the unmarried among them to find a wife, about their dreams of opening a small shop, tearoom, or restaurant in Chengdu or Chongqing with their savings. They had originally only wanted to stay two years, but now they had been there for five or six years and there was no end in sight. Their salaries supported their families in their villages. He saw the sadness in their faces, their melancholy, their exhaustion, and their fatigue. He knew their stories. They were the typical stories of the migrant workers, who could almost never save enough money to open their own businesses, who worked until their bodies were completely worn out and sucked dry, only to return to families who had grown strangers to them over the years and with whom they no longer had anything in common apart from a terrible wordlessness.

The more Zhang listened, the more the men told him. Getting people talking was one of his gifts. Mei sometimes asked how he managed it: why people said things to him that they normally kept to themselves. He himself did not know why.

When they had eaten almost all of the hot pot and the row of empty beer bottles filled half the table, the men started talking about their work at Cathay Heavy Metal. They did not complain. The management did not treat them better or worse than in many other factories. They worked twelve hours a day, six days a week, sometimes more, and they had one week's holiday per year. They slept eight to a room and earned about a thousand yuan per month. That was enough for a beer in the evening and a meal out now and then; they sent most of the money back to their parents and brothers and sisters in Sichuan. They couldn't complain; life was work, wasn't it, and they were better off in comparison with their fathers, who had worked much harder hauling boats up the Yangtze against the current, day in, day out, barbarous drudgery that had caused many of them to collapse and die from sheer exhaustion. And they had not even been able to feed their families properly from the few yuan they got for that work. They would think of their fathers whenever their work seemed too hard or too dangerous for them.

"Why dangerous?" Zhang asked casually.

The circle of men laughed at Zhang's naïve question. The men raised their glasses of beer and toasted Xu and Yang, who had died in a work accident two weeks ago. There had been an increase in accidents at Cathay Heavy Metal in the last few months. When production was being increased so rapidly and so many inexperienced young men were being employed, it was bound to happen. They had told the management that many times already, but anyone who complained too much would end up like Yee. The security guards had beaten him half to death one evening and had cast him and his few possessions out of the factory gates after that.

Two weeks ago there had nearly been a riot. A young foreigner— supposedly the American joint venture partner—had visited the factory, and a few workers had wanted to speak to him about the lack of safety measures in the factory. On management's suggestion, they had drawn up a petition that they wanted to present him with. A fight broke out and the petition had fallen on the ground; the foreigner stepped on it and some of the men took this as an insult and a loss of face so it really fired them up. In the end, the foreigner had fled in his car, which the workers had surrounded, shaking it as though they wanted to overturn it.

"And the security guards?" Zhang asked, surprised. "Where were they?"

"They had looked on and only intervened at a very late stage."

"Why?"

The workers considered this. They had asked themselves this question before, but not come up with a conclusive answer. They were certain that it wasn't because of inattention or carelessness.

———

Back at the police headquarters, Zhang checked the Mercedes's number plate. The car belonged to one of Tang's companies, so Victor Tang had likely been at the factory. He called the booking office and asked who had used the two service limousines that afternoon. He did not know the man on the other end of the line; he was probably temporary.

"No one," the unfamiliar voice told him.

"Are you sure?"

"Nothing is recorded."

"I'm pretty sure I saw the cars," Zhang said, baffled.

"Where was that?"

Zhang hesitated. Why did the man want to know that? Who was he speaking to? "Never mind. I must have been mistaken," he said, hanging up.

He hated being suspicious.

———

Chief Detective Luo Mingliang called the homicide division to a meeting. Luo had been friendly with Zhang in the past; they had solved a few difficult cases together and Zhang had come to appreciate what a tough and sharp-witted investigator he was. Apart from that, they shared a passion for Chinese sayings and aphorisms and had often gone out for meals together, engaging in heavyweight verbal duels in which each proverb had to be countered with another until one or the other of them ran dry. Since Luo had been promoted to the head of the division five years ago, they had seen each other less and less outside of work. Luo was now mainly occupied with official matters to do with the authorities and the party and their easy relationship of the past had now turned mistrustful, more and more so with every "gift" or "token of appreciation" that Zhang turned down.

———

Luo Mingliang greeted his colleagues briefly. He was in a great hurry, but he still wanted to let them know about the pleasing developments in the case of the murder of Michael Owen. The very first investigations, ordered by him, had led to a promising trail. There was already a suspect. Zu, a thirty-year-old worker from Henan Province, who worked in the foundry operations at Cathay Heavy Metal, was the man. He had fought with Michael Owen at the factory gates the evening before Owen had disappeared. It had been about the low pay and the poor safety conditions for the workers at the factory; the American and Zu had left the factory grounds together; several security guards had witnessed it. The next day, Zu had not appeared at work. They were now searching for him. Luo told his colleagues that all they had to do now was to help with this search; until further notice, no independent investigations were to take place. With any luck this sensitive case would be solved by the next day.

Zhang saw how his colleagues all exhaled with relief.

"What do we know about Zu?" Zhang asked. Even the sound of his voice made most of them wince.

"Not much yet. He's been working at the factory for a year. We'll get a photo and all the personal details from the HR department at Cathay Heavy Metal this afternoon. I'll let you all know once we have them."

The policemen got up and returned to their desks. While leaving the room, Luo asked Zhang to come with him.

His office was a large, bright room at the end of a corridor, with a reception area in front and two secretaries. Zhang took note of the new furniture: a red couch and two red armchairs, with white cloths protecting the armrests.

"Take a seat," Luo said, offering him a cigarette and tea. "Zhang, how long have we known each other now?"

This familiar tone is a bad sign, Zhang thought. What does he want from me? "I don't know. Nearly fifteen years, I think."

"A long time. Enough to get to know each other a little, to know some things about each other, isn't it?" Luo replied, sipping his tea. "You told me that the killed American was a friend of your friend Paul, right?"

That was not a question but a statement, and Zhang did not know what his boss was getting at. He decided it would be better to stay silent.

"The death of a good friend of one's best friend cannot leave a person untouched, and of course one wants to do everything to find the murderer. No, what I should say is, one will not rest until he finds him, am I right, Zhang?"

He rephrased it, "One would, especially since one is a detective, leave no stone unturned to solve the case, so that the murderer can be properly punished for this cowardly and dastardly deed. Friendship calls for that, doesn't it?"

Zhang did what Luo expected him to do: He listened attentively and nodded.

"One would conduct investigations, follow up every trail, independently, if necessary. We all know what we owe our friends. Am I right?"

Before Zhang could nod once again, the slow, lecturing tone fell away from Luo's voice and it became so hard and severe that it reminded Zhang of party meetings and their endless self-criticisms.

"Is that why you were at the Cathay Heavy Metal factory this morning? What were you doing there?"

"I . . . I . . ." Zhang was so surprised that he started stammering. Why did he have to justify himself for perfectly everyday investigative work? How did his boss know about it anyway? Had the driver told him? Had he been seen at the factory, or was Luo hiding something from him?

Without waiting for a proper reply, Luo continued speaking. "You did not discuss that with me. Making these kinds of wayward inquiries could jeopardize the whole investigation. You must stop immediately. Do you understand?"

"Yes," Zhang replied. He felt sick. Not now. Just don't throw up on Luo's couch.

His boss's voice suddenly grew calmer and sounded almost friendly. "Perhaps there's an older case that you can occupy yourself with for a few days?" Luo watched him, dragged on his cigarette, and blew the smoke slowly out of the corner of his mouth. "The wise man adjusts to the circumstances like the water fits in the vessel. They knew that even during the Tang dynasty."

"The greatest victory is the battle we do not fight," Zhang responded.

"Exactly right. You've understood me," Luo said. "It sounds like a Tang dynasty one." He paused for a moment, as though he was considering whether to counter with another saying.

His boss could not have given him a clearer warning. At the same time, he was offering him a way out which meant that no one would lose face. "Anything else?" Luo asked, in a tone that left no doubt about the fact that, for him, the conversation was over.

"Be friendly to unfriendly souls; they need it the most," Zhang heard himself say, regretting the words as soon as he said them. That was neither a fitting proverb nor a pleasant reply; it was nothing but an unnecessary provocation.

Luo pulled at his cigarette again and was silent for a moment. Their eyes met and Zhang saw in the eyes of his counterpart that he was thinking very hard about if and how he should react to this challenge.

Suddenly, a smile flitted across Luo's face. "Well said, but that can't be a Chinese saying, Zhang. You can't tell me that. Perhaps the Buddha might have said that, but surely not someone Chinese," he said, laughing, quietly at first, then louder and more heartily until he started coughing.

———

When Zhang left the police headquarters half an hour later, the two black Audi limousines that he had seen that morning on the grounds of Cathay Heavy Metal were parked in front. The drivers were in their seats, sleeping. He knocked on a window and woke one of them.

"What do you want?" the man grumbled.

"I need a car urgently," he lied. "Is one of you free?"

The driver shook his head. "No time. Call the car service. We're driving Ye and Luo today."

"All day?" Zhang asked, as casually as possible.

"All day," the man repeated, closing the window and turning to one side.

———

He made his way home. The longer he thought about the case, the more mysterious it seemed. He had rarely seen Luo so tense and worked up. Why was this case so explosive that the party secretary was getting involved and Luo was warning him, Zhang, off further investigations so urgently? It had to be more than the fear of reports in the international press and of frightening off a few investors. There was definitely more behind this story.

Zhang thought about what he ought to do next. He could obey Luo's orders and work on the murder of that prostitute last year, a hopeless case. But something in him resisted being pushed out of solving the Owen case just like that. The police were already looking for a man; when they would arrest him and put him forward as a key suspect was only a matter of time. Even though he would probably not be able to do anything for this man, he did not want to give up at the first warning.

He wondered who had been in Michael Owen's apartment and what they had been looking for. The hard drive and memory chips that were now hidden in his fridge at home under the bok choy vegetables? It would be best for him to see this apartment for himself, but how was he to get in there without arousing suspicion? He could only do it with Paul's help, and Zhang was not at all sure that his friend would do him this favor. He had already asked so much of him.

He had no time to lose. He decided to take the quickest route to Lamma. Before that, he had to get Michael Owen's things from their hiding place. They would be better hidden with Paul in Hong Kong than with him in his fridge. And in case Luo was tapping his phone, he wanted to lay another false trail. He rang Paul, and was glad that he did not pick up the phone.

"Hello, Paul, it's Zhang here." He spoke slowly and clearly into his cell phone. Paul would think he was crazy when he got this message. "I got your call. You didn't sound too good. I'm very sorry that you're so badly affected by this death and that you're not well. It's almost five PM now, and I'm on my way to see you. If I get a cheap ferry, I'll be in Lamma in two or two and a half hours. I've taken tomorrow off and can stay till tomorrow evening. See you soon."

Then Zhang rang his boss and asked for a day off because he wanted to visit his friend in Hong Kong, who wasn't well. Luo Mingliang agreed at once. The relief in his voice was clear.

XIV

The water was warm and soft and ran down Paul's body as if he were standing under a shower. He had gotten soaked through walking just a few steps so he had given up shielding himself against the rain. He had closed the umbrella, which was far too small, wrapped his cell phone and his wallet in a thin plastic bag, and now sat unprotected on the pier, waiting patiently for the ferry. He estimated that Zhang would be on one of the next two vessels.

It was pouring so hard that the lights of Cheung Chau and Lantau had vanished behind a wall of rain. Only the children among the passersby took any notice of him. They pointed at him, the madman who was simply ignoring the storm, they laughed or waved, and he smiled back.

Zhang came on the express just before 8 PM. He wobbled down the shaky gangway, lost for words at the sight of his friend soaked through, stared at the rain for a few seconds, weighing up the chances of even reaching the Sampan with dry feet, and turned down Paul's offer of his umbrella with thanks. They walked down the jetty, past the post office and the fish tanks in which lobsters, crabs, snails, and mussels awaited their end, and entered the restaurant. They sat in the covered terrace right by the harbor, and Paul ordered sweet and sour soup, a steamed fish, and vegetables for them both. The rain drummed loudly against the plastic roof and they had to lean far forward over the table to hear each other.

"Sorry about the somewhat confusing message earlier," Zhang said, after he had rubbed a hot towel over his face.

"What was wrong with you? I had no idea what you were talking about."

"I'm sorry. I wanted to put my coworkers off the trail in case they really are spying on me."

"Spying on you? Do you really think so?" Paul asked.

Zhang told him everything about his conversation with the workers from Cathay Heavy Metal and his meeting with Luo.

"I still don't think he's having you watched. After all, your visit to the factory wasn't a secret."

"That's true. But why did Luo give me such a stark warning? I've never seen him behave like that."

"You told me yourself that the murder of a foreigner in China was an unusual thing."

"So it would have made more sense to press on with my investigation rather than to tell me not to do anything."

"I thought he was already on the trail and had a suspect."

"That's right. Surely that should be another reason for him to be a bit more relaxed about what I was doing."

Paul didn't know what to say. He himself was not even sure he really wanted to know anything more about this case. Michael Owen was dead, and he could do nothing else for his parents. Their son's murderer would be caught sooner or later and punished; Paul believed the Chinese police would do this. He had promised Christine he would neither get further involved nor travel to China again, and he wanted to keep his promise.

"You don't want to have anything more to do with this, do you?" Zhang said, as though reading his mind.

Why was he giving him such an angry look? "I don't know if there's anything else I can do," Paul said evasively.

"Go to Michael Owen's apartment with me, for one thing."

"Are you serious?"

Zhang nodded.

"I don't have the key."

"But his mother does. We could arrange it with her tomorrow morning."

Paul leaned back in his chair, thinking. "What do you want to do there?" he said, after a long pause.

"Someone was there looking for something and it's very likely that that someone is directly or indirectly involved with Michael Owen's murder. Where did he get the key for the apartment? What was he looking for? Maybe he left traces that you and the parents didn't notice? In my bag here I have Michael's hard drive and memory chips, all secured with passwords and PINs. It's possible he wrote them down somewhere or that his parents know what they are."

Paul sighed. "He who perseveres wins in the end. Which dynasty does that saying come from?"

"None of them. The saying is 'Perseverance means victory,'" Zhang corrected him. "And that was what the great Chairman Mao said."

———

The next morning they met the Owens at ten o'clock in the Harbour View lobby. Paul had told the couple quite candidly that Zhang wanted to have another look at the apartment. Elizabeth Owen had agreed immediately, but her husband had been very much against it. He could see no reason for it: The investigations were being carried out in Shenzhen; the murder had taken place in China and not in Hong Kong; what could there be to find in the apartment? But his wife had prevailed against him.

They rode the elevator to the thirty-eighth floor in silence. Elizabeth unlocked the apartment door, led Zhang and Paul into the study, and went back into the living room. Richard Owen followed them and stood by the entrance to the study.

"What's going on here, a search?" he asked, after Zhang had pulled out several drawers in the desk and rummaged around in them.

Paul knelt down on the floor and leafed at random through the

files that were scattered around. He had no idea what he was looking for.

Zhang turned on the computer. The screen showed a prompt
for the password. He looked over at Richard Owen, who shook his
head. "No idea." He seemed to think for a moment then he said with
a sigh, "Try my name."

The computer showed an error message.

"Or VinceLombardi. All one word."

"Vince Lombardi?" Paul asked, sounding surprised.

"That would be like Michael. He's a football fan, really crazy for
it. His team is the Green Bay Packers from Wisconsin. Lombardi
was their top coach in the 1960s. A legend. You're American and you
don't know who Vince Lombardi is?"

Paul felt a short sharp prick inside and felt himself shrink back to
the awkward, skinny little Paul Leibovitz standing around in a New
York schoolyard, not being chosen for any of the baseball, football,
or basketball teams because he could neither run fast nor throw or
catch a ball well. Back then, the boys had looked at him with the
same mixture of pity, astonishment, and contempt that Richard
Owen was regarding him with now. He had hated sports ever since.
"No," he said, much more quietly than he intended to. "Never heard
of him."

Another error message flickered on the screen.

Suddenly, Richard Owen's cell phone started playing the first few
notes of Frank Sinatra's "My Way." He rushed to answer the call, as
if he had been waiting for it for hours.

"Oh, Victor, it's good to hear from you. Is there any news?"

Paul closed the files and stood up. Zhang had turned around in
shock at the sound of the name "Victor." Zhang did not understand
a word of what Richard Owen was saying but the excitement in the
man's voice and his widening eyes told him that something extraordinary had happened.

"My God . . . are you, are you sure . . . so quickly . . . I know . . .
of course . . . unbelievable . . . I can't believe it."

Richard Owen let himself sink into the chair by the desk. In the meantime, his wife had come into the study from the living room. When he saw her, he nodded at her vigorously and started laughing, as though he had just been told that they had become grandparents.

"Yes, Elizabeth is right next to me. I'll tell her everything . . . Thank you . . . no . . . there's no doubt . . . already signed? By him . . . fine, I'll be in touch later on. Thank you so, so much for calling . . . of course . . . what a relief."

Richard Owen put his cell phone down on the desk, took his wife in his arms, and pressed her close.

"Elizabeth. They've arrested Michael's murderer."

His wife broke free of his embrace and stared at her husband. "How do you know?"

"That was Victor. The police just called him."

"Who was it? Who killed Michael?"

"A worker from the factory. Shu, Su, or Zu; Victor told me, but I've forgotten the name. He had a fight with Michael and hit him with a pipe. There are two eyewitnesses. Then he ran away. The police caught him yesterday at the train station and interrogated him all night. He confessed this morning."

Paul translated quietly for Zhang, who, agitated, pressed his lips together.

Elizabeth Owen was struggling to gain her composure. It had taken a while for her husband's words to sink in. Tears ran down her cheeks, and she clasped her hands to her face, sobbing. As though she had hoped until that moment that the arrest of the murderer would bring her son back to life.

Richard Owen looked at his wife helplessly. When he had told her the news he had looked strangely relieved, almost euphoric. Only now did his lips begin to tremble; he turned his back to them abruptly. After a few seconds, he had command of himself again. He turned to Zhang. "Your colleagues have done excellent work," he said in a formal voice. "My wife and I owe you many thanks."

Paul translated, and Zhang nodded politely, but Paul could see from the look on his face that he was not really listening at all.

"Do you still have anything left to do here? If not, I'm sure you will understand that my wife and I would like to be left on our own now."

Richard Owen walked them to the door. He could hardly wait to get rid of them. They said good-bye, got into the elevator in silence, and took a taxi back to the ferry terminal in Central.

The next ferry was an old vessel; instead of sitting in the air-conditioned cabin, Paul requested that they sit in the open air on the stern. There was an unpleasant smell of diesel there, but there was a light breeze blowing and they had a good view of Kowloon and Hong Kong Island. It was an oppressive, overcast day; the blue-gray clouds hung so low that they surrounded the Peak and the tops of the IFC and the Bank of China tower. The ferry chugged wearily through the churning waters of the harbor, and Paul looked at the Hong Kong skyline, where the western end of the island between Sai Ying Pun and Kennedy Town was almost entirely filled with thirty- or forty-story apartment buildings.

They left Hong Kong behind them and crossed the East Lamma Channel, passing two enormous container ships that were anchored in front of Lamma. They had not exchanged a single word yet on the ride, and Paul was beginning to find his friend's silence a bit odd. What was he thinking? Their search in Michael Owen's apartment had not been successful, but the case seemed to be solved. So why did Zhang look so depressed?

"What are you thinking, Zhang?"

Zhang gave him a long look. His eyes looked tired. "I don't know what to think of the whole thing. Perhaps you can help me."

"Me? How?"

After a long silence, Zhang said, "Tell me if you believe what you heard. And be honest."

"Why wouldn't I be honest with you?"

"Because you want to believe it."

He could not deny that. Paul had felt more and more relieved as he had heard the news about the arrest and the confession, and he did not want to give any further thought to the possibility that a mistake had been made.

"Why shouldn't it be true?" he replied.

"Sure, nowadays it's not unheard of for a worker to kill his boss in China," Zhang said, as though thinking aloud. "But a foreigner?"

"But the workers told you that there had already been a fight and a brawl a couple of days ago. Why shouldn't that have escalated?"

"To murder?"

"Why not? Perhaps this Zu or whatever he's called is related to one of the men who died in the accident at the factory? Maybe he wanted revenge. Who knows?"

"Maybe."

"Apart from that, he confessed to the crime. Does that count for nothing?"

Paul saw the doubt in Zhang's face. His friend had once told him how confessions came about in Chinese prisons. There were two rooms in the basement of the police headquarters that practically no one was allowed entry to, into which particularly silent or intractable suspects vanished for a few hours or even for a few days. But would they name an innocent man as the murderer in such a sensitive case as this one? Paul could not believe they would.

"What will happen now?"

"The wretched fellow will be assigned a defense counsel and in a few weeks or months the trial will take place. He'll be sentenced to death and soon after that he'll be shot."

"Shot?" Paul exclaimed in amazement, regretting his naïvety as soon as he said this.

"What else? Murder gets the death penalty in China. Have you forgotten?" He paused briefly. "So you don't have any doubts about what you heard?"

"Zhang!" Paul shouted fiercely. "I have no idea, goddamn it. Maybe the worker struck out in rage. Maybe the Triads are behind it because Michael Owen did some shady business. Maybe it was an assassination ordered by a competitor. How should I know? What do you want from me?"

Zhang took two deep breaths in and out before he replied. "All I'm asking you is to take a few seconds, close your eyes, and listen within yourself. That's all."

"My inner voice tells me . . ."

"You didn't even stop and close your eyes," Zhang interrupted.

Paul fell silent.

The ferry stopped at Lamma. They disembarked in silence, bought water, fruit, vegetables, tofu, and rice for lunch at Yung Shue Wan and climbed the hill to Tai Peng.

Of course he knew what Zhang wanted from him. They had had many discussions about their inner voice. They both agreed that everyone's was unique to them but that only very few people listened to theirs; yes, it was often difficult enough to even be aware of it with all the distractions of the everyday. Paul had often ignored his inner voice—and had always had to pay the price. But since Justin's death, his inner voice seemed to have practically died away. There was a bottomless silence within him, and on the rare occasions when a whisper rose, he ignored it. The voice would disrupt the order he had painstakingly constructed in his life. He did not want that. He wanted to go on walks, be alone, and clean the dust of his child's boots.

When they arrived at the house, Zhang went straight to the kitchen and started cooking. Paul sat down at the counter and started cutting the tofu into cubes.

"I'm sorry I shouted earlier," he said. "I don't know what to say. You're asking too much of me."

"I was afraid of that, but I'm serious. I need your help. If this worker really is the murderer, who searched Michael's apartment?"

Paul sighed loudly, took hold of a bunch of spring onions, and sliced them thinly. "If I think about it long enough of course I have doubts. But what would they lead to?"

Zhang turned around and gave him a questioning look.

"Many years ago," Paul continued, "I was in love with a woman who was afraid of how her family would react and who refused to have a relationship with me, saying, 'I'm from Hong Kong. The first thing I always ask myself is, What will this cost me?' I've never forgotten those words and I hear them again now. I have no idea what it will cost us—you and me—if Michael Owen's murderer is still at large, but my instincts tell me that it would be a high price indeed, and I'm not sure that I really want to pay it. I'm no police detective."

Zhang reflected on this for a long time. Then he said, "I understand. But would you at least do me the favor of trying one more time to get into the hard drive this evening? Maybe we'll be lucky and find the right code. I'll read the report on the interrogation of the suspect tomorrow. Maybe we really do have the murderer already and we're wasting our time with these thoughts."

"Okay," Paul promised. The probability of getting into the hard drive was practically zero.

After dinner they sat on the terrace, drank tea, and played two games of Chinese chess before Zhang left for Shenzhen. He had told Luo that he would be back at work the next day.

———

When he was alone again, Paul cleaned the house, swept the garden, and wondered what else he could do to put off getting to grips with the computer.

What password would a football fan use? Vince Lombardi and the Green Bay Packers already presented thousands of possibilities. The name of Michael's favorite player. Or his date of birth. The name of the quarterback who had played the last time the team won the Super Bowl. The number of touchdowns he made. Paul looked up the team's website. They had won the Super Bowl four times. He typed "Lombardi4" into the password field. Error message. "Lambeau," the name of their stadium? Error message. "Bart Starr," the quarterback in the 1960s? No. Paul stared at the screen and thought again. He had used "Justin95" for all his accounts, PINs, and passwords. A name and a year. Which year would be the most important for a team's fan? The year it was founded? "GreenBayPackers1911." No way, Paul thought. Which fan would be interested in when a team was formed? What counted was championship titles; he'd gathered that much about sports. "GreenBayPackers1967," the year in which they first won the Super Bowl. No. He remembered how the other boys used to talk about the Yankees, the Giants, or the 49ers. Sports fans loved team nicknames, "Packers1967." Wrong. "Packer67." Right. The password window disappeared, and Paul startled. As though a stranger had suddenly put a hand on his shoulder.

The screen now showed a photo of the Great Wall of China, covered with at least two dozen folders: Letters, Photos, Heavy Metal, Vic, and so on.

Paul felt his heart begin to thud more heavily. Something deep within him stopped him from clicking on the mouse again, as though there was an invisible barrier that he must not cross. One more click of the mouse and there was no turning back. Paul ran his hands through his hair. Finally, he opened the folder labeled Photos, which opened up a series of subfolders. He clicked on Shanghai. Instead of the travel snapshots and views of the city he expected to find, he found himself looking at photos of a large construction site. Cranes, diggers, a cement foundation. Michael Owen and a short Chinese man wearing hard hats, standing shoulder to shoulder and smiling. In Tang, he found photos of a tall man about his own age who faced the camera rather stiffly every time. Here he was with an arm around a young woman at a dinner, sitting in an office behind a large desk, sitting on a plane. The folder A contained only photos of the woman who Tang had his arm around at dinner. She was a young, very good-looking Chinese woman with a challenging, almost provocative, smile. She was standing with a Prada bag on the Bund in Shanghai, in the Forbidden City in Beijing, in the lounge of a luxury hotel. Here she was in a pink bathrobe at a breakfast table, lying asleep in bed or naked, with legs half spread, on the couch with one hand over her vagina. Paul magnified the photo so that he could see her features more clearly. She had the fair skin, high cheekbones, and oval face of a northern Chinese woman; she was smiling, but something about her gaze disturbed Paul. He felt like an intruder, like a stranger in a world that he really did not want to enter. He clicked through various files and folders randomly. They were all secured with different passwords. All he could open was a letter that was still on the virtual desktop. He read it, once, twice, closed the document, shut his computer, and wished that he had never opened it.

Paul rang the number that Zhang had left him, but the cell phone was switched off. He wandered aimlessly through the house. It had grown dark outside and a strong wind was blowing, the sign of a possible typhoon. He heard the leaves rustling and the loud cracking and creaking of the bamboo swaying in the wind. It was the first time since he had lived here that he found the place eerie; he wanted to talk to someone, to hear a human voice. He checked the time. If he hurried he could still get the 8:30 PM ferry and meet Christine in Wan Chai for a drink or to have dessert in a coffee shop.

He left the house and rang her number on the way. She was no longer in the office. She was at home with her son in Hang Hau and would be very happy for him to visit.

Hang Hau. Paul was not sure if he still had the strength for it.

XV

There were days when Zhang felt an almost physical revulsion on entering the police headquarters. The strong smell of disinfectant stung his nostrils after taking only a few steps into the hall, and the constant roar of the air-conditioning hurt his ears; the cool air made him feel cold, and the obligation to spend hours with several people in cramped smoke-filled rooms reading through files or phoning people made him feel like retching. On days like this he withdrew like a snail into its shell; he only spoke when necessary, hid behind mountains of folders, and read reports for hours until he practically knew them off by heart, went for lunch alone, and dragged the lunch hour out into the afternoon.

Today was such a day. The mere sight of the young men and women in uniform at the entrance made him shiver, as if he were cold. Perhaps, thought Zhang, perhaps Mei was right, and it was time to leave the police force and do something else. In the long term, it was impossible to be a police detective who felt that no punishment was just because punishment and justice bore no relation to each other; what was more, he could not trust the people he worked with. Mei always said he would have been a better lawyer than a police detective; he was much too soft for the work and would always have sympathy for a criminal, however wretched, and try to find an explanation for every crime, no matter how abominable. He did not contradict her; in the last twenty years he had not met a single murderer or person who had committed an act of violence in whom he had not glimpsed at least a shadow of himself. Weren't all human beings capable of anything? Did we not have to be humble and grateful every day for our destiny, our Karma, our god, for not putting us in situations in which the most destructive forces within us flowered in full force? After the Cultural Revolution, the Chinese people surely could not have the slightest doubts on this front.

Three lousy peppercorns.

———

In the office, people were standing around in small groups drinking tea and talking about the Michael Owen case. Zhang's request for a copy of the interrogation report made them fall silent. Why did he want it? The case was practically closed according to Luo. They were hours away from a confession.

Was there no signed confession yet?

No. What made him think so?

His thoughts turned to Tang. Why had he told Richard Owen that they already had a signed confession? Had Luo or Ye told him they already had one after the first interrogation? Or was it the other way around: Had Tang decided that there had to be a confession and told the Owens it existed, so Luo and Ye were working on getting one now?

Zhang asked where the suspect was being held.

In one of the rooms in the basement.

After a brief exchange, a colleague gave him a few sheets of paper containing a summary of yesterday's interrogations and the personal details about the suspect.

It was the typical story of a migrant worker. Zu also came from Sichuan Province, from a small village near Chengdu; he was the son of farmers. Thirty-two years old, married with one child, he had lived in Shenzhen for eight years and had worked in the foundry at Cathay Heavy Metal for a year. The report stated that he was a good friend of the worker who had died there a few weeks ago. Filled with grief and rage at the bad safety conditions in the factory, Zu wanted to take revenge on Michael Owen. He lay in wait for Owen near the factory and blocked his path with a bicycle in order to speak to him. The American did not understand him and responded with shouting and dismissive hand gestures, which made Zu even angrier and gave him the feeling that the foreigner was treating him without the slightest respect. Even though he, Zu, was only a worker, he had his pride. When Zu refused to move out of the way, Michael Owen had grabbed hold of him; there were two eyewitnesses who saw this from a nearby coffee shop. Zu defended himself; he picked up a piece of iron pipe lying by the roadside and struck Michael Owen several times in rage. When Owen was no longer moving, Zu panicked, put his victim in the car, and drove to Datouling Forest Park, where he hid the body in the bushes, stealing the cash and credit cards in order to make it look like the murder was a robbery case.

The police had found the iron rod and had recorded the witnesses' statements.

Everything was there, Zhang thought, after he had read through the report several times: a motive, eyewitnesses, the murder weapon. The only thing missing was the murderer's signature. He wouldn't have been surprised if Luo had simply signed it himself.

How probable was it that this was indeed how the crime had taken place? Would a worker really have the courage to attack the owner of the factory, who was also a foreigner? It wasn't out of the question, Zhang thought, if there was enough anger. The death of a friend could give rise to it. An iron pipe by the roadside? Also very possible; there was a lot of scrap metal and junk on the roads of Shenzhen. How would the fight have taken place? Was Zu strong enough to fatally wound Michael Owen, who was younger and probably taller and stronger? Zhang imagined the scene: Owen getting out of his car and trying to talk to the Chinese man, getting angry because he was not being understood or was being shouted at, turning away at some point to get back into his car, and being attacked from behind. Possible. But how had Zu gotten the body to the park? Farming people like him could seldom drive, certainly not a Mercedes or a BMW, which Michael Owen had probably driven. And why had Zu taken the body to Datouling Forest Park, of all places? To make it seem like the murder had taken place because of a robbery, the backstreets in Shekou with the bars for foreigners would have sufficed. The autopsy report stated that Michael Owen's left arm had been broken in several places, his chest had been crushed, and his right shoulder dislocated. Could Zu have done all that alone? Or had he had accomplices who were being protected by this confession?

No one would be looking for the answers to these questions. For the police, the case would be closed the moment Zu signed a confession. Every court in China would find Zu guilty as a result, and no judge would ask how the confession had come about. And if he really was being held in the basement by Luo and Ye, his signature was only a matter of time.

Zhang could no longer stand the confines of his office and the voices of his colleagues. He muttered something about his knee hurting and a doctor's appointment and left the building by a back door.

He wanted to be alone, to think while walking through the city, but he came to a standstill only two streets away next to a building site. It was the size of two football fields; on one side four skyscrapers with almost complete exteriors towered into the sky and on the other side were the skeletons of four more. Zhang knew this area well; he remembered building work on this spot a few years ago: A dozen eight-story buildings had been built then. They had been demolished last year to make room for these taller, bigger, more modern apartment buildings. He was fascinated by building sites; he loved watching them, how a building was created, grew larger, took shape, and multiplied. He thought of the construction workers as representatives of the millions of people who worked out of sight in the factories producing shoes, shirts, lights, toys, and goodness knows what else for the rest of the world, who no one ever took an interest in. For him, building sites were a glimpse into the heart of this city.

He watched the workers through the fencing. They were tanned a deep brown, wearing shorts only, chests bare because it was far too hot for a T-shirt, far too hot to do anything, really. Under the burning sun they schlepped iron rods, wooden slats, and doors, mixed concrete, and shoveled sand, sweating away, torturing their young bodies, already so worn out, carrying out their work in silence, concentrating, with a seriousness and dignity that Zhang found moving. These workers he knew would move from building site to building site, working seven days a week, fifty-two weeks a year, until the day they just couldn't do it anymore and were packed off home without any notice, or, worse still, until the day they fell from the scaffolding out of sheer exhaustion or, in a moment of inattention, were killed by a falling plank or rod or were run over by a digger.

He could so easily have been one of them himself. He had scraped through the entrance exams for the police academy with the minimum score. One more wrong answer, one more careless mistake, a small error, and he would have been on a building site. At least that had been his plan if he had failed. He would be back in Sichuan now with a broken body, squatting by the roadside in Chengdu, perhaps, mending bicycle tires or selling lottery tickets. That is, if he were even still alive. Zhang thought about the young man he had once had to pick up from a building site. He had fallen from the thirty-first story of the shiny glass façade of a building in what had at first been mysterious circumstances. Zhang discovered later that the man had initially refused to work so high up because he was afraid of heights and got dizzy; it was only when they had threatened to send him home otherwise that he went up there. He had likely panicked on the bamboo scaffolding and lost his grip.

Zhang had never passed one of the new skyscrapers without thinking about that man.

Watching the workers, he knew exactly what he had to do. The voice in him could not be ignored, even if he had wanted to do so.

Like Paul, he had ignored it often enough in his life and paid heavily for it. But we don't have a choice, he thought, as he hailed a taxi.

————

Zhang took the precaution of making a big loop around the Cathay Heavy Metal grounds. Neither Luo nor anyone else from work must know what he planned to do. He directed the taxi to drive to the Old Sichuan and asked to be let off a few blocks away. The factories were clearly having their lunch break at the moment, for the streets were full of young men and women running errands, standing in line outside telephone shops, strolling up and down, or simply relaxing in the shade under trees. Zhang walked past several restaurants, looking for workers wearing Cathay Heavy Metal overalls. At a table at the back of Old Sichuan, he recognized three of the men he had shared a hot pot meal with the day before yesterday.

Did he greet them a little too enthusiastically? Was he a little too loud? Had they grown suspicious because he had turned up again and sat down with them as if they were old friends? Zhang did not know, but he could feel immediately that something had happened. All of them were distant and silent; they were very clearly not as glad to see him as he was to see them; they ignored his remarks about boring Cantonese food all being the same and the delicious spicy hot pot. His pushy behavior and inappropriately hearty tone soon made him feel uncomfortable too. He grew quiet and tried to make sense of the fragments of conversation he was hearing.

The men were angry because one of their coworkers had been arrested two days before; they did not know why. The man's wife and their six-month-old son, with whom he shared a room in the factory quarters, had had to leave the factory grounds the next day, which was just as bad if not worse. A woman friend who worked in a textile factory nearby had secretly given them shelter, but they would not be able to stay with her for long. No one knew where she should go; of course she did not want to go back to Sichuan while her husband was in prison.

Zhang hesitated. Should he offer to help? Would that awaken more suspicion or would the fact that he came from the same province dispel any doubts? He raised his voice and said something about how he could probably take the woman and her child to stay with a friend from Chengdu who lived in Shenzhen, though of course he would like to meet her first. The men looked at him in amazement. One of the Cathay workers stood up suddenly, as if there was a danger that Zhang could change his mind, and beckoned him to follow.

They crossed the main road and went down one of the narrow backstreets that led straight to the grounds of a small factory that consisted of a flat-roofed building with white tiled surfaces. In the background, Zhang could hear the monotonous hum of sewing machines. Behind that was a long brick building, the workers' quarters. They walked up to the first floor, picking their way past buckets and washing lines full of underwear, socks, shirts, trousers, and skirts, to a room at the end of the corridor.

The door was half open; they entered without knocking.

Inside were four bunk beds, a small table, and eight red plastic stools, which were stacked on top of each other in a corner. There were several posters of Chinese pop stars on the walls, and there was a metal grille in front of the only window. On each bed lay a thin raffia mat with a big stuffed toy and a bulging plastic bag. It was unbearably hot. Zhang could not see anyone, but he heard breathing behind a curtain that was obscuring one of the lower bunk beds.

"Don't be afraid, Liu, it's me," said the man who had led Zhang there, as he pushed the rags aside. A delicate young woman with a baby in her arms was hiding behind them. "Here is someone who may be able to help you."

The woman did not move, but looked at Zhang with her small narrow eyes. "Who are you?" she asked.

"My name is Zhang Lin," Zhang replied.

"What do you want?"

"To help you."

"Why?"

"Because I've heard that you need help." Zhang knew that the woman in front of him would have to be a Buddhist already in order to believe in this reason.

"Are you a policeman?" she asked suspiciously.

He had been afraid of this question. He did not want to lie but if he told the truth he would endanger both himself and her.

"I'm also from Chengdu," he said in a way that implied that someone from that city could never become a policeman in Shenzhen.

A brief smile flitted across her mouth. "Me too."

"I've heard that you and your child need a bed for a few days."

The fear returned to her face immediately. "Yes, and what about it?"

"I have a friend who is from Chengdu. He has a restaurant in Shekou and there are two rooms above it for his waitresses. There is often a bed free there. He may even need a worker. I could give him a call."

She put her baby down on a pillow carefully and crept out of the bed. How small and delicate Zu's wife is, he thought, as she stood in front of him. She looked as if she was in her early twenties, and there were dark shadows in the hollows under her eyes. Her lips were stretched thin and her eyes had the look of a person who had never found much reason to trust a stranger.

Zhang understood why she was frightened. Every year, tens of thousands of young women vanished overnight without a trace, lured into a trap by strangers who promised them a good job. Well-organized gangs smuggled them right across the country to remote provinces and sold them to farmers who often treated them like slaves. The newspapers and the television were full of stories like these. How was she supposed to know that he did not belong to one of these gangs?

"How long do you need somewhere to stay?"

She looked at him for a long time, expressionless, as though the time had now come for her to decide whether to believe him or not. Their eyes met. He felt uncomfortable; he hated lying or concealing the truth, and always thought that the person being deceived must see that immediately. But for her this was not a question of trust. As far as he could see from her eyes, she had no other option.

He repeated his question.

"I don't know. My husband was arrested the day before yesterday. I don't know when he'll be released."

"Arrested?" Zhang asked, looking as surprised as he could. He was not a good actor.

"Yes, arrested. Two days ago three policemen came and took him away. They wanted to talk to him, they said. I have no idea what about. He can't have done anything recently. He's been sick."

"Sick?" The word slipped out of him much too quickly and loudly, but she had either not noticed his agitation or had decided that it didn't matter who this stranger was.

"With stomach problems."

"Since when?"

She thought for a moment. "For quite some time now. He couldn't even work in the last few days. He's been lying in bed all the time."

XVI

The taxi took them to Shekou via the Guangshen Expressway. The traffic had gotten heavier with every passing kilometer; they were only moving very slowly now and jolted to a sudden standstill every few meters, making the photo of Mao hanging from the rearview mirror dance back and forth wildly. The air in the car was sticky; the air-conditioning was merely blowing warm air into the back; they had rolled the windows down, but even the breeze created as they drove along was warm. Zhang watched the young woman and her baby from the corner of his eye. The child was half asleep, dozing on the lap of the mother, who was looking out of the window silently. She had given short, brusque replies to his few questions about her husband. He felt sorry for her and he felt a pall come over him at the sight of her.

"I used to work there," she said, tipping her head toward the factory grounds not far from the expressway.

"What did you do there?"

"I painted wings."

"You painted wings? What kinds of wings?"

"Angel wings. Small white angels made of clay were delivered, and we had to paint them. Red cheeks, blue eyes, blond hair, and golden wings. They were sold to America. Our boss said the people there would hang them on trees. I don't know if that's true."

"And?" Zhang asked.

"And what?"

"I mean, what was the work like? Were you treated well?"

She turned to face Zhang and looked at him as though he were mad. "What strange questions you ask." After a pause she added, "It was fine. I got thrown out when they noticed that I was pregnant." She turned away again and looked out of the window.

Zhang slid around on the backseat trying to find a position in which his legs did not hurt so much. Ever since the young woman had, without knowing, provided her husband with an irrefutable alibi, his whole body had rebelled. The pain in his knee had increased with every passing minute; he felt it creeping slowly but mercilessly and relentlessly up his back; it would reach his head in a few minutes. The old Chinese physician whom he had consulted regularly for years and who, with great dedication, brewed him herbal teas that tasted awful, claiming that they would do Zhang good, was proved right yet again. Everything was connected to everything else; nothing in the body, or, as the doctor liked to add, in life, was to be viewed in isolation. The stomach problems, the nausea, the rheumatism pains, yes, even the knee, was directly connected to his soul and the burden that it bore. It had not taken much for the physician to convince him of this, but Zhang was still constantly surprised at how quickly his body reacted and how little he could outwit or deceive it as he grew older.

The old man claimed that this was a good thing; the detective should count himself lucky that his body was so sensitive. He just had to stop ignoring the signs it was giving him. Zhang was not so sure. There were days like this one when he would have liked to be a little more robust, would have preferred to have a body that reacted a little more leniently to stress. He knew exactly what his knee and his back were protesting against. An innocent man was sitting in a harshly lit, white-tiled room in the basement of the police headquarters and was in the process of signing a confession that had every likelihood of leading to his own death sentence.

Even with the cabdriver's help, he had difficulty finding his friend's restaurant. He had not been there for at least half a year, and the street looked different now. On the corner, a large supermarket had just opened on what had once been a piece of empty land. It was flanked by two new pink-tiled buildings that had gilded columns and swan statues at the entrances. The two buildings that had stood there six months ago had disappeared.

The restaurant owner greeted Zhang in a friendly manner but looked skeptical when he sized up the young woman and child. Zhang could see that he did not believe that they were distant relations who needed a bed for a couple of days, and a job if possible. He seemed to be calculating what advantages and disadvantages doing this favor could bring him. After few moments' thought, he clearly concluded that the pros outweighed the cons; doing a police detective a small favor could not possibly be a mistake. He led them up to the second floor. There was a bed free there and Zu's wife could help out in the kitchen while the baby was sleeping.

Zhang thanked him, turned down an invitation to stay for dinner in a pleasant but firm manner, and promised to be in touch over the next few days.

He had hoped that the pain in his body would recede a little, at least for a time, after doing this good deed, but he had fooled himself. Now he felt as if someone was sitting on his shoulders, striking him on the head over and over again.

He went to the supermarket, bought a bottle of water and a packet of aspirin, sat down in the pedestrian area in the shade cast by a meter-high plastic inflatable beer bottle, and thought about the possible courses of action left to him.

So many thoughts flitted through his head that he had trouble concentrating. He had to find out more about Michael Owen in order to get any further. Who could help him? Who knew how Michael Owen had spent his time in Shenzhen? Had he always just come over from Hong Kong for the day or had he stayed the night here? Did he have any friends or acquaintances in the city? Zhang had no idea where he should start looking. Maybe Owen's parents knew more, but they would only talk to Paul at best, not to him. There were probably clues about contacts in Shenzhen on his computer, but Zhang had already asked Paul for help with that and not heard anything back. He really didn't want to ask him again, not because of his pride but because Paul had told him quite clearly that he did not want to have anything more to do with this. He had sworn to himself that he would respect this wish, but there was no one else whom he could turn to right now.

"What will this cost me?" His friend's words still echoed in his ears. It was a strange thing for Paul to say. Paul was not the type who subjected everything he did to a cost-benefit analysis beforehand; he was often remarkably generous. He must have felt very much under pressure from Zhang to have responded as he did. Apart from that, the question was quite justified. The probability of them finding Michael Owen's murderer on their own was very small, and even if they got on the trail of the murderer, it would be practically impossible to bring him before a court. This much was certain: Whoever was behind this had powerful friends in Shenzhen.

As his melancholy worsened, he closed his eyes and tried breathing calmly to meditate for a short period to soothe his nerves, but he could not do it. Instead he saw the young woman and her child before him once again. The image of her cowering on the bed, crouched with her child in her arms and looking at him with fear and suspicion, would not leave his head. Now he knew what he had found so moving about this woman. It was the deep suspicion, distress, and loneliness in her eyes. It reminded him of the frightened look in his own eyes when he was her age. But he was a child of the Cultural Revolution; he had been forced to spend years in the countryside; he had seen Hu die and experienced things that he had not even told Mei or Paul about before. She, on the other hand, was a child of the new era; more than a generation and the economic reforms lay between them; she had left her village of her own accord and moved to the city to determine the course of her own life. Discovering a familiar fear in her eyes made him feel shaken and confused.

Zhang started at the sound of his cell phone ringing. A new era, an old fear.

"Zhang, where are you?"

Zhang had to swallow a few times before he could say anything.

Luo raised his voice. "Zhang, for God's sake, can you hear me?"

"Not very well. My phone is running out of battery. I'm waiting for a taxi. Just left the doctor's. My knee . . ."

"We have the murderer, Zhang," his boss said, interrupting him. "It was that worker. He signed a confession an hour ago."

Zhang did not know what Luo expected him to say. Congratulations? Well done? Liar? It wasn't Zu; he had an alibi? Who are you covering up for? He could think of neither a stock phrase nor a Chinese saying so he said nothing.

"Did you hear what I just said?"

"Yes."

"Zhang?" Luo's voice now sounded severe, almost threatening.

"That's . . . that's . . . that's . . . great news," Zhang stuttered.

"You can tell your friend in Hong Kong. The parents are being told right now. And so the case is closed, Zhang."

"It certainly looks like it," Zhang replied.

"It doesn't look like it, Zhang. It is." After a brief pause he asked, "Are you coming back to the office now?"

If he said no, if he made up some reason not to go back to the police headquarters now and share in Luo and his other colleagues' pleasure at the case being solved, then there would be no going back. Then he would have to start looking for work. He thought about Mei. He thought about his son. He thought about their apartment, having dinner together, and the wonderful gentle smile that often lit up his wife's face when he cooked for her. He thought about the hours that he spent in front of the computer with Zheng playing chess together. What would it cost his family? Did he have the right to make them pay any price? If he, Zhang, fell foul of those in power in this city, if even one of those people felt threatened by him, his family would have to pay for it. That was how it had always been in China and that was how it was now. He felt his heart pounding more heavily. Did he have any chance of getting something out of it? He would have liked nothing better than to jab the red button of his cell phone and toss the phone straight into the fountain in the square at the end of the street. But that wouldn't have changed anything. He had to make up his mind.

"Zhang?"

"Luo," he said in a shaky voice. "Luo, I was just at the doctor's. My knee. I can hardly take a step. You know my problem." Zhang took a deep breath and continued. "He said it would be better if I moved as little as possible in the next few days. Lying down would be best, he said."

Now it was Luo who was silent.

Did he suspect anything? Was he calculating if Zhang could still do any damage or were his thoughts somewhere else altogether?

"Hm," was all Zhang heard. His battery beeped once more. He had to hurry.

"I'm sure I'll be fine in three or four days. Call if you need me. I'll be lying on the couch at home."

Maybe it was this that allayed Luo's doubts or maybe his boss had decided that Zhang was no longer a threat, no matter what he got up to. "All right. Get well soon," he said, and hung up.

Zhang listened to the hiss of the phone for a moment before he put it back into his pocket with trembling hands.

Had he really made up his mind?

If Mei were in front of him now, he would not have been able to put into words why he was doing what he was doing. Because right now in Shekou, in a shabby room among all the bars and brothels, there was a young mother with a baby whose father was to be executed for a murder that he did not commit? Because he felt that he would be partly responsible if he did not try to find out who was responsible for the crime? Because as a Buddhist he feared the bad

Karma that would result? Because he had looked away more than once before in his life when an innocent man had died? Because three miserable little peppercorns still haunted his dreams?

No, that all sounded much too honorable. He was anything but a hero. He was a human being, small and fearful, defenseless and vulnerable. A human being who wished he had a choice, who wished he could just hide away now, look away, or shout "kill the traitor" when he was ordered to, but he could not. Something in him revolted. It was that simple, that complicated.

Zhang tried to reach Paul. He let it ring through to voice mail, then he hung up. He did not want to leave a message. He wanted to speak to Paul; he tried again and again, without success. Where could his friend be? Why wasn't he picking up his phone? He wanted to call Mei and let her know that he needed to go over to see Paul urgently and that he would be back by tomorrow at the latest, but his phone battery had finally run out. He would call his family from Paul's phone in Hong Kong.

Zhang looked for a taxi and told the driver to take him to the pier by the quickest route possible. He could take one of the express ferries straight to Hong Kong from there.

Paul was now the only one who could help him.

XVII

The storm whipped up the sea so much that the *Yum Kee*, with its diesel engine, only made very slow progress. The ferry was almost empty, and Paul, unusual for him, had taken a seat on the upper deck by the window. Heavy waves pounded the side of the ship and made the whole vessel shake. The white spray of the breaking waves slapped against the window with such force that Paul flinched when it first hit.

Everything indicated that a typhoon was on the way. He had not paid attention to the news; the authorities had probably already issued a warning.

Paul wondered if all his windows were closed and if the gutters on his roof terrace were clear. He had left home in such a hurry that he had even left his cell phone on the kitchen counter.

He did not quite know what he was doing. He had lived alone on Lamma for almost three years and had always found his own company sufficient; he had relished the quiet and solitude, had set up his world around him and never had the feeling that he missed anyone or anything, apart from Justin, of course. He was surprised and unsettled by his longing for Christine, his need to hear her voice and to see her, not tomorrow or the day after, but now, immediately. Did she mean more to him than he wanted to admit? Or had the death of Michael Owen, the photos and the letter that he had found on his computer stirred things up so much that he suddenly could no longer stand being alone?

Was missing her a betrayal of his son? What was he to do with all these new impressions and experiences? They were certainly not going to fall away from him, drop by drop, like the water on the window in front of him. They left traces and awakened longings. Could he stop them from overlaying and gradually dulling his memories of Justin?

He thought about his dark hallway, about the door frame with the markings, the rain boots and the raincoat, and felt that he would like to go straight back there if he could. He felt guilty, as though he had left his son alone at home, breaking his promise. He would have mango pudding with Christine; he would see her and calm down, and if he hurried he could still comfortably make the last ferry back to Lamma.

The journey to Hang Hau took much longer than Paul had expected, and the longer he spent on the metro, the clearer it became to him what he had let himself in for. Hang Hau, of all places. He, who went out of his way to avoid a group of even five or six hikers on Lamma because they were just too many people for him to cope with, was now making his way of his own accord to a satellite town with several hundred thousand inhabitants.

He was to get off at Hang Hau and go to Exit B1, where Christine had promised to pick him up. It had sounded quite simple on the phone. Now Paul stood lost on the platform, confused by the many different signs. He felt as if he were taking the Hong Kong metro for the first time. To the left was Chung Ming Court. Hau Tak Estate. On Ning Garden. Exit A1. A2. To the right for Wo Ming Court. Yuk Ming Court. La Cite Noble. Exit B2. B1.

Paul took the long, seemingly never-ending escalator and went through the turnstile hoping to see Christine immediately. Instead, he found himself looking into the faces of strangers waiting for others, and saw their eyes pass over him. They looked at the other people arriving and one face after the other lit up once they had met the eyes of a friend or acquaintance. He did not see Christine anywhere.

Paul walked hesitantly toward the exit. It had stopped raining, and he walked out onto the plaza but stopped abruptly as though he had come up against an invisible wall. One high-rise building after another stretched out in front of him in the night sky. He looked left and right: It was the same everywhere. Even though he had lived in Hong Kong for over thirty years, he had never seen such a concentration of tall buildings before. He leaned his head back and tried to count the number of stories in a building but lost count somewhere between twenty-five and thirty and gave up. There had to be fifty, maybe sixty stories.

He turned around and saw Christine coming toward him with quick, light steps. She was smiling at him, and he knew immediately that it had not been a mistake to come. Nothing else in the world soothed him as much as that smile did. He felt as if he had never seen her looking so beautiful before, even though she was wearing just a simple white T-shirt and floral pants in a light fabric that billowed around her legs with every movement. Before she could say anything he had taken her in his arms, feeling her slim, muscular body and her soft breasts. He stroked her hair to one side and kissed her carefully on the neck.

"What a way to say hello," she whispered in his ear, and he felt her body relax in his arms. They held each other tight for a few long seconds and said nothing. "I'm sorry you had to wait. Josh showed me his homework again, at the last minute, just before going to bed."

"No problem."

"What shall we do? What do you feel like?"

Paul shrugged his shoulders. He didn't care what they did as long as Christine was by him. They stood next to each other shyly for a moment like two teenagers on their first date.

"You wanted to have dessert, didn't you?"

Paul nodded.

"There's a pretty good café in the mall. Let's go there."

They took another escalator up, crossed two streets, and entered a shopping mall. It was thronging with people inside; Paul stopped walking after a few steps, knitted his brows together, and felt goose pimples forming. He would not be able to stand being here even if he had wanted to. Not for any smile in the world.

Christine saw immediately how he was feeling.

"The old village of Hang Hau is ten minutes away. There are a couple of open-air restaurants there. Do you feel like taking a walk even in this weather?"

"Sure. Let's just get out of here."

They walked down the main road and were the only pedestrians to be seen far and wide. Only in the small park did Paul see two couples walking around and around having heated conversations.

"This is our crisis park," Christine explained, when she saw how surprised he looked. "This is where couples come when they are quarreling and don't want the children or the neighbors to hear them."

They walked hand in hand down a narrow path that was barely lit. When an occasional, especially strong gust of wind blew, they stopped in their tracks and Christine sought protection behind Paul. After a few minutes they came to a traffic junction with several unremarkable restaurants around it. Their kitchens were on the sidewalk. Bare-chested men were standing in front of open fires clanging away at woks with ladles and chopsticks. They were clearly good at what they did, Paul thought, for there were many customers. The diners were sitting under tarpaulin coverings that were flapping vigorously in the wind, chattering away loudly. The air was filled with the smell of hot groundnut oil, stir-fried vegetables, and soy sauce.

Christine got them a table and two stools. Paul ordered tea, a mango pudding, and sticky rice dumplings filled with black sesame.

"*Tong yuen,*" Christine said, smiling.

Paul knew what she was hinting at. The roundness of the rice dumplings signified unity and togetherness.

"You can decide whether I've ordered them for their taste or for their symbolic value."

"I'll tell you after I've tried them."

They looked over at the high-rise buildings of Hang Hau, which

looked even more impressive from where they were sitting, but at
the same time as unreal as a film set for a science fiction movie.

Christine watched him for a while, leaned her head to one side,
and asked, "Why have you come all the way to Hang Hau? Something must have happened."

"I don't know," he replied hesitantly. "I felt alone on Lamma.
For the first time. I sat at the kitchen counter listening to the wind
rustling the bamboo leaves and . . ." He fell silent.

"And missed me?" she said, finishing his sentence with a question.

"And missed you," Paul repeated, smiling. He had not missed the
trace of irony in her voice.

"That makes me glad," she said, waiting.

"And there's also a new development with this murder case."

Christine's lips thinned and her eyes narrowed; she lifted her
head and straightened in her seat.

The waiter brought them their desserts. Paul cut a rice dumpling
in two, took a spoonful, and offered it to her. She opened her mouth
slowly, but kept her eyes fixed on Paul as she did so. If he was doing
this to distract her or calm her down, it was not working. She knew
that this was not the whole story yet.

"The police in Shenzhen have arrested a suspect."

Paul waited for a reaction, but there was none forthcoming.

"Apparently, he's admitted to the murder."

"What do you mean 'apparently'?"

"Zhang himself is not sure. He knows very well how some of
these confessions in China come about. I just took a look at Michael
Owen's computer and . . ."

"What did you do?" she said, interrupting. "How did you get
that?"

"The first time I went to his apartment I took a few things like
Zhang told me to. One of them was a hard drive and . . ."

"You've committed a crime, Paul. Do you know that?"

"Why do you think that?"

"You removed a hard drive and goodness knows what else from an apartment!"

"A police detective asked me to."

"That has nothing to do with it. That was theft."

"I just borrowed it. I'll return everything to his parents. Don't worry."

"At the very least, you tampered with some potential evidence," Christine retorted. "I don't think the Hong Kong police will have much understanding for that."

"They won't know anything about it."

"Paul, stop it with the excuses."

They said nothing for a few moments, feeding each other spoonfuls of dessert until they had calmed down a little.

"Okay," Christine said, when both plates were almost empty. "What did you find on the hard drive?"

"Do you really want to know?"

"I wouldn't ask otherwise."

"Most of the folders and documents were locked with a password, but the ones I could open were interesting enough." He leaned forward and added in a whisper, "Michael Owen clearly had a girlfriend in Shenzhen."

Christine looked at him as though he was trying to make fun of her, but then she realized that he was being serious, and started laughing so loudly that the diners at the neighboring table turned to look at them curiously. "That doesn't really surprise me. I know one or two people in Hong Kong who have girlfriends there. Like my ex-husband."

"But his family knew nothing about it."

"Yeah, that's really unusual. If that doesn't make him a suspicious character . . ." She practically choked out her reply, and Paul had to join in laughing at the clumsy way he was telling this story.

"He was with her in Shanghai on a building site."

"A building site? And in Shanghai too? I thought there weren't any of those in Shanghai?"

"Christine, stop it," Paul asked halfheartedly. She seemed to find his efforts at playing the assistant detective amusing at best.

Maybe she was right and he was overestimating the importance of the information he had found.

The only really unusual document he had found was a letter Owen had written to Victor Tang last week.

"I also found a letter to his business partner. In it, Michael Owen is threatening him with legal action. It seems Tang tried to intimidate him in some way."

"Is that all?" she asked.

"Yes, but the letter shows that there was a pretty serious disagreement between them."

"What about it? Even business partners can have a fight without murdering each other as a result. You should take a look at some of my business correspondence sometime. If that were proof of anything, I'd have been in jail long ago." She spooned up the last of the mango pudding, waved the spoon in front of Paul's face, and put it into her own mouth. "So that doesn't sound especially suspicious, Mr. Detective."

"Maybe not suspicious, but it's a start on finding out what else Michael Owen did in China."

"Why do you want to know that when someone has already confessed to the murder?"

He took a deep breath preparing to explain Zhang's doubts to her in detail once again, but he exhaled without saying anything at all. If he were honest with himself, he really had no answer.

"Paul, I've already pleaded with you not to travel to China on this matter anymore," she said in a serious but quiet tone. "You know why. You know I'm frightened."

She pushed the plates aside, took his hands in hers, and looked straight into his eyes. "It's because of the things I have lived through, which my family suffer from even today, which I can't forget and don't want to forget. Not ever. That would make me feel as if I were betraying my father and my brother, and siding with the murderers. They want us to forget but I will never do that. Do you understand?"

Of course he understood. Every word. Forgetting was betrayal.

"You made a promise. Does it still hold?"

"Yes, of course," he said. He took the last rice dumpling from the plate, bit it in two, and gave her the other half, which disappeared into her mouth with a slurping noise.

The wind had let up, as though the typhoon were gathering strength for its full force tomorrow or the day after. They continued sitting under the tarpaulin as one fellow diner after another left, and until the cook doused the fire and started to fold the tables and chairs up. They watched the lights in the high-rise buildings go out one by one until some of the buildings could only be made out in the darkness by their towering outlines.

Paul told her a bit about Justin, about the first pancake he made by himself, which landed on the kitchen floor, about his tears on his first day at school, about the nights watching over him when his dreams about witches and ghosts just would not go away. It was the first time he did not feel uncomfortable talking about these things. For the last three years he had had nobody with whom he had wanted to share his memories, and whenever he had hinted at them to Christine in the past, he had always regretted it soon after. In his mind these moments with Justin were so alive and so present to him that they could have happened yesterday; it was as if his son might walk through the door any moment and start making a new pancake. But as soon as Paul had put his memories into words they had become something final, part of the past, as though Justin had died a little more with each sentence.

He did not get that feeling today. He knew she was the right person to share these memories with. On this wet and windy night, they drew the two of them closer together.

By the time they got back to Exit B1, the last metro train had long gone. Under the streetlamp was a taxi that could take him back to Central.

"Would you like to stay the night?" Christine asked.

Only a short time ago, he would have thought such a question showed a lack of sensitivity. Now he remembered their night in the Mandarin Oriental hotel and suddenly felt unsure of himself. He was happy that she had asked him to stay, but what would she be expecting?

"I don't know," he said.

"Just stay the night. Nothing else."

He was constantly amazed at how well she could guess at his thoughts, doubts, questions, or fears.

"What about your son?" Paul asked.

"He's sleeping. By the time you get up tomorrow he'll have left for school. I've told him so much about you anyway."

They went up to the twelfth floor of a building in Wo Ming Court. The higher floors, Christine explained, had been too expensive.

The entire apartment was barely larger than Paul's dining room and living room combined. Right behind the front door was a tiny kitchen, then came a room with a round table, four chairs, and a couch. On the other side was a shelving unit with a DVD player and stereo system, with a big flat-screen television on top, and there was an ironing board and a basket full of laundry in front of it.

They walked down a short narrow corridor: The bathroom, a walk-in closet, and Josh's room led off it; at the end was Christine's small bedroom. The double bed in the middle practically touched the walls on either side. Christine closed the door behind them, flung her arms wide, and whispered, "Make yourself at home."

"I love your sense of humor," he whispered back.

"The bathroom isn't big enough for us to be in at the same time," she said. "Shall I go first?"

"In a moment," he said quietly, pulling her T-shirt over her head carefully, taking her trousers off, and kissing her on her tummy. His desire grew with every breath he took; he would have liked nothing better than to pull her onto the bed and make love to her. But not here, he thought, not with her son sleeping in the next room. Maybe tomorrow. They would go to Lamma tomorrow. He would get groceries and cook her favorite soup in the afternoon, buy flowers, and a bottle of champagne, and fill the house with candles.

"Will you come to Lamma tomorrow evening?" he whispered. "To stay the night?"

She held his head in her hands and looked at him; he saw in her eyes that she knew exactly what he was thinking.

"If you don't change your mind by then."

———

Paul stayed awake for a long time. Christine had fallen asleep in his arms. He stared at the ceiling, listened to the dull hum of the air-conditioning, and was much too keyed up to be able to fall asleep. Since he had lived on Lamma, this was, following the night in the hotel a few days ago, only the second night that he had not spent in his own bed. He longed for the familiarity of his own house but loved having Christine's warm, soft body next to him, her delicate skin, the lovely smell of her, and her breath on his shoulder; that was what made this night magical.

He felt incredibly thirsty, so he nudged Christine's head onto her pillow carefully and got up.

He crept down the corridor to the living room, where he stood still for a moment. The furniture reminded him of all the other living rooms of his Hong Kong acquaintances. There were no books on the shelves but black and white photos of some ancestors with a stalk of plastic flowers next to them, and a statue of a shiny golden cat that was perpetually waving its left paw, a symbol of luck and wealth. There were several piles of DVDs behind it. On the wall above the black imitation-leather couch there was a framed poster of European alpine scenery with a lake, snow, and blue sky, probably from an airline or a foreign tourist agency.

Paul thought about her tiny, badly ventilated, noisy, and hopelessly overcrowded office in which she had to work long and hard to be able to afford this small apartment for her and her son. How proud she should be of herself. How much he respected her for it.

Placed tidily next to the sink in the kitchen were a red plastic container with the logo of an English football team on the lid and a water bottle with the same logo. Someone had gotten Josh's lunchbox ready for school the night before. The sight of it was so unexpected and so painful that he had to bite his lips in order not to cry out. He bit down until the tears trickled down his cheeks and blood dripped onto the counter.

Christine was strong, but was she strong enough for them both? Was he not too difficult a proposition? He went back into the bedroom, thought for a moment about whether to get dressed and slip away, out of the flat, out of her life, but he did not have the will. Instead, he lay down next to her in bed once again, curled up to her, and fell into a sleep like death after a few seconds.

———

Morning voices woke him. Josh seemed to be looking for something and was swearing under his breath. The Filipina housemaid also did not know where the missing pencil case was, and was complaining about his mess. Christine kept asking her son to keep quiet and to hurry up. She was clearly running late. There was a smell of fresh coffee and baked goods. After a while the voices faded away, and Paul heard a door closing. Shortly after, Christine came into the bedroom holding a tray.

"Did we wake you?"

"No, I was awake already," he lied. "What do you have there?"

She put the tray down on the bed. There were two cups of coffee, milk, sugar, and two croissants on it.

"You're amazed, aren't you?" she asked. The pride in her voice moved him. "Josh loves croissants. They have chocolate in them. I had two left in the freezer. Real French croissants!"

"But I'm not French," he said, regretting his blunt reply immediately. He hated croissants, but he did not want to dim her happiness.

"Neither is Josh. Don't you like them?"

"Yes, yes, I do. Great," he said, sitting up.

Only now did she see his wound.

"Paul, what have you done to your lip?"

"Nothing. Had a bad dream. Must have bitten on it in my sleep. I didn't notice."

She gave him a considered look but let it pass without probing.

They traveled into the city together. Paul took her to the office, and Christine promised to come to Lamma that night. At the door, they kissed with such passion that neither of them knew how they were to pass the day without the other.

From Wan Chai, he took the metro to Queens Road, bought the groceries for the soup he was going to make, flowers, candles, and a bottle of champagne in the IFC Mall, and took the 12:20 PM ferry to Yung Shue Wan. The hydrometer on the pier displayed 96 percent humidity; it was one of those overcast hot days that never seemed to brighten up. The ash-gray clouds hung over the harbor like a giant lid. The water was still choppy but the wind had let up. Paul hoped the typhoon had either weakened or changed direction unexpectedly.

In Yung Shue Wan, he took a seat at the Green Cottage Café on the harbor and ordered his usual—a freshly pressed apple and carrot juice with a little ginger—and tried to imagine the night ahead. Would the house be big enough for three? Would Christine forgive him again if he lost the strength? Did he have "all the time in the world," as she had promised him once before?

He bought some more fresh tofu, mangoes, and water in the village and climbed the hill to Tai Peng laden with two heavy bags.

The storm had raged through his garden and terrace: leaves, small branches, frangipani flowers, geraniums, and bougainvillea petals were scattered everywhere. The wind had blown the rain through the old wooden window frames; the puddle of water pooled over the entire kitchen counter, with his cell phone in the middle. It was still working and was showing twelve missed calls from an unknown number. Who would have tried to ring him so many times? The Owens? Zhang? He wanted to ring his friend, but first he had to mop the kitchen. Then he put the flowers in a vase and the champagne in the fridge, put candles in all the holders he could find, and distributed them all over the house. He went upstairs, cleaned the bathroom, changed the sheets, dusted his and Justin's room, cleaned the living room, swept the terrace, and had completely forgotten about Zhang until he heard footsteps and a familiar voice calling from the path.

"Zhang? Goodness, what's happened?"

His friend was in a pitiful state. He was dragging his left leg behind him and walking with stiff and jerky movements, as though he had used up his last reserves of strength struggling up the hill. Paul had seen that slightly absent look in his eyes before whenever Zhang was suffering from his severe headaches or joint pains. "Come in. Shall I make you some tea? Have you eaten already?"

"Tea would be good, thank you."

They entered the house. Zhang lay down on the couch, and Paul made some tea and sat down next to him.

"Tell me what's going on."

"I'm afraid I have a problem."

"Michael Owen?"

Zhang nodded. "I couldn't let it go. This morning I went to a restaurant near the Cathay Heavy Metal factory once again and talked to a couple of the workers there. They were pretty worked up about Zu's arrest and didn't know what he was being accused of. One of them took me to see Zu's wife and child after that."

He paused, slurped a mouthful of his hot tea, and looked his friend straight in the eye. "Paul, the man has an alibi. This Zu guy was sick. He had been lying in bed for days. His wife and his child were with him all the time."

"Are you sure?"

"Yes. His wife told me, quite innocently, without knowing why her husband had been arrested. I have no doubt whatsoever."

Paul took a deep breath, looked down at his shimmering light-green tea, looked over at Zhang, closed his eyes, and tried to concentrate. He felt as if someone were shaking him so hard that he was on the verge of losing consciousness.

After a long pause, he asked, "What does that mean?" so quietly that Zhang barely understood him.

"That means the murderer is still a free man."

"And what else?"

"That an innocent man is being sentenced to death and will be executed, that a woman will lose her husband. And a child his father."

Paul had the feeling that this was not all that it meant, that he could not go on pretending that all this was none of his business. He said nothing for a while, sipped his tea, and then asked a question.

"What do you want to do?" Why had he said "you"? Had it slipped out of him unconsciously or had he meant it that way? Was he trying to distance himself from Zhang, his dear friend, his only friend? Would Zhang ever forgive him for that?

"I can't do much yet, not now. I need your help. I'm sorry to be asking at all; you've already said that you don't want anything to do with . . ."

"What can I do?" Paul interrupted him brusquely.

"I have to find out what Michael Owen got up to in China. Who was he in touch with? Did he have friends or acquaintances? At the moment, I can think of only two ways for me to find out about him: via his computer and his parents. And I don't have access to either."

Paul could not bear sitting on the couch any longer. He stood up and started pacing up and down the room. The computer and the parents. Would it stop at that? Could he turn down these requests from Zhang? He had already had a look at Michael's computer and a telephone conversation with the Owens would only take a few minutes.

"I got to work on the hard drive right away yesterday. I wanted to tell you about it, but couldn't get hold of you. I stumbled across the password to get in: It's Packer67. I didn't get very far. The computer is full of documents that are almost all secured with passwords too, and I haven't tried to crack them yet. I was able to open a folder of photos, and there was a letter saved on the desktop. I'll show you."

Paul fetched the hard drive and his laptop, put them on the table in front of Zhang, and turned the computer on. They looked at the photos without saying anything, then Paul opened the letter and read it aloud, translating it sentence by sentence:

"Dear Victor,

I told you this yesterday on the telephone and want to express it one more time very clearly in this letter. Our last meeting was more than unpleasant. I do not want to experience anything like it again, or I will feel forced to act out the consequences. I find your threats impertinent. Your accusations and blame are entirely without foundation. What you say is hurtful and outrageous. You insult not just our company but our family too. If we were in America, I could sue you for something like this. I am asking you herewith to apologize unreservedly by the weekend.

Michael."

Paul looked at his friend out of the corner of his eye. Zhang had sunk into himself; he was cowering on the couch, his eyes roaming aimlessly across the room; his lips had thinned and his eyes had narrowed. If Paul was not mistaken, he looked frightened. Almost in a whisper, he asked Paul to repeat what he had just read.

"This doesn't sound like the usual kind of disagreement between business partners, does it? What do you think?" Paul said, after he had read the letter out one more time.

Zhang did not react at all. Had he not heard him or was he lost in thought? What was he so frightened of?

"Zhang, what's wrong with you?"

He still did not react.

"What are you thinking about?"

"Me?" he replied in a sluggish voice, as though he were slowly returning from another world. "Absolutely nothing. I'm just exhausted. What did you say?"

"That the letter doesn't sound like a normal disagreement between business partners."

"No, it doesn't."

"Perhaps the parents know something about it. Shall I call Elizabeth Owen now?"

"No," Zhang blurted out in a raised voice. "Not now. On no account."

"Why not? You said . . ."

"We . . . we have to be careful."

Paul had known his friend for over twenty years, but he had never seen him look so frightened before. "Zhang, you're not well; something's wrong."

Zhang shook his head. "No, no, Paul, it's nothing. I'm just saying that we can't make any mistakes now. We don't know what kind of relationship the parents have with Victor Tang and how much they are in touch with him at the moment. If you ask them about a quarrel now, they'll wonder how you know about it and why you're asking so many questions anyway since the murderer has now been caught. They're likely to tell Tang about it; he absolutely must not find out that we—that I—am still not letting the matter rest. He'd tell Luo about it right away, and I really don't want to think about what would happen then. Apart from that . . ." He did not finish his sentence.

"Apart from that, what?"

"Nothing, Paul, nothing."

"You wanted to say something."

"Yes, but not right now."

"Why not?"

"Because it has nothing to do with this case."

"So? It's on your mind, isn't it?" Paul said in a gentle tone that indicated that he was ready to listen to whatever Zhang wanted to talk about. But Zhang did not take him up on the offer. Instead, he jiggled his left leg nonstop and drummed his fingers on the tabletop.

"Do you know the woman in the photos? Does it have anything to do with her?"

"No. She looks like someone you'd see in a karaoke bar."

"Does it have anything to do with Tang?"

"Why do you think that?" Zhang retorted sharply. He did not seem to like Paul's question at all.

"I don't know. Just a feeling I have."

"Nonsense."

"Didn't you say he came from Sichuan?"

"Yes, and what about it?"

Why was Zhang being so vague? Why was he so slow to reply? "Does he come from Chengdu?"

"I . . . I think so."

"He must be our age. Early or midfifties, right?"

"Why do you think that?" Zhang responded.

"Do you know him personally?"

"Why are you asking?"

"That's not an answer," Paul replied. He saw in Zhang's eyes that he felt cornered; he had a secret that he did not want to divulge. He had gone too far. This was not an interrogation; he had no right to question his friend like this. He had to accept that even a friendship like theirs had boundaries, that there were taboos, ghosts, or demons that it was better not to awaken. Nevertheless, he trusted Zhang without reservation; this unconditional trust was the foundation on which their friendship rested. He did not want to disturb it. "I'm sorry," Paul said.

"That's okay."

"What do you think about the letter?"

"It's difficult. It doesn't get us much further at the moment because there's nobody we can ask about it. Later on, maybe."

"Should I call the Owens again now anyway?"

Zhang nodded. "Okay. Try, but be careful. It would be best if you could ask Mrs. Owen a few questions about Michael's life in China in as casual a way as possible. I hope she has a lead."

———

Paul rang Elizabeth Owen and said something about the investigations in Shenzhen being wrapped up and two or three final questions that the police still had that they'd passed on to him to handle in order to make things easier; a pure formality, as he said, just so they could write a full report; that was how it was with the bureaucracy in the Middle Kingdom.

Elizabeth's replies were not very useful. She knew neither any friends nor any acquaintances that her son had had in China; he had never mentioned any names. When he had stayed the night in China, which he had done often, he had always stayed in the Century Palace Hotel near the station; she remembered that. There was a very good massage parlor in the basement there, which he had visited often after long days in the office, and a bar, which he had liked. That's all she knew. Paul thanked her.

"The bar is called Glass. It's a club, a karaoke bar, and an expensive brothel," Zhang said in a tired voice, after Paul had told him about the conversation. "I've never heard of the massage parlor, but many of these places are also brothels. We still don't know much, but it's better than nothing. I'll be on my way."

"On your way. Where?"

"To the Century Hotel."

"Do you know anyone there?"

"No."

"What are you going to do there, then?"

"Look around, see if anyone can tell me anything about Michael Owen."

"As what? As a detective? As soon as you start investigating or questioning people there, word will spread. If there's a high-class brothel there, the owner will certainly have contacts with your people."

"With us?"

"With the police," Paul clarified. "They'll probably even have a stake in it, won't they?"

"Probably. Do you have a better idea?"

Paul thought for a moment. He went into the kitchen, put some more water on to boil, and returned to the living room, where his friend was still huddled helplessly on the couch.

Yes, he had a better idea. But should he say it? What would Christine say if he broke his promise? Would she ever forgive him? But the question of whether he could allow Zhang to travel back to China in this condition weighed just as heavily on him. Paul suddenly felt paralyzed; he felt a leaden heaviness in his whole body and was unable to make a decision.

What would Justin do; what would he tell him to do? Paul knew that this was an absolutely idiotic thing to imagine. His son would have been eleven years old now, and he would never have burdened him with a question like this, with such a difficult decision. But still, the thought of talking to Justin and having to account for himself to him helped. He was helping a friend in need.

———

"The hotel," Paul said slowly, "is the only lead we have. I can think of only one realistic way of investigating without putting you further into danger. I'll travel there, book a room, get a massage, visit the bar, and tell everyone I meet that I'm a good friend of Michael Owen's. If he stayed there often, someone will know him and be able to tell me something about him."

"Let me do that."

"You? A friend of Michael Owen's? I think I would be more convincing in the role, don't you think?"

"Of course. But what about Christine?"

For an instant, Paul thought about simply not mentioning his trip to Shenzhen.

"I'll call her later from the ferry."

Zhang did not look as though he wanted to carry on objecting. Paul went upstairs, packed a few things in a bag, got his passport, cash, and credit cards, and came down again. He felt better now, relieved; the wretched feeling of paralysis had gone. It had been good to make a decision, no, to make *this* decision.

His friend was lying on the couch with his eyes closed; he looked as if he were meditating.

"Zhang?"

"Yes," he replied, without looking at Paul.

"I'm going now. The sheets on my bed are clean. There's food in the fridge. If you need something, you'll have to go down to Yung Shue Wan. Do you have any Hong Kong dollars?"

"Not many."

"I'll put five hundred on the kitchen counter for you. I'll call you as soon as I'm at the hotel. Are the telephones in the Century safe or are they tapped?"

"As long as they don't suspect anything they're safe. And why should you seem suspicious to them?"

"Do you need anything else? Aspirin? Something to read?"

"No." Zhang opened his eyes. "Be careful. And thank you. I know what it is that you're doing for me."

———

Paul had to hurry. He walked down to the village in long strides. He was moving so uncharacteristically quickly that the old men and women weeding in the fields lifted their heads and looked at him in astonishment.

The ferry had barely set off before he rang Christine.

"It's Paul."

"I knew that, whether you believe it or not. I knew it was you from the first sound of your voice." The tenderness in her voice. He did not want to hear it now.

"Christine, I'm very . . ."

"Is it about this evening?"

"Yes," he said abruptly.

"Have you changed your mind?"

"No. But Zhang has arrived from Shenzhen. He needs my help. He's found the wife and the child of the supposed murderer. The man has an alibi. I have to find out something for him so I'm on my way to China now."

That was it. Final. No argument. Paul could hear his own voice. He was surprised, shocked at how cool it sounded, how hard it was. He did not apologize, did not want her understanding or to ask for her forgiveness because he was breaking a promise. He was telling her. He was sorry about that, but there was no other way. He did not have the strength for a discussion, for questions or doubts about his decision. If she got angry with him or even started swearing at him, he would hang up immediately.

Christine said nothing for a few endless seconds. Would she start shouting at him? Throw accusations at him? Cry?

"Where are you now?" she asked in a calm voice.

"On the ferry to Hong Kong."

"When are you arriving?"

"In about twenty-five minutes."

"I'll wait for you at the ferry terminal at Central," she said, and hung up.

XVIII

Her initial reaction was an ominous mixture of fear and rage. How could he do this to her? Why was this Zhang person more important than she was? Did his promise to her count for nothing? It had only been a few hours since he had asked her if she wanted to stay the night with him.

Will you stay the night?

She'd been waiting for these words, this request. She had imagined many times what she would do when he spoke them. Had dreamed about his body, about his bed in the house on Lamma, how she would lie under the white mosquito net, how she would feel him, his strength, his desire, how they would become one.

He was more tender than any man who had touched her. Like a teenager, she felt a desire that she would give herself up to immediately, if he would only let her. He defended himself against every one of her attempts to seduce him; they were shy and tentative, but scared him off nonetheless, made him withdraw and seek distance rather than closeness. Sometimes he took her hands gently from his chest or from his neck, and sometimes he pushed her away like a wrestler freeing himself from a claw hold. Many times she had been in a state of high arousal when she left him, and been unable to calm herself on her return journey, so there was nothing for it but to meet her own needs at home, alone in bed, with Josh and Tita sleeping in the next room, which she did not like, and which made her angry with him. Others, she knew, saw her as strong, stubborn, maybe. But she too was vulnerable. She was needy, and, like every needy person, she was very vulnerable.

Now he had finally asked her to stay the night with him and she had thought about nothing else that whole morning in the office, but then, once again, it was all over? Did he not know what he meant to her?

His voice. She hated it when he sounded so cool and hard. He had not even apologized.

She sat motionless on her chair for a long time after she had ended the call. Quiet tears ran down her cheeks and she felt for an instant that she had metamorphosed into a five-year-old child who had been abandoned by everyone. She was small and defenseless, her life was slipping through her fingers, she would lose everything. Her son. Her apartment. Her small company. Paul.

No, she heard herself say. No, you won't. You were small and defenseless once, but this is today. You are a grown woman, over forty years old. You are not a victim, you are strong. Strong. Strong. You have the power of self-determination.

No one was forcing her to be with Paul. She could break up with him. She could meet him at the ferry now and tell him that he was hurting her and abusing her trust in him and that she never wanted to see him again. For a split second she felt a strange relief at this thought. Like a person who had been expecting bad news for some time and found it liberating when it arrived. But did she really want to be without Paul? She loved him, believed they belonged together . . . Only children believed that the moon did not have one side turned away from the earth.

She did have a right to be furious with Paul. Love allowed that. He had said something about an innocent man and an alibi, but she was completely uninterested in that. Could she expect him to have more understanding for her fear of the Chinese in the People's Republic? What was a suitable time period within which to stop being frightened? Five years? Ten? Twenty? How long, she asked herself, was fear a natural defense mechanism? The thought of the uniformed men who had pushed her father from the window still having power over her life today was the most awful of all.

Christine looked at the clock. In less than fifteen minutes Paul would arrive at Central. She had to hurry. She grabbed her bag, said that she didn't know when she would be back, and left the office quickly.

It was almost impossible to get a taxi in Johnson Road at this time of day. In her high-heeled shoes, she walked swiftly through the market in Tai Yuen Street. She knocked over a box of children's clothing on the way and heard the stall keeper cursing behind her. She brushed past several passersby who swore at her, then snatched a taxi away from a woman with two children on Queens Road East. She was not especially superstitious, but she began to fear that she would have to pay for all her rudeness. The punishment followed in the form of a traffic jam because of an accident on Man Yiu Street, less than three hundred meters away from the ferry terminal. She was already more than five minutes late. She paid her fare, got out of the cab, took off her shoes, held them in her hand, and ran barefoot on the road between the stationary cars toward the pier.

Paul saw her from a distance and walked toward her. Instead of saying anything, they embraced. She felt how he was holding his breath, his body stiffening slightly, as though he was expecting an attack, verbal at least, at the next breath. But she said nothing and did not let him go, held him tight until he gradually relaxed and started breathing evenly again, and his muscles were less taut.

"Do you have time to take the Star Ferry?" she asked.

"The Star Ferry?" He looked at her in total astonishment.

"Yes, why not?"

He nodded, and they walked past the piers which the boats to Cheung Chau and Peng Chau stopped at, past the taxi stand and the bus station, turned left behind the General Post Office into Connaught Place and, in a few minutes, reached the old white and green terminal from which the boats to Tsim Sha Tsui departed.

She had taken this ferry very often before. Even after the opening of the much faster metro, which traveled beneath the harbor and took less than five minutes for the journey from Central, she had initially preferred taking the ferry, which was much slower. As time passed, she had taken the ferry less and less, and more out of nostalgia, and she had not been on it at all for years now. The ferry was a relic of another world, Christine thought, as the boat made its sedate approach to the quay. Even embarking and disembarking took more time than the entire journey with the MTR. The boat was so slow, so inefficient and uncomfortable, that taking it was an act of defiance against the laws and the logic that defined this city. Why did she want to take the Star Ferry now, of all times?

They sat on the lower deck, which had no protection from the wind, and stank of diesel and oil. All through their bodies, they felt the vibration of the engine, which was chugging so slowly that they felt as if they could count every single stroke of the pistons.

After a deckhand had cast off, she asked Paul, "You once asked me about my dreams. Do you remember what I said in reply?"

"Yes. You said that you were from Hong Kong and that you didn't have any dreams. Plans, yes, but no dreams."

"That's right. And what did you say to that then?"

"I was surprised, and I felt a little sorry for you," Paul replied. "I said to you that dreams could be beautiful, and you laughed and shook your head as if you did not know what I was talking about."

"That's right. For the last few hours I've been trying to imagine what it would be like to have a dream. It's different from actually having a dream, but it's still a start, isn't it?"

"Yes."

Paul looked at her waiting for a further explanation or an accusation. That he was destroying this tentative beginning, that she had been right not to dream, that now she saw how quickly a dream could be destroyed. But she did not say anything.

"And?"

"And nothing."

He looked at the dark, almost black, water.

After a while he said, "I still owe you an explanation."

"You don't owe me anything."

"I'm very sorry about tonight, and that I couldn't keep my—"

Christine put her hand on his mouth and kissed him on the cheek.

"I can . . ."

She shook her head. "I don't want any explanations. I love you. That's enough."

As if trusting was only for fools. As if we had a choice.

XIX

Zhang heard Paul putting on his shoes, opening the door and closing it gently behind him, walking over the terrace, down the steps to the path toward the ferry station, opening the squeaky garden gate and closing it again, standing still for a moment, and then hurrying away.

After that there was silence. Zhang heard nothing at all for several seconds, apart from a barely audible hissing in his ears; only then did he become aware of the birdsong and the rasping and scratching of the bamboo plants in the garden. It was a silence that he no longer knew in Shenzhen. There, human or machine noises were ever present. Even at night, when he lay awake next to the sleeping Mei, the noise of construction or from traffic, the humming of air conditioners, or the voices of the brothel visitors floated up to intrude on him. In contrast, he noticed, the stillness that reigned in this house did him no good. It spread through him and pushed all thoughts of the case of Michael Owen, of Mei or Paul, to one side, and made space for memories that he did not want to engage with. Stillness, thought Zhang, is not good for people who want to forget.

He got up from the couch and looked around the living room, trying to find something to distract him. He noticed the fresh flowers on the table and the candles everywhere. Both were extremely unusual for his friend. Had Christine planned to visit him this evening? If Paul had gone to so much trouble, that was a good sign. It meant he was venturing out of the world he had withdrawn to with his memories of Justin. But why had he not said anything about it? Maybe it was better that he hadn't? If Zhang had known about the plans with Christine it would have been even more difficult for him to ask Paul to do him a favor. He was thankful that Paul had spared him this embarrassment.

Zhang went to the table and looked at the furniture in the living room. He was struck anew by the beautiful Chinese antiques his friend owned. The long, chestnut-colored elm-wood dining table with its eight chairs was from the Qing Dynasty, as was the deep-red, carefully polished wedding chest with the round brass clasp in the middle. Both were over a hundred years old and in very good condition. Their simple classic shapes radiated a calm that had impressed him at first sight. On the shelves were several blue and white porcelain bowls and plates. Paul had once told him how old they were and which province they came from, but Zhang had forgotten the details; he saw only the delicately traced patterns and the fine glazing, which had been applied with great care. There were two paper scrolls on the wall with popular motifs from traditional Chinese paintings: a bamboo grove and a scene of a temple in the mountains, done by an eighteenth-century master that Zhang had already admired many times.

Did a person have to be from the West to have such an impartial appreciation of such specimens of Chinese art? He had never seen any antiques in a Chinese person's flat, neither in his friends' houses nor when he visited homes in the course of his investigations. Old cupboards and tables, beds and benches, yes, but they were not in good condition; they were not appreciated for their age or their quality; their owners only still had them because they could not afford anything else.

Zhang wondered whether he would have one of Paul's pieces of furniture or art in his apartment if he could afford it. He doubted it. He did not see in them the old China, whose art and culture his friend admired so much; to him, they signified something quite different. He did not see the skilled artisanal craftsmanship, the classical forms, or the traditions and experience of hundreds of years that lay behind them. He saw their destruction. He saw them lying in broken pieces on the street, how they had been smashed and set on fire, how he and his schoolmates had thrown them out of the windows and stamped around on them in the name of the Revolution. It was not possible for him to separate these memories, even if he wanted to.

High up on the shelves was the sculpture of a Buddha. Zhang knew it well. He had tried to ignore it for a long time; for years, he had crept around it like a frightened child in front of a nasty uncle. It was a present from a Chinese person from Nanjing who had rescued it from the ruins of a temple and asked Paul to smuggle it out of the country in order to bring it into safety. You never knew how things would go in China.

Zhang stood on a chair and took the figure down. It was made of wood, and the workmanship was not of particular artistic value. The facial features of the enlightened one were far from delicate, and his body, the crossed legs and the raised right hand, were very crudely carved. Despite this, Zhang thought the sculpture had an extraordinary aura. Its creator had not been a gifted artist but he had given it something that moved Zhang. It was familiar to him; it was, now that he was touching it, stroking the porous wood with his fingers, alive in a shocking way. He had tried for so long to forget, but there was no denying it. He saw himself standing at the edge of the village to which he and the other school pupils and university students from Chengdu had been sent. Little Zhang, a sixteen-year-old boy full of fear and questions, who had no one with whom he could share his feelings. He was small, much too small for his age; the faded blue Mao suit was two sizes too big and hung from his puny frame like a cut-out sack that someone had pulled over his head. He was so shy that he only ever spoke in the group when he was asked a question, and then not more than a few words.

He smelled the warm, humid mountain air, he felt it on his skin, he felt the wind blowing over the mountains, bringing damp cold in the winter and lung infections that they could not fight off. No one was supposed to acknowledge it, but everyone knew a quarter of the kids never recovered, were left for dead. He heard the voices of the others, their singing, their screaming, their rejoicing. It was all suddenly so clear to him again, as though forty years were nothing more than the blink of an eye, as though there was no difference between yesterday and tomorrow. As though a lifetime was not enough to forget in.

To distract himself he went over to the stereo system, switched it on, and pushed a random CD in. Piano music came out of the speakers, the quiet, enchantingly beautiful music of a Western composer. Zhang thought it was Chopin; he and Paul had listened to this album often while they played chess. It made him feel calm and strong then, but now it did not help. The beauty of the music made everything worse. Despite his efforts, the film in his head played on.

A misty autumn day in the mountains of Sichuan: the clouds lie low in the valleys and swallow up the paddy fields in the distance, as though heaven and earth could be one. A troop of Red Guards marches on a muddy dam straight through the field, the leader of the brigade in front as always. Some of them hold red flags and wave them in the air vigorously, singing songs of the Revolution; their clear, loud singing echoes through the valley. They are young voices, full of faith; they do not yet have a trace of doubt. Zhang is walking barefoot; mud swells between his toes with every step. He has no idea where the path is leading. Some say they are walking to a show trial against the "bourgeois elements" and "counterrevolutionaries" in the next village, others say they are heading for the old temple farther up the valley. He doesn't care where they are going; he just wants to go with them.

After a long march—he doesn't know any longer how far they walked—they finally reach their destination. The temple is hidden by a bamboo grove; it is not big, twenty meters square maybe, and surrounded by a wall with a mighty wooden gate. The gate is barred, and the young men and women are outraged. Who dares to bar entry to them, the avant-garde who are spearheading the great proletarian Cultural Revolution? They call, they shout, they demand entry, and with every minute that entry is denied to them, they grow more enraged. They rattle the wooden gate. They try to climb the wall, in vain. They throw stones at the green, glazed tiles of the temple roof and cheer loudly whenever a stone breaks a tile. Suddenly the heavy wooden bolt is drawn back from within. Out of the gate steps a monk, the sole remaining inhabitant of the temple. He is an old man, wrapped in a dirty gray cloth, emaciated, his head shorn bald, with legs like sticks. His cheeks are sunken and his eyes deep in their sockets; a long, thin beard straggles from his chin. The young people are shocked at the sight of him. They shrink back and fall silent, unsettled, undecided about whether this old man really is the decadent bourgeois element, the counterrevolutionary, the revisionist, who they have heard is hiding here.

The leader of the group punches a fist in the air and calls out, "Long live the great Chairman Mao!" He sees the doubt in the faces of the others; he can feel that, right now, they need someone to tell them what to do, that they need to be led. He pushes the monk aside and orders them to storm the temple. All of them throng inside, pushing impatiently to get through the door as if there were not enough space for everyone. Zhang is among them. He is fired up; he senses that something exciting is about to happen, and he is happy he is allowed to be there.

The first few Red Guards press into the meditation hall; they carry books, manuscripts, wall tablets, and Buddha statues into the courtyard and dump them in a pile. Others have discovered the corner of the temple where the monk sleeps; they defecate on his quarters, throw his notebooks on the pile in the courtyard, and set it alight. The flames shoot up high.

The old man stands to one side, not moving, not saying a word. In his eyes is not even a flicker of fear. His silence only makes the pack more furious. They destroy the meditation hall, they tear the carvings from the walls, they burn every Buddha, every sculpture that they can get their hands on, and what they can't burn, they smear with excrement. Only the monk himself remains untouched. His stillness, his pronounced serenity, unsettles them.

At some point they begin to flag; a few of them squat on the ground amid the rubble, worn out. The fighters of the Cultural Revolution are tired from the battle against the "old thinking" that lived in this temple. Finally, they make their way back to the village. Only their leader stays, and with him, Zhang.

The two of them stay in the courtyard and have a look around. The eighteen-year-old Tang Mingqing is tall, towering over Zhang by more than a head. His features are striking and he looks so handsome and strong and confident that he could have stepped straight out of a Communist Party propaganda poster. Zhang feels uncertain; he does not know what Tang plans to do, and if he wants him to be there. Why does he not follow the others? Is he staying out of curiosity? Or does he want to help Tang, do him a service, whatever he plans to do? He has known him for years, after all; they grew up on the same street in Chengdu and went to the same school before the Cultural Revolution. When Zhang and his group were sent to the village six months ago, Tang was there too and was the only person he knew. But that had not been enough for them to become friends and it would never be enough, for Zhang was too quiet and Tang was too loud, and the older boy had absolutely no respect for the puny kid from his neighborhood.

The monk withdraws to the interior of the temple. He is sitting in the midst of the chaos in the meditation hall, his legs folded over each other in the lotus position, his thin hands lying on his bent knees. He looks at Tang and Zhang as if he knows exactly what is coming next.

Tang strides toward the old monk, stops next to him, glances down at the man, looks around the room, points at a wooden beam in the corner, and asks Zhang to bring it to him.

Zhang obeys.

Tang steps behind the old man and looks over to Zhang once more. He looks focused and very calm at the same time, as if he were about to pass a probation period, to fulfill a duty entrusted to him, one that a prospective member of the Communist Party of China could not shirk. In the name of the Revolution. In the name of a new China. In the name of the Great Chairman.

Tang strikes.

Zhang looks on.

———

They do not exchange a word on the way back to the village.

Zhang says nothing and he does not want an answer, although the question—why did the monk have to die?—had shot through his mind once. A terrible question that he was immediately ashamed of; it showed him how weak his foundation was and how much work he still had to do on himself to overcome his decadent thinking and become a good revolutionary like Tang.

Zhang is silent when the others ask why they are so late. He is silent when he hears the official version of events weeks later. The old temple in the mountains had long been a crumbling wreck and had finally collapsed; the monk living in it had been crushed by a falling beam from the ceiling when it happened.

He has maintained his silence to this day.

He has never told Mei about that day, and never told Paul. He has blotted it out of his memory, just like the crimes of those years have been excised from the Chinese history books. For over two decades he had not thought about it at all; he had been much too busy with the return to Chengdu, finishing school, moving to Shenzhen with Mei and his son, and his police work.

Almost thirty years had passed before the memory had caught up with him after all, for reasons that he did not understand. At first it had returned intermittently, at long intervals, in his dreams; on those nights Mei had woken him up because he had been crying, or screaming so loudly that he woke their son. For some time now, it had popped up every few weeks, even during the day, at home, and Zhang could see no reason for it. It could be triggered by the sight of a wooden beam or a Buddha figure, but also by the sight of an old man with sunken cheeks and stick-thin legs crossing the road slowly. Memory operated by its own rules.

In the past few months, he had, more and more often, found himself looking into the faces of people his own age and wondered: What did you do thirty-five years ago? Did you betray people or were you betrayed? Were you a victim or perpetrator, or both? Where are your memories? Are you only hiding them? When will they reappear? How can you stand the silence?

That he would never get an answer to all these questions made him prone to regular periods of self-doubt. Was he perhaps the only one still troubled by what happened back then? Was it his mistake, a very personal failure of his, not to be able to leave the past in peace? There were millions of perpetrators and victims, so that was a ridiculous notion, absurd, really, he reassured himself when these thoughts came up. But because public discussion of the crimes that had been committed was not allowed and he himself had not mustered the strength to do so with the people closest to him, he felt unsure of himself, and this uncertainty plagued him.

How did that day figure in Tang's memory? Had he suppressed the murder? Did it haunt him, and, if so, how? Or maybe wealth helped him with forgetting? Is it easier to extinguish memories when you live in a big house with servants? And buy yourself a new luxury car every year? Eat at the most expensive restaurants, set up companies, build factories, buy apartments and sell them, fly back and forth across the country nonstop from one meeting to another, and when you have one or two lovers who are constantly available to offer their young bodies as distraction? Can a person escape his past that way?

Zhang thought about how quickly the face of his country had changed. He thought about Chengdu, Chongqing, Shanghai,

Wuhan, and all the cities he had visited in the last few years that he no longer recognized because the historic quarters in the city center had been bulldozed and a forest of high-rise buildings put up in their place. In a very short time, buildings hundreds of years old that had borne witness to the past had disappeared in those cities. Razed to the ground as though they had never existed. At times like these, it seemed to him that this untrammeled building frenzy and the incredible rate of change were a desperate attempt to flee from history, and the new high-rise buildings, roads, highways, airports, and factories were not so much signs of progress as giant memorials to the desire to forget. As if you could brick up memories. As if you could cement them all away and plaster over them. As if you could leave your shadow behind if you only walked fast enough.

It was a ridiculous endeavor, bound to fail; Zhang felt this in his own body. He understood for the first time what power that moment still had over him, nearly forty years later. He had been witness to a murder. Could he have stopped it? Refused to give Tang the wooden beam? Charged at him while he was striking the blows? He might have been able to save the monk, but at what cost? Either Tang would have beaten him, Zhang, to death, or he would have had to answer to the Red Guards or to the party for his contemptible deed; he would no doubt have been cast out. There would have been no place in the new China for someone who saved the life of an old Buddhist monk.

He saw his sixteen-year-old self before him, standing in the meditation hall, watching as Tang clutched the stick firmly with his strong hands, lifted his arms, higher and higher, torso twisting like a quill drawn taut. He saw the piece of wood whip through the air and he saw how everything was shattered with one stroke: belief in the Great Chairman and in the party, the permanent revolution and its young fighters, and, much worse, the young person's belief in his own innocence. Destroyed, in a split second without him realizing it at the time. Measuring the consequences of that blow occupied him to this day.

He did not feel guilt, only shame, bottomless shame about his own inadequacy, about how easily led he had been, and, most of all, about the cowardice within him that had showed its ugly face then.

This shame had led him, though he had not understood the connection immediately, to the teachings of Buddha. One year after the murder of the monk, Zhang had seen the old cook Hu die, and his death was the event that gradually made him able to grasp the atrocities that were being perpetrated before his eyes. Beaten to death because of three lousy peppercorns. He had liked the mule-headed Hu; he had thought of him often in the years since, but the monk had been buried deep in his memory.

How had this outbreak of violence become possible? How could pupils rise up against their teachers and children betray their parents? How had two pillars of Chinese culture simply collapsed in the space of weeks? How could he have participated in it?

He did not find any answers to these questions in Buddhism, but the teachings gave him clear and simple instructions and rules of behavior, a kind of moral compass that he thought China had lost, certainly by the time of the Cultural Revolution. Apart from that, he was fascinated by the Buddhist idea that he was responsible for his own fate and did not have to pray to any god, any saints, or any Great Chairman on the path to enlightenment.

That was why he was not at HQ celebrating with his colleagues now. Twice now he had looked on from the sidelines without taking action when innocent people had been executed. He would not do it a third time. Not for anything in the world.

But where should he be now? With Mei in the kitchen? If she knew the truth, would it destroy their love? Probably not, but would she understand him? Zhang was not entirely sure. She was ten years younger than he was, and had lived through the worst years of the Cultural Revolution as a small child. As far as Zhang knew, her family had not been politically active, and had been spared the purges. She had also never witnessed public humiliations or executions that might have traumatized her. She had never spoken of them, at least.

But that meant nothing, Zhang thought, she probably thought the same about him.

Where should he be? With Tang in the office? He did not have the strength for that. Not yet. Zhang had seen enough photographs of Tang in the newspapers to know that he had not paid the price of losing any of his charisma. The broad shoulders, the upright posture, the striking features, the confident look in his eyes: All made him look like the natural focus of every picture. Would he be able to stand firm against that look today? It was only a matter of days until they would be facing each other again, and when it came to it, he would have to be well prepared, otherwise . . . Otherwise? Was it possible that Tang might wield power over him once more? An absurd notion. He had proved his courage often enough in the years past; every gift he had turned down as a policeman was proof of his strength. But now that the thought had entered his mind, it would not be chased out again, no matter how ridiculous Zhang found it.

Victor Tang knew what to take aim at in order to destroy a man.

XX

He left the station and walked up Jianshe Road, his brisk pace meant to deter anyone who tried to approach him with offers of a shoeshine, a cheap hotel room, a massage, or a woman. He either ignored the few who still tried their luck or shook them off with vigorous arm movements. Why had Michael Owen chosen the Century Plaza? It was one of the oldest and best hotels in Shenzhen, but its guests were mainly Chinese businesspeople. Visitors from Hong Kong or abroad preferred to stay in the chain hotels they trusted, such as the Holiday Inn or the Shangri-La.

A uniformed doorman opened the door, bowed slightly, and greeted him with a loud "Welcome, sir."

While registering at the reception desk, he said that his good friend Michael Owen had recommended the hotel to him, but there was no reaction to the mention of the name. Paul asked if it would be possible to stay in the room that Mr. Owen had always stayed in on his visits; he heard it had superior views. He did not know the room number, no, but perhaps they could check on their computer system.

The receptionist tapped away at his keyboard without looking up and shook his head. He couldn't find an entry. Paul had to spell "Owen" several times, and he felt glad that Michael's surname was not Abrahimovich.

After a while the young man's face lit up. Owen, Michael, yes, there he was. On his visits he had stayed most often in junior suite

1515 but he had not been a guest at the hotel for quite some time now.

Where in Shenzhen had Michael Owen spent the night before his death, if not in his regular hotel?

Paul persisted. Perhaps there was a computer error? He was fairly sure that his friend had stayed at the hotel just a few days earlier.

Absolutely not. His last visit was almost exactly six months ago. Before that he had indeed been a regular guest.

The junior suites were all reserved, so were the deluxe rooms, so, a few minutes later, Paul found himself in a small nonsmoking room that reeked horribly of cigarette smoke, with a window looking out onto train tracks, a highway, and two building sites. The faucet in the bathroom dripped, and he could hear several loud Chinese voices and a television in the room on his left. He thought about Lamma, the flowers for Christine, and the bottle of champagne in the fridge.

The Emperor's Paradise was in the basement of the hotel. Paul had no idea what he was letting himself in for here. When he had traveled through China in the 1980s and the early 1990s, there had been neither erotic massage salons nor brothels, or they had been off-limits for foreigners and so hidden away that he had never noticed them. Was the Emperor's Paradise a proper massage salon or would the hands of the masseuse not stop at certain places? How would she react if he turned down all erotic play? Would he be able to ask about Michael Owen without attracting attention?

Four tall young women in long pink evening dresses with fake white pearls in their permed hair greeted him. From the excitement in their faces he could see that a Western guest was unusual here. A man in a black suit came up to him. He smiled, but it was one of those Chinese smiles that was more a showing of teeth than a friendly gesture, and covered up suspicion and uncertainty. The man labored to formulate a sentence in English, and breathed a sigh of relief when he heard Paul speak Chinese.

"A good friend of mine, Michael Owen, recommended this salon to me," Paul said as casually as he could.

"We're very glad to be able to welcome a friend of Mr. Owen's," the man replied, still somewhat formal but a little more relaxed. The young women giggled and whispered something among themselves that Paul did not understand.

"Michael raved about your massages." Paul was amazing himself with his own acting talents.

"I'm happy to hear that. I think perhaps, then, that you will also want to be massaged by Number Seventy-Seven?" the Chinese man responded.

"Very gladly. Michael recommended her to me warmly," Paul replied, speaking as if no other woman would do.

"Then please follow me."

They walked past a small fountain and several plaster statues of cherubs before they came to a changing room, where the man passed Paul to two attendants who helped him to undress, folded his clothes, and stored them in a numbered locker. They wrapped a bathrobe around him and led him to a kind of spa with two swimming pools, showers, and sauna rooms. Several Chinese people were lounging in the whirlpool chatting; they looked up briefly, sized Paul up, and then continued talking.

Paul sat down in a sauna for a few minutes. He wanted to think about how best to begin his conversation with Number Seventy-Seven. But he was too flustered to concentrate. He showered and went to the quiet room.

There was a guest lying on almost every lounger here. Some of them had closed their eyes while others were talking in whispers or looking at one of the four flat screens on the walls, on which live stock exchange data from Hong Kong, New York, Tokyo, Shanghai, and Shenzhen flashed. As far as Paul could tell in the half darkness, he was the only foreigner there. What had brought Michael Owen to this place? Was it a recommendation from Victor Tang, pure curiosity, or simply coincidence? Had he just had a massage or had he been looking for a young girl to take up to his room?

Paul had barely sat down when a young woman came to stand in

front of him. Her beauty surprised him. She had an unusually narrow face, a large mouth with thick, sensual lips, and long black hair
that hung down her back. She was wearing a blue and white striped
smock that barely covered her bottom. The skin on her slender legs
was so white that they shimmered in the dim light of the quiet
room. She spoke in a low voice and asked him to follow her. They
walked through the twists and turns of the corridor into a pleasantly
warm room that smelled of essential oils, in which two candles were
burning. Paul took his bathrobe off and lay down on the massage
table on his stomach. The young woman closed the door and slid
the inside bolt.

She stood next to him, put a towel over his naked lower body,
rubbed oil on her hands, and started her work with slow movements.

A shudder of pleasure rippled through Paul at the first touch.
It was more stroking than massaging; her fingers played with him,
gliding over the oiled skin from his tailbone to his shoulders and
back again, down the sides beneath his underarms, over his arms,
pressing gently into his flesh at certain points.

"That feels good."

"Thank you. Why are you so tense?"

"Am I?"

"Yes. Do you often have headaches?"

"Sometimes."

"Your shoulders, your arms, and your back are very stiff and much
too hard." She pushed the towel aside a little and massaged his lower
back with gentle circular motions.

"Too much work," Paul claimed.

"It doesn't feel like that," she said, spreading more oil on his legs.

"What, then?"

"I don't know. That's why I'm asking."

Paul closed his eyes. "What's your name?"

"When I'm working, they call me Seventy-Seven."

"And when you're not working?"

"Pu. And you?"

"Paul."

She started massaging his thighs with gentle movements. Was she trying to relax him or to arouse him?"

"Michael asked me to say hello from him."

"Thank you. I've been told that you're a friend of his. How is he?"

"Fine."

"I haven't seen him for a while. Not for two weeks at least," Pu said.

"He has a lot to do at the moment."

"He always does."

"You're right. When was he last here?"

"No idea. After Anyi stopped, he no longer came, and that was almost exactly half a year ago." After a long silence she asked, "Do you know Anyi?"

"No, not yet, I'm afraid."

He felt like he was a poker player who was bluffing and raising his stake with every remark he made. One wrong question, one wrong answer, and he would be exposed. Was Anyi the woman in the photos on Michael Owen's computer that were saved under A?

"She's never talked about you either." Was that a hint of suspicion in her voice or mere surprise?

"I haven't seen Michael for a long time. I live in Chicago and . . ."

"Chicago?" she interrupted him, astonished. "Where did you learn such good Chinese, then?"

He was a terrible liar. Chicago! Why on earth had he chosen a city he had never been to in his life! If he was unlucky, she would start telling him about an uncle who owned a restaurant there and ask him where he lived exactly. He had to talk as little about himself as possible; the more he had to make up, the greater the danger of getting entangled in a net of contradictions. "I lived in Hong Kong for a long time before, and have traveled through China a lot. That's how I learned the language."

"You speak it very well."

"Thank you."

Pu continued massaging his upper legs, kneading the muscles and stroking his inner thighs gently. He had walled in his emotions, his senses, for so long but now he had to will himself not to be seduced by this young Chinese woman.

"You can turn over now," she said.

No, he could not do that right now. It was impossible for him to lie on his back in his current state. "In a minute. My shoulders often ache a great deal," he said apologetically. "Could you massage them a bit more?"

She moved to the upper end of the massage table and stroked his curly white hair and the thick hair growth on his arms. His hirsuteness had fascinated every Chinese woman he had met so far. "You're older than Michael, aren't you?"

"Yes, quite a bit," he said, laughing. Did she mean to compliment him or did she really find it difficult to guess his age?

"I'm actually more a friend of his father's. That's how I know Michael."

"His father's?" Her voice was disbelieving, almost astonished. If he did not think of a good explanation now he would not get a single word more out of her. "I mean, I was a friend of his father's before."

"Before? You mean before the big quarrel?"

"That's right. Before the quarrel," he replied, hoping that she didn't hear the relief in his voice. "After that, even his friends found Owen Senior difficult to cope with. Have you met him?"

"No. And after everything Michael has said about him, I don't want to."

"And his mother?"

"I haven't met her either."

Paul stayed silent for a few moments while Pu massaged his shoulders, neck, and head.

"I'm meeting him later tonight, actually," he said suddenly, without giving it great thought.

"Who?"

"Michael, of course."

"In Hong Kong?"

"No, here in Shenzhen."

"Is he coming to the Century Plaza?"

"No."

"Are you going to see him at the apartment?"

"Yes, probably."

"Then you'll meet Anyi."

"I hope so. Michael said he would ring me. How long will it take to get there by taxi?"

"About half an hour, I think."

"That long?" he asked.

"In the daytime it takes twice as long."

"Isn't there a shorter route?"

"To Diamond Villas? What shorter route would you take there? If the traffic is very heavy, watch out that the taxi driver doesn't take the Bao'an, but the Hongling Road; it's less busy. Tell him he should go via Nigang West Road, then turn left, go past the hospital; you'll see the Villas then. Anyi always took that route from here, and I do the same when I visit her."

"Thank you. I hope I can remember all that."

"Please turn onto your back now."

He turned over gladly. Pu was still standing behind his head. She massaged his torso first, teasing his chest hair, and slowly leaned so far over him that he could feel her breath as she used both hands to stroke his stomach all the way down to his groin and back to his chest, and down again, her arms reaching farther every time. But she could do what she liked now, no part of him stirred. He was too distracted. His mind was occupied with thoughts of Diamond Villas, a Chinese lover, and a young American man who had clearly sought and found much more than a new location for the family business. Why had he not told his parents anything about his girlfriend, with whom he was clearly sharing a flat? Or had Elizabeth Owen known about it and not told him, Paul, about it? Every family had its secrets and taboo subjects that no one discussed, and most certainly not with a stranger. Paul wondered what secrets the Owens had shared with each other. What had the father and son quarreled so violently about, so that even Pu, the friend of Michael's lover, knew about it?

At the end of the massage, Paul added a generous tip to the bill he was asked to sign, and Pu thanked him sulkily. Toward the end of the session she had grown more and more frustrated and impatient with the lack of reaction from her client.

Paul hurried back upstairs to his hotel room. He could hardly wait to tell Zhang about what he had found out in the Emperor's Paradise.

The telephone in Lamma rang and rang. Paul counted every ring and grew more and more uneasy. He hung up and tried again. Finally, he heard his friend's voice. Zhang sounded strained, as though he could barely breathe.

"Zhang, is everything all right?"

"Fine. I just lay down for a while. Where are you?"

Paul told him about his conversation with Pu.

"Do you know Diamond Villas?" he asked when he had finished sharing what he had learned from Pu.

"Yes, it's not far from Lake Silver, if I'm not wrong. It's one of the new settlements that have sprung up all over Shenzhen—Golden Dream, Honey Club, Rich Man's World, and so on—pretty expensive areas with big town houses and luxury apartments. Most of them are owned by civil servants and party officials from the north who invest their corruption money here. As far as I know, the rest of the property has been bought by businessmen from Singapore or Hong Kong for investment or for their mistresses."

"Have you been there?"

"No. They all have private security guards so we don't have much to do there. They're surrounded by high walls and there are mostly strict checks on entry."

"Sounds like a modern-day Forbidden City," Paul said.

"For the new little emperors, yes, absolutely right."

"Will I be able to get in?"

"You? You're a foreigner so should have no problem. Just put on an arrogant Don't-you-even-dare-speak-to-me-you-good-for-nothing-little-Chinese-security-guard expression and walk confidently past the guardhouse and you'll be left alone. Just don't peer in looking hesitant and unsure like you usually do. That will not be the right moment to look pensive or sensitive."

"I'm glad you're back in the mood to annoy me."

"Just a tip for my assistant detective," Zhang said in jest. "Seriously, though, shouldn't I come with you?"

"No. If both of us turn up, it will only put the woman off. I think I played my role as Michael Owen's friend pretty well in front of Pu. Why shouldn't it work with Anyi too? Do you think someone's already told her that Michael is dead?"

"I can't think who would have. And she would surely have told her friend about it."

"That's right. There you see again what an amateur you're working with. I'll call you again tomorrow once I'm back in the hotel."

It was an awful night. At first Paul could not get to sleep because the men in the next room, from what he could understand from the roaring, were having a party to celebrate signing a contract. Just when he had finally nodded off, a knock at the door woke him, and he opened it unsuspectingly to find a plump young woman in a kind of black leather bikini, holding tissues and a bottle of oil in her hands. She asked him if he wanted "room service." It was 3:50 AM.

During the hours that followed, he was much too keyed up to sleep properly. How should he introduce himself to Anyi? As a representative of the family, who was looking for the missing Michael? As a friend of Michael's, who was just stopping by to visit on the off chance he was home? He had to use his intuition to decide which role he should play, and that meant he would be ill prepared for any questions she might ask him. He lay dozing in bed till shortly after eight AM, had some cold, over-salted scrambled eggs for breakfast, and took a taxi to Diamond Villas.

After they had passed the entrance to the development, Paul asked the driver to turn into the next side street and let him off.

The development was surrounded by a wall that was at least three meters high, with broken glass embedded into the top of the wall. There was an entry barrier with a small guardhouse next to it, in which two watchmen sat. Paul did not feel up to putting on a don't-you-even-dare-speak-to-me-you-good-for-nothing-little-Chinese-security-guard expression.

Paul walked along the whitewashed wall. Two big limousines came out of the exit and several women carrying shopping bags disappeared through the gate. He immediately realized his first mistake. Only domestic staff entered Diamond Villas on foot. Anyone who lived there drove air-conditioned cars in, of course. He was only a few steps away from the barrier. He straightened up, puffed his chest out, walked tall, ran his hand through his sweaty hair one more time, and did not even give the guardhouse a look. Let them dare to even speak to him or stop him.

They did not dare to.

Exhaling with relief, he walked up a long driveway, looking around him. At first glance, this development had nothing in common with the world beyond its gates. Its exclusiveness and isolation did indeed remind him of the Forbidden City. There was a tidy paved sidewalk and there was no rubbish on the streets. The grass between the paths was freshly mown and the buildings were well maintained. The complex consisted of eight high-rise buildings, each named after precious stones.

He asked one of the women with the shopping bags if she knew where Michael Owen lived. He received an uncomprehending stare in reply. He described Michael in a few sentences and she suddenly knew who he meant. The young American man lived on the top floor of the Sapphire building. Paul should go through the parking lot and take the elevator straight up to the penthouse. After a Porsche four-wheel drive shot out between a Ferrari and a Mercedes and nearly ran Paul over, he found the building.

The doorbell markers had numbers instead of names on them. He pressed the button on top and waited.

"Hello?" said a stern female voice.

"I'm looking for Michael Owen."

"He's not in. Who are you?"

"Paul Leibovitz, a friend of Michael's from Hong Kong."

"Are you Chinese?"

"No, American."

"Who are you?" she repeated, this time in heavily accented English, as though she was trying to find out if he was really a foreigner by testing his accent.

"My name is Paul Leibovitz, and I'm a friend of Michael's and the Owen family. I have to speak to you urgently," he replied slowly in English, pronouncing each word very clearly.

There was silence for a long moment, then there was a light buzzing noise and the door opened.

She was waiting for him at the elevator. Paul recognized her face immediately, though she was far more beautiful in person than in the photos. Her features were more delicate and her skin was paler. With her high cheekbones, dark-brown almond-shaped eyes, and generous bee-stung lips, she was the very cliché of Chinese beauty. She was surprisingly tall and slim, but not scrawny, her hair was piled in a topknot fastened with a chopstick, and she was wearing baggy gray jogging pants and a sweatshirt with NYU printed on it.

She sized him up in one glance with suspicious eyes and then stepped aside without saying a word. Paul walked past her into the apartment. She closed the door behind him and led him into the living room.

The room was bright. It had a wall of windows opening out onto a balcony, from which the view stretched over the water reservoir to the hills beyond it. There was a black leather couch against the wall and a small oval table in front of it with a plastic flower arrangement on it; there was a large flat-screen TV opposite. On the other side of the room was a kitchen area with a breakfast bar and four stools.

Anyi sat down on one of the stools, folded her arms over her chest, and said, in Mandarin once again, "I didn't catch your name."

"Paul Leibovitz."

"What do you want from me?" she asked in a brusque tone.

"I'm looking for Michael Owen."

"Who sent you?"

Paul said nothing. He wondered if she was really as brisk and confident as she appeared to be or if she was behaving like this just to hide her fear and insecurity.

"His mother. She's worried."

"Are you with the police?"

"No. I'm a friend of the family."

She cast him another suspicious look. This was no relaxed chat over a massage that Paul could bluff his way through. The two people sitting here were circling each other warily, exercising great caution, waiting for a sign of weakness from the other. He had no idea if he ought to assume a more forceful manner or if he should try to win her trust with a more sensitive approach. She did not appear to be the kind of person who was easily intimidated, nor did she seem like someone who was quick to trust others. And she was certainly not, as Zhang had surmised from seeing the photos of her, one of those karaoke bar ladies. The young women who worked there, hoping that one of their rich clients would take them as a mistress, were mostly migrant workers. They streamed into the city and worked initially in factories. The most attractive among them would eventually start working in disproportionately better-paid club or bar jobs. For the most part, these girls came from villages and small towns and were too frightened and shy to get involved with a foreigner. Anyi's story was different. Her tone, her body language, and her gestures impressed Paul, even though the ambition and confidence that they expressed were unfamiliar to him.

"May I sit down?"

Anyi did not say anything, but nodded slightly.

Paul took a seat on the couch.

"Do you know where Michael is?" he asked.

"I thought he was in Hong Kong."

"He's not there."

"And not here either," she said coolly.

"Perhaps he's in Shanghai?"

She stared at him with a cold, calculating look almost devoid of emotion.

Anyi shook her head.

"When was the last time you saw him?" Paul asked.

She shook her head again.

"When was the last time you spoke to him on the phone?"

Silence.

"Is it usual for you not to hear from him for days?" His voice had sharpened involuntarily. Her silence was annoying him. "Aren't you at all worried? Something could have happened to him."

A tremble of her lower lip betrayed her. She was not keeping silent out of defiance or ignorance. She was silent because she was frightened the next sentence would make her lose control of herself.

"Maybe he needs your help."

That was one sentence too many. The young woman slid off the stool as violently as if someone had pushed her from behind and ran into another room. He heard her sobbing through the open door.

Paul wished Zhang were with him. He had no idea what he should do. He was not a police detective. An experienced officer would probably press the point now, take advantage of the weakness, increase the pressure by making just the right remark in order to get the woman to talk. He could not do that. He felt sorry for Anyi; his instinctive reaction to someone who was crying was to offer them help, and he followed his instincts. He got up and went into the next room, where Anyi was lying on the bed with her face buried in a pillow. He sat down next to her and stroked her head.

She allowed him to carry on. He looked around the bedroom as she collected herself. A large Mickey Mouse plush toy was propped against the head of the bed with a pink heart-shaped pillow next to it. There was another flat-screen television on the wall opposite and a desk with a computer on it in the corner. There were several intermediate English language course books on the floor.

When she had stopped crying, Paul asked, "How long have you known Michael?"

She turned her head toward him, wiped the tears from her face with a pillowcase, and said, "Almost exactly one year."

"Are you learning English for him?"

"Yes. He doesn't speak much Chinese. And we want to go back to America later."

"And you're preparing for it by sleeping with Mickey Mouse and wearing NYU sweatshirts?"

"Yes," she said, a brief smile flitting across her face.

"Where do you want to live in America?"

"Hopefully, in New York, if everything with the new company works out the way Michael plans."

"I grew up there." Paul hoped that this information would relax her a little and make her ask more questions, but Anyi had fallen silent again.

"Where are you from?" Paul asked after a pause.

"From Shenyang. It's north of Beijing, in Manchuria."

"I know."

"Have you been there?"

"Many times." In the early 1990s Paul had been a consultant for a large American brewery that had wanted to buy a state-owned enterprise in Shenyang, and he had traveled to the city often in the course of the negotiations. He remembered clear, deep-blue skies and terribly cold winter days, when the maximum temperature was below minus four degrees Fahrenheit.

Anyi was impressed by the fact that he knew her hometown. She smiled at him again, this time, it seemed to him, for a longer time and more warmly. She sat up, reached for a paper tissue from the bedside table, and blew her nose.

"You speak good Mandarin. Almost like a Chinese person. Amazing."

"Thank you. I've lived in Hong Kong for thirty years and have traveled through China a lot. Do you speak Cantonese?"

She shook her head.

"What brought you from Shenyang to Shenzhen?"

"I thought you were familiar with China," she said, pushing a few strands of hair away from her face.

Paul could clearly detect the disappointment in her voice. She had not expected such a stupid question from him.

"Where are you from?"

"I was born in Germany and grew up in New York."

"And have lived in Hong Kong for thirty years. Why?"

He was not sure if she expected an answer. Why did people leave their families, their home countries, the places where they were born? He had not asked himself these questions for a long time. They had occupied him a great deal before, but he had never found a conclusive answer to them. A desire for adventure and an urge for freedom, he had used to say in answer to similar questions from strangers, receiving understanding nods, and he had marveled anew at how easy it was to stifle any conversation with the right words. How little people really listened or probed. So he had never had to tell them about the loneliness of the outsider or about the distance he had felt lay between him and his parents even as a child, one that was much easier to bear when it could be measured in miles.

Anyi's voice fetched him back to the present. "I was watching Hong Kong TV before you came. A program about Chinese migrant workers was on. Apparently there are now over one hundred and fifty million people in China who have left their villages for the cities. One hundred and fifty million! Can you imagine? Most of them are even younger than I am—sixteen, seventeen, twenty years old. They leave their villages without any idea of what is to become of them in the cities. Why? What are they thinking? I'll tell you why: because they can't stand it at home anymore!" She slid back to the top of the bed, leaned against the wall, took the pink cushion, and held it in front of her stomach.

"But you don't seem to be the daughter of a poor farmer who ran away from the country to the city because of poverty."

"No, I'm not. My parents are minor party officials in a truck factory. I have no idea why they never rose higher in the party. They probably weren't ambitious or ruthless enough. I don't mind. I didn't lack for anything as a child."

She looked past Paul out of the window, looking pensive and doubtful, reluctant to share more childhood memories with this stranger. After a long silence, during which Paul heard only himself and her breathing, she carried on, "I was born in 1982. Compared to the years before that, it was a politically peaceful time. For me, the Gang of Four was a group of boys in the neighborhood, not Mao's widow's gang, if you know what I mean. My parents had a small factory apartment with its own kitchen and toilet, which was a great luxury back then. After I finished school I could have worked in accounts or administration at the factory, but I didn't want to. I wanted to get away, just get away."

She looked him straight in the eye. "Maybe for the same reasons that you could no longer stand being in New York? As long as I can remember, I always wanted to get away. Away from Shenyang. When I was a little girl I stood in front of a world map at school one day and I still remember very clearly understanding in that moment how big the world is. I picked out three cities in China that I wanted to travel to: Beijing, Shanghai, and Shenzhen."

"Why did you go to Shenzhen and not to Beijing or Shanghai?"

"Random happenstance. Someone I knew worked at the front desk in the Century Plaza and wrote to tell me that the city was exciting and that the hotel was still recruiting young women. So I got on a train and came south."

"And your parents?"

"Do you know what my father said to me when he was saying good-bye? 'Anyi, you are doing the right thing. My generation wanted to sacrifice itself for the country and the Revolution, but nothing good came of it. You young people think of yourselves first, and that is good.' It's actually pretty sad, isn't it?"

Paul nodded without saying anything.

She continued. "I worked a couple of months at the hotel reception. Then I applied for a position in the Emperor's Paradise and was successful and got it. The job was pretty well paid and not difficult. You had to like men and naked bodies, and I like both. And you had to be good with your hands. Don't get me wrong, that was not a brothel. We didn't disappear into a back room with the men."

"But into the hotel."

"No, not that either. If at all, it was entirely of our own free will. The Emperor's Paradise had nothing to do with it."

"And where did you meet Michael?"

"He was one of my customers. He came in one day, and I liked him immediately. He was very handsome, very polite, and obliging, and so shy that he didn't even dare to remove the towel. I only had to massage his thighs and he would have an erection, which he found terribly embarrassing. He only spoke a few words of Chinese, and constantly mixed the tones up, but he did try."

She paused, perhaps to give him the chance to ask questions. Or to see if Paul was judging her.

"You can just say it," she continued. "I know what you're thinking. For someone who wants to see the world, Michael came in very handy, right? A kind of plane ticket on two legs. But you're wrong. Even before I met Michael I had been made very decided offers by other men. I could have been the mistress of a construction magnate, a factory owner, a Hong Kong banker, or a senior party cadre in Beijing, and those were only the more interesting options. All of them had much, much more money than the Owens, believe me. But I did not want what they offered. I don't want to be a pretty bird that some rich man keeps in a cage. I could claim that I waited for Michael, but I am not that romantic. The right man came at the right time. I love him and I think he loves me too." The longer she talked and the more serious the conversation grew, the more unsettled he felt by her. He had underestimated her. She was smart. And she possessed the strength and the energy of a woman who knew exactly what she wanted. In that way, she reminded him of his ex-wife, Meredith. Those qualities had been alien to Paul all his life, and made him feel uncomfortable. But they fascinated him too.

What she said about Michael Owen sounded honest. Anyi probably really loved him, which meant that he would be the messenger bearing this terrible news. He had not considered this at all beforehand; without thinking about it, he had factored Anyi in only as a source of information. The thought of having to tell her that Michael had been murdered left him short of breath. He felt pressure against his chest, as though someone had wound a chain around his torso and was pulling it tighter and tighter.

"Are you unwell?" Anyi asked. "Would you like something to drink?"

"Yes. Some water, perhaps."

She got up, went into the kitchen, and came back with a glass of water.

"Would you like to lie down for a while?"

"I'm fine now, thank you," he lied.

She sat down on the bed again, held the pillow like a hot water bottle to her belly, and kept staring at him. He felt uncomfortable under her gaze; he could not fathom it. Was she looking at him with concern or had his sudden attack of weakness awakened her suspicions?

"I've told you so much about myself," she said. "Now I'd like to ask you something."

"Yes, please do."

"What's the matter with you? Is it because of Michael?" Uncertainty lay over her voice like a shadow.

He replied by asking another question. "Have you really no idea where he might be?"

"No."

"Apart from you, does he have friends or acquaintances in Shenzhen?"

"Not that I know of."

"Who could he have quarreled with?"

"What makes you think he quarreled with anyone?"

"Who would benefit from his disappearance?"

"You're asking questions like a policeman."

"What did you do together in Shanghai? Which building site did Michael visit there?"

Paul could see that the brief moment she had trusted him had vanished, that she was unsure of herself again, and tried to conceal it with a brusque manner. "Which new company were you talking about just now?" he asked.

"What do you mean?"

"You said just now that you and Michael wanted to live in New York if everything worked out with the new company."

She said nothing and gave him a piercing look, as if she was seeing him for the first time. "Who are you, really?" she burst out. "Who sent you? You're supposed to be a friend of Michael's and you don't know anything about Lotus Metal?"

"I'm a friend of the Owens'."

"I don't believe you. You're lying."

"You can trust me."

"I don't trust anyone."

"You trusted Michael Owen, I hope."

"I was sure that he held no danger for me. That is worth a great deal. If you call that trust, then yes, I trusted him."

"Then I am sorry for you."

Anyi rolled her eyes toward the ceiling. "No pity, please. Thank you."

"What reason have I given you not to trust me?"

"Since when did I need a reason not to trust someone?"

"If you're naturally suspicious, then no, of course not."

"What nonsense you're talking. Naturally suspicious. There's no such thing. Don't you have children? They are not suspicious. Cautious, maybe, but not suspicious. If they are, they were made so."

"What made you suspicious?"

"That's absolutely none of your business." She got up from the bed, tossed the cushion back against the wall, and walked into the living room.

Paul followed her.

She was standing in the kitchen with her back to him.

"What are you frightened of?"

"Who told you I was frightened?"

"I can see it in your eyes."

She turned around. Paul noticed for the first time the shadows under her eyes: much too large and dark for someone her age. "If you're so clever and can see so much from the eyes of a Chinese person, then you will have to answer your questions yourself." She took a step toward him. "And now I must ask you to leave. I would like to be alone."

Paul suddenly saw the photo of her and Victor Tang before him. Tang had his arm around her and was smiling into the camera. She looked strained in the photo, with her head turned to one side as if she wanted to free herself from his hold.

"How well do you know Victor Tang?"

"Not at all."

"You're lying. I've seen photos on Michael's computer in which Victor Tang has his arm around you."

"I want to be alone. Leave!"

"He's the one you're frightened of."

"Didn't you hear what I said? Please go!" she shouted, slapping the palm of her hand down on the kitchen counter. It was meant to be a decisive gesture, but like every demonstration of strength, it exposed fear and weakness above all. Paul knew that he was right. He saw it in her clenched fists, in her rigid pose, in her eyes.

"Why are you frightened of Victor Tang?" he said slowly and clearly, repeating the question in English.

Silence. She did not look at him, but stared down at the floor.

Paul thought about the dead Michael, about Zhang, about Christine, about the supposed murderer, who had signed a false confession.

"Michael Owen," he suddenly blurted out, "has been murdered. His body is in the basement of the police headquarters. I want to know who murdered him and for that I need your help."

She stared at him. Her narrow eyes widened, and her mouth formed into a silent scream. Her knees buckled, and her hands lost their grip on the kitchen counter. For a split second, Paul thought she would faint. He reached his arms out to catch her if she fell, but then he saw her body stiffen again, saw a person turn to stone before his eyes in just a few seconds. Her face still twitched for a few moments, involuntarily. She bit down on her lower lip, and tears ran down her cheeks. Paul took a step toward her to comfort her.

"Don't touch me," Anyi whispered without looking at him.

Paul thought about Elizabeth Owen and the despair in her face when he had had to tell her that her son had been murdered. He saw Meredith when she saw her son's lifeless body, and he thought about how everyone had their own language in love and in sorrow, in joy and in pain, and that it was a miracle of this life we understood each other at all. Then he had the feeling that with every breath she took, a little more life drained out of Anyi's face; the twitching had stopped and no more tears flowed. Her skin was as white as snow, and she gazed past him.

"I'll answer two questions for you and then you must go, do you understand?" she said in a toneless voice.

"Yes," Paul said quietly.

"What do you want to know?"

"What did you do in Shanghai?" Paul asked without taking any time to think about it.

"We went there often in the last few months. Michael had meetings with Wang Ming, the head of Lotus Metal, but Michael's parents know that. I don't have to tell you that."

"Where will I find Wang Ming?"

"Is that your second question?"

"No." He thought for a moment. "Why are you frightened of Victor Tang?"

"Why am I frightened of Victor Tang?" Anyi repeated, as if she wanted to make sure she had understood the question correctly. "Do you know him at all?"

"No."

She nodded. "Otherwise you certainly wouldn't ask that question."

"That's not an answer."

She said nothing for a while and kept looking past Paul into empty space. Her voice had regained neither color nor expression. "I think anyone who knows him is frightened of Victor Tang."

"Michael Owen too?"

"No. I mean everyone Chinese. Not Michael and his parents. That surprised me at the beginning. Michael seemed so brave, so strong, so confident, just what I imagined an American to be. He wasn't frightened of the police, he wasn't frightened of officials, he didn't get intimidated, even when Tang threatened him. That impressed me. But it gradually became clear to me that he did not understand Tang at all. Michael did not realize what danger he posed. 'The law is on my side, don't worry,' he used to say. Then I knew that he had understood nothing. The law? In China!"

Her voice slowly filled with expression again. She sounded astonished, still surprised at such naïvety. "He tried. You can't accuse him of not trying. He tried to learn Mandarin. He read a couple of books about China and was convinced that America and China were not so dissimilar after all despite all the differences. Sometimes we really fought about that. We're in China here, not in Wisconsin, I told him. And he always said the same thing back. 'Darling, that doesn't matter. In the end we all dream the American dream.' I told him he was wrong, that we would dream the Chinese dream, but he only laughed and said that it was the same as the American dream, just in different colors. He was quite convinced of that."

"Why did Tang threaten him?"

"He kept asking why I was so frightened. I told him, 'Michael, everyone has enough reasons to be frightened, but Chinese people probably have even more reasons.' He didn't understand," she replied.

"Why did Tang threaten him?"

Instead of replying she simply shook her head.

"Does Tang have anything to do with the murder?"

"I don't know. You'll find that out. Or maybe not. I said I would answer two questions and I've done that. Go now. Please!"

"Can't I help you?"

"I wish you could."

"Perhaps I can—"

"No," she interrupted him. "You can't do anything for me now except leave me alone." She turned away and walked toward the door.

Paul followed her. He had no doubt that she knew more than she was prepared to say, but it was also clear that he would not find out more from her right now. He had to call Zhang as soon as he had left Diamond Villas and ask him to come over. With his experience he would have more success; he would get her to talk.

Anyi opened the door. "Don't worry about me," she said in parting, looking him in the face as she said this.

Had he ever seen a face as lonely and despairing as this one?

XXI

Is there a life without lies? A life not permeated by falsehoods? Zhang was not thinking of the small untruths that make everyday life easier. Nor of the made-up excuses for arriving late or the tales concocted to cover up forgetting a birthday or another act of carelessness. He was thinking about a big secret that he, and perhaps everyone, carried around. What was it for other people? The misappropriation of inheritance funds? An illegitimate child whom the wife knew nothing about? The forbidden love for a close relative? The betrayal of a friend or a business partner? He wondered if Mei lived with a big secret. Was she perhaps secretly in love with another man? Had she had an affair that Zhang knew nothing about? He could not imagine so, but could a person ever be certain? Wasn't every life based in some way on a lie, a fiction, a pretense? Could a person conceal it until his deathbed, or did it force its way out of its hiding place at some point? What will Mei and, later, his son say; how will Paul react, when they find out what he had kept silent about for over thirty years? Zhang wondered. Will they see everything that he has done and said in another light? Will they turn away or will they be able to forgive?

Sitting on the express ferry from Hong Kong to Shenzhen, he wondered if he had a choice in the matter. He probably had no choice back then, back when hysteria had ruled the whole country and the sixteen-year-old Zhang had longed for respect and recognition; he had wanted to belong too badly. Aside from that, he had not met anyone in his life so far who had dared to question Mao Zedong and his commands, the pervasive power of the Communist Party and the official propaganda, or who had even prompted Zhang to at least think about it. He had been a blind man who had believed he could see.

But the Cultural Revolution lasted for ten years. By 1976 he had choices, like everyone who had been part of the madness. From then on, every day had been a choice, every day Zhang had decided anew to stay silent instead of telling the truth and asking for forgiveness. He bore the responsibility for that, and, if he were honest with himself, he could not pin the blame for his silence on society or on any political party, political chief, or great chairman. He had learned that from Buddha. We are the masters of our actions, we create our own Karma. It is *our* life. This late revelation, a revolutionary one for a Chinese person of his age, had been a liberation, but like every liberation, it brought uncertainty and many new questions with it.

Zhang was so tortured by his thoughts that he felt nauseous, and he had to go up on deck.

As the ferry zoomed toward the harbor at high speed, the warm air ruffled his hair, and the water, whipped up by the many vessels, looked like a bathtub in which children were splashing around. The waves slapped against the side of the ferry in quick succession, and some of them raised the ship high up in the air, only to let it dip again immediately. The constant up and down motion only made Zhang feel more sick. He leaned against the railing and tried to meditate, but retched loudly twice instead, feeling his stomach in revolt as the fried noodles and wonton soup he had eaten not long before rose like a wave and burst out of him. Part of it landed in the water and the wind spread the other part on his pants and shoes in equal proportion. Stomach acid burned in his throat and he wished he could crawl off somewhere to hide and find protection from what was awaiting him in Shenzhen.

He shuddered at the thought. Interrogating Anyi.

She was hiding something and was frightened of Tang, Paul had said.

Zhang thought about his own past with Tang. One lie always led to another, and the second to a third until a web of untruths, attitudes, distortions, false assertions, and excuses was created. Was it ever possible for it to stop at one lie?

He was not sure. He knew only that *he* would no longer be running away, that his lie had caught up with him, just as one day the lies would catch up with Tang and with the whole country.

––––––––

Zhang was one of the last to disembark. When he saw the border guards, the sight of a uniform made him nervous again for the first time in years. Were they already looking for him? Would they take him off to some side room on a pretext, take his police ID from him, and get in touch with the homicide division?

Nonsense! Luo thought he was at home on the couch resting his damaged knee. Since yesterday, Zhang had not done anything that would arouse suspicion. But now he was about to cross a line and after that there would be no turning back, he knew that.

Until now he had simply withdrawn from the system. Despite several invitations he had not joined the Communist Party again and was not on any committees or commissions. That was possible in the China of today without being immediately branded a counterrevolutionary. His colleagues did not understand him; they found him eccentric but harmless. Now, he was setting himself against the system, acting in opposition for the first time in his life, and that was dangerous, just as it had been before. It was only a matter of time, of hours or a few days at most, before his investigating encroached on the interests of other people, influential people who would know how to defend themselves. Apart from Paul, Zhang was on his own.

The young border official guessed nothing of these thoughts. He glanced at the passport, the Hong Kong visa, and the computer, and waved Zhang through.

He took a taxi from the ferry terminal to a café near Diamond Villas, where Paul was waiting for him.

"You look a mess! Were you sick?" Paul blurted out when he saw his friend.

"The crossing was rough. I was a little seasick. It's not so bad," Zhang replied. "I'll just go to the restroom and clean my shoes and trousers."

They found the best taxi they could—a shiny new black VW Passat with tinted windows—and traveled the short distance to Diamond Villas. They passed the security guard, who greeted them with a snappy military salute, and got the car to drop them off in front of Sapphire.

"I may ask you to leave after a while," Zhang said as they walked through the parking lot.

"What do you plan to do?" Paul asked in astonishment. "Do you want to intimidate her?"

"No, but I have to see if she begins to trust me. If I succeed in making her do that, it may be better for the two of us to be on our own for a while."

Paul nodded.

They stood in front of the iron grille gate that separated the garage from the elevator and looked at each other without exchanging a word. Zhang gave his friend a sign, and Paul pressed the button for the penthouse.

They waited and buzzed again, but there was no response.

"Maybe she's asleep? She was pretty exhausted when I left," Paul said.

Zhang pressed his lips together as he thought, passing both his hands through his hair. "I hope nothing's happened to her. She told you more than can be good for her. We have to get into the apartment."

They went back to the security guard at the entrance and asked for the building manager.

The building manager lived in the basement of Sapphire; he sized up the two strangers with a skeptical look. Of course he had a key, but he could only open the door to an apartment if he had specific instructions from management to do so in an emergency or if the owner of the apartment was present. Even Zhang's police ID did not impress him at first. Only when he read the words "homicide division" did he start, fetch the key, and take them up to the top floor.

After ringing the bell and getting no reply again, the building manager opened the door. Zhang gestured with his head to indicate that they wanted to be left alone now. The building manager reluctantly took the elevator back down to the basement.

"Anyi?" Paul called out hesitantly.

No reply.

"Anyi," he repeated in a louder voice.

Silence.

Zhang was the first to enter the apartment carefully. The curtains in the living room were closed and it took a moment for their eyes to get used to the half darkness. They listened and flinched. Both of them had the feeling that they had heard a sound from the bedroom.

"Hello, is anyone home?" Zhang called out. His voice sounded more hesitant than a police detective's ought to, he thought.

No reply.

They looked around the living room. The glass of water Paul had drunk from was still on the table, as were the plastic flowers. Next to them lay a pile of magazines.

"Anyi," Paul said again, loudly. But he no longer expected a reply.

Zhang shook his head and began walking toward the bedroom. The door was slightly ajar. He stopped, held his breath, and pricked his ears to try to make out if someone was breathing quietly in the room before he slowly pushed the door open.

The bed was covered with shoes, tops, underwear, dresses, and skirts, and the closet doors were open. On one side were piles of men's clothes; the shelves on the other side were almost empty.

Paul had followed Zhang in. "She's gone," he whispered, as if to himself.

"And not to run errands," the detective said. "This looks like she's run away."

They searched the flat but did not find anything suspicious.

"What do we do now?" Paul asked.

"No idea," Zhang replied, letting himself flop onto the couch with exhaustion. "Hey, Paul, what exactly does 'I am so sorry' in English mean?"

"Please excuse me. Or, my mistake, pardon. Forgive me. Why are you asking?"

"Richard Owen stammered those words when he was identifying the body of his dead son. Could that have some meaning?"

Paul thought for a moment. "I don't think so."

Zhang leaned back, crossed his arms behind his head, and stared at the ceiling. After a while he asked, "What do you think about meeting Elizabeth Owen again?"

Paul paced up and down in the living room. Finally he said, "I'd be happy to, but I'm afraid she won't be able to help us any further. Remember how little she knew when I rang her yesterday."

"That's true. But now at least we have two names, maybe we can do something with them. Apart from that, I want to know what the father and the son had their big fight about. She should at least be able to tell us that."

———

Elizabeth Owen picked up the phone on the second ring, as if she had been waiting for his call. She was in the hotel resting, and her husband was at the US consulate seeing to the paperwork. She was happy to speak with Paul at any time. They agreed to meet two hours later in the bar of the InterContinental.

———

On the way back to Hong Kong, Paul told Zhang again about his conversation with Anyi, this time in detail.

Zhang's cell phone rang while Paul was talking. He looked on the display screen and got a shock. It was Luo, the head of the homicide division.

"Zhang, how are you?"

"Thank you for calling, but I'm afraid I'm not well yet. Rather the opposite, in fact."

"Where are you? It's so noisy in the background. I hope that's not the brothel beneath you making such a racket."

"No, I'm on the ferry to Hong Kong," Zhang replied, so nervous he was unable to think of an excuse.

"What are you going there for?" Luo asked, astonished, in a tone of voice that did not sound at all sympathetic.

"I-I'm on my way to see a specialist. My knee is quite swollen and is terribly painful. My friend Paul has booked me a last-minute appointment with an orthopedic specialist."

Luo said nothing for a few seconds, as though he was trying to decide if this was another thing to be suspicious about. "I'm only calling to tell you that the trial of Owen's murderer has been brought forward. The Americans pushed for it. It's taking place the day after tomorrow. Since we have a confession, it won't take longer than a day. I thought you'd like to know about it."

"Of course."

"Maybe you can tell the parents about it through your friend. We're informing them via official communication channels, but that takes a bit of time."

"I'll do that."

What did his boss want from him? Did he suspect him of not sticking to the official line? Or did he really only mean to ask him to tell the Owens about the trial?

"It will be a relief for the parents, won't it?"

"Of course, Luo, of course." His boss was suddenly talkative, which Zhang found odd. He wondered how they had gotten the factory worker to put his signature to a made-up confession. What had they threatened him with? The arrest of his wife, and his child ending up in an orphanage? The arrest of his relations in Sichuan or their expulsion from the village? They had probably promised him at the same time that he would be spared the death sentence, and that his family would be given a generous allowance during his time in prison. That would be an attractive offer for the poor fellow; if he had even the least experience with the police and the courts, he would know that there was no alternative for him.

"Most bereaved people in these situations only consider the case closed when the murderer has not only been found, but been judged and sentenced by a court, yes?"

"Yes, you're right," Zhang replied obediently.

"When will you be back at work?"

"In a few days, I hope." He heard Luo's heavy-smoker's breathing on the other end—he still seemed to have something on his mind.

"Zhang, just think. He who seeks revenge should not forget to dig two graves."

Zhang tried to think of a saying that defined the difference between justice and revenge, but nothing occurred to him. "I know. How does the saying go? Of the thirty-six possibilities open to one, flight is always the best option."

"Who said that?"

"Sun Tzu in *The Art of War*, I think."

"You are right. Don't forget it," Luo said, hanging up.

What made Luo think that he was trying to take revenge? Did he know something about Tang's and Zhang's past? Impossible. Luo probably thought that revenge was the only possible motive for him; why else would a policeman look for a murderer when a confession was already at hand?

Paul had followed the conversation with interest.

"Tell me, does Mei actually know where you are and what you are doing?" he blurted out.

"Not exactly," Zhang replied evasively.

"What does that mean?"

"I told her the same thing I told Luo, that I'm with you because you booked an appointment with a knee specialist."

"Why don't you tell her what you are really doing?"

Zhang hesitated before replying. Yes, why didn't he? Because there was a time for every truth to be told and the right time for him to tell this truth had long passed? Because he loved his wife immeasurably and did not want to inflict his pain on her? Because she would be in danger if she knew? Because he was a pathetic coward?

"I didn't tell her anything because it would only worry her," Zhang said in a subdued tone.

"And because she would have tried to stop you?"

Of course she would have done that, Zhang thought. By every means possible. He nodded instead of saying anything.

"That is . . ." Paul searched for the right words. He wanted to voice an objection, but at the same time not to make any terrible accusations.

Zhang interrupted him. "I know what you want to say, and you're right. But there was no other way. If I had told her anything I would not be here right now. I had no choice."

They fell silent and looked at the sea and the container ships in the roadstead being unloaded by smaller vessels.

"What should I tell Mrs. Owen?" Paul asked.

"Everything we know. That her son's murderer is still at large. That an innocent man is in prison. That he will be sentenced to death tomorrow and executed soon after. If Elizabeth Owen does not help us once she hears us out, then she or her husband have something to do with the murder."

Paul stared at him incredulously, as if to check that Zhang really meant what he said.

"What are you making that face for? Do you think that's out of the question?"

After a long silence Paul said, "I don't know. I don't even want to imagine such a thing."

———

When he walked into the bar of the InterContinental about two hours later, Elizabeth Owen was already waiting for him.

XXII

The dry martini was good, very good, in fact, even better than at the Drake in Chicago, where she normally treated herself to one at the end of a long shopping trip on Michigan Avenue. The martini there was sometimes too warm and a little watery; this one here was blissfully cold and strong, and it did not take long to take effect on her. After the second sip, Elizabeth already felt a warm shudder of well-being course through her whole body. Much better than the tranquilizers that she had been taking for days. They made her terribly tired, every movement was an effort, sometimes even speaking was too much. What had the doctors been thinking? If Richard had not insisted on them she would have stopped taking the medication yesterday. This morning she had pretended to swallow the pills to please him, but flushed them down the toilet later.

The martini worked wonders, giving her an inappropriate but nevertheless wonderful feeling of lightness. It soothed her soul without numbing her; on the contrary, she felt wide-awake after half a glass. She was able to be impressed by the view of Hong Kong's skyline from the large windows, with the colorful lights reflected in the water of the harbor. When she scrunched her eyes up a bit, it looked like a display of fireworks that went on and on. This was a fascinating view, she conceded to herself, even if she couldn't otherwise stand the city. She liked it as little as Shenzhen, Shanghai, and Beijing and all the other places she had been to in the past few years. She did not understand what her son had found so wonderful about this country. Nowhere did Elizabeth Owen see what her son had rhapsodized about so passionately: the magic of thousands of years of ancient history, the supposed intelligence of the people, their optimism, or their creativity, which was said to be so similar to the American mentality. Everywhere she went she saw dirt and rubbish. She saw far too many people who, whenever she came into contact with them, pushed and shoved, who burped and farted while eating, who had bad breath and who dared to smile at her despite their terrible teeth. She heard a language in which not a sound was familiar to her. To her, Chinese sounded like a series of strange, often sinister-sounding noises. Sometimes the people made themselves understood by purring, piping, and almost singing, only to change to a hard, brusque tone the next moment, hissing, growling, and shouting, so that every sentence sounded like a dangerous threat or an order that brooked no resistance. It hurt her ears.

At some point she had decided to simply suffer through the trips to Asia patiently, the price for seeing her son on a regular basis. The country itself meant nothing to her; the business in China existed to make the company flourish and ensure that there was enough money in the bank account and that they would not, as Richard had once feared, go bankrupt and have to compromise their retirement.

Now Michael had paid for his enthusiasm and his trust with his life, battered to death by a totally insignificant worker who probably couldn't even read and write. Who could ever understand this?

From afar, she saw Paul Leibovitz enter the bar and look around for her. He was a handsome man with a striking face and his curly white hair suited him. The look in his eyes was a little too weighed down, but this melancholic air did give him a certain aura, something mysterious. She raised her right arm and waved at him to come over.

"Paul, here!" she called, making the other hotel guests around her pause their conversations for just a moment. That had been too loud. Much too loud.

She had to be careful. The martini. One too many and friends would turn into enemies.

Elizabeth Owen stood up and greeted Paul, going through the motions of an embrace and a kiss on each cheek.

"I have to talk to you about something," Paul said. His voice was almost as melancholic as his eyes. "There've been a few developments."

"I know. The court case against Michael's murderer has been pushed forward. It starts the day after tomorrow," she said, pleased at the surprise on his face.

"How do you know that?"

"From Mr. Tang. He rang this afternoon."

"Did he also tell you that the man who will stand before the court is not the murderer?"

She must have heard wrongly. "Can you please repeat what you said?"

"The man who will be sentenced to death on Friday is innocent."

"Innocent?" she repeated, as though he was speaking a foreign language she was not fluent in. "How do you know that?"

"My friend Zhang and I have done a little independent investigation. The man has a cast-iron alibi."

"I thought he signed a confession."

"He did. But he was probably forced to do so. That is not unusual. It happens every day in China."

"You really mean that?"

"Yes."

"I don't understand. I mean, if the man can prove his innocence, why is he still in prison?" Even she recognized how naïve this sounded but right then she could think of nothing else to say.

"We think it's because the real murderer is being protected." Paul said nothing more for a moment. He clearly wanted to give her time to process the news, but he could have kept silent until sunrise and it would not have helped her. She merely looked at him questioningly.

"Your son must have been involved in some kind of situation and made powerful enemies. Do you know who or what they could be?"

Elizabeth Owen simply could not focus. Michael had had enemies? Her baby, her little Michael? Out of the question. In America he had only had friends. In America, they had called him the gentle giant from high school through to college; he had gotten along with everyone.

"No, my son had no enemies."

"Or someone who he had fought bitterly with, who might have felt threatened?"

She shook her head. "His father, at most," she blurted out with a short, almost hysterical laugh that she choked down immediately.

"What did you say?"

"I didn't mean that seriously," she replied, when she had calmed down. "But the two of them fought almost constantly."

"Over what?"

"Over everything. My husband was terribly jealous of our son, he always was. I think from the day of his birth. Don't ask me why. I have no idea. How can a grown man be jealous of a baby? But no matter how much they fought, Richard always loved Michael, of course. He was his son, after all. He never wanted to harm him." The rest, thought Elizabeth Owen, was none of Paul's business. The tears. The threats. The sleepless nights when she heard the shouting of the two men in her life echo through the house.

"Did they also argue over the business?"

"As I said before, over everything, but I kept out of the discussions about the company and our investment in China. In our family, business is for the menfolk, if you know what I mean."

"Does the name Wang Ming mean anything to you?"

"No, I've never heard it."

"Lotus Metal?"

"No."

"Did you know that your son often traveled to Shanghai?"

"Did he?"

"Can you tell me why?"

"No, I have no idea why. My husband may know more. He's on his way back to the hotel."

"Did you know that Michael had an apartment in Shenzhen?"

Did you know, did you know . . . She wished he would stop these did-you-knows. *No.* No, she did not know. She would have liked to shout it out loud, so loud that the cocktail and champagne glasses shattered in the hands of all the well-groomed people in this hotel lounge. What was he telling her? Michael had had a second apartment in China. He had had a Chinese lover. Who he had wanted to move to New York with. Which Michael was this Leibovitz man talking about?

Was it possible that she knew so little about her son? After nearly thirty years? Why had he kept all this from her? Why did he not trust his mother? Had he been afraid that she would immediately tell Richard everything? She had never done that. She had been loyal to him, always, all through the years and the endless fights between father and son. She had been on his side, even if she had not always been able to show it. She would not have betrayed him. Not this time.

"I expect my husband any moment. He will certainly be able to answer some of your questions," she said, seeing Richard at the reception desk just then. He looked like a stranger, face flushed red, damp, tousled hair, and light-blue shirt covered with dark wet patches.

Richard Owen sat down with them reluctantly. Elizabeth could sense that her husband was not at all keen to have a conversation with Paul.

"Mr. Leibovitz, please could you repeat for my husband everything you have just told me?" She wanted to see how Richard reacted.

Paul cleared his throat and took a deep breath. "I've come to tell you that the man who will stand before the court charged with murdering your son is innocent."

Richard Owen did what he always did when he was surprised by bad news: his head jerked a few times and his mouth fell open. It looked like he could no longer control his body movements.

"Mr. Tang told me that the murderer had signed a confession."

"That's right. But that was a confession under duress."

Elizabeth Owen saw how her husband was seething. She saw how he struggled, how he fought not to lose control of himself. And she saw exactly how, after a few seconds that must have seemed endless to him, he calmed down and his features relaxed a little, as though he knew, after a moment of being at a complete loss, exactly what he had to do.

"I'm sorry, but I don't know what you mean. After a big investigation, the police in Shenzhen arrested a man who confessed to the crime. As far as I know, there are even eyewitnesses, who saw the fight with my son. And you say the confession is not genuine? The man could be sentenced to death for it. Why should he sign a false confession?"

"We think he was probably forced to."

"Who exactly is 'we'?"

"My friend Zhang and I."

"The two of you, conducting your investigation, wish to call the work of the entire homicide squad into question? Who asked you to look further into this case in the first place?"

"No one. Zhang discovered a few inconsistencies in the confession that he followed up on. There's no doubt the accused has an alibi: he was ill in bed that day. And there are no reliable eyewitnesses for the crime."

"I suggest we wait for the court case. In America the courts are there to establish whether the accused is innocent or guilty. As far as I understand, it's no different in China."

Richard Owen started to get up. For him, the discussion was over.

"May I ask you nonetheless to answer a few questions?"

"You may, but I will not answer," he said, and stood up.

"Then answer *my* questions." Elizabeth Owen had followed the conversation intently. She felt a rising rage inside her as she saw Richard dodge Paul Leibovitz's questions. Her body stiffened, as it always did when she got angry.

She took a deep breath. The soothing, relaxed feeling the alcohol had given her was completely gone. But her mind was clear and focused: Her husband was hiding something, and she wanted to know what and why.

Richard Owen looked at his wife, completely confused. This force, this sharpness in her tone, and in front of a stranger too. The way she gazed at him. He did not want a scene, not here in the lounge, so he sat down again.

"Did you know that Michael had an apartment and a lover in Shenzhen?"

"No."

He was lying. She could tell, but she did not want to stop now. They would discuss that later.

"Who is Wang Ming?" she asked as calmly as she could.

"The name means nothing to me."

"What is Lotus Metal?"

Richard Owen gave a deep sigh before he replied. "That was a crazy idea of Michael's. Our business was going so well he wanted to set up a second joint venture with a company from Shanghai. It was to be called Lotus Metal. I didn't think it was a good idea, and nothing came of it."

"Did you fight about that two weeks ago?"

"Darling, I don't know if this is the right time to . . ."

"Did you fight about it?" she insisted.

"Yes."

"What does Tang have to do with it?"

"With Lotus Metal? Nothing. I . . ." The ring of his cell phone interrupted him.

"Richard Owen speaking. Victor, what a coincidence. I'm sitting here in the hotel with Elizabeth and our friend Paul Leibovitz and we've just been talking about you."

Richard Owen nodded a few times while he listened to the long reply, his gaze moving from his wife to Paul and back several times.

"Yes, that's right. You're right. It's a good idea, thanks. I'll ask them now and let you know right after."

He ended the conversation with a tap on his phone.

"That was Victor Tang. He's invited us to dinner at his house tomorrow evening. He'll send a car. He would be very pleased if you, Mr. Leibovitz, would come with us. Would you be fine with that? Is that all right with you, Elizabeth?"

She nodded. A dinner with Victor Tang, why not? Her husband wasn't sharing everything he knew, she could tell. The only other person she could think of who would know about Michael's secret life in China was Tang.

Maybe it was all her own fault, Elizabeth thought. Maybe this was just the end of something that had started much earlier. She was wondering when exactly she had stopped asking questions. It must have been after the wedding, when her father-in-law told her in plain words that in the Owen family women were highly regarded but not involved in anything that concerned the company—and the company, Elizabeth had to learn soon after, was what the family was all about. It was not a time to challenge the orders of an old patriarch, not in Wisconsin, anyway, and she did what was expected of her. Gave birth to a son. Raised him. Hosted guests, entertained business partners, organized charity events for Michael's schools and the hospital. Enjoyed, at least to a certain extent, the life and privileges of being the wife of the local magnate. Somewhere along the way, she thought, one of her greatest strengths got lost, her inquisitive, curious mind.

She should have raised questions. She should have challenged her husband and her son. She should have gotten involved in their arguments early on, trying to mediate between them. It was too late now. Nothing would bring Michael back, but she wanted to know the truth. Who killed him and why? She owed it to her son—and to herself—to find out. Her sense of guilt demanded that much. She *had* to talk to Victor Tang.

XXIII

The second martini after the Owens had left had been one too many. He had emptied the glass in two long gulps and could still feel the clear, cold taste of the gin in his mouth. He would have liked nothing better than to spit it out in a high arc into the water of the harbor beneath. He took the few steps down to the ferry stop, bought a ticket, and walked down the heavily juddering and squeaking bridge onto the 9:30 PM ferry.

It was not that he felt unwell, quite the opposite, in fact. He felt the pleasant and unfounded happiness that alcohol can conjure up. But he knew this feeling too well to trust it. He knew how quickly it could turn to an equally unfounded low mood with him. He had to concentrate now. He wanted to think about the conversation with the Owens and Tang's invitation, and he needed a clear head for that, not an artificially stimulated or depressed mood. How did Tang know about the signed confession? He must have a very good contact in the upper ranks of the police. The ferry sounded its muffled horn three times and started reversing. After making a labored turn, she finally set off into the night. Paul could tell exactly when the captain turned the engine up to full speed ahead. He enjoyed the familiarity of this moment. If only he were going to see Christine, instead of Zhang who was waiting for him in Yung Shue Wan. He would visit her in her office tomorrow on his way to see the Owens.

He wanted to take her in his arms, touch her, and bury his head in her neck, if only for a few seconds.

The green and white pier on Yung Shue Wan shone brightly in the darkness and was almost deserted. Hardly anyone wanted to take the ferry back to Hong Kong at such a late hour. Zhang was leaning against the railing, and it looked like his eyes were closed. Paul was a little shocked when he saw him. He looked tired, exhausted, and even smaller than usual, with his shoulders drooping weakly and his head slightly tucked in as though anticipating some calamity. Paul felt that his friend had visibly grown older in the last few days.

Only the joy and relief reflected in his friend's eyes when he saw him gave Paul comfort.

They walked away from the pier, past the Man Lai Wah Hotel, the post office, and the Island Bar, to Sampan. The waiter greeted them with a brief nod and led them to a table right by the water. Paul ordered some fried noodles, a sweet and sour soup, some bok choy vegetables, chicken with cashew nuts and peppers, and told Zhang about the last few hours.

Zhang listened in silence.

"I thought about the conversation I had with the Owens the whole time I was on the ferry," Paul said at the end, "and there are a few things I don't understand. Why did Richard Owen not want to answer my questions? Why was Elizabeth not just a grieving mom but so angry at her husband? And most of all, what is Tang up to? Why is he inviting me to dinner?"

"I suspect he's heard about our investigating and wants to find out what we know," Zhang said.

"But from whom?"

Zhang thought for a moment. "I can only guess Anyi," he said at last. "They know each other, and who knows how close they are?"

"I can't imagine that. She's frightened of him. You didn't see her face when she was talking about him."

"If Tang has something to do with the murder, and Anyi knows something, the safest place for her to be is near him."

"Why do you think that?"

"That would show him that she's changed sides, that he can trust her. A sign of her submissiveness. Like an animal that rolls over on its back when it realizes that it has lost a fight. It hopes that the opponent will show mercy."

Paul shook his head decidedly. "I didn't get that impression from her. She's not the type who gives in. I think it's more likely that she's in hiding somewhere."

"In hiding? From Tang? Impossible. Sooner or later he will find her and treat her like an enemy and she . . ." Zhang did not finish his sentence.

"And she?"

"And she will not survive."

"What do you mean?"

Zhang cocked his head and looked at him as if he wondered if Paul was being serious. "She would disappear without a trace. And no one would ever hear anything of her again."

"Aren't you exaggerating?"

"Paul. You don't know who we're dealing with. You have no idea," Zhang said loudly and unusually insistently. "You don't know about people like this."

Paul watched his friend sitting bent low over the fried noodles as he pushed his plate to one side and stared at him helplessly. Where had the pleasure they felt in meeting again gone? Paul thought he could see a flicker of it in his eyes.

"Do you know Tang?"

"You asked me this question once already, two days ago," Zhang replied, still worked up.

"Yes, but you never answered it." Why was he being so testy? "And you don't have to reply now either," Paul added in a conciliatory tone. "I know that you would never keep anything from me. It's just . . ." He searched for the right words. "I'm not used to seeing you so upset. I'm worried about you."

Zhang looked away. He stared in silence at the half-empty plate of bok choy, the bowl of soup, the chicken that they had not touched yet. "Yes," he said after a long pause. "I know him."

"How?"

"From Sichuan. We were in the same work brigade in a village in the mountains during the Cultural Revolution."

"And?"

Zhang lifted his head and looked at him once more, but his expression was immeasurably tired and sad.

"And nothing," he said at last. "It was not a happy time."

"Why didn't you say so before?" Paul was amazed at the relief in his own voice.

"You know how I dislike talking about it," Zhang replied. "I don't enjoy remembering those years. I'm sorry."

"At least now I understand why you're always so unnerved whenever Tang is mentioned."

"There's something else you ought to know," Zhang said after he had calmed himself a little. "We're not just dealing with a very powerful person, we're also flouting one of the most important rules in our culture."

"What do you mean?"

"We haven't formed any alliances. We are alone, you and I. Only crazy people dare to challenge the authorities in China without building a network before that."

"Who should we have tried to build a network with?"

"No idea, but it's too late now anyway. It's certain that Tang has not only friends but also opponents and enemies in the party, in the administration, and among the rich people in the city. You know how it is in China nowadays: There are different factions and interests that fight each other. They fight about money and power, from the politburo to the smallest party cell. I've seen these power struggles for years in the police. I have no idea who Tang's opponents could be and where they are. In Shenzhen? In Sichuan? In Beijing? I'm convinced they exist and that, if we find enough incriminatory leads, evidence, or witnesses, they are our only chance."

They ate their sweet-and-sour soup in silence.

After a while, Zhang asked, "Did you hesitate before you accepted Tang's invitation?"

"No. Why should I?"

"Out of fear. The dinner could be a trap."

Paul was disconcerted. Until then, he had not thought for a moment that his personal safety could be compromised. He had seen himself as an outsider until now, as someone who just happened to be able to help a stranger, and someone who was standing by his friend, not as an interested party or an accessory and certainly not an active party whom someone could feel threatened by. "I hadn't thought about that at all. Do you think that's possible?"

"It's not likely, but it's not out of the question."

What made Zhang think that there might be a trap? Paul had traveled through China for almost thirty years now and he had never felt threatened or worried about his own safety. The very idea of it was so unpleasant that he did not consider it for long. "No. I'm just interested in seeing what will happen, and what Tang wants from me. But I don't feel frightened. Not a bit."

Paul called for the check and paid.

They did not speak on the way home to Tai Ping. It seemed to Paul that each man was deep in his own thoughts. Zhang took a deep breath several times and seemed to be about to say something, but nothing came out.

———

Paul lay under the mosquito net and concentrated all his attention on the silence. He had turned off the fan and opened the windows wide. He thought about the nighttime ferry ride and the short walk from the ferry point to the village; he thought about his walks on the Lo So Shing Beach and the sounds from his garden at night; the voices of the night, the smell of the sea, and the humidity of the air, which had him sweating even while having breakfast on the terrace in the morning. Without him really realizing it, he had grown fond of Lamma in the last three years. He was living a life that Justin knew nothing of, had never had the least idea of, and the longer he thought about it, the more it hurt him. He wished there were a way his son could be part of this. Paul decided to write him a letter—no, not just one, several, in which he would describe his life here in detail. *Letters to Justin.* It was a strange idea, one that probably nobody would understand, but it comforted him. So much so that he finally fell asleep.

———

It was late morning by the time Paul woke. He heard Zhang's voice in the living room. Did they have a visitor?

Paul got up, knotted the mosquito net together, and had a shower. Even the cold water was too warm in this season, much too warm. He went downstairs and saw Zhang sitting at the long dining table in front of Paul's open laptop, with a ballpoint pen in one hand and the phone in the other. Paul went into the kitchen, made himself a pot of jasmine tea, peeled a mango, and sat down on the terrace. Zhang soon came out to join him.

"Good morning. How did you sleep?" Zhang wanted to know.

"Not bad. Did you lie awake long?"

"Yes. The lack of noise drives me crazy. I can't sleep in this silence. I used the time to surf the Internet instead, to see if I could find anything on Lotus Metal."

"And?"

"There's not much, not on Google China or Baidu. But a friend who works in the Department of Commerce was able to help. Lotus Metal is a registered company that is owned by the Ministry of State Security. It has a factory in Shenyang and is one of the suppliers to a German car manufacturer that operates a plant there. Lotus Metal seems to have very ambitious expansion plans. A big factory near Shanghai is under construction and a second one is in the pipeline. Wang Ming is its CEO. I found a brief interview he gave to the *China Economic Daily* a couple of months ago on their website. Their questions were quite critical; they asked him why he was investing so much money when the Chinese car industry was clearly suffering from overcapacity. As a justification for the construction of the new factory, he mentioned a future joint venture partner who he was not allowed to name yet, but who had a great deal of experience in metal processing and had excellent contacts with big American firms. Some of the agreements had already been signed and the rest were practically on the table ready for signature.

"Do you believe that?" Paul asked. "If I remember correctly, Richard Owen claimed that the name Wang Ming meant nothing to him and that Lotus Metal was a crazy idea of Michael's that nothing ever came of."

"Maybe Mr. Owen is lying. Or maybe the negotiations didn't get very far or they broke down, and Wang Ming only mentioned them in the interview as a public justification for his investment, or to intimidate his competitors."

"That wouldn't surprise me."

"I'll have more information from Beijing by this evening. My friend knows one of the top officials at the Ministry of State Security, who is responsible for industry and commerce. He will probably know the name of the joint venture partner and whether an agreement has been signed yet or not."

"I didn't know that the Ministry of State Security had anything to do with industry," Paul said, surprised.

"It has a great deal to do with it. All unofficially, of course, but they boost their income with their dealings. Just like the army does."

"Do you think Victor Tang knew about Lotus Metal?"

"I'm assuming he did. I can't imagine Michael Owen would have been able to keep something like that from him. That would also explain the disagreement between Tang and him."

"But why should Michael Owen set up a second company that would compete with another firm in the group? Without Tang? From what we know Cathay Metal is a gold mine."

"Maybe. But maybe the figures weren't quite right. Tang might have gone behind his back, or at least Michael must have believed he had been betrayed. Or Lotus Metal simply made him a better offer. You know how little contracts count for among us. We'll have to find out, and fast. If Michael Owen wanted to change partners, that would be our potential motive for a murder."

Paul pushed his hair away from his face; his hair, nearly white now, had grown so long that he could almost have tied it back in a short ponytail. What Zhang was saying sounded strangely, almost unnervingly, familiar. Paul thought about his travels through almost all the Chinese provinces in the past three decades. Hubei, Shandong, Fujian, Gansu, Liaoning. Regardless of which part of the country he had been to, his experiences had often been similar. He thought about the American and European companies he had advised about their investments, the negotiations he had attended and translated, and, in a few cases, even led. There the American managers sat, opposite their Chinese business partners, and neither side could even pronounce each other's names correctly. He had always marveled at how people who knew so little about each other managed to do business together. One side saw a simply inexhaustibly large market for its products and the other side thought it had found a kind of golden goose in a suit and tie, a never-ending source of gold for its companies. These illusions popped like soap bubbles, followed quickly by broken contracts, embezzlements, and the complete loss of trust and respect. What Zhang had just described was more than plausible; it was a realistic scenario. The only thing Paul had never heard of was a disagreement between Chinese and foreign business partners ending in a murder.

"We don't have much time," Zhang said. "The supposed murderer's trial starts in two days. You have to try to find out something from Tang and Richard Owen, and, in the process, give as little away as possible about what we've discovered. Tang must not know that I'm involved or that we have spoken to the prisoner's wife. As she is the alibi, she would certainly be in danger. Tang would not take long to find out where she is hiding."

Paul remembered that he had blithely mentioned the alibi to the Owens; he hoped they would keep that to themselves.

"He invited you to dinner," Zhang continued, "so he wants something from you. He will try to interrogate you. You must wait, be patient, and at some point you will be able to ask questions."

"By the way, Mr. Tang, your old friend Wang Ming asked me to send you his regards."

"Something like that. But I'm sure you'll be able to do it more elegantly than that."

At last, his friend was smiling again.

"Should I come back to Lamma after the dinner or should we meet somewhere in Shenzhen?"

"Lamma is safer."

"The dinner starts at seven in the evening and the last ferry leaves at half past midnight. I should be able to catch that."

Paul watched a gray-green rat snake, slithering through the grass at the other end of the garden. It was long and thick and harmless. "Are you afraid of snakes?"

"No," Zhang replied. He had also noticed the snake, and he sat down on one of the chairs on the terrace as if to add emphasis to his reply.

Paul got up, fetched him a cup, and poured him some tea.

Shortly after, Christine rang and asked Paul if he could come slightly earlier. She had not been able to get anyone to cover for her and was only free between one and two. Paul looked at the clock. If he hurried, he could still catch the express ferry at 12:15 PM. He quickly changed his clothes and tried to say good-bye to Zhang, but he was on the phone. Zhang put his hand over the receiver for a moment, whispered, "Someone I know in Shanghai" and "Good luck, be careful," turned away again, and continued his conversation.

———

Paul's heart was beating fast when he climbed the stairs to Christine's office. He wanted to put it down to the two flights of stairs, the heat in the stairwell, the high blood pressure that his father had suffered from, but he knew himself how foolish all that was. He was happy to see Christine, there was no other reason, and it was both a wonderful and a strange feeling. He could not remember the last time his heart had thudded so furiously in anticipation of seeing someone. Standing in the hall for a moment, he heard Christine's voice through the door, a voice that sounded so energetic, businesslike, and decisive in the office, and so tender in his ears.

He rang the bell, went in, and suddenly felt transformed into the shy young man he had once been, who had only been able to say a few sentences throughout an entire long evening in the presence of women.

Christine took his hand as they walked downstairs. They crossed Johnson Road and cut through Southorn Playground and a few minutes later, they were sitting in a small, crowded coffee shop. Paul could hardly wait to tell her about the Owens and Anyi and how he had found Michael's lover, but Christine ordered first, without consulting him: a portion of black sesame rice dumplings, a mango pudding, and two caffe lattes.

"Is that okay?"

Paul smiled and nodded. He would have chosen the same things. "Christine, you won't believe this, but I found Michael Owen's . . ."

She interrupted him with a vigorous shake of her head. "Paul, please don't be angry with me, but I don't want to know."

"Why not?" He struggled to hide his disappointment.

"Because I can't help you."

"But I don't expect you to help."

"Because I can't share it with you. I didn't sleep last night. I'm not exaggerating. I lay wide awake in bed, as if I had taken some kind of stimulant."

"There's no reason . . ." He started contradicting her but stopped. After everything Zhang had said to him, he could not pretend to her that he was going to Shenzhen on some kind of leisure trip.

"That doesn't count at all. What you say and how I hear it are two totally different things, and nothing will change that. Everything that you tell me, every person you tell me about, will only make me more frightened for you. You have decided to help your friend. I respect that. When you go to China my thoughts are with you every minute—no, what am I saying—every second. I won't ask you not to go any longer. I trust you, but nevertheless, or perhaps because I do, I don't want to know what you do there. Can you understand that?"

Paul was afraid he could not. If the situation had been reversed he would have behaved quite differently—he would want to know about everything, every detail, every meeting; he would want every conversation to be recounted as fully as possible. And even before that he would have asked her not to go—no, not just asked but put pressure on her, he would not have given her any peace until she gave in, and if she had not, he would have taken her refusal to consider his wishes as clear proof of her lack of affection for him.

"I don't know if I would be so understanding in your place."

"It's not understanding."

"Then courageous."

"It's not courageous either. I love you. That's all."

He wanted to respond to her. The same three little words. I love you. He wanted to shout them out. I love you. Or to whisper them in her ear. But he could not. He couldn't get a single sound out, and he did not know why. He knew what he ought to say, and it would not have been a lie, it would not have been a pretense, yet not a word passed his lips. It was as if he had forgotten how to speak. As though there was nothing but a gray, cold, and silent emptiness within him. She would surely ask, "Do you love me?" next. That's what all women did in situations like this, and he had no answer for her apart from a sad, seemingly endless silence. His silence drove him crazy. She must doubt him. He tried to force himself. He opened his mouth, but she just gave a gentle shake of her head.

She did not ask questions. She just looked at him, stroked his mouth and his lips gently, and took his face in her hands as though she had never held something so precious before.

"I love you," she repeated, kissing him with such passion, so full of tenderness and desire that he felt as if he was fainting for a moment. "I love you."

XXIV

It had been a mistake to go up to his bedroom to see Anyi one more time. She had just had a shower and was sitting on the bed with the remote control in one hand and a plate of rice crackers in the other, staring at the screen. Her skin was pale, barely distinguishable from the white silk sheets, so her black hair, dark-brown eyes, and plump, deep-red lips stood out all the more. Her bathrobe was a little askew. Tang could see the edge of an almost-pink nipple, and the sight aroused him so much in that instant that he lay down on the bed with her. She must have sensed his arousal, and clearly saw it as her duty to fan it and to give herself to him. She put the rice crackers and the remote control aside, leaned over him, and started unbuttoning his shirt. She trailed the tips of her fingers over his chest and unbuckled his belt.

Before long, Victor Tang was lying half naked on the bed, with Anyi sitting astride him. She moved her hips rhythmically up and down, and he massaged her small, firm breasts with both hands, thinking about the Owens and Paul Leibovitz and wondering what his role was in all of this. Anyi breathed heavily and sighed out loud, but her orgasmic cries were too shrill and sounded too exaggerated to convince him of her ecstasy. The television was still on, and Tang saw from the corner of his eye, in the upper right-hand corner of the screen, that the stock market in Hong Kong had fallen.

When she realized that, despite the distraction, he had come and was slowly getting limp, she got off him, lay down next to him, and reached for the remote control.

She can't have felt much. Tang did not kid himself, but this was not the time to think about Anyi's pleasure. She was a mistress, an exceptionally intelligent and good-looking one, but still nothing more than a mistress, of which there were tens of thousands in Shenzhen.

Until a few days ago she had been Michael's, but now she belonged to him. He was supporting her. He would continue to pay the rent for the apartment, give her a generous allowance and, when he felt like it, spoil her with presents. In return, she had to be at his service at all times. That might not always be satisfying for her, but it was certainly better than packing plastic toys or lightbulbs into cardboard cartons on some conveyor belt for five hundred yuan a month and sharing a room with seven other young women. She knew that, so it would never occur to her to complain. Only people who were stupid or presumptuous did that, and she was not one of those. It was a temporary arrangement, a business relationship, if you like, based on a cost-benefit analysis like any business relationship, existing for as long as both parties benefited from it, and it would end the day one of the two parties found a better deal. It was the opposite of love.

Why had that been so difficult for Michael Owen to understand? He had tried to learn Chinese history, read books in which the role of concubines in ancient China had surely been explained in detail. Why had he still not understood? When Tang had realized that things were becoming serious he had tried to explain the principle of the concubine and its renaissance in modern-day China to him. Michael had only stared at him in horror and grown terribly angry, saying that he had not the slightest idea what Anyi meant to him. She was different. She was not a concubine, she was his girlfriend. He loved her above all else and she loved him, not his money or his citizenship—he did not doubt it for a second. She was learning English for him, and he was determined to marry her and take her back to America with him one day. This impulsive show of anger that did not accept any other point of view had troubled Tang. Michael's outburst reminded him of the laughter of the students at Harvard when he had told them about his vision of China as the factory of the world. They had laughed at him; they did not understand this country and its culture, even if they, like Michael, tried to. They simply could not grasp how hungry the people here were. They did not know what it meant to have been deceived for decades of your life. Neither the Harvard students nor Michael, let alone his father, could understand how often people in China had been lied to, how much unlived life they were carrying around with them, and how strong the desire was to live it.

But Tang had not forgotten Michael's outrage. Michael Owen had been so convinced and spoken so convincingly that day that Tang had grown curious. What if he, Tang, was wrong? Perhaps this young woman was one of the rare exceptions. Tang wondered if he would be disappointed or delighted if that were so.

The next time Michael traveled to Wisconsin for a few days, Tang invited Anyi to dinner. She certainly did not seem like one of the mistresses of Chinese businessmen; he had gotten to know many of them and they were so interchangeable that he could not remember a single one. She was different. More intelligent, more beautiful, and more confident. It was clear that she was proud not to have worked her way up from a factory conveyor belt to a karaoke bar to the bed of the first available rich man. She could afford to be choosy, but she obeyed the same rules the others did. He saw it in her eyes. He saw it in her face. He saw it in the way she moved. He smelled it, like a dog picking up the scent of a wounded animal. She could deceive Michael Owen but not him, Victor Tang. She had escaped the misery of her childhood and would not go back there for anything in the world. She knew that the economic reforms had produced many winners and at least as many losers. She had understood that on the free market everything was a matter of supply and demand in the end and that nowadays everyone had a price. Anyi too.

It had taken a second meeting the following day to persuade her, with a mixture of charm, promises, and veiled threats, that she had nothing to lose and everything to win if she accompanied him home. She was too clever to turn him down. After all, no one could guarantee that Michael would keep his word and take her to America. That night, Tang screwed her three times, and if he really thought about it, those were the only times he really enjoyed it. But perhaps that was only because of the pleasure he took in having been right.

Tang got up, put on his clothes, and cast Anyi a look that she did not respond to. He left the bedroom and went downstairs again without exchanging a word with her.

The dining room table was laid with silver chopsticks and blue and white china to set off the dark rosewood. The cold appetizers were already on the table; they looked delicious. Tang had told his cook to prepare a twelve-course Chinese meal and also to put a bottle of Dom Pérignon on ice and to fetch two bottles of Pétrus 1989 from the cellar.

Tang did not want to leave anything to chance this evening. He did not know Paul Leibovitz. From what he had heard from Richard Owen, he seemed to be one of the few foreigners who had lived in Hong Kong for a long time and managed not to become rich. Tang wondered how that was possible; did this man simply not have the ability or was he one of the few people who was not interested in fast cars, fine food, or expensive wines? Tang wondered if he should leave the yellow Ferrari in the garage, then he called one of his drivers and asked him to move the car and park it in the driveway. That never failed to impress his Chinese visitors. Most of them were not able to tell the difference between Dom Pérignon and cheap sparkling wine, but more and more often now at least one of the party had some idea of what expensive and exclusive wines Tang was treating them to. It was not long, then, before word got around and everyone in the group raised his glass gratefully and a little reverentially to their host. If they were not impressed by the wine, the champagne, or the shark fin soup, the Ferrari by the front door or the gold golf clubs in the hallway did the trick. Tang was always fascinated by how reliably these techniques worked, by how people were awed by wealth. He himself did not care much for expensive wines; he merely sipped at them and never drank more than one glass in an evening. He had just as little interest in cars, and there was nothing he found more tedious than playing golf, but no one could have guessed. The luxurious lifestyle that he displayed to the world consisted of carefully chosen symbols, gestures, and signs to ensure that every guest would immediately understand Victor Tang's place in the new hierarchy of modern-day China.

Paul Leibovitz, too, would immediately know who he was dealing with. As long as Tang did not know why this man was involved in the Owens' affairs, and therefore also in his, and why Leibovitz was snooping around, he had to be on his guard.

Was he really acting on behalf of the family, as Anyi had told him? That would be bad news, for then he was probably a kind of private detective who had been employed by Elizabeth to nose around, without Richard knowing anything about it. Or perhaps Richard knew all about it and had been playing the innocent to him for days? Was he working alone or was he working with someone in Shenzhen? Was detective Zhang helping him? Luo had told him that Zhang had been seen near the Cathay Metal factory a few days ago.

Zhang? It was a common surname; he knew many Zhangs and he remembered one of them in particular, but it couldn't possibly be that one. He had not thought to ask Luo if his subordinate came from Sichuan. The thought of them meeting again over thirty years later, in a country as big as China, in these circumstances, was inconceivable.

Tang heard the hum of the electric motor that opened the cast-iron gates to his property. He opened the front door and stepped out. His black Mercedes rolled up the driveway almost silently past the Ferrari and Lamborghini and came to a stop right next to him.

He stepped toward the car, opened the door for Elizabeth, and inclined his head slightly in a bow. She greeted him with a tense smile. Richard looked a sight. He must have lost several pounds in the last few days. His face was ashen and he stood bowed as if he had a hunchback.

"Mr. Leibovitz? A pleasure. I've heard a great deal about you."

Anyi had not been exaggerating. Tang could see that this was a stranger he had to take seriously. He could not say what impressed him the most at first sight; was it the way Leibovitz looked at him steadily? A gaze that held his for many seconds and in which there was no fear? Or the shadow Tang recognized in his face that seemed strangely familiar to him? If he was going to find out anything from him he would have to be patient and not let him out of sight for the whole evening.

Tang invited his guests into the house. A server stood there with cold moist towels for them to refresh themselves after their journey. Another server brought a tray with glasses and champagne; he opened the bottle and poured the champagne with the label facing upward, as Tang had taught him. Tang watched Leibovitz and immediately realized that he was not one of those people who could be impressed by Dom Pérignon.

Perhaps he would be impressed by the ancient Ming Dynasty vases that he had recently bought for fifty thousand dollars at an auction in New York. Exquisite pieces. They had been owned by a foreigner for more than one hundred and fifty years; now, thanks to Victor Tang, they were finally restored to their homeland. He planned to make a permanent loan of them to a museum in Shanghai.

Leibovitz listened attentively but did not even start when Tang mentioned the price of the vases. Richard, on the other hand, gave a loutish whistle and clapped him on the back. Elizabeth didn't seem to be impressed either. Was she listening at all?

XXV

She did not like champagne, no matter which unpronounceable French name it had. It gave her headaches. The conversation with Paul yesterday had left her no peace; she had not been able to get his questions, Richard's hesitant replies, and her own role in all of this, out of her head. She had lain awake brooding next to her snoring husband the whole night. Surely it was possible that an innocent man was in prison because he had signed a forced confession. Elizabeth Owen could just not fathom it, but if it was true she was determined to get to the bottom of it.

They were standing with Tang in front of two old vases with blue snakes and dragons on them. Rare and precious antiques from the Ming Dynasty. Beautiful ceramics, she had to admit, but she was not here to listen to a lecture about Chinese antiques.

Elizabeth watched her husband and thought he looked old. His tan notwithstanding, he was no longer handsome. The pinup. The crush of all the girls at college. Where had the golden boy gone, the high school and college football legend Elizabeth had not been able to resist? Where was the glow, that confident the-world-belongs-to-me smile that seemed to know no defeat, that had so impressed her that she fell in love with him and abandoned her plans to move to New York to become a buyer at a department store? He had courted her for two years; she had been reluctant at first because New York had been her dream but in the end she could not withstand his charm, his persistence, and the promise of a life free of materialistic worries.

Richard was still tall, but he seemed fragile next to Paul and Tang. Especially in comparison to the Chinese businessman, who was standing bolt upright next to him holding a glass of champagne, swaying back and forth on his feet a little, always at eye level with her husband. He was wearing one of those Chinese jackets with a mandarin collar, all black; it made him look stern, perhaps a little reserved, and pretty handsome, she had to admit. There were certain moments when he seemed to her like the image of her husband when he was younger, even though there were fewer than fifteen years between them. The same confidence, the same decisiveness and strength that Richard had projected before, though Tang did not wear the smile of the victor but looked serious and focused instead.

She did not like him, but no one could accuse him of being in-gratiating. He had good manners and taste. He was courteous but never obsequious.

Elizabeth asked one of the servers for a glass of ice water. Her throat was getting dry, as it always did when she was tense and nervous. All afternoon she had thought about how to approach Victor. Whether she should wait and start a casual conversation while they were eating to see how or if she should confront him directly with straightforward questions. Sitting in Tang's limousine she had decided to wait; standing here next to him, however, she felt differently. She felt increasingly short of breath and dehydrated as Tang carried on about the Ming Dynasty. Her heart was beating fast, she was getting more stressed and strained by the second, with each new detail about the Ming vase. She knew the longer she waited the worse it would get. If only Paul or Richard would give her a reassuring look, but they did not pay attention to her, instead they listened attentively to Tang.

She was on her own.

"Mr. Tang?" That might have sounded rather sharp, admittedly, and it was probably the wrong moment but it didn't matter. She could not wait any longer, and at least the three gentlemen had finally looked up and in her direction.

"Mr. Tang, I am very sorry to interrupt you but does the name Metal Lotus mean anything to you?"

He looked at her with a polite smile. "I'm afraid that means nothing to me. Perhaps you can tell me more? What is it about? A company?"

"That's what I want to know from you, Mr. Tang."

He paused for a moment. "In which context did you hear about it?"

"Michael mentioned it as an aside once. Metal Lotus or Lotus Metal, I don't quite remember." She tried to sound as casual as possible but to no avail.

"I'm sorry, Mrs. Owen. I have nothing for you."

Was he telling the truth? She could not read Chinese faces. Somehow they all looked the same.

"And Wang Ming?" she asked, clearing her throat with a sip of water. "Is he a friend of yours?"

"Wang Ming? Who is that? Why are you asking? Did Michael mention the name?"

There it was. That was what she had been waiting for, for this hint of uncertainty in his otherwise relaxed voice. *Did Michael mention the name?* Why did he want to know that? His question had sounded strained, just a little, but Elizabeth Owen had not missed it.

"Yes, Michael talked about him often, also in connection with you," she lied.

"There must be some mix-up. I've never heard the name before."

He was lying! And how! There was no question. Richard and Paul could not have missed that. The clipped sentences, the edge in his voice; that was how a person spoke when he had something to hide. She had to press on; she couldn't give him any peace now, could not let herself be distracted by excuses. She was on his trail and she would eventually corner him and get him to disclose what he knew.

"Mr. Tang," she held her breath, weighed her words, "who murdered my son?"

Silence. She heard the ice in her water melting. In place of a reply, an ominous silence spread in the room. She waited. Why was Tang not answering? Was he too cowardly? Why were the other two men not saying anything? This embarrassed silence. The looks they were exchanging. As though Elizabeth were nothing more than a nervous wreck, a pitiful, hysterical woman who would not keep quiet rather than a grieving, devastated mother who wanted to know who had killed her son.

"Mr. Tang, I asked you a question."

He could look at her as coolly as he liked for as long as he liked. "Who murdered Michael?"

"As far as I know it was the worker who is now in prison. He has signed a confession."

"The man has an alibi."

Was that a tightening of his face? Had his lips grown thinner than usual? Or was she imagining it?

"Then you know more than I do, Mrs. Owen."

She couldn't stand that dismissiveness in his voice.

"Ask Mr. Leibovitz if you don't believe me. He and his friend from the homicide division found the wife of the supposed murderer. The man cannot have been the murderer. On the evening that Michael was murdered he was with his wife. He was lying ill in bed. There are witnesses."

Bulls-eye. She would have had to be blind not to notice how that affected Tang. He was grinding his teeth; she could see it from the movement of his lower jaw. The others were still not saying a word.

"Is that correct, Mr. Leibovitz? Am I right?"

Paul was silent. Yes, she had promised not to mention what he told her to Tang. But did he really think that was possible? He was a fool to have believed her. Why else had they accepted this invitation of Tang's? Surely not to exchange small talk or to enjoy fine dining. Her Michael was dead and what Paul had told her yesterday had awakened her doubt in the official version. Without him she would never have thought to question Tang's version of events. How could he leave her in the lurch now?

"Mr. Leibovitz!" She wanted to yell at him, but her voice was getting weaker. "For God's sake, say something. I'm only repeating what you told me yesterday. Wang Ming! Lotus Metal! The alibi! I haven't just made it up. You told me all that! Why are you keeping quiet?"

That had no effect. Paul Leibovitz remained silent.

"Were you lying to me?"

At least he did not dare to look her in the eye. Without his help she was trapped. Tang would not answer any of her questions in a meaningful way, she was only making a fool of herself. She felt betrayed and debased and wanted to get away, away from here, as quickly and as far away as possible.

"My dear Mrs. Owen."

That tone of voice. That was how people spoke to someone who was sick, not to her. Tang's hypocritical understanding was even more intolerable than his derision. "You know how terribly sorry I am about what's happened. I know that you feel very upset and that you want to see the actual murderer of your son punished. Let me assure you that's what we all want. Whether the suspect has an alibi or not and whether he signed a confession wrongly or not will all be established by the court on Friday. There are judges, public prosecutors, and defense attorneys for that. That is no different in China from the way it is in America. Mr. Leibovitz will surely be able to confirm that, won't he?"

He nodded. Paul nodded. How dare he do that after all that he had told her yesterday in the hotel about forced confessions in Chinese prisons? Whose side was he on?

"I want to go back to the hotel immediately."

"But Mrs. Owen . . ."

Elizabeth interrupted her host. "Not another word. I want to go, and right now. Call me a taxi."

"You don't need a taxi. Of course I'll ask my driver to take you.

He would have taken you back to Hong Kong later anyway, so he's waiting outside," Tang said, walking to the door.

Elizabeth Owen took her bag from the chair and looked at her husband. Why didn't he say something? Where was the man she had fallen in love with?

Richard put his glass down and made ready to accompany her. She had no idea how she would be able to stand him being near her.

XXVI

He felt his grief mingle with rage as he thought about Elizabeth and Michael. If only this one time Michael had listened to him. He should not have insisted on looking for a new business partner when the business with Tang was going so well. They had been earning more than ever before, and if Tang siphoned off a little more for himself than was due under the contract, so be it. There was more than enough for them. Richard could not understand Michael's indignation on that count, especially when he could not even prove the misappropriation of funds. When did the ostentatious display of wealth that initially attracted Michael begin to repel him? The first time Michael expressed displeasure, Tang's cars were parked in front of the entrance to the house. A yellow Ferrari and a golden Lamborghini had stood there like sentinels. Tang had told them that the Lamborghini wasn't a standard make but that he had had a mechanic in Hong Kong take the car apart and gild the parts separately. That had excited Richard—a golden Lamborghini! He had even squashed himself behind the small black leather steering wheel and taken it on an imaginary drive, but his son had reacted extremely negatively.

Michael ought to have showed a little interest in Tang's sports cars. As a courtesy. Instead, he had asked Tang if he were not afraid of getting into trouble by flaunting his wealth like this. It was a strange question, especially from an American, he had to agree with

Tang there. That was just one of the many times when he hadn't a
clue what his son was thinking. The Chinese man had not allowed
himself to be provoked by this, but had shaken his head, smiling,
and quoted the words of Deng Xiaoping: "Some people can get rich
first."

That was Victor Tang for you. Never short of a quick reply—that
was why Richard liked him. Michael could not deal with his ready
wit and humor. Richard sometimes felt that he was the only one in
the family who really knew what they had in Victor.

———

And now, Elizabeth had lashed out. Metal Lotus? Metal Lotus!
She could not even remember the name. Metal Lotus. He could
feel himself growing hot in the face. What would Tang say in reply?
Yes, Mrs. Owen, I'm familiar with Lotus Metal. It's another firm
that supplies the car industry and a competitor of ours. An up-
and-coming company, with a lot of financial backing from Beijing,
that made a very attractive offer to your son. Luckily your husband
was clever enough to let me know about it, so I was able to prevent
Michael from succumbing to the temptation and doing business
with them behind my back and to my detriment. Yes, Mrs. Owen,
you heard right—your husband told me about it.

That would be the end of their marriage. Elizabeth would never
understand it, and she would never forgive him for it. He, of all
people, had given Tang the information. But who else should he
have turned to for advice? Her? He would have liked to, but she
had never wanted to know anything about the business. Michael
had been on the verge of destroying a partnership that worked
fantastically well. He had not wanted to listen to his father's advice.
And it wasn't just advice. It was still Richard's company, after all. So
strictly speaking his son had ignored his boss's orders, had defied
the requests, instructions, and orders from Wisconsin every day, negotiating contracts in the family's name with people Richard didn't
even know. Who should he have placed his trust in and who should

he have turned to for advice? He trusted Victor. He was not just a clever and respectable businessman who was good with figures, but he was also quick and decisive when he wanted to get something done. Richard saw in him the same fire that had motivated him before. He confided in Victor as a precautionary measure. He had wanted to protect Michael from a mistake with grave consequences.

Mr. Tang, who murdered my son?

Why did she have to provoke Victor so? There was a murder suspect, more than a suspect, to be precise. Whatever Leibovitz claimed about forced confessions in Chinese jails, Richard Owen simply could not imagine someone going against his better judgment and signing his own death sentence, for that was what Victor had explained it amounted to. A murder confession in China was equivalent to an execution. No judge would ask how the confession had arisen, whether alcohol or drugs had played a role or whether the murderer had been abused as a child or suffered from racism or discrimination or other so-called mitigating circumstances. In our country, Victor had said, a murder is a murder and it is punishable by death, just like in America. The ridiculous investigating by Leibovitz and his friend could not bring their son back to life again anyway. Elizabeth should let the case take its course.

Victor had spoken to him the day before Michael disappeared. They had talked about how to prevent Michael from conducting further negotiations and whether it would make sense to give him a clear warning. Richard had agreed without asking for details of what Tang meant by that. In the end, all this was in Michael's interests, even though he saw it as the opposite. Tang would never have gone so far as to inflict bodily harm on Michael. That was simply unthinkable. If the murderer had really not been arrested yet and if the story about the alibi was really true then the murder must have been the result of robbery, an accident, or mistaken identity.

XXVII

―――――――――

Ask Mr. Leibovitz if you don't believe me. He and his friend from the homicide division . . .

Paul had closed his eyes for a minute and hoped he had misheard. How could she have done that? Had he not told her in the hotel in Hong Kong that she would have to be patient that evening, that she must not, under any circumstances, mention the alibi and Zhang, or she would put the lives of his friend and the suspect's wife in danger? She had looked absently across the lobby when he had said that, but she had been listening to him, and she had promised to say nothing, not just once, but twice. He had trusted her. But she kept talking and talking as though the danger she was placing others in did not interest her in the least.

Is that correct, Mr. Leibovitz? Am I right?

When all eyes were suddenly on him, Paul's legs buckled a little, as though someone had pushed the backs of his knees. He tightened his leg muscles, tried to stand up straight, and hoped the others had not noticed.

Mr. Leibovitz! For God's sake, say something. I'm only repeating what you told me yesterday.

Paul had ignored Elizabeth Owen because otherwise he would have shouted at her: Shut the fuck up. I don't want to hear a single word more, do you understand? Not a word more, in the name of your son. If you carry on talking like this, an innocent man will be sentenced to death. If you don't stop talking immediately we will get nothing out of this—nothing at all.

Instead of saying anything he looked past her as if he did not hear what she was saying at all. He could not have helped her, even if he had wanted to. They were not going to find out a thing from Tang that way.

He heard Victor Tang reply in a voice that seemed muffled even though he was standing right next to him. *My dear Mrs. Owen . . . how terribly sorry I am . . . the suspect . . . an alibi . . . will all be established by the court . . . the way it is in America. Mr. Leibovitz will surely be able to confirm that, won't he?*

Paul sank his head into his chest and nodded. He did not have the strength to look at the others. He had rarely felt so ashamed in his life. Elizabeth Owen left him no choice. If this evening was to have any purpose at all then he had to let Victor Tang make an accomplice of him; he had to agree with him, whatever he said.

He had watched Elizabeth storm out of the house, followed by her husband and Victor Tang, who had called for his driver.

From one second to another, the room was silent. Paul thought he could hear the quiet sound of a television somewhere, but perhaps he was wrong.

The sudden peace did him good. He watched the two servers, who had observed the quarrel without changing their expressions, and were standing motionless in a corner like mannequins. He signaled to them to bring him another glass of champagne and sat down on one of the couches in front of the fireplace. He had not hesitated to accept Tang's invitation to stay for dinner without the Owens. Zhang's warning about a trap crossed his mind, but listening hard to his feelings, he could detect no fear in himself. Victor Tang was an impressive phenomenon, but he did not intimidate him, and the absence of the Owens actually made things easier.

Paul looked around. Next to him were the precious Ming vases and the two servers in their Chinese silk suits. Through the window he could see the yellow Ferrari in the driveway. He thought about the prostitutes in the building Zhang lived in and their two dozen or so pink panties, which they hung out to dry on the roof terrace every day. The shameless flouting of laws in front of the police reminded him of the shamelessness with which Victor Tang was displaying his wealth. If anything disturbed him, it was this lack of shame. He had encountered prostitutes in China before, but they had always conducted their business discreetly. What he found so surprising about where Zhang lived was how openly the law was broken in the face of official propaganda. No one bothered in the slightest to preserve even the appearance of observing the law. He had asked Zhang who the party secretary of his area was and why the police did nothing, but he had only smiled and shrugged his shoulders. He asked himself the same questions now, sitting in this living room. The Ferrari, the Mercedes 500, the gold golf clubs in the hall, this ostentatious neo-Baroque villa, the champagne—they were all carefully chosen symbols, gestures, and markers to make every guest immediately understand Victor Tang's place in the hierarchy of China today. But their symbolism went far beyond that, for this was all ill-begotten wealth, and every Chinese visitor to this house knew that. Paul too would never have believed that Tang had accumulated his wealth purely through legal means. He knew China too well for that. What kind of society was it where the robbers did not hide their loot but flaunted it with pride?

Paul heard car doors slamming and the crunch of the gravel path as the car rolled over it. But a few minutes passed before Victor Tang came back into the house.

"Excuse me for having left you to wait so long, Mr. Leibovitz. I was trying to calm them both a little."

"Did you succeed?" Paul asked.

"I'm afraid not. Mrs. Owen was very upset. But that is more than understandable after everything that's happened." Tang sat down on the couch opposite and beckoned at a server, who immediately brought him a glass of champagne and who also topped off Paul's glass. "May I ask if you're American?"

"Yes. I was born in Germany but grew up in America."

"Where?"

"New York City."

"Wonderful. Amazing city. I went there often when I was at Harvard. Do you know the Chongqing Grill in Chinatown, by any chance?"

"No."

"It's on Mott Street. The corner of Bayard, if I remember correctly."

"No, I'm afraid not."

"They make the best hot pot outside of Sichuan. Incredible. Or that dim sum restaurant on East Broadway, what was it called?" Tang tapped his fingers on the arm of the couch and stared at the ceiling as though the name of the restaurant would appear there any moment.

Paul had no idea what his host was up to. This man was not one of those people who simply talked away; he weighed up every sentence. An American would have started cross-examining him long ago, would have wanted to know who this friend in the homicide division was and why they presumed to conduct their own investigations. What did Tang want from him? To confuse him? Distract him? Make him nervous? Or was he merely applying some ancient Chinese strategy to avoid confrontation as long as possible and only address the key issue just before the conversation ended, almost as an aside?

"It doesn't matter. I can't remember it now. Here's to you," Tang said, raising his glass.

"Thank you. And here's to you."

They sipped their champagne and were silent for a moment.

"The Owens told me how helpful you were to them in Hong Kong, Mr. Leibovitz. I want to thank you for that. But I know very little about you. I don't even know what you do in Hong Kong."

Paul thought for an instant. He had told the Owens almost nothing about himself, so Tang really could hardly know anything about him. "I manage two China investment funds. Hutch & Hutch and Go Global," he said.

"How interesting. What kinds of investments?"

"Venture capital for Chinese start-ups."

"In which industries?"

"Various industries. We're very diversified."

"Any specialties?"

"Yes, lie detectors."

"I'm sorry?"

"We're financing the development of a completely new type of lie detector, which a Chinese company in Shenyang is working on." Paul could see clearly from Victor Tang's otherwise poised expression that he was disconcerted by this. He had often experienced that in conversation with Chinese people. Many of them found it as difficult to guess his age as to understand his sense of humor. They never knew exactly when he was joking and when he was being serious, and Victor Tang also had this problem. He stared at Paul, nodding uncertainly.

"We've invested a lot of money in a joint venture, the Truth and Trust World Wide Cooperation, TTWW for short," Paul continued in a serious tone. He had to muster all his self-control to suppress a smile. He could guess what would happen next. Tang could not admit that he was unnerved. If Paul was having him on, it would be the same as losing face so he would have to find out the truth in the course of the conversation.

"Lie detectors?" Tang asked, as if he had misheard.

"Yes, lie detectors," Paul said.

"But they already exist. What is new about your machine?"

"A revolutionary technology. We don't measure the electrical currents in the brain but the heart rate. The heart reacts to a lie much more quickly than the brain."

"The heart?"

"Yes, you can't fool the heart. It's amazing, I wouldn't have believed it before but our tests prove it. The method is absolutely reliable. The machine will be small and portable, not too expensive and easy to operate. The first domestic lie detector, so to speak."

"For use at home?" Tang's voice sounded more and more perplexed.

"Of course not just for the home. It will work on a wireless basis up to a distance of twenty meters. So you can use it in the office or at presentations or press conferences without wiring anyone up to it. We think there'll be a big market for it. Especially in these times. Don't you think so?"

"I . . . I don't know. Which markets do you have in mind?"

"China, Europe, America. Everywhere lies are told."

Tang said nothing and gave him a considered look. It was not a look intended to intimidate; he had a questioning, searching expression on his face and Paul was surprised to realize that this man was not as unlikeable as he had thought he would be. How would he react now? Admit that he did not know what was going on? Paul was eager to hear his reply.

"Advantage Leibovitz," Tang finally said. "I like you. I still can't tell if you're kidding or not."

Instead of saying anything right away Paul allowed himself a grin that spread right across his face for a second. "We're still looking," he said, again perfectly seriously, "for a suitable name for the product. What do you think about iLie?"

Now Tang laughed out loud. "You're doing that very well. You're an incredibly good actor." He shook his head in disbelief and, after a brief pause, asked, "Are you hungry? Shall we have something to eat?"

"I'd like that."

Tang got up, still shaking his head in wonder, and led the way into the dining room, a large hall with high ceilings, blank white walls, and a dark wooden floor. An impressive chandelier hung in the center of the room, with white candles burning in it instead of lightbulbs, and there was an oval table below it, made of dark-brown rosewood, long and wide enough to seat a large group of people.

Now it was set for only two. Tang and Paul were to sit opposite each other in the middle of the table with more than a dozen dishes, big and small, of cold appetizers in front of them. The two servers stood behind the chairs waiting for Tang and his guest to take their seats.

Paul could not remember if he had ever seen candlelight in a Chinese dining room. They were usually lit with harsh fluorescent light. The flickering candlelight gave this room a festive atmosphere that seemed almost ghostly to Paul because it was so unusual.

"I told my cook to prepare a menu of Sichuan dishes. I hope you won't find them too spicy?"

"I like spicy food."

"Then you must try the chicken in chili oil and Sichuan pepper sauce. It's one of my cook's specialties."

Paul picked up a slice of cold chicken with his ivory chopsticks and dipped it in the sauce. Tang had not been exaggerating. The meat was tender and the sauce was wonderful—spicy but not too spicy. He tasted the typically earthy aroma of the Sichuan pepper, which left a slight numbness on the tongue. He tried the cucumber in mustard sauce, the tea-smoked pigeon, and the cold pork with garlic sauce.

"Delicious. Your cook is a genius."

"Thank you. I ate at his restaurant in Chengdu a year ago and employed him the same evening. Try the bang-bang chicken. It's unique."

Paul was familiar with this specialty from Zhang's kitchen, and he loved the bizarre combination of different tastes: sweet and sour and then spicy and salty in turn and with a nutty undertone too. It was almost as good as his friend's. Paul nodded approvingly.

"Your idea of the lie detector was not only very amusing," Tang said. "The longer I think about it, the more interesting I find it. Assuming that this machine was about to be launched on the market, do you think it would have a chance?"

"Why not?"

"Don't we all like to be lied to now and then?"

"You might, perhaps. Not I," Paul replied, with his mouth half full, instantly startled by his own reply. He had meant to speak lightly, as if he was making a joke, but his voice sounded entirely humorless and free of irony; he had sounded brusque, almost aggressive. But he did not want to have a confrontation. Not yet.

"Let's assume you have this machine with you now. What would you ask me?" Tang responded in a friendly manner, as though he had not heard the undertone in Paul's voice.

Paul thought for a moment. "What did you argue with Michael Owen about before his death?"

"Who told you we had an argument?"

"I found a letter addressed to you on Michael's computer."

"We disagreed about the future direction of our company."

"Why were you so insulting and abusive to him?"

"Was I?"

"Michael set you an ultimatum, asking you to apologize."

"It's possible," Tang replied curtly.

The conversation was getting more serious at every turn.

"What did you know about Michael's negotiations with Lotus Metal and his talks with Wang Ming?"

Tang replied with a question. "Who are you working for?"

"For no one."

"Did the Owens employ you?" he asked in a sharper, more demanding tone. Paul could hear that this man was not used to encountering opposition.

"No," he said, in as relaxed a manner as he could manage.

"Who is paying you?"

"I'm not getting paid."

"What are you after, then?"

"The truth," Paul replied, hoping that this did not sound too pathetic.

Victor Tang moved his head from side to side, picked up a slice of chicken, dipped it gently in the chili sauce once, and put it into his mouth. He wiped his mouth with a napkin and lifted his glass.

"To the truth," he said, sounding once again as jovial, almost play-ful, as he had been at the beginning of their conversation. Paul had never met anyone who could change the atmosphere so quickly and disconcertingly.

"Are you sure that you really want to know the truth?" Tang asked, after he had drunk from his glass.

Paul thought about this. He did not want to let himself be intim-idated by Tang, so he took his time before he replied. *No cheating, Daddy. Tell the truth.* "I think so."

"You think so?" Tang repeated, looking a little disappointed. "You should be very certain about such an important matter."

"You're right. I take that back and give you a clear yes."

"That doesn't sound entirely convincing either. Think about it. The truth can be very dangerous," Tang said with an almost devilish laugh. Now it was his turn to leave Paul guessing about how serious he was about what he was saying.

"I know," Paul said evasively.

"The search for the truth can sometimes bring great danger."

Paul was not sure if they were talking about truth in general or about the case of Michael Owen. "Let me put it this way. I al-ways want to know the truth. I don't know if I will always have the strength to take it."

Tang put his chopsticks down and looked him straight in the eye. The two servers remained frozen in their places. It was so quiet that Paul could hear the barely audible flickering of the candle flames.

"Mr. Leibovitz," Tang said, speaking quietly, almost whispering, so that Paul had to lean forward to hear him. "What will you do if the truth is too much for you? Will you suddenly realize that you don't have the strength to take it? Will you give it back then?"

Paul shook his head, feeling a slight uncertainty rise in him. Had he not expressed himself clearly or was Tang deliberately misunder-standing him? "Who should I . . . ?"

"That's right," Tang interrupted immediately. "That's exactly what I was talking about. Who should you return the truth to? Who will take uncomfortable, awkward, complicated truths back? No one. It's not like a suit that you realize does not fit you when you get home, that you can exchange. Once a truth is spoken all the weapons in the world will not suffice to catch it again and lock it away or extinguish it. For a time, perhaps, but not forever. You know a little bit about us Chinese and you know what I mean: We think long term. Once a truth has been spoken there is no going back. Do you agree?"

Paul nodded. It was a rhetorical question, and this was not the moment to contradict Tang.

"That means that we have to be very, very cautious and carefully weigh the risks to ourselves and to any confidants before we start searching for the truth, don't we? Because the truth can do many things. It can heal. It can comfort. It can give us wings, yes, give us almost superhuman strength. But it can also do exactly the opposite. It can destroy marriages, tear friends apart forever, bring governments down, start wars. In other words, truth has its price. Do you follow me, Mr. Leibovitz?"

Paul barely dared to move. Tang did not wait for a reaction.

"Knowing the truth can sometimes be tantamount to a death sentence, Mr. Leibovitz. Are you ready to accept this price?"

XXVIII

———

"You're lying, you miserable, dirty little traitor. Tell the truth now, do you hear? We want to know the truth! The truth!"

They had grabbed him by the back and forced him onto his knees. He was surrounded by half a dozen young men and women who could easily have been his children and they were taking turns shouting at him, spitting at him, and kicking him. He cowered at the edge of a raised platform with his head lowered; a heavy wooden placard on which someone had written "traitor" hung from his neck. He was bleeding from a wound on his forehead. He was trembling all over and was not making a sound. Several thousand people had streamed into the old city square of Chengdu that hot summer's day, and they were watching the spectacle of this public tribunal with rapt attention.

"The truth! The truth! We want to know the truth!" The voice of the screaming young man cracked with rage. He spat in the face of the man kneeling in front of him one more time and kicked him in the back so he lost his balance and tipped over, his upper body hitting the boards with a dull thump.

The fourteen-year-old Tang Mingqing stood on a small side street that led to the square, not thirty meters away from the stage, which he could not tear his eyes away from. He was crippled with fear. The tall and powerfully built man who was lying there was his proud, strong, beloved father. Weak like an old man. Helpless as a beetle that had fallen on its back.

He could not believe what he saw. If his father could be arrested in the name of the Great Chairman and publicly put on trial like this then anything was possible. If it had not been enough for him to leave the family as a boy to join the Communists, if it had not been sufficient that he had fought for Mao in the civil war and then supported every one of his political campaigns, then, Tang thought, there was nothing in this world that could be relied on. Then everything was possible and it was really randomness that ruled life, hiding behind the everyday routine. Then any feeling of security was an illusion. At any time and without notice, from one moment to another, evil could take over the entire country and the lives of every individual.

The young Tang leaned against the side of a building, closed his eyes, and felt the tears running down his face. He felt cold even though the sun was burning his skin. "Dissenter, counterrevolutionary, friend of capitalism." He heard this from thousands of throats. No, he wanted to scream at them, it's a mix-up! You're wrong, my father is not a traitor—most definitely not!

But what if they had not got it wrong? What if they were telling the truth? It was a monstrous thought that he would have liked to banish but that spread like lightning through his head. Could he really rule out, with absolute certainty, the possibility that there was any truth in their accusations? Of course not, for he saw his father so seldom. Who knew what he had talked about in the barracks with the other officers who had almost all been arrested in the past few weeks on counterrevolutionary charges? The Red Guards must have found out something about his father from them, something that had escaped him. There *had* to be some basis for their accusations; after all, they were acting in the name of Mao. He himself had called upon the Red Guards to liberate the country from old ways of thinking and not to show anyone mercy, not even the older people who appeared to have earned it. And who wanted to doubt the orders of the Great Leader? The Red Guards knew something that no one else knew, that was surely how it was. Then everything that Tang had experienced in the last few hours made sense—their apartment being stormed, the plunder, his mother's fear, and his father's silence. He had something to hide; they both had something to hide, otherwise why did they say nothing? His parents clung to old ways of thinking that had to be stamped out. Had his father not been very reserved in his support for the Cultural Revolution at the start? Had he not questioned the point of this great proletarian movement with his mother just a few days ago? Of course he had. Tang had been lying in the next room and he had heard everything even though they had spoken quietly, practically whispering. He had gotten up, stood next to the door, and listened, making out every word. How had they dared voice even the slightest doubts in Mao's politics? What were they thinking? Tang felt ashamed of his parents.

He opened his eyes and turned around once more. Two Red Guards were kneeling next to his father on the stage; one of them clutched his hair so he raised his head with his face frozen in a grimace. Traitor. They were all shouting it—the people on the stage and the men, women, boys, and girls who surrounded him. Tang joined in. Quietly at first, barely audibly, then louder and louder until he was screaming with all his might, "Liar! Traitor! You miserable, dirty little traitor! Tell the truth now!"

But his father said nothing, and they continued beating and torturing him until he lost consciousness. Eventually they dragged him onto a truck, drove away, and locked him up. Almost ten years passed—during which time his mother died—before Tang saw him again, and he barely recognized him. The proud PLA commander had turned into a broken old man who could barely speak a coherent sentence and who survived for exactly two years, two months, and two days after his imprisonment ended. He liked to spend his days sitting in a rocking chair in the semidarkness of his bedroom, letting his son care for him until his heart stopped beating one night.

He was officially rehabilitated two years later.

Tang was called to the party secretary's office, where he was handed a letter in which the party informed him that, according to the latest findings, the charges that had been brought against his father during the Cultural Revolution and led to him being jailed for almost ten years had been proved to be false. The deceased's file and his family's files would be amended accordingly. That was all. No compensation. No declaration of who might have been responsible for this and how they would have to be brought to justice. Not a word of apology, not a trace of regret in the face of the party functionary. The party secretary had looked at Tang as though he really ought to be grateful for this generous gesture. "Any more questions, Comrade Tang?"

———

Tang wondered whether he should tell his guest this story. Maybe then Paul Leibovitz would understand that there was no such thing as *the* truth, that to seek it out was to search for an illusion, for the truth could be bent at will and warped, if necessary even completely dismantled and constructed anew, assuming, of course, that you were one of those who gave orders rather than took them, who was standing upright and spitting at others rather than one of those lying helplessly in the dirt. Victor Tang had sworn to himself long ago that he would never belong in the latter group. Never! And if doubt sometimes crept over him he only had to look around him or out of the window. The Ferrari outside the door, this villa, the Dom Pérignon in his glass. To Victor Tang, the meaning of these luxury goods was that they constantly reassured him that he was one of those who was standing upright. One of those who could determine the truth. These luxury goods were much more than expensive toys or status symbols—they were a part of his protection against his fear of randomness. If he had learned anything from the fate of his family, it was the realization that anything was possible in his country and that there was nothing on earth that you could rely on. Every feeling of security was an illusion. Anarchy could be lying in wait around the next corner, to seize power and destroy everything.

Why was he thinking about this now? It had been a long time

since he had given his father so much thought. He could not remember when he had last conjured up that afternoon in the summer
of 1966 in his mind's eye so clearly. The memory had stirred him
up, and he did not like it. People who felt ruffled made mistakes.
His guest, on the other hand, was sitting across the table from him
without expressing any obvious emotion. If Victor was not wrong,
this Leibovitz guy was impressed neither by threats nor by symbols
of wealth. The lie detector had been a good joke, and Tang was
extremely unhappy that he had fallen for it at first. Leibovitz sat
in front of him listening very carefully, but there was no fear in his
eyes—he had that in common with Michael Owen. Owen had also
never understood who he was dealing with.

Tang felt himself growing warm. Was it the many candles or was
the air-conditioning not working properly? Maybe, he thought, it
would not be a bad idea to tell Paul the story of his father. It could
not hurt for his opponent to know where Victor was coming from.
Perhaps then he would understand that this was about much more
than a couple of half-finished contracts between Michael Owen and
another company. Their joint venture, Cathay Heavy Metal, was a
gold mine that, thanks to the hunger of the Chinese for cars, yielded
more and more every month, and he would not let anyone destroy
it, not at any price.

So Tang began to tell his story.

When he had finished, there was a long silence in the room. Paul
Leibovitz listened thoughtfully to what he was being told. Now he
put his chopsticks down and cleared his throat. "I'm sorry for you
and your family."

"You don't have to feel sorry. We are anything but a tragic exception. Ask other Chinese people my age and you will hear similar
stories."

"That's true, but I'm still sorry. I'm also asking myself why you've
told me all this."

"Certainly not to awaken your pity. But perhaps so that you'll
understand me better?"

"Or so that I'll stop searching for *the* truth because it doesn't exist?"

"That too, yes."

"I suspected that, and I'm telling you this: You're wrong. In your father's case there was a truth. He was innocent. And in the case of the murder of Michael Owen there is also a truth. The man who is sitting in prison is just as innocent. The murderer is still a free man."

Tang took a deep breath. He had to control himself, not let his anger show too clearly. Did this man not want to understand him or was he taking him for a ride? "That's not the point, Mr. Leibovitz. Why don't you get my meaning? It's about who establishes what the truth is, and in this case that has been done. The man is guilty, that has already been decided. Tomorrow he will go to trial. Judgment will be passed on him and he will be executed. Anyone who wants to stop that puts himself in danger. In this respect not much has changed in this country."

"Are you trying to frighten me?"

"What makes you think that?" Tang responded, making an effort to speak in just the right innocent-sounding tone of voice that would leave Paul unsure about how what he said was meant. "I merely wish to warn you. You and your friend the detective. The head of the homicide division, Luo, is a friend of mine. I'm afraid he won't be very pleased to hear that one of his men has disobeyed his orders. It's not only you who are putting yourself at risk, it's your friend too. What was he called again? Zhang, yes?"

Paul looked at him without replying.

"In Sichuan I knew . . ."

"I know," Paul interrupted him immediately. "You and my friend Zhang know each other from before. He told me."

Keep eating, slowly, Tang thought to himself. Don't let him notice anything. Take a piece of smoked duck and be careful not to let it slip from the chopsticks. Put it in your mouth calmly, without trembling, and chew leisurely. Sip a little from your glass. How long had it been? When did a murder become no longer punishable? Did this Leibovitz fellow know about it? Tang could not imagine that Zhang had told anyone about the afternoon they had spent together in the temple. Zhang had not betrayed him then so why should he have broken his silence to a foreigner?

"How long have you known him?"

"For over twenty years."

"Oh, how unusual," Tang replied, trying not to let his surprise show. "What did he tell you about me? Only positive things, I hope."

"Not much. It's a long time since you last met."

Tang had no idea if he could trust what Paul was saying, given that he had proved his talent for acting so impressively already. "I couldn't say when I last saw him. It would certainly be interesting to meet him again."

"I doubt that will happen. Both of you have very different attitudes, at least to the truth."

"Are you quite sure?" Victor Tang asked.

"Yes. Zhang does not lie. I'd trust him blind."

"That's always a mistake."

"You're a cynic. I've known Zhang for a long time—he has no reason to lie to me. There isn't a person I trust more than him. Anyway, I really think that in the end we don't have any choice other than to trust people."

"You're a dreamer. I'm convinced of exactly the opposite. We don't have any choice other than not to trust people."

"Zhang has never given me a reason not to trust him."

"He is Chinese."

Paul laughed, surprised. "And what about it? You're not trying to tell me that I can't trust any Chinese people?"

"I don't. At least not those from my generation."

"You're crazy. That's absurd."

"Weren't you listening to what I just told you? I wasn't telling you a fairy tale!" He had to keep his voice in check. Paul Leibovitz was not someone you shouted at.

"I know," Paul said calmly.

"Then I don't have to explain to you how often in the past a truth was declared a lie and a lie the truth. How many children betrayed their parents. How many pupils their teachers. How many supposedly 'best' friends denounced each other. Do you have to experience that yourself to believe in it?"

"No, but the Cultural Revolution ended over thirty years ago."

"So? What are thirty years? Not even half a human life. Anyone who lived through the purges will never forget them as long as they live. Never, do you hear me, never! Anyone whose father . . ." Tang broke off.

Paul also said nothing for a moment. "I understand."

"You don't understand anything," Tang interrupted. He could barely conceal how worked up he was. The memories had flooded into him with a force that he would not have thought possible.

"I'm trying to understand," Paul continued undeterred. "But in the last thirty years a great deal has happened in China."

"Yes, I've noticed that too. The buildings have grown taller and the streets wider."

"You're not being serious."

"Of course not. But this country cannot reinvent itself. Only the Americans could think that. We all have something to hide. Your friend is no exception. And I would not trust anyone who has anything to hide, they'll do anything to keep their secrets private."

"My friend has nothing to hide from me. You will not convince me that I cannot trust him."

"No?"

"No!"

"Did you know that he lived in a village in the countryside during the Cultural Revolution?"

"Of course."

"And do you know what he did there?"

"Like the others, he helped the farmers with the harvests. He worked morning to night to prove that he was a good revolutionary and he is still paying for it today. He has problems with his knees and suffers from rheumatism."

"Ah, knee pains and rheumatism. I would say he was a lucky man if they were all the problems he had."

"What do you mean?"

"Did he tell you that we were in the same work brigade?"

"Yes."

"Did he let you know how well we worked together?"

Paul shook his head. He had no idea what Tang was getting at, and that was good as far as Tang was concerned, very good, in fact. Victor Tang had decided that an accessory to the crime did not really matter. He took a deep breath. He wanted to savor this moment. He had the feeling that the two men's search for the truth about Owen's murder would end right here at this candlelit table laden with Sichuan delicacies. In a few minutes Paul Leibovitz would understand that we have no choice but not to trust people.

"Did he ever tell you," Tang said, dragging out every word, "about the story of the old monk in the temple?"

XXIX

Paul felt the life force drain out of his body. Every breath, every movement, yes, even sitting upright and motionless, seemed too much for him. Although Tang had only spoken a few sentences, Paul knew quite well that this was no mere anecdote he was telling to entertain or distract him, but a report that had only one object: to destroy the trust between him and Zhang forever. He saw it in Tang's face. There was a new glint in his eye, a coldness that announced a terrible evil. The man had to put some effort into injecting his voice with a cheerful, excited tone.

Paul wondered if he could interrupt him and simply tell him that he was mistaken, that he knew this story already. But that would have been cowardly. He wanted to know what event had been so awful for Zhang that he had kept it from him for over twenty years. He owed that to their friendship.

"We were all extremely agitated when the monk did not immediately open the gate . . ."

Paul could tell how the story would go. Certainly by the time Victor told him that he, Zhang, and the old man had stayed behind without the others in the temple. With every sentence, this tale led toward a terrible, unavoidable ending. Zhang, his Zhang, this reliable and beloved friend, had watched while an old defenseless man was beaten. Not only watched; he had fetched Tang the weapons and later covered up for the murderer with his silence. Zhang—a murderer's accomplice. With every sentence, this truth sank in deeper. He could not believe it but he also had no doubt that what Tang said was true.

Paul could only guess what had kept Zhang from talking about this. The shame, a bad conscience, the fear that Paul would judge him and turn away from him?

Trust was a part of life, trust without boundaries. It was the basis of every human contact, every friendship and every love; Christine had reminded him of that. "He who trusts risks disappointment. Living without trust is far worse than any disappointment."

As if trusting was only for fools. As if we had a choice.

Thinking about what she had said, he felt such a longing for Christine as he had hardly ever felt for a person before. He felt weak and helpless, and could only hope that Tang had not noticed it. He loved Christine. He loved her with all he had to give.

Tang did not bother to conceal his pleasure at the success of the surprise he had sprung. On the contrary, he reveled in everything he said that could further disquiet Paul. The sweet sound of victory was in his voice. Paul wanted to counter with something, but what? What was more powerful than a friend's betrayal?

"Don't you believe me?" Tang asked, clearly wondering why Paul was silent.

"I do. Every word." Paul felt unable to think clearly. "But it doesn't change anything." He had not given this sentence any forethought; it just slipped out of him. An act of defiance, because he didn't want to allow Tang his cheap victory. Or was he trying to protect himself because he wouldn't have been able to cope with this revelation otherwise?

"What do you mean?" Tang gave him a searching look.

"Exactly what I said," Paul said bravely. "It doesn't change anything. It doesn't change my friendship. It doesn't change my belief in Zhang. It doesn't change my trust in him. It doesn't change my affection for him."

Tang started laughing, a cold and loud laugh, almost hysterical.

"You're no romantic. I got that wrong about you. You're a pathetic coward. You find out a truth and you're too frightened to act on the consequences."

Paul did not have the strength to defend himself. He wanted to object, he wished that he really felt the way he had just involuntarily claimed he did, but there was a second voice within him that would not be silent. It kept whispering to him that Tang was not wrong. When did trust turn into unintelligent credulousness, loyalty to a childish defiance? "Zhang will have had his reasons for not telling me this story," he said flatly.

"Of course he had his reasons," Tang mocked. "We all have our reasons when we lie."

Paul stared at the candles on the table. The pressure in his eyes had grown intolerable; he would not be able to hold back his tears for much longer. "Please excuse me. I have to use your bathroom."

"Please do," Tang said in a contemptuous voice. "Go up to the second floor. The two bathrooms on the ground floor are out of order."

Paul could barely feel his legs as he rose from his seat. He felt as weak as if he had spent weeks in bed. He crossed the dining room and the entrance hall, taking tentative steps, and climbed the curved marble staircase slowly, holding on tight to the gleaming gold banister.

Tang had not told him whether to go left or right or which door he ought to open. The first on the right-hand side was not the bathroom, it opened onto an empty room without any furniture in it. The second led to a big bathroom without a toilet in it. Only after he had opened the third door did Paul realize that it could not have been the toilet. A television was on in the room. In front of it was a bed. On it was Anyi.

She looked at him with horror, as though he was a contract killer sent to silence her.

"What are you doing here?" Paul stammered.

"Get the hell out of here! Close the door at once!" she growled at him in a strangled voice.

Paul closed the door behind him.

"Are you crazy? Tang will kill us both if he sees us together."

"What are you doing here?" Paul asked again.

"Go away! Now. Please." Her anger had turned to pleading.

Paul was shocked by the fear in her face.

"How long have you been here?"

Anyi did not reply.

"Why are you so frightened?"

"If you don't go at once I'm going to scream for help," she threatened.

"What do you have to do with Michael's murder?"

"Mr. Leibovitz." Tang's voice came up to them from the dining room.

Anyi froze on her bed.

"I forgot to tell you where the toilet is," he shouted. "The second door on the left."

Paul opened the door slightly and said, "Thank you," loudly before closing it again.

"Go away! Go away!" Anyi whispered.

"Not before you answer my question."

"I don't have anything to do with it."

"I don't believe that. Why are you here, then?"

"You wouldn't understand."

"Then explain it to me."

"I can't."

"Tell me one thing. What does Tang know about Lotus Metal?"

"Everything."

"Were you the one who told him about it?"

"No," she insisted.

"You knew about Michael's talks with Wang Ming and Lotus Metal. You were with Michael in Beijing and Shanghai. You were with him on the building site for the new factory. I saw the photos. Tang found out from you."

"No. No. Not from me."

"But of course. Who else?"

"I don't know either. But I never told anyone anything."

"Mr. Leibovitz?" Tang's voice sounded from the hallway now.

"Please, please go now. Maybe he'll let you go, but he won't spare me."

"Why did you betray Michael?"

"I didn't."

"I thought you loved him."

"I did."

"Who else knew about the negotiations?"

"No idea. His father, maybe."

"His father?"

"Yes, I think so."

"Mr. Leibovitz, where are you?"

Paul and Anyi both held their breaths. They heard the footsteps on the stairs clearly. Tang seemed to hesitate at the top. "Mr. Leibovitz?" He walked in the direction away from them and knocked at a door. When he got no reply he turned around and walked slowly toward Anyi's room. Paul took his hand off the door handle and stood against the wall next to the door. He saw the handle being pushed down slowly and the door opening wide.

"Mr. Leibovitz?"

Anyi did not say anything. Her lower lip was trembling and her face was ashen.

Tang stepped into the room and saw Paul immediately. "I didn't know you wanted to play hide-and-seek with me," he said sarcastically. "If I'm not wrong I don't have to introduce you; you know each other already. Anyi-yi, my darling, did my guest disturb you?"

She shook her head absently.

"Mr. Leibovitz, what do you want from my girlfriend?"

Paul looked first at him and then at Anyi. She sat in the bed defensively.

"Nothing," Paul said.

"Did you have a question?"

"No."

"If that is the case I'd like to ask you to leave my girlfriend's bedroom. I get the feeling that your presence here is not welcome."

Paul looked at Anyi, but she did not look back at him.

He left the room with Tang right behind him.

"The toilet is over there if you still need it."

————

Tang waited at the foot of the stairs and led Paul back to the dining room.

"Who told you about Michael's negotiations with Lotus Metal?" Paul asked once they were seated again.

"Why does that interest you?"

"I want to know who betrayed Michael Owen."

"That is completely unimportant."

"Not for me. Was it his father?"

Tang did not reply.

"Or Anyi?"

"I've told you already, it doesn't matter who told me. The consequences are the same."

"I have never met anyone as cynical as you."

"It will not surprise you to learn that I take that as a compliment."

"Why did you kill Michael Owen?"

"I absolutely reject that accusation," Tang replied with a lightly ironic tone. How can this man feel so completely secure? Paul asked himself. "But if you're convinced that I'm the murderer," Tang continued, "you can also answer this question yourself. Michael conducted secret talks with a competitor firm behind my back. Our joint venture had made a lot of money, but at least until now it would not have worked without the Owens' contacts and supply agreements. So I had a motive, yes? But I'm going to tell you three things that you should take very seriously. First: I did not murder Michael Owen. Second: The truth has been decided. Third: You have to watch out that you're not fighting against the rest of the world. You don't want to become a martyr for the truth, do you?"

"I'm not alone."

"Are you sure?"

"Yes."

"I hope for your sake that you are not deceiving yourself."

"What do you mean by that?"

"Tell me where you got the story about the murderer's alibi," Tang said.

"From the wife of the man who you've put in jail. Mrs. Owen already told you that."

"Have you spoken to her?"

"No. My friend Zhang did."

"Were you there?"

"No. He told me about it."

"I see. He told you about it."

"What's so unusual about that?"

"Are you still sure that everything Zhang tells you is true?"

Paul rejected the implication immediately. "Of course. Why not?" Let his host think he was naïve or stupid, but he would not let Tang realize he had any doubts about Zhang's honesty.

"Only the very wise and the very stupid never change their opinions. That's an old Chinese proverb. What makes you so sure? Maybe the last time I met Zhang was not thirty years ago but two days ago. Maybe he changed sides and you haven't noticed?"

That was enough. Paul stood up very suddenly, as though he was about to lean over the table and grab Tang by the collar. His chair fell backward and clattered loudly against the floor.

"That is ridiculous," Paul shouted, raising his voice for the first time that evening.

"If you're so sure, why are you getting so worked up?"

Paul wanted to have nothing more to do with this person whom, he had to admit, he was no match for.

"I'm going now."

"Do that. I won't stop you. You won't get far with what you know."

"You're threatening me again."

"I'm not threatening you. I'm merely stating how it is. Don't overestimate what you can do. The bee may have stripes on its back, but they do not turn her into a tiger."

"Another Chinese saying?"

"And not a bad one. May my driver take you anywhere?"

"No thank you." Did Tang really think that he would get into his car and trust himself to his driver after this conversation?

"Shall I ring for a taxi for you?"

That could also be a trap. Paul remembered Zhang's warnings; anything was possible. He just wanted to get out now, onto the street, where he surely would find a taxi before long.

"No. I'd prefer to go on foot."

"As you wish. It's a long way from here to the ferry or to the next train station, and it won't be a pleasant walk, I assure you."

Paul strode through the dining room and the reception room to the front door, where he turned around. Tang had followed him and was looking at him with a mixture of wonder and pity.

"You're making a mistake, Mr. Leibovitz."

Paul could not think of a suitable reply. He opened the door and disappeared wordlessly into the night.

———

Paul had never walked through such a bleak and disquieting residential area in China before. The broad, newly paved streets were clean but there was no one around and hardly a car to be seen. The multistoried villas were protected by high walls and several rolls of barbed wire. Now and then a Mercedes or a BMW glided by almost silently, stopped before an entrance, and then disappeared behind a large gate that closed once more with a quiet hum.

It was already past eleven PM and Paul realized that it would be difficult for him to get a taxi at this hour. At the next crossroad he looked around in all directions to see if he could make out the lights of a main road in the distance. He saw nothing but dimly lit avenues and walls whose edges melted into the darkness. He carried on walking in a straight line, hoping to get to a main road. He thought about Tang and his threat and looked around to see if a car might be following him, but the road was empty. Paul felt a physical unease, a real revulsion, when he thought about the conversation he had just had. The blithe enthusiasm with which Tang had told the story of the old monk. The satisfaction in his face when he saw how deeply his guest was affected by the tale. Paul could have continued feeling indignant about Tang's cynicism for hours, but his discomfort would not hide the fact that Tang had succeeded. Something that Paul would never have thought possible had happened: A seed of doubt about Zhang's honesty, about their friendship, had been sown.

It doesn't change anything, he had claimed bravely, but the more Paul thought about it, the less true it seemed. He wanted to fight against feeling suspicious and mistrustful, but he was too weak right now, or the feeling was too strong; yes, it was growing now, feeding on itself like jealousy or paranoia. Zhang had hidden the fact that he knew Tang from before for a long time. What else was he keeping from him? "Trust once lost can never be regained." This was a Confucian saying that had stayed in Paul's mind.

Suddenly he heard the sound of an engine behind him and turned around. A dark Audi had drawn up a few meters behind him and there were four men in it staring at him. He tried to cross to the other side of the road, but from the other direction a second car drove toward him at high speed. Paul froze with fear. The car made a sharp turn, mounted the sidewalk with a dull thump, and stopped right in front of him. The doors flew open and several young men in suits got out and started running toward him. In a few seconds they had surrounded him. Paul looked to the left and to the right and realized that he could neither run away nor defend himself, and he could not call for help either. One of the men ordered him in crude Mandarin to get into the Audi; he was not to try anything; the more cooperative he was, the less violent they would have to be.

Paul went over to the car and sat in the rear seat. Two heavyset muscular Chinese men moved to sit on either side of him and the driver started the engine while one of the men blindfolded him quickly. He felt a sharp smell shoot up his nose. Christine was the last thing he remembered thinking about before he lost consciousness.

XXX

It was the piercing pain in his head that woke Paul. A tension pulling from his neck over the back of his head to his forehead and over his face that reminded him of the migraine attacks that had occasionally overcome him while Justin was ill, forcing him to spend a day or two lying down in a darkened room. Justin had often come to lie down beside him after school then, and Paul had not had the heart to tell him that even the sound of his high voice caused him pain. He listened to it until they both fell asleep together.

Paul swallowed. His mouth and his throat were completely dry. He opened his eyes gingerly; bright light would only make the pain worse. The room he was lying in was in a twilight of half darkness. Where was he? It took a while for him to remember the dark avenue, the two cars, the men, and the blindfold, which had stunk of a sweetish scent. Surely only Tang could be behind this. He had not predicted that he would have an extremely uncomfortable walk without reason.

What else do you know? Tang had asked almost casually during the dinner. *Don't expect an answer now,* Paul had replied lightheartedly, almost jokingly, enjoying the thought that his host feared that he, Paul, had more information with which to incriminate him. Maybe that had been a mistake. Maybe he should have simply told the truth: Nothing. I don't know anything apart from what I've told you. He had not wanted to admit this yesterday. Would Tang still believe this "Nothing"? Christine had been right to be frightened. He had been incredibly stupid.

Paul tried to sit up and groaned. With every movement he felt his pulse pounding in his temples. This pain could not be withstood for long without pills. He felt nauseous and he was afraid that he might throw up any second. He looked around him. There was no toilet and no bucket in the room, only a sink. If he vomited in there, the sour smell of the vomit would stink up the whole room. He took a few deep breaths in and out that helped a little with the nausea.

His bed was a kind of pallet with a thin, uncomfortably firm mattress on it that he could barely lie on. Paul stood up slowly with considered movements. He was still wearing the suit he had on yesterday but the pockets were empty. They had taken away his cell phone and his briefcase, his ID, and his belt. The laces had been taken out of his shoes. He saw a plastic bottle of water and a plate of rice on a small wooden table. He went over to the table and drank half the bottle in a few short gulps.

Paul wondered if there was any way of escaping, but the only window in the room was small and had a grille over it; it was at the top of the wall, almost right under the ceiling. The door was secured with a locked metal grille. He got up and shook the grille and shouted "Hello" a few times without getting a reply. Paul carried the only chair in the room over to where the window was and stood on it. He could only see a little through the window; more than half of it was underground and a strip of blue sky as wide as a hand showed through the rest. He was able to open the window slightly, and soon heard a car driving up, car doors slamming, and footsteps. The car drove off again. Was he about to have a visitor? He listened hard. He got down from the chair, walked over to the door, and listened. Nothing.

Where had they brought him? This room was neither a cell—he was certainly not in an official prison—nor a guest bedroom. He was in a kind of basement. He remembered that Zhang had told him about two rooms in the basement of the police headquarters in which confessions were forced out of people. With violence if necessary.

Strangely, this thought did not make him feel frightened. Fear was nothing more than a function of an overactive imagination, at least with regard to nontraumatic experiences. That was how he had often comforted Justin when he had been frightened of the dark. People imagined everything that *could* happen and felt afraid. So those who had no imaginations could not be afraid.

He thought about Michael Owen. Perhaps he too had not wanted to accept till the very end how far his enemy would go.

Paul kept thinking about Zhang and the death of the old monk. Tang had told the story at such length and in such detail that images of that afternoon rose before Paul's eyes, haunting the half dark of the room. The ruined temple. The scrolls with excrement on them. He saw the Red Guards marching over the fields with their flags, he saw the monk, and how Zhang passed the wooden rod to Tang and how Tang struck the blow. The worst thing was that he was observing these images as a disinterested spectator. He felt nothing now apart from a terrible coldness within him, an indifference to the deed and toward his friend. He had had the same feeling in the months after Justin's death; he remembered it as a kind of numbness of the heart, and the paralysis had been awful. To feel nothing felt like a relief at first, but in the long run it was worse than any pain. It had taken him a long time to free himself from this coma of the feelings. He did not want to return to that state, not at any price, but whenever he thought about Zhang now it seemed to come upon him. He felt nothing. No hatred. No disappointment, not even anger. It was as though there had never been any closeness between them.

Paul sat down on the bed, leaned against the bare gray concrete wall, closed his eyes, and tried to find a position in which his headache would be easier to bear. From time to time he walked up and down below the window hearing the cars that drove past, sometimes voices that quickly died down again.

It was dark by the time he heard a key in the lock. The door opened, the metal grille was pushed aside, and the light was switched on. Two men came into the room. One of them was carrying a tray with two bottles of water, a big bowl of rice and stir-fried vegetables, and the other was holding a tin bucket and a roll of toilet paper. They did not react when he asked where he was and who they were and merely gave a brief, glum nod when he asked for something for his headache. A few minutes later one of them returned with a packet of aspirin. After that, all was quiet and dark. Paul took four pills immediately, undressed, and lay down. He curled up with the blanket pulled up over his chin and fell asleep shortly after.

He was awakened by the sound of a deep male voice and a hand shaking him roughly by the shoulder. It took Paul some time to realize that he was not dreaming. Three tall powerfully built Chinese men were standing in front of his pallet; they did not look like policemen or like contract killers; in their dark-blue suits, they reminded him more of businessmen. One of them ordered him to get dressed immediately and follow them.

They led him down a long narrow corridor to a small elevator that they had to squeeze into in order to fit the four of them. When the door closed, Paul had the feeling that the entire elevator stank of the same sweetish scent he had smelled in the car. The muscular bodies of the young men were pressed up against him, and he felt their breath on his face, stinking of stale cigarette smoke. He grew more and more uncomfortable. He suddenly realized how defenseless he was among them. The men did not even bother gazing at the ceiling or the floor out of politeness, but stared at him brazenly. Their eyes met several times and the expression in their eyes was unfamiliar to him. He could not fathom what they had in store for him.

They brought him to a room that looked like a junior suite in a rather run-down average Chinese hotel. The light-colored carpet had several stains on it and there were two couches with worn brown covers and a coffee table with a vase of dusty plastic flowers on it in front of a large window. According to the clock on the wall it was just after 5:30 AM. A man was sitting at a desk bent over a folder of papers. He looked up briefly when they entered the room and then continued reading. The men motioned to Paul to sit down on a chair in front of the desk, left the room, and locked the door.

The man did not make any move to start a conversation.

After sitting in silence for a few minutes Paul asked, "Who are you? What do you want from me?" He intended to sound indignant and angry, but when he opened his mouth to speak he was short of breath and he sounded tense and strained.

The man did not even look up from his papers.

"Why are you holding me prisoner?"

Now he raised his head and looked at Paul expressionlessly.

"Do you work for Victor Tang?" Paul asked, undeterred.

The man closed the file, pushed it aside, leaned forward a little, and looked Paul directly in the eye. "I'd like to make this clear from the start, Mr. Leibovitz. There is only one person here who asks the questions and that is me. Do you understand me? You can either stay silent or answer the questions. That's up to you. But I would personally recommend that you do the latter in your own best interest."

Instead of replying, Paul looked out of the window and tried to look as relaxed as possible. He did not want to let himself be intimidated. This man did not look like what Paul imagined a henchman of Tang's to look like, but he did not look like a respectable detective from the police headquarters in Shenzhen either—his attitude to a foreigner was too confident for that. He was in his early forties at most, and was also wearing a suit. He spoke Mandarin without a discernible accent so he was probably from Beijing. His voice was sharp and decided.

Leaning far back in his chair, he said, "You obtained access to Michael Owen's apartment in Hong Kong and stole several items, including a cell phone and a hard drive."

Paul started in surprise and sank deep into his chair.

"Why did you do that?"

"Who told you that?" Paul blurted out. Only Zhang and Christine knew about that and they would have told neither the police nor Tang. Would they?

"Did you not understand what I said earlier? Answer the question or say nothing," the man told him.

"Was it Zhang? Did he tell you about it?" Paul couldn't help asking.

A brief smile flitted over the man's face. "And if he did, does it matter? You committed a theft. Why, Mr. Leibovitz?"

Who was this man? How did he know Zhang?

"What do you live on in Hong Kong?" the stranger asked.

"That has nothing to do . . ."

"What do you live on?" the man interrupted him in an icy tone.

"From the interest on my savings," Paul replied, immediately feeling annoyed at himself for replying. He was letting himself be intimidated.

"Why are you taking such an interest in the murder of Michael Owen?"

Paul said nothing. If the man did not tell him who he was he would not answer any questions.

"Did you know Mr. Owen before? Who asked you to conduct investigations?"

Paul closed his eyes. He did not want to give the impression that he was about to answer a single question.

"Mr. Leibovitz. You're not doing yourself any favors. You're making a mistake."

Tang had taken leave of him the previous evening with exactly the same words. The more Paul thought about it, the more convinced he was that only Victor Tang could be behind his abduction. Why did he not interrogate him himself?

He shook his head. "Tell me why you're asking these questions and who you are working for and I may answer them. Until then you'll get nothing from me."

The man sized him up, as if gauging how serious Paul was. He stood up and walked around the desk. For a moment Paul was afraid that he was about to be violent to him. But he walked past him to the door, opened it, and called the men waiting in the corridor to take Paul back to the basement. He disappeared into another room without saying anything more.

———

Paul lay on the bed and stared up at the ceiling. His headache had mostly gone, apart from a slight tugging over his left eye. He tried to get his thoughts in order, not knowing what Tang intended to do with him. Or what Richard Owen's role in this was. If Anyi was not lying it might have been he who had betrayed his son to Tang. But was Anyi telling the truth? He was losing any instinct for whom he could trust or not.

He heard cars driving up in front of the building again. Gravel spattered against the window and brakes squealed. He went over to the window and climbed onto the chair. There seemed to be more cars arriving and he thought he heard not only the voice of the man who had interrogated him today but—he could hardly believe his ears—the voices of Tang and Zhang. They were farther away and he could not hear what they were saying, but that was Zhang's light singsong, his melody. No, he was not mistaken, and the impassioned voice that was answering was Tang's. The voices quickly faded into the distance and nothing could be heard after a few seconds.

Paul pressed his mouth against the crack in the window and shouted his friend's name and thumped his fist against the glass, but no one replied.

Breathless with excitement, he spent the next hour pacing up and down in his room. Every so often he climbed up onto the chair to listen for sounds and rattled the iron grille over the door, and he kicked the narrow gray metal closet that looked like a locker next to the sink until there was a dent in the side. Gradually he started imagining what might happen again and with that came the fear. He was completely defenseless against them. He felt faint all over.

He grew dizzy and breathless and a piercing pain stabbed him in his left breast.

He lay down on the bed and tried to calm himself, concentrating on the breathing exercises that Zhang had taught him a long time ago. Very slowly, breath by breath, his heart slowly regained its normal rhythm. He lay there for hours and thought about Zhang, trying to banish the thought that he might have betrayed him as he watched twilight and darkness falling outside. Lights came on in front of the building and one of them cast a narrow beam into his room; other than that, everything was dark.

Suddenly, he heard footsteps and voices in the corridor. Someone unlocked the door and the metal grille. Two men he did not know came in, followed by a third, who switched on the light.

It was Zhang.

Paul flinched. Several times in the past few hours he had imagined how he would react when they met again. Now the time had come, and he was speechless at the sight of his friend. Zhang tried a smile, but Paul did not return it. He still felt nothing. He felt as if he was staring at a blank wall. Paul was shocked at himself. Where had this coldness come from?

Zhang took a step toward him. Paul retreated.

"Stay where you are. What do you want?" he asked suspiciously.

"What's wrong with you? I've come to fetch you." Zhang seemed amazed by Paul's reaction.

"To fetch me! What do you two have in store for me?"

"What do you mean by 'you two'?"

"You and Tang."

"Me and Tang? Are you crazy? What makes you think that we . . ."

"What makes me think that?" Paul interrupted brusquely. "Because you were once his henchman, weren't you?"

"I'm sorry?"

"Don't look so surprised. Tang told me everything," Paul said in a voice full of contempt. "About the temple. The monk. And your readiness to help him." Paul felt as if he was hearing his own voice from afar, as though it belonged not to him but to a stranger he did not know and did not like.

Zhang's narrow eyes widened. His mouth fell open, and he clasped his head in both hands. Paul would not forget his look of horror. It was as though he were imploding in front of him, sinking into himself like a building expertly rigged for demolition. Zhang seemed at a loss for a moment. He gasped audibly a couple of times and seemed about to leave the room but turned back, sat down on the chair, and asked the other two men to leave and close the door behind them. He propped his elbows on the table and buried his face in his hands. It was so quiet that Paul could hear both of them breathing.

"I'm sorry, Paul, that you had to hear it from him."

"I'm sorry, too." He heard how self-righteous and annoyed he sounded. "Why did you never tell me about it?"

"I don't know," Zhang said without looking up.

"You don't know," Paul echoed, his voice slightly raised. This reply was not only cowardly, it was an insult. "You don't know? How many times did we sit in your kitchen and talk about the Cultural Revolution? I asked you about your experiences, and you told me about them. But you kept the most important one to yourself."

"I know."

"We talked about the crimes that were committed then and I still remember exactly what you said about this country and how it was still in the shadow of those times. You talked about how important it was to discuss it and got worked up about nobody having the courage to do so. That's what you said, wasn't it?"

"Yes."

"Oh, Zhang! It's always other people who are the cowards. You looked me in the face with such indignation and I believed you. Every word." Paul could hear his voice getting louder and louder, how he was losing his composure with every sentence.

"But you yourself were one of them. One of the murderers, one of the people who said nothing." He was standing right in front of Zhang, and was practically about to grab him by the shoulders in rage. "Did you even tell Mei about it?"

"No. No one."

"Not even your wife? How could you live this lie? How could you stand it, sleeping next to her and waking up next to her and hiding a murder from her?" Paul did not wait for a reply to his question, but continued talking. "And your son? How will you explain it to him? And now you expect me to believe that you haven't been sent by Tang to collect me?"

Zhang sat motionless on the chair and said nothing.

"How am I supposed to know that you're telling me the truth? 'Trust once lost can never be regained.' Isn't that what Confucius said?"

"Yes."

Paul turned around and kicked the closet door so violently that it came free of its hinges and clattered onto the floor. He kicked it again and again until it was at the other end of the room. He grabbed the footstool in front of the sink by one leg and smashed it with all his might against the wall so splinters of wood flew across the room. He would have liked to destroy the table and the chair too, charge at his friend, and beat him up. He stood in the middle of the room, holding the leg of the stool in his hand, exhaled, and struck the bulb that was hanging from a wire in the ceiling.

At first it seemed there was complete darkness, but when his eyes had gotten used to it he saw that Zhang was still crouched motion-less on the chair.

Paul felt as relieved by his outburst as he was shocked by it. The inner paralysis, that terrible numbness, was gone and had given way to this rage that he and Zhang now had to work through. There was no shortcut that he could take back to Zhang.

"Why didn't you say anything?" Paul said. His voice had lost all strength.

"I don't know," Zhang said again, tonelessly.

"Were you dropping hints all those years that I didn't pick up on?"

"No."

Paul sank down on the pallet. Zhang emitted a series of strange sounds: deep sighs, gasps, and dry sobs in turn. They sat there for a long time without saying anything. Suddenly Zhang sat up and turned toward him. Paul could clearly make out the outline of his narrow frame in the darkness.

"It had gone," Zhang said with great care and very quietly. "For years. I had erased it from my memory. As though it had never happened. It always cast a shadow over my life but I did not notice it or did not want to notice it. Then this shadow started whispering. The memories returned in images and in words, even the musty smell of the old temple filled my nostrils again but I could not talk about it. I was too ashamed. Can you understand that?"

Zhang got up from the chair, took a few steps back and forth, and sat down next to him on the bed. The faint light was enough to see his face. He was a miserable little heap of a human being cowering in front of Paul, and Paul did not know what to say.

"How could I have done such a thing, Paul?"

"That's what I ask myself too." The sentence had slipped out of him and he regretted it immediately. Who knew how he would have behaved in the same situation? He did not want to judge the deed, he only wanted to know why Zhang had not had the courage to talk about it and if he was hiding anything else.

But Zhang had clearly not heard him. He continued, as though talking to himself, "How could I have been so easily led astray? Why was there nothing in me that rebelled against it? I used to think we were afraid of other people: the party, our parents, the teachers, the leaders. But we must have been most afraid of ourselves."

"Are there other deaths that you haven't talked about?"

Zhang nodded. "Old Hu. A cook from our work brigade who added peppercorns to his soup. But the soup was supposed to taste the same to everybody. When the Red Guards caught him they beat him to death."

"You did too?"

"No. I didn't join in but I stood by without helping him. I'm afraid I thought then that he deserved his punishment. Soup had to taste the same to everyone. I used to believe in this madness."

"Killed because of a few peppercorns?"

"Yes. Since then I've never not felt fear when I add seasoning to food. That's how far the shadows reach."

The land of the whispering shadows, Paul thought. One of those shadows had been with him for years, and he had neither seen nor heard it.

"And I thought all the time that I knew you," he said quietly.

"You do know me," Zhang replied. "As well as anyone can expect to know another person. Everyone has a few secrets."

They sat in silence on the bed for a long time. Paul would have liked to hug his friend, but he did not dare to.

"Shall we get out of this basement, then?" Zhang asked eventually.

"And go where?"

"Wherever you want," Zhang said, taking a deep breath. "You're free. Go back to Hong Kong. Open the bottle of champagne in your fridge."

"And what about Tang?"

"They arrested him last night, interrogated him overnight, and brought him here this morning. He's in the basement of the building next door."

"Who are 'they'?"

"The Ministry of State Security. These buildings belong to them. We're near Shenzhen airport."

"What has state security got to do with this case?"

"When you set out for the Owens' yesterday I was on the phone, remember?"

"Yes."

"I was talking to my friend in the Ministry of State Security in Beijing. He confirmed that Lotus Metal had been in negotiations with Michael Owen. When I told him that Michael Owen had been murdered he was shocked. Ten minutes later a colleague of his who was responsible for industry at the ministry rang me up. He was with Wang Ming of Lotus Metal, who just happened to be there. They too had not heard about Michael Owen's death yet. They had merely been very surprised that he had not been in touch for a few days. You can't imagine how they reacted to the news of the murder. The project meant a great deal to them. Wang Ming was so angry that he was sitting in the minister's office only minutes later getting a warrant for the police to take action."

"And then?"

"They asked me to bring everything that you took from Michael's apartment—the hard drive, the cell phones, the memory chips—to them in Shenzhen."

"I thought the ministry was in Beijing?"

"Yes, but Wang Ming and a dozen officials from the ministry took the next flight to Shenzhen. It all went incredibly quickly. You left the house just after noon to see Christine first. I was on the phone to Beijing until one-thirty, and at three o'clock they were already on the plane. We met shortly after seven-thirty in the evening at the Shangri-La Hotel near the Shenzhen train station. Half of them were IT engineers, experts in computers and cell phones. It barely took them half an hour to gain access to the entire hard drive and all the memory chips."

"And was what they found useful?"

"Useful? It produced almost all the clues and the evidence that we have. I have the feeling that we all made a mistake about Michael Owen. Tang, at least, was completely wrong about him."

"What do you mean by that?"

"He negotiated the contracts with Lotus Metal very skillfully— they were much more lucrative for the Owens than the ones with Tang. He planned every step carefully, and after Tang discovered the negotiations and started threatening him, or at least trying to, the American documented every communication meticulously. Every e-mail was saved."

"Wasn't it stupid of Tang to put his threats in writing?" Paul asked.

"Of course it was. He probably felt overly secure because of his contacts with the police, the city administration, and the party in Shenzhen. He couldn't imagine that anyone would bring charges against him for anything. The memory chips that you found were actually much more useful than the hard drive."

"What's in them?"

"They were all SIM cards for cell phones. Michael Owen had two cell phones on which he could record conversations. We found at least six conversations from the ten days before the murder, in which Tang made serious threats to Michael Owen and to Anyi."

"How did Owen react?"

"He didn't take the threats seriously. I listened to the recordings a few times, and they made me feel very anxious. They were constantly at cross-purposes. I don't know if they didn't want to understand each other or just couldn't. Owen kept insisting that the law was on his side. Apparently, there was a clause in the contracts with Tang that gave him a right of cancelation in special circumstances, and he wanted to invoke that clause. Sue me if you will, he challenged Tang several times. He could not have imagined that Tang would turn to violence."

"And then you got the police involved?"

"No." Zhang shook his head. "All the men here, including the leader of the investigation who interrogated you this morning, flew here yesterday morning from Beijing on a special flight."

"Why?"

"You know how Tang has close contacts in Shenzhen. No one here would have arrested him."

"Not even with the evidence?"

"I suspect we wouldn't even have gotten as far as showing anyone our evidence. He is too powerful. We've been very lucky."

"Why is Tang important enough for Beijing to bother with?"

"I think there are two reasons for it. He chose the wrong enemy in Lotus Metal. No one should cross a company owned by the Ministry of State Security. But even more important is that Tang acts as an example. You know the old Chinese saying, 'Slaughter a chicken to frighten the monkey.' Tang and his people are the chicken."

"And who are the monkeys?"

"The many thousands of big and little Tangs all over the country who are doing as they please and thinking that 'the mountains are high and the emperor is far away.' That's a beautiful saying from Confucian times, by the way."

"You mean that every now and then, the emperor has to show that he has long arms?"

"Exactly right. Just wait. I'm sure that we'll see, read, and hear about this case a great deal in the next few days. Two teams from CCTV and several reporters from *Xinhua* were already here today. The *China Daily, China Youth Daily, Beijing News,* and *Shanghai Daily,* all the big national newspapers will carry detailed reports. This story comes very handy for Beijing. It fits in with the current anticorruption campaign and is a good opportunity to show that the government is clamping down hard. Imagine, they've not only arrested Tang but also the entire management of his conglomerate firm. Luo and countless colleagues at police HQ were suspended from duty today, as were two party secretaries and several department heads in the municipal administration that Tang had many dealings with, along with an official who worked closely with the mayor. You know how the political campaigns and propaganda work in China. The purges of today are no longer called by the same name but they haven't changed a great deal in principle."

"And why," asked Paul, "did they abduct me?"

"It was a security measure at first. They wanted to make sure that Tang didn't do anything to you."

"If that were the case they should have simply asked me to follow them. Why have they left me in this basement for almost two days and interrogated me like a prisoner?"

"For the same reason that they interrogated me for one night, even after I had given them all we had and had listened to the recorded conversations with them. Because they wanted to make sure that we were telling the truth and that this was not a trick or one of Tang's many ruses. Because they didn't trust us. Because no one trusts anyone here. Ever."

XXXI

The air was uncomfortably warm, but not so hot that it made Elizabeth Owen sweat. The deep-blue sky over the city reminded her of the wonderfully cold and clear winter days in Milwaukee; even the smog that otherwise hung like a brown mist over the skyscrapers and the harbor had disappeared. This was the first day of beautiful weather since she had been in Hong Kong.

The sea had also taken on a different color. Here, near the Yung Shue Wan harbor, it shone in a light turquoise like she had seen in the Bahamas. Elizabeth was glad that she had made her way here to visit Paul Leibovitz and was only sorry that her husband had not come with her. Why had Richard resisted coming so much? He had made an incredible scene in the hotel; he had gotten all worked up and cursed and sworn, and even warned her that she should not believe everything Leibovitz told her. She had no idea what he was talking about. Everything Paul had suspected and claimed so far had been true. Richard was behaving as if she had gone off to meet a lover; he surely could not be seriously jealous of Paul. Sometimes she got the feeling that her husband was afraid of him, but when she asked Richard this he flew into a terrible rage.

After a good half hour the ferry docked at the jetty. She was one of the last to leave the rocking vessel; the gangway wobbled dangerously and a ferryman offered her his hand, but she preferred to hold on to the railing.

What a strange place. There were no skyscrapers, only unremarkable small buildings; no cars and no roads. A couple of fishing boats were bobbing up and down in the bay. The smell of the sea was strong, and white smoke was puffing out of four chimneys that rose up beyond a hill. Elizabeth pulled out of her bag the piece of notepaper on which she had hurriedly scribbled directions this morning. She walked along the pier, past grubby fish tanks full of fish, crabs, and sea cucumbers. On the left was Green Cottage and the ATM, on the right was the rusty container cabin where the police station was. She was to turn off here.

She saw the small vegetable plots that the old farmers were working on. Right after that came the path uphill, just as Paul had described.

The path was steep and difficult to climb, and when Elizabeth Owen finally got near the top of the hill she was out of breath and soaked with sweat. She sat down on a bench to rest before turning left again and climbing up a little way more before seeing the house less than a hundred meters away behind a thick bamboo grove. She could tell she was in the right place when she saw it shimmering white behind the green of the thicket.

The terrace was a gardener's dream. Paul clearly shared her passion for flowers. Everything was in bloom: roses, hibiscus flowers, geraniums; red, white, and pink bougainvillea; and a beautiful frangipani tree. The plants had been so carefully tended that she did not see a single wilted bloom anywhere or any brown leaves in the pots or on the red and brown tiles.

He had seen her coming through the kitchen window and opened the door.

"There you are. I was starting to get worried."

"Did I take a long time?"

"Goodness, no. I was only afraid that you had gotten lost."

"No. Your directions were excellent, but the climb up was more difficult than I'd anticipated. You really live far away, as if in exile."

"Alone, but not in exile," he replied, inviting her into the house.
"I chose to retreat a little for a while."

"A while is fine. How long do you plan your retreat to last, if I
may ask?"

He had to laugh at that. She realized that she had never seen
him laugh, and thought the laugh lines around his mouth and eyes
suited him.

"That's a good question. I don't know. I think I'll know when the
time comes."

"How will you know?"

He gave her a thoughtful look and took his time with his reply.
"How do we know that the time is right for something?"

Elizabeth was not sure if he was directing the question at her or
at himself. It was a strange question, one that she had never asked
herself.

"By thinking it over and deciding that it is time," she said.

"Maybe. But it's never worked like that for me."

"What happens instead?"

"I hear a kind of inner voice instead. Do you know it?"

"No. What do you mean?"

"A whisper in your head or your heart, deep down, that tells you
what you have to do in difficult times."

"No. I wish I would hear that now and then," she said with an
embarrassed laugh.

"It's difficult to explain. Let's put it this way: I'm sure that I'll
know when the time comes to engage more with the world."

"You've already done that in the last few days. More than you
wanted to, I suspect."

It was meant as a joke but Paul did not laugh. He laid his knife
down and looked her so pointedly in the eye that she felt uncomfortable.

"You may be right. I hadn't thought about that. Perhaps the time
has come."

"You've made an extraordinarily beautiful place for yourself here," she said before his gaze disconcerted her any more. "Your terrace is wonderful. May I look around a little? You must forgive me. I'm terribly curious."

"Go ahead. I'll make some tea."

She went into the living room and marveled at how beautiful old Chinese furniture could look, and at the fresh flowers on the table and the windowsill. It looked so clean, as if several conscientious cleaners had just cleaned the house top to toe. She saw a pair of small rain boots in the hall. "Do you have children, Mr. Leibovitz?" she called out in amazement.

"A son," he replied from the kitchen.

"You never said anything before," she said, walking back to him. He was standing at the kitchen counter peeling a knob of ginger and he shrugged, as if it had not been worth mentioning. "What's his name?"

"Justin."

"An unusual name. How old is Justin?"

Paul thought for a moment and looked at her for a long moment as though he could see the age of his son in her face.

Typical of a man, Elizabeth thought. First he forgets to mention his child, then he doesn't even remember the year he was born in. Richard had also never known how old Michael was; she had almost always had to revise his reply to this question upward or downward by a year.

"Eleven," Paul said at last.

"Eleven! A good age. Where is he at the moment? In school?"

"In school?" he repeated wonderingly, as though that was a very odd idea. "No, here."

"Here in the house?" Elizabeth had not heard a child's voice or sounds of any sort. "You mean upstairs in his room?"

"In a way, yes," he said, looking past her and smiling gently as if he was amused by her confusion.

"Why doesn't he come downstairs? Don't you want to introduce him to me?" He seemed not to have heard her, even though he was standing right in front of her. "Don't you want to introduce him to me?" she repeated.

"No, he's very reserved, shy even, and when there are strangers in the house he likes to hide away."

"What a pity," she said, disappointed.

"Maybe he'll come out of his own accord. Sometimes he makes a surprising appearance." Paul poured some tea, sniffed at his cup, and took a sip.

"I don't really understand what you mean, but it doesn't matter," she said somewhat brusquely. "I came here because we're flying back to America tomorrow and I didn't want to leave the city without seeing you one more time. I want to thank you."

"What for?"

"My husband and I owe you a huge thank-you. If you and your friend had been happy with the official findings of the police investigation we would still be doing business with our son's murderer."

Paul felt very uncomfortable about what she was saying. He took another sip of tea and looked over her head out of the window. "What's going to happen to your joint venture now?" he asked, as though he wanted to change the subject quickly.

"We don't know yet. My husband wants to sell our interests as quickly as possible."

Paul went back to the kitchen counter. There were several small bowls on it with sliced spring onions, garlic, bamboo shoots, and all kinds of vegetables that she did not recognize. He started dicing the ginger. He seemed to be expecting quite a few people to dinner.

"I won't take up any more of your time," she said, finishing her tea. "But I still wonder about two things. What happened to the man who was suspected of the murder?"

"He's been released. I don't know any more than that."

"And my son's Chinese girlfriend, what's she called again?"

"Anyi."

"Anyi, that's right. Was she arrested?"

"I don't know. Why should she have been?"

"For being an accomplice to murder, of course. My husband said Tang could only have learned about Michael's secret negotiations from her. She was with Michael in Shanghai and Beijing. She knew about the plans with Wang Ming."

"That's what your husband says?"

"Yes. Why do you look so surprised? He's sure of it. How else would Tang have known?"

"I've no idea," Paul said hesitantly.

He was once again as serious as when she had first met him, and he was avoiding her gaze. She could feel it.

"Do you know how else?"

Paul shook his head vigorously. "No. I don't know who else was involved in your son's plans."

"We don't know either but we think she was the only one. Apart from my husband, of course."

He turned away and rubbed his eyes.

"Is something wrong? Mr. Leibovitz, you told me a few days ago that my son had been murdered. I can't imagine what else that you could tell me that would be more terrible than that. What is it that is so terrible that you cannot tell me now?"

He still had his backed turned to her and his hands over his face.

"You can see why I want to know," she continued. "Because if Tang had only found out after the agreements had been signed then Michael would surely still be alive."

"You mustn't think like that," he exclaimed, whipping around to face her.

"Why not?"

"Because it can't change anything," he said curtly. "Because no ifs in the world can bring Michael back."

"I know that," she stammered, surprised by his outburst. "I just want to know who betrayed my son."

"We know who murdered him. Isn't that enough? The truth

sometimes comes at a terribly high price, Mrs. Owen. The truth can't always be borne."

"Mr. Leibovitz, are you all right? You're crying."

"It's the onions, Mrs. Owen, the onions."

———————

Paul Leibovitz was a strange person. Every meeting she had with him confirmed this thought, but she felt strangely happy in his presence and would have liked to stay longer and talk about Michael as a child and a young man, about the profusion of rosebushes they had that Paul would like, about the Milwaukee house that he was of course always welcome to visit. But Paul had told her on the telephone that he did not have much time because he was expecting dinner guests and was getting ready. When she started making motions to leave he did not ask her to stay for another cup of tea or call for his son to say good-bye to their guest. He walked her to the door, hugged her, and wished her all the best and a safe flight back.

She walked down the hill noticing for the first time the greenery growing wild and high all around her by the path. The ferns and grasses to the left and the right were a meter high and many of the leaves on the bushes and the trees were as tall as she was. The path was so overgrown in places that it seemed the undergrowth was about to reconquer the space. Climbing plants had wound themselves around the tree trunks and branches overhead as though they wanted to devour them, and for a moment she feared she might be their next victim. She imagined the branches above her rearing up and growing bigger, fatter, and stronger in seconds, wrapping themselves around her and pulling tighter and tighter until they had swallowed her up. She knew it was a horrible and silly thought, but she still felt a little frightened. She started walking more quickly and would have liked nothing better than to run down the hill to the village.

Everything here was strange to her: the people, the food, the noise, the dirt, yes, even the plants and trees in their exuberant, unchecked growth. She could hardly wait to finally get home and walk through her garden, sit on her terrace, and look at the rosebushes. It would not be easy—she was not going to deceive herself. They had to organize Michael's funeral first, put his affairs in order, and clear out his apartments. Perhaps only then would she really gradually realize that he was no longer there. And she also had to find a way back to Richard. Like everyone else, he also had had too much to deal with.

She thought about the many evenings they had spent with Tang and had absolutely no idea how they could have been so deceived by him. It was strange how well he and Richard had gotten along. The more she thought about it the more uncomfortable she felt, and she did not want that, not again. She closed her eyes and tried to smell the sweet, heavy scent of her roses on a summer's day but the air stank of salt and water. She wanted to think about Richard and their morning breakfasts on the terrace, their laps in the pool, their walks on the golf course. But she couldn't do that either. Instead, she kept seeing images of Tang and Richard together. How they had constantly filled each other's whiskey glasses at the end of their first evening together. How they had toasted each other, laughing. How they had roared and slurred through "My Way" together in the karaoke bar. She saw the images, heard the music and the singing, and did not understand a word. Was that the voice that Paul had spoken about? She hoped not. It brought more confusion than clarity to her.

Elizabeth Owen could hardly wait until she was sitting on the plane tomorrow. Whatever awaited her in Milwaukee, at least she knew who she was dealing with there. Who she could trust and who she could not.

XXXII

He had not noticed any of the men. Not the four men by the side table nor the two men by the door nor the group having an unusually silent meal at the big round table on the way to the washroom. Victor Tang was sitting in the Golden Dragon and was too deep in conversation with new steel suppliers to be alert to anything around him. Only when he had paid the bill and gotten up to go did he notice that over a dozen young men in the restaurant stood up at the same time, and that gave him an uncomfortable feeling. The next thing that he noticed was that the restaurant manager, who usually fluttered around him and thanked him for his generous tip when he left, was nowhere to be seen. Even the waiters were keeping their distance from him. They were looking away or giving him strained smiles, not daring to bring him his coat.

On his way to the cloakroom, two of the men planted themselves in front of him and told him to follow them outside. Whoever was behind this, Tang thought, must be incredibly sure of himself to arrange for him to be arrested in public.

A convoy of cars was waiting outside the door: six limousines that were soon driving at high speed on the highway, bringing him to a large building on the outskirts of the city. If he was not wrong, it used to belong to the Ministry of State Security before that ministry moved to new quarters near the airport. The policemen were probably from Beijing. That was not a good sign, but he was not too worried. He had clearly made a mistake; now he had to find out who he was up against. Would it be Wang Ming and his pathetic Lotus Metal? If the ministry was trying to call him—and thereby also parts of the party and municipal authorities—to justice, then he had miscalculated badly. Tang could not imagine that was the case and it didn't matter to him either way. As soon as he knew who he was dealing with he would assemble his allies and counterattack.

His watch showed that it was just after ten when they arrived at the building. Lights were on on the top floor, but the rest of it was in darkness and looked unoccupied. They climbed over a pile of rubble in the entrance hall and walked up a staircase without a banister and through empty, barely lit corridors to a large room with a high ceiling, with only a red couch and an empty desk and chair in it. A bulb hung from a long black wire, and the walls were bare. Plaster was peeling from several places on the wall, and it looked like a place earmarked for demolition. The men told him to wait there, and they left him alone. When he sat down on the couch he sank so deep into it that it felt like he might as well have been squatting on the floor. His knees were practically at eye level. A dwarf could have sat on the chair opposite and appeared like a giant to him. He was about to clamber his way out of the couch when a man entered the room.

"Don't stand on ceremony, please. Stay seated and make yourself comfortable," he said, sitting on the chair behind the desk.

As least he had a sense of humor, Tang thought, falling back into the pathetically flabby upholstery.

The man looked down at him for a long moment without saying anything. He was young, probably not even forty yet, and he had a piercing stare that Tang could not avoid. Surely he didn't think that Tang would be intimidated by that.

"Tang Mingqing" the stranger said eventually, drawing out the syllables as he spoke.

"Yes. And who are you?"

"My name is Wen. I belong to the Central Commission for

Discipline Inspection and I'm heading the investigation against you."

"When did this investigation start?" Tang asked, astounded. His surprise was not feigned.

"It officially started yesterday. Unofficially, it started some time ago."

Was it this damn couch or the intolerable arrogance in the man's voice? Tang started to feel uncomfortable, and slid back and forth in search of a comfortable position in which he would not look so ridiculous with his long legs.

"To what do I owe this, if I may ask?"

"The list is long. Several serious cases of corruption. Misappropriation of official funds. Tax evasion and," he paused here as if to give the next word extra weight, "murder."

"That's absurd," Tang blurted out. "I think you don't know who is sitting in front of you. A phone call from me will be enough to clear up this ridiculous episode."

The inspector took Tang's cell phone out of his bag, which the men in the car had taken from him, and tossed it to him.

"Please try your luck. To be honest, we would also be very interested to see who you turn to in such a situation."

The cell phone thudded next to him on the couch. Tang stared at it and felt himself growing hot. Please, he couldn't show any sweat on his brow now. He had not expected this coldness. This man was of a different stature to the party cadre heads, fat cats, or local officials he usually dealt with. Threats did not impress him. He had been sent from the capital, and possessed the remorselessly self-righteous manner of a person acting on behalf of those in power. I must change my tone, Tang thought, to get this official to realize how important I am.

"Inspector Wen, what do you actually know about me?" he asked in as jovial a tone as he could manage.

"A great deal."

"I mean about my personal life."

"You were born in 1952 in Chengdu, son of an army officer."

"That's right," Tang said, interrupting him. "I was one of the Red Guards and led a work brigade in the countryside during the Cultural Revolution. Four years later, I went to study at Harvard. The first Red Guard to make it to an elite American university. Did you know that?"

The inspector merely nodded. He did not look amazed or impressed. Tang comforted himself with the thought that he was from another generation—much too young to grasp what an achievement that was.

"It was my own long march, if you like."

Silence. Not even the hint of a smile passed over the apparatchik's expressionless face at this allusion.

"When the economic reforms started I established several companies here in Shenzhen for the Sichuan government, and earned about a hundred million American dollars for the province."

No reaction. It was like speaking to a wall.

This conversation had taken a turn for the worse, and Tang could feel himself growing more and more uneasy. He had wanted to demonstrate how superior he was but he felt smaller and smaller as he went on. As though this was a magic couch that was shrinking him back to the size of a fourteen-year-old.

"Then I set up my own company and, as you know, became a very successful entrepreneur."

"Not by legal means. That's why we are sitting here."

"Inspector Wen." Perhaps a joke would help to lighten the situation. "Behind every great fortune lies a great crime."

"And?"

"Do you know who said that?"

"No. Chairman Mao? President Hu?"

Tang gave a deep sigh. "Balzac."

"Who?"

"A French writer. Forget it."

He could not believe that he was supposed to answer to this young man. Did he have to give him a history tutorial first? What in damnation was he accusing him of in the first place? It would be very difficult for them to prove that he was responsible for the murder of Michael Owen. What remained were crimes like fraud, misappropriation of funds, and corruption. Laughable. What kind of China did this man live in? This was a time of establishing new horizons, a gold rush period in which everyone was out to get as much as he could for himself. Every great power in their history had experienced a time of change like this. It was a time for chancers and gamblers, speculators and robber barons. Tang was convinced that it was people like him who helped the country make progress. Without them, the people would be sitting in the dirt and chewing on tree bark like the North Koreans. How did the inspector think that the Rothschilds and the Rockefellers had come by their fortunes? By honest reckoning of every cent or centime? By keeping their word on agreements?

"If you're suddenly trying to crack down on these types of crimes in China," Tang said in a trembling voice, "then you can arrest the majority of party cadre heads, officials, and entrepreneurs in the country."

"I'm not investigating the majority, Mr. Tang. I'm investigating you."

"That is completely arbitrary. Today I've fallen into disfavor. Tomorrow you'll seek out another victim. And what about the rest of them? Do they stay under the carpet? What do you have in mind? A show trial?"

"I understand a show trial to be for cases where the accusations are unfounded and the judgments have been decided before the start of the process. Our charges against you are based entirely on the facts. An independent judiciary will decide on the outcome."

"You can't be serious. Based on the same facts you could lock up tens of thousands, no, millions of people."

"My task is to conduct an investigation of you. The rest do not interest me right now." He paused and smiled briefly. "We'll have to start somewhere."

It was this smile that made Tang feel a deep, bottomless fear, a fear that he had thought he had left behind him forever. He recognized this smile from when he had smiled the same way. It was the evil smile of contempt that the powerful cast at their victims.

This interrogation was only the beginning. They had probably already searched his offices and his house and arrested his managing director. Victor Tang no longer held himself upright. He was suddenly no longer one of those people who could bend and twist the truth or even completely dismantle it and make something else out of it entirely.

He saw his father. The pack was on its way to the market square. He could hear their cries already.

If anything could save him, it was the fact that Inspector Wen was not an independent investigator who was bound to observe the rule of law. He was a tool, a henchman for the powers that be, and those could change, Tang thought.

A second man came in, walked over to Wen, leaned down to him, and whispered something in his ear. The men talked in low tones so Tang could not make out a word of what they said. While they talked, the stranger looked at him as though he was regarding a dog warily, unsure of whether he was about to attack him. He was shorter and quite a bit older than the inspector and seemed somehow familiar to Tang. He stood up, walked around the desk, and stared at him without saying anything. They had met before, but where? Why was his usually excellent memory letting him down now, of all times?

"Do we know each other?"

The man nodded.

"How?"

"From a temple."

"Where did we meet?" Tang could not remember when he had last been in a temple.

"At an execution."

"Whose?"

"A monk's. But mine too," he said, stretching his arm out and making a movement as if he was holding something and striking downward with force. Where was that musty smell coming from? What was that horrible sound that cut Tang to the bone in his spine and his legs? Wood splintering.

"Mine," Zhang repeated. "And yours."

XXXIII

She had wanted to come unburdened, without the terrible fear of the past few days and nights when she had hardly been able to sleep because she was worrying about him and wondering what had happened. Most of all, though, she had wanted to come without the weight of high expectations. He had rung her that morning and asked her to dinner and also asked her if she might like to stay the night. His voice had sounded quite different from before: very relaxed, cheerful, in fact, and she did not want to bring anything with her other than the happiness and lightness that had been with her all day since they had spoken on the phone. She simply wanted to spend the evening and the night with him, to simply see what would happen, and not be disappointed if it turned out to be nothing much.

But by the time she had made her way through the hedges and the bamboo grove, opened the garden gate, closed it behind her, and seen the house and the terrace, all the longings and expectations that she had wanted to leave behind in Hong Kong had returned.

Paul had turned the garden into an enchanted forest. Tea lights placed close together marked out the terrace and several white and red lanterns were hanging from the trees. A string of fairy lights was wound around the frangipani tree and an eight-candle candelabra was on the table next to two glasses, a big bouquet of red roses, and a bucket with a bottle of champagne in it. The doors and windows were open, and the only light in the house came from the candles on the tables and windowsills in the kitchen and the living room.

Paul lay quietly on his deck chair and pretended to be dozing. She could see perfectly well that he had opened one of his eyes by a tiny slit and was following her movements. She had never received such a welcome from anyone before.

She went to the table and saw how much care he had taken to decorate everything. There were more than a dozen small bowls full of delicious things; she could see eggplant, hundred-year-old eggs with mustard and ginger, and steamed crabs, all her favorite dishes. White frangipani petals and many more small red bougainvillea petals were strewn on the table. Her place setting was a disc of deep-red silk and a tea light flickered on both plates. She heard Paul getting up carefully and creeping up behind her. Then he was standing behind her and covering her eyes with his hands.

Her knees gave way. For a moment, she was afraid that this was all a dream and that she would wake up any minute and find herself on her couch in Hang Hau, staring at the test screen on the television. Then she felt his lips on her neck and her skin prickled. How could a person kiss so tenderly? She wanted to turn around, but he took her in his arms, lifted her up, turned in a circle with her, and carried her into the house and up the stairs like a sleeping child. He laid her on the bed and started undressing her. There were candles burning in the bedroom too. By their light, she watched his every move and she saw that he would not lose his strength today. She could hardly hold still with excitement and she wanted to tear off her skirt, her blouse, and her bra, or at least help him with the buttons and the belt to hurry things up, but he stroked her hands to her side and whispered, "We have time."

The gentleness with which he undressed her, the way his fingers glided over her skin, aroused her so much that she would not be able to take much more, would explode if he did not release her soon. How could he control himself for so long? How could he cover her with kisses for so long, until she was practically floating from the touch of his tongue?

When the moment came, she felt as if she was losing consciousness. As though he was sending waves of happiness through her body, waves that swept everything in their way along with them, that lifted her high and carried her into another world she had never been to, where there was no fear and no doubt, where there was one answer to every question. A world she had not even thought existed and that she never wanted to leave again. She felt indescribably weak and at the same time stronger than she had ever been in her life.

Their bodies were so intertwined that they were like one body. She held Paul tight and knew that she would never let him go again.

After some time she heard him laughing quietly as he lay in her arms. She took his head in her hands and saw that he was laughing and crying at the same time. He got up and carried her through the dark house down to the garden, where all the tea lights had burned down to the wick and gone out. He put her down on a chair gently, went back into the house, fetched two bathrobes and a basket full of tea lights, lit them one after another, and soon the garden was lit as it was when she arrived. He brought some warm rice from the kitchen, opened and poured the bottle of champagne, handed her a glass, and kissed her on the neck again, making her heart pound with excitement once more.

"You're driving me crazy," she whispered. "If you don't stop, the candles will go out another time without us."

"Again? I'm not a young man of twenty anymore," he whispered back.

"What a shame," she said, kissing him on the forehead.

Paul began feeding her. He picked up a piece of eggplant with his chopsticks, circled it in front of her open mouth, and let it drop in. He fed her some chicken in lemon sauce, cold duck, and tofu cooked in seven spices. She knew Paul was a keen cook, but his food had never tasted so good.

"This is incredible," she said, amazed. "How long did you spend in the kitchen?"

He was clearly pleased by her praise. He poured more champagne into her glass and clinked glasses with her.

"What are we toasting?" Christine asked, curious.

"You."

"Why me?"

"Because I want to thank you."

"Me? What for?"

"For your love. 'As if trusting was only for fools. As if we had a choice.' When you first said that to me I thought you were crazy. Of course we have a choice."

"And now?"

Paul sipped from his champagne, leaned his head to one side, and gave her a thoughtful look. "Now I know that you're right. When I had dinner with Victor Tang your words suddenly came to me. I missed you terribly and I quoted you."

"Did he know what you were talking about?"

"He knew very well. But he thinks the opposite is true, that we have no choice but not to trust."

Christine thought about her brother and her father and she thought about the story that Paul had told her yesterday on the telephone about Tang's father. "That's very Chinese."

"He said something similar."

"What?"

"That he wouldn't trust any Chinese person from his generation."

"I wouldn't either. In love, we have no choice but to trust. But apart from that, yes we do have a choice."

Christine listened in silence as he talked about the past two days, trying to imagine Tang and his world—the mansion, the gold golf clubs, the servants, Anyi—but she could not. It was too alien to her. It was as if Paul were telling her about his journey to the land of darkness, not about a place she could get to by train in an hour. What Paul was describing confirmed her worst fears and left her feeling indifferent at the same time. She was interested only insofar as she was still worried about Paul. She didn't care about Tang, and the Owens meant nothing to her. Only when the conversation turned to Zhang, and Paul spoke slowly and increasingly hesitantly about the temple and the old monk, did she grow uncomfortable. She could see how difficult it was for him to tell this story.

There was a long silence in the enchanted forest after that.

"Why did he never say anything?" Paul said in a half whisper, tipping his head back and looking up into the night sky as though the stars might have an answer for him.

Christine marveled at his question. Was it really so difficult for him to understand that Zhang could not share this secret? "Paul, your friend was just too ashamed, and he never found the right time. I think that after the right time passes, every minute of silence becomes another lie and they mount up so quickly that at some point it becomes simply impossible to talk about. Don't you know that feeling? Are you sure that you would have said anything in his place?"

He was still staring up at the stars in the sky. "No," he said, without looking at her. "Confucius claims that trust once lost can never be regained. Do you think that too?"

"Stop that," she said, rolling her eyes. "Even the Chinese philosophers get it wrong sometimes."

"Hmm. I'll think about it."

"Paul, it's not the head that forgives but the heart."

He smiled. "But even the heart takes time."

"Especially the heart."

He nodded and fell into a long silence again.

"What are you thinking?" Christine wanted to know.

"About Elizabeth Owen. She was here this afternoon. She wanted to thank me. It's strange, but I had a bad conscience after she went."

"After everything you've done for her?"

"Yes."

"Why?"

"I got the feeling that I should have told her that it was her husband who told Victor Tang about Michael's negotiations."

"Why?"

"She thinks it was Anyi."

"I would too, if I were her."

"But I know the truth," Paul retorted.

"And you think she doesn't?"

"No, she doesn't."

"Paul, Elizabeth Owen is not stupid. I'm sure she has a sense of who it was but she doesn't want to know. You can't force the truth on someone who doesn't want to see it. Anyway it's none of your business. It's a matter for the two of them."

Paul gave a deep sigh. "Sometimes I envy your pragmatism."

"You mean my simple view of the world?" she asked in mock indignation.

"No," Paul laughed out loud. "Not at all. But things like that bother me for ages."

He shook his head, got up, and fetched another bottle of champagne from the fridge. He put his arm around her and kissed her. "It's exactly that which I am grateful to you for, Christine. For your sense of humor and your belief in people, even though I can't always share it."

"Then watch out: the ability to trust is contagious."

It was still wonderfully warm so they pushed the chairs together and sat facing each other with their legs on each other's laps. They talked and ate and drank the second bottle too, until they heard the first birdsong and the sky above them gradually grew lighter. Christine could not remember when she had last spent the night outdoors in Hong Kong.

At some point they went upstairs and crawled into the bed, which still smelled of them. Paul lay next to her with his arms crossed under his head and his eyes open and Christine was reminded of her son. Not that there was the slightest resemblance between them, but the look in his eyes made her think of Josh when he was three or four years old and how he had greeted her in the mornings sometimes with such boundless happiness. It was not long before Paul fell asleep and Christine watched him, far too happy for sleep to cross her mind. She had taken the day off—her first in many years. Even on the day of her grandmother's funeral she had gone to the office in the afternoon. After a while she got up to surprise Paul with breakfast. She crept downstairs, tidied up in the garden, made some tea, and took the raspberry jam and the croissants out of the bag she had brought with her. She warmed them up in the oven, put everything on a tray, brought it up, and sat down next to him on the bed.

She listened to his quiet, even breath and watched his face at peace in the warm glow of the early daylight, and she asked herself whether she was frightened that he would pull away one more time, as he had so often in the past few months. Whether she was afraid that he would leave her or cheat on her, just like her husband had left her and cheated on her. Whether she was still haunted by the pain that her husband had caused her. No, she thought. No, she was not. She would not surrender to the power of mistrust. Because of that, her best friend said she was naïve and credulous, and her mother scolded her for being innocent, simple, and unworldly about love. Christine knew that she was none of those things. How could someone who loved be simple? How could anyone call her unworldly when there was almost nothing more important in the world than to love and to be loved?

She thought about the cold and rainy day in February when she had first met Paul. She had thought that he was about to shatter into thousands of tiny bits of glass like a car windshield on impact. He had been silent as if he had lost the power of speech; she remembered the wounded look on his face. This last night, in the flickering of the candlelight, he had looked no less vulnerable, but something was back in his eyes, a light that she had not seen all these months but that she had always known existed. He had laughed and joked and loved her more gently than any man ever had, and he had found his speech again. He would never lose her again, that she was sure of. He had carried her in his arms through the house and into the bedroom.

Past the rain boots and the raincoat.

EPILOGUE

November, Hong Kong

Dear Justin,

    It's still very early in the morning. The sun just woke up about half an hour ago and it's bright red and "crawled" out of the sea, as you always used to say. (Do you remember the first time we saw it sink into the sea? You were afraid that it would go out forever and when it rose again the next morning you were convinced for a very long time that it slept in the water and that is why the sea was so warm.)

    I woke up much earlier than usual today and couldn't settle down again because my head was full of a very special experience I had yesterday. But I'll tell you more about that later. Anyway, I hadn't slept much and couldn't lie in bed anymore so I got up when the birds and the little children were still sleeping. Now I'm sitting, as I have every morning for the last few weeks, on the roof terrace. There is a pot of tea in front of me and in the distance through the bamboo I can see the sunlight dancing on the sea. Today will be a good day—I feel it. The air is clear, which it only ever is in November in Hong Kong, and my garden is honey scented because the frangipani tree is blooming with more flowers than ever before.

    There is a big pile of paper next to me, covered in closely

*written handwriting—all the letters I have dedicated to you. I
had the idea of writing to you a long time ago but never had the
courage to. Who writes letters to his dead son? It was only after
I returned from my trip to China as an assistant detective that I
dared to start. I felt very strange writing the first few sentences,
but Christine strongly encouraged me to keep on writing, for
she wanted to get to know you, and this is the only way. Every
letter became easier to write, and a few days ago I thought about
an older French journalist I used to meet often in Saigon at the
end of the war. Maybe I already told you about him before. No
matter what time of the day or night it was, I always saw him
writing on the terrace or in the lobby of our hotel. He even wrote
while having his breakfast or during his dinner. One day, I went
up to his table and asked him why he did it. "Writing helps!"
he said. I was in my early twenties then and did not know
what he was talking about. What was writing supposed to help
with? Now that I have written over fifty letters to you, I know
what he was talking about. Writing really does help. It helps
with loneliness. It helps with fear. It helps with the terror of
forgetting. It helps with the melancholy of the everyday. Writing
has an almost magical power—and I don't need anything other
than an empty piece of paper and a pencil. (Yes, yes, and a pencil
sharpener, I hear you say.)*

*I have written down everything that has been important
to me since you were born: The moment I first held you in my
arms, the first bath I gave you. I have described our trips to the
Peak, the many bruises that suddenly appeared and that we did
not recognize as symptoms, and everything else up to the story
of Michael Owen and his parents. I have felt better with every
sentence, with every line. (Now that reminds me of the afternoon
when you lay ill on the couch and refused to let go of your book.
And when I asked you over and over again to rest properly
and finally getting annoyed, you claimed that reading helped.
What did it help with? I wanted to know. You didn't reply for a*

long time. Finally you said in a very firm tone, "Tummy aches, boredom, bad moods, scolding dads." So writing and reading help!)

Yesterday afternoon I cleaned the house thoroughly. Since your illness I have a mania for cleaning that I can't get rid of. I suddenly stopped in the hall—it was as though I heard you calling me. I was standing in front of your yellow rain boots and the red raincoat with the blue polka dots. I looked at the markings on the door frames that I had moved here from our apartment in Repulse Bay. The last one was dated February 28 at four feet two and a half inches. You were a small child. Even at birth.

I wonder how tall you would be now. If you would reach up to my chest, and what shoe size you would have. I saw you standing in front of me—your curly blond head, your deep-blue eyes, and that smile that could soften my heart like nothing else in the world. I felt the pressure behind my eyes building again, and suddenly something happened that I had thought never would. I wasn't filled with sadness when I thought of you, but with a different, completely new feeling. At first I didn't even know what it was or how I should describe it. I thought about it the whole evening and half the night, and I think I now know what I can call it: gratitude. I can't think of a better word for it. Now I hear you saying quite clearly, "What do you mean by that, Daddy? Why gratitude? What have I done for you to be grateful to me?" That's the way you always used to ask me questions when you didn't understand something.

I'm grateful to you for every smile. Now don't look at me like that, as if a smile were nothing that a person had to be grateful for. I mean it seriously. For every time we went looking for shells on the beach. For every good-night story that I was able to tell you. For every morning that you crawled into our bed. I'm grateful for every question that you asked me, every moment that I was able to share with you. Grateful without end. I did not *always feel like that before because I took that all for granted, but your illness taught me never to take anything for granted again. I know now that some memories may fade or even disappear altogether, but it doesn't matter. I don't have to think about you all the time to know you are with me.*

I think that yesterday afternoon was the first time that the gratitude was stronger than the sadness. Before, the pain of your physical absence, the fact that I can no longer touch you, that you no longer walk beside me and grab my hand when you're startled by something—this pain overshadowed everything. I knew the power of fear. I knew the power of jealousy and sorrow, but not the power of gratitude.

Now you ask me why I felt it yesterday of all days. Why not a week ago, a month ago, or a year ago, as your mother did, maybe? I don't know. I can't answer that question. I only know that there are no shortcuts in life, no matter how much we long for them, and that everyone goes at their own speed and that any attempt to significantly influence this speed in any way either fails or exacts a high price. My path to this feeling went via the route of separation from your mother, living in Lamma, endless hours of loneliness, a dead young American man, and, most importantly, Christine, who I have always written a great deal about to you. This path took me exactly three years, two months, and eleven days.

I remember that our doctor, Doctor Li, predicted something like this in the days after you died, but I rejected what he said brusquely. No, more than that, I was really angry because I found the very thought a betrayal of you, of my sorrow. How was a person who had just been robbed of his son by death to feel grateful? That was asking too much.

So, it's almost time to stop now, for I still have to go to the village to get my groceries. I'm expecting visitors in the late afternoon. You won't believe it, but Christine and her son, Josh, are coming and Zhang and his wife, Mei, are coming too, with their son, Zheng. Of course I'm quite excited about it. I've never had more than two people at a time come to visit on Lamma and I hope that this won't be too much for me. These friends are all I have left, and I want very much for them to meet. Will they like each other? Will they have anything to say to each other? I feel the way you used to before one of your birthday parties.

Mei moved back in with Zhang again two weeks ago, I think. She loves him so much that she couldn't do anything other than forgive him eventually. They want to make him the head of the homicide division, by the way, but I don't know if that would be the right thing for him. I made up with him a few weeks ago. Christine was right, and it's good when Chinese philosophers sometimes get it wrong—trust that is lost can be regained.

Don't be sad, but this could be the last letter for some time, for I feel as if I have told you everything now.

"Paul, life goes on," your mother said to me once, and I was terribly appalled by that, because it sounded heartless to me, like she wanted to forget. But that's not possible. You've become a part of me. The person who is writing these words would not exist without you. You have no idea how rich you have made me. Life, though very different now, does go on, and that's good.

It's the only answer we have.

With love,
Your Daddy

ACKNOWLEDGMENTS

This book is fiction. The plot and characters are imaginary. I got the ideas for them on the many journeys I have made to China since 1995. I was also inspired to write this novel by the innumerable conversations that I had with friends, acquaintances, and strangers in China and in Hong Kong, where I lived for a time. Countless people helped me on my travels and with my research, and I feel incredibly grateful to them for their trust, their openness, and their support. Special thanks go to Zhang Dan, Ted Fishman, Clara and Derick Tam, Paul Chiu, Bessie Du, Angela and Carsten Schael, Lamy Li, Greg Davis, Aaron Fu, Werner Havers, and Thomas Bohlander for their help. Also to my parents and my sister, Dorothea.

I owe my wife, Anna, a very special thank-you. She gave me her advice, her encouragement, and her suggestions at every stage of this manuscript, and was an indispensable help to me. It is her love that has made this book possible.

ABOUT THE AUTHOR

Jan-Philipp Sendker, born in Hamburg in 1960, was the American correspondent for *Stern* from 1990 to 1995, and its Asian correspondent from 1995 to 1999. In 2000 he published *Cracks in the Great Wall*, a nonfiction book about China. *The Art of Hearing Heartbeats*, his first novel, is an international bestseller. He lives in Potsdam with his family.

ABOUT THE TRANSLATOR

Christine Lo is an editor in book publishing in London. She has also worked as a translator in Frankfurt and translated books by Juli Zeh and Senait Mehari from German into English. Her most recent translation is *Atlas of Remote Islands* by Judith Schalansky.